Love or Desire

Fiery Tenderness

ISBN: 978-609-08-0682-1

DEDICATION

A huge thank you to my dear friend Yamine who encouraged me to write this story and supported me throughout the journey of its creation.

CONTENTS

CHAPTER 1: MORNING

It was one of those rare autumn mornings that made you smile the moment you opened your eyes. I, however, wasn't in a hurry to open mine, greeting the unusually clear and warm Saturday through my eyelashes pressed tightly together.

After a cold week of rain that felt like an endless torture, the absence of raindrops tapping against my windowsill was a welcome surprise. Yet, what surprised me even more was how it had no energizing effect on me at all. Good weather usually filled me with vigor, pushing me to rush toward new challenges rather than linger in bed. More importantly, though, my internal clock always kicked in whenever I had something important planned. It would wake me long before the alarm, leaving me to fidget in bed, waiting for it to go off. But that morning, I was as calm as a tranquil lake, even though what I had to do felt as important as a semester exam.

Apparently my sense of responsibility had gone on strike. First, it let me sleep through the night without setting my alarm, and then it was indifferent as I dozed, ignoring the growing risk of missing the bus. So I stayed in bed, savoring the sweet, sinful half-sleep. I felt good—better than I had in a long time.

Through the haze of sleep, I heard Dean's quiet footsteps. I'd always wondered how he managed to walk so silently, despite the creaky floors of my dorm. I'd spent hours trying to figure out his secret, but eventually gave up, chalking it up as just another one of Dean's many virtues.

Dean leaned over the bed, the fresh scent of shaving cream lingering on his skin. I inhaled deeply, giving myself away—I wasn't really asleep. Dean smiled and whispered softly, "Morning, babe."

Too lazy to open my eyes, I smiled faintly and murmured, "Mmm..."

"Maybe this will wake you up," Dean teased, his voice playfully threatening as he stole a kiss.

A wave of pleasure spread through me, reaching every inch of my body before fully taking over. Excitement quickly replaced sleep, forcing me awake. I turned my head to avoid another kiss and, smiling playfully, uttered, "If you keep this up, we're definitely going to be late."

Dean pulled back, giving me space as he sat on the edge of the bed. I yawned and sat up. "What time is it?"

"6:30," Dean said after checking his watch, then gently pulled me closer.

Damn, I was supposed to get up half an hour earlier, echoed somewhere deep in my mind. Still, I chose to ignore that wise inner voice. Instead of jumping out of bed and rushing to the shower, I stayed where I was, staring at the sexy contours of Dean's athletic body, savoring the warmth of his hands sliding up and down my waist. His gaze, full of tenderness and adoration, made him even sexier in my eyes. It was all so pleasant, yet it felt sinful.

Trying to sound indifferent, I said, "One more kiss, and then we go." I tilted my head and leaned forward slightly, inviting him to accept.

Dean, however, seemed to have his own plans and no intention of obeying. His lips dodged mine, teasingly brushing my neck. His breath hot against my skin, he whispered in a seductive tone, "Just one?"

With more effort than I'd like to admit, I held back a moan and said, “Dean, we need to hurry. We can’t be late.”

“Alright, you’ve convinced me,” Dean said with mock surrender, before passionately pressing his lips to mine.

***

We arrived at the meeting point five minutes before the bus was set to leave. There weren’t many people around, so it was clear we weren’t the last to arrive. That made me feel a little less guilty about my morning carelessness. I hate being late, and it would be downright foolish to be late for the excursion I’d been looking forward to for so long.

I quickly scanned the groups of people near the bus. Aside from a few familiar faces from my course, there were several I didn’t recognize. Some looked sleepy, while others were full of energy. Two guys were talking and laughing so loudly that their voices echoed irritatingly in my ears. Those two were definitely morning people.

Gladys stood by the bus driver’s cab, nervously checking her phone. Against the white backdrop of the bus, her dark skin and lush black curls took on a mysterious quality, adding a menacing edge to her appearance. Her red plaid shirt, tied at the waist, combined with her stern expression, gave off a warning vibe, amplifying her intimidating presence. Gladys was angry, and she had every right to be. Unlike me, she was never a fan of age-old secrets or ancient cities. The only reason she agreed to spend the day on this excursion was because she’s an amazing friend.

You might be wondering about Dean. Well, I only found out yesterday that Dean was coming, and I was shocked—he’s even less of a fan of antiquity than Gladys. Honestly, I often wonder what the two of them are even doing in the archaeology department. Still, I can’t imagine my life or studies without them, so I figure it’s a good thing they’re my friends, no matter the reason.

My relationship with Dean is complicated; it’s like a zebra pattern.

For every stripe of the honeymoon phase, there will be an immediate breakup. Honestly, the last time we fought, I hoped I'd finally have the strength to end it once and for all… but fate had other plans.

Gladys, a regular witness to my suffering after each quarrel, did not like Dean, to put it mildly. It was fundamentally unclear to her why someone like me, in my right mind, would need such trouble in life.

Generally, straightforwardness was typical of Gladys, while tactfulness was not. She always spoke her mind and called a spade a spade, even when her names for things crossed the boundaries of censorship. Because of this, getting along with her could be quite difficult at times. Gladys often voiced the unpleasant truths I was afraid to admit to myself. Her words often acted like a cold shower of reality. Sometimes, however, I didn't want to sober up; I preferred to put on rose-colored glasses and believe in the best. And that's exactly how I felt in that moment.

I knew there was little chance of getting Gladys's approval for my reconciliation with Dean, so I focused on finding ways to avoid her indignant remarks or at least lessen their intensity.

If I show up in front of Gladys holding hands with Dean, a storm is guaranteed. I need to talk to her alone first and explain everything. But how do I gently let Dean know I need him to be temporarily absent?

As my mind raced to solve this tricky problem, an opportunity came to my rescue. Dean's phone suddenly rang, prompting him to stop and answer the caller. I seized this opportunity and rushed toward Gladys.

"Hi!" I tried to make my voice sound as innocent and airy as possible.

"Are you kidding me, Tayra? Where have you been?"

I was about to answer when the expression on Gladys's face shifted suddenly. I wondered if she saw Dean behind me, and within seconds, my assumption was confirmed.

"Hi, Gladys!"

"Hi, Dean," said Gladys in a neutral voice, vainly trying to mask her disapproval behind a facade of calm.

I didn't know if Dean noticed his friends or sensed Gladys's fury and decided to retreat before she could burn him to ashes with a lightning bolt from her eyes, but he said, "Babe, I'll greet the guys and be back in a minute." Before I could blink and mumble, "Of course," my boyfriend disappeared into the crowd.

That's when Gladys finally voiced the question I was desperately hoping to avoid: "How do you plan to explain this?"

I looked down and sheepishly rubbed my cheek. "Well..."

I felt like a schoolgirl explaining to her parents why she had gotten bad grades on tests. Yes, Gladys was just my friend, and I wasn't obliged to report my personal life to her, but we were very close, and she was the only person I could talk to about things like this, so "it's none of your business" wasn't an option. Moreover, the rational part of me shared Gladys's opinion on the matter and agreed with the reasoning I assumed she would present. I felt stupid, guilty, miserable, and utterly lost. Yet, since staying silent, even when there's a direct threat to my life, is out of character for me, I was determined to fire back to avoid giving up without a fight.

Meanwhile, Gladys kept attacking: "Are you two dating again?"

"It's a bit complicated…" I said uncertainly, bracing myself for the icy shower of Gladys's ironclad arguments.

"I don't understand you! You two fight all the time; you literally don't match in anything!"

"Except sex…" I said quietly, inwardly scolding myself for being so stubborn. Had I admitted defeat at that moment, the conflict would have been resolved sooner. However, that wouldn't be me if I did.

"Well, indeed," said Gladys, rolling her eyes.

"I know, Gladys," I sighed. "This is hopeless, and I should've broken up with him long ago. But yesterday he came, and I… I just couldn't resist." I paused and shyly rubbed my cheek again. "He's so good in bed."

"You do know he's not the only one with a dick on campus, don't you? He's also not the only one with good abs. Besides that, I don't know what you're holding on to. Haven't you had enough, Tayra? Isn't it time to grow up and admit you have no future together?"

"You're right. I know you are. It's just… after each reconciliation, I start to believe that things will change for the better. I'd love to be realistic, but I can't help it."

"You just don't want to," said Gladys, shaking her head in disapproval.

I said nothing and fixed my gaze on the ground.

Those few seconds of tense silence felt like an eternity, but finally, Gladys sighed and spoke in a slightly warmer voice: "Listen, Tayra. I understand. But you can't keep doing this to yourself. Just cut the rope and move on with your life."

"I'll try, I promise," I said, looking up just in time to hear footsteps behind me. I assumed it was Dean, but the lack of total hatred in Gladys's eyes made me doubt. I turned my head and saw my boyfriend with his friend Caleb, a handsome blond with almond-blue eyes.

Caleb likes Gladys and tries his best to get closer to her. Gladys is positively inclined toward Caleb, but she's wary of him because he's Dean's friend. When I saw Caleb, I thought maybe I wasn't the only reason Dean joined the excursion group. Maybe he agreed to accompany Caleb, who decided to go because he knew Gladys would be there.

We're worse than kids, even at twenty years old, I thought, turning back to the bus. *The funny thing is that in this kindergarten, I seem to be the only one actually interested in the ancient city we're going to visit.*

Soon, we heard the voice of our guide inviting us to board the bus and take our seats. When the engine started, I turned my head to the window and began to study the objects outside: buildings, trees, and fields. They changed much faster than I could follow. Nevertheless, this activity helped me organize my thoughts and finally shift my focus from the love drama in my life to the actual goal of our trip: the ancient city Tiamon, which I had wanted to visit ever since I saw its mention in a history encyclopedia.

The place has always been surrounded by mysteries and often appears as a venue in myths and legends. Interestingly, even a large number of related findings haven't shed light on most of the secrets the place is said to have.

I've always had a soft spot for hidden secrets, especially the ancient ones. This is probably why I chose archaeology as my major. When I heard that an excursion to the "Tiamon Catacombs" was organized at our university, I was the first to sign up. Of course, I knew that since it was a museum, all the objects there had already been studied carefully and checked diligently, so the chance of finding something new was close to zero. However, the anticipation of visiting this place in person filled me with excitement. I had a strong feeling that the trip would be remarkable, dividing my life into before and after. I had no clue why that should happen, but I had no doubt it would. And, the closer the bus brought me to Tiamon, the stronger this exciting feeling became.

CHAPTER 2: TIAMON CATACOMBS

We arrived at Tiamon in the late afternoon. Since the parking lot for tour buses was quite far from the museum itself, we had to walk another fifteen minutes to reach it. On the way, the guide told us that once upon a time, Tiamon was a colossal city, the center of trade, commerce, culture, and education. But only one building has been preserved to this day: the Tiamon Catacombs, a multi-level system of underground labyrinths located beneath the ancient temple of Tiamon.

While some tunnels have been well investigated, most of them are part of the excursion route, the majority of the underground catacombs remain unexplored and closed to visitors. Some of the closed areas were in disrepair and unavailable for sightseeing due to the risk of floor collapses.

The museum complex, "Tiamon Catacombs," was situated in a large field. Its above-ground section consisted of a large ancient temple. The temple's structure resembled two truncated prisms of different sizes, set atop one another. The building was bulky and lacked elegance in its design. However, when I looked at it, my heart was shackled by a reverent horror I couldn't comprehend, and I thought that perhaps this was the effect the building was meant to evoke.

Offices and service areas flanked each side of the building. They were arranged neatly, allowing for a sizable open area where visitors could admire the temple's magnificence. The museum's grounds were fenced, with several security points and surveillance cameras along the perimeter.

It was crowded at the catacombs entrance; several excursion groups were waiting for their turn to enter. Our guide went to the museum administration building while we waited outside with the other tourists for the next set of instructions.

Gladys studied the temple with an appraising look, then winced and yawned.

The total absence of respect for this ancient architectural monument, I thought disapprovingly, scanning the crowd for like-minded people. I couldn't be the only one who appreciated the impressive forms and unique spirit of the historical marvel we were about to visit. Fortunately, I spotted a few faces filled with awe and respect, and, reassured, I was about to return to admiring the temple when it suddenly struck me that I didn't see Dean anywhere.

It was hard to miss him. Dean's thick black curls, rising 185 cm above the ground, made him easily recognizable even in crowded places and at a distance. His signature black leather biker jacket, always unzipped regardless of temperature or wind speed, made Dean's figure even more noticeable.

Just to be sure, I scanned the crowd at the catacombs entrance again and, not finding Dean this time, began to worry. For some reason, the first thought that came to mind was of the tunnels closed due to the danger of collapse. Dean's knack for getting involved in wacky stories and finding adventures out of the blue was as significant as his ability to quietly navigate the creaky floor. When I added his adventurous spirit and passion for exploring anything marked "Forbidden" or "Do Not Enter," my imagination painted a vivid picture of a weak and barely breathing Dean trapped under a pile of heavy stones with no hope of escape. The image felt so realistic that I was seized by genuine horror. Frightened, I turned to Gladys and asked, "Have you seen

Dean?"

Not sharing my concern, Gladys nodded indifferently toward the smoking area. "There he is, with Caleb."

I looked in the direction of Gladys's nod and saw Dean theatrically blowing a ring of smoke while Caleb studied the toe cap of his right sneaker.

"Oh," I sighed with relief, which soon turned to a bit of concern and disappointment. Did my overreaction mean I cared about Dean more than I should?

As if reading my thoughts, Gladys looked at me and said, "You know, you should learn to care less."

"Just a habit," I shrugged guiltily. "I thought he might have gotten into trouble..."

In such situations, Gladys would usually roll her eyes and say something like, "Big deal!" In fact, I expected to hear something similar then, too. By that moment, I was so tired of discussing the matter that I was ready to accept any comment just to end it. However, Gladys surprised me. Instead of sniffing or making a venomous remark about Dean, she approached me, placed her hand on my shoulder, and, looking me in the eyes, said, "His problems are not yours. Try to get used to it."

I nodded and changed the topic. "What do you think of the building?"

"It's huge," my bestie shrugged. "I tried estimating how many stones were needed to build it. Got a number with five zeros for just the foundation and gave up. Also, how did they lift them to the top? Those rocks must be heavy."

She did think about the building, I thought, glancing at Gladys with newfound respect. *In her own way, but she did show interest.*

At this point, our guide finally returned. Since he didn't signal for the group to gather, I figured we still had to wait in line, which meant

I could ask him a few questions.

"Mr. Teudos!" I called, hurrying over to him.

"Yes?" the guide said, turning toward me.

"Do you know any legends about these catacombs?"

Mr. Teudos raised a brow, gave me an attentive look, then smiled. "Places like this are often shrouded in myths. Is there something in particular you're curious about?"

His enigmatic smile made me feel a bit embarrassed. As soon as I mentioned "legends," people began inching closer, curious to hear more. By the time I answered the guide, we were surrounded by a tight circle of onlookers, and I wasn't sure how to ask my question without either satisfying my curiosity or sounding ridiculous in front of the crowd.

"Um..." I began hesitantly, "it was about a priest. After he caught his beloved cheating, he turned to black magic and made a potion that made any woman who drank it fall in love with him. But these women could never love anyone else. The priest never loved them back, though. He treated them with contempt, taking revenge for the hurt he'd suffered. The secret room where he made the potion was hidden deep in the Tiamon Catacombs, and it's said the recipe is still there."

When I finished, I glanced at the onlookers. Their faces were mostly serious—no one giggled, which I found reassuring. The guide stood still, looking thoughtful, maybe even puzzled. After a long pause, Mr. Teudos finally spoke.

"Wow," he said, rubbing his chin. "That's interesting, really interesting. I've never heard that version, but I think I know what it's based on. I believe you read this story in a children's book, right?"

"Well, it was a long time ago, so I don't remember exactly where I read it. Probably in a kids' book. Does it sound too fairy-tale-like?"

"Well, no, that's not what I meant. Your story seems to be an adapted version of the legend of Tiendal—well-known around here.

But the original isn't about love or heartbreak. It's more about vanity and wounded pride, pushing an otherwise remarkable man to use his gifts for evil. It's a tale of lust, power, and magic."

"No wonder the children's book left that part out," I said, impressed. "But it seems like we're all adults here, so maybe you could tell us the real legend? Please? And since it's tied to the Tiamon Catacombs, it's still relevant to the tour."

I looked at Mr. Teudos pleadingly, and so did the rest of the group, giving him no choice but to agree. After a few seconds of hesitation, he glanced at his watch. "Alright, but I'll have to keep it short, or we'll miss our spot to enter the catacombs."

"Just don't leave out the spicy details," said Gladys, suddenly appearing behind me.

The crowd burst into laughter, and even Mr. Teudos smiled. I shot Gladys a disapproving look and hissed, "Gladys!"

"Well, Tayra, don't be a bore," she whispered back, unapologetic. "Those old stones have been there for centuries; they can wait another half-hour. A story about sex and magic sounds way more fun."

And this is my best friend, I thought with quiet exasperation. Sighing silently, I prepared to listen.

CHAPTER 3: THE LEGEND

"Tiendal was the high priest of Pharaoh Milcentep and possessed an extraordinary gift—he could see the future. Because of this, Milcentep relied on him for every decision, elevating Tiendal to a position of great power and privilege.

One day, by the river, Tiendal encountered Ilze, a slender, dark-haired girl—the daughter of a wealthy merchant. Enchanted by her beauty, Tiendal was determined to have her. But Ilze's father, knowing the priest's notorious habit of discarding women, refused. The Pharaoh, however, intervened, and by his order, the girl was taken to the palace to become Tiendal's mistress.

While with Ilze, Tiendal forgot about other women. But despite her obedience, Ilze's heart seethed with hatred—no surprise, since she had been taken to the palace against her will.

Before long, Ilze fell in love with a young slave. The two lovers would meet in secret whenever Tiendal was away. Oddly, despite his ability to see the future, Tiendal remained oblivious to the affair happening right under his nose—until the day he caught them in each other's arms.

Tiendal was furious, his heart heavy with pain. But what stung him most might surprise you—it wasn't the betrayal itself, but the undeniable fact that Ilze found more pleasure in the slave's touch than in his own. Unaccustomed to making mistakes or losing, Tiendal couldn't bear the thought of being outmatched by a mere slave. He wasted no time brutally killing both Ilze and her lover, but even their bloodshed didn't satisfy his thirst for vengeance. Tiendal vowed that, from that moment on, no other man would ever surpass him as a lover.

He struck a pact with ancient dark forces, gaining a new ability. Any woman who had once been touched by Tiendal would become numb to the touch of any other man. This curse made women addicted to him, incapable of loving another. And yet, Tiendal discarded his lovers without a second thought, tossing them aside like refuse when he grew bored. Driven mad by his rejection, women would lose their minds, even take their own lives. But Tiendal cared only about one thing—ensuring he would always be the greatest and only lover in their hearts."

The guide finished his tale, glancing at me as though gauging my satisfaction with his storytelling. I was impressed, but not entirely satisfied. Too many questions still nagged at me. I didn't hesitate to voice the most pressing one: "What does this have to do with the secret room?"

The guide seemed to expect this. He smiled, a hint of mystery in his tone. "They say the ceremonies that sustained Tiendal's powers over women were performed in a secret room. The entrance was hidden, and the passage leading to it was sealed with powerful magic."

That makes sense, I thought, then quickly followed up. "And what happened after Tiendal's death?"

The guide's eyes lit up with a mischievous glint, a sly smile playing on his lips. "This," he said, his voice brimming with enthusiasm as he theatrically raised a finger, "is the most interesting part! Tiendal discovered how to make women the source of his immortality."

Mr. Teudos paused, scanning the crowd to gauge their reaction. Dozens of eager eyes urged him to go on, and so he did.

"After Tiendal's death, a woman would enter the secret chamber, unwittingly triggering his reincarnation. Days after the ritual, Tiendal would reappear in the city, reborn in a new body, resuming his role as the Pharaoh's adviser. The woman who initiated his rebirth became his first slave in his new life.

For centuries, Milcentep's descendants performed the ritual of Tiendal's resurrection—until one fateful day when the lustful priest and Pharaoh Pilzernath set eyes on the same woman. As a result, Tiendal was poisoned, and Pilzernath ordered the destruction of the secret room. However, the magic protecting the room rendered its destruction impossible. Consequently, Pilzernath ordered the tunnel leading to it to be sealed with stones. This effectively ended the centuries-old reign of the priest."

Wow, I thought, preparing to ask my next question, when the guide received a signal from one of the museum employees. He waved to attract the attention of the rest of the group and announced in a louder voice, "Attention, everyone, it's our turn. Let's go."

As we approached the temple, I remained deeply affected by the legend I had just heard. Ilze, her lover, and Tiendal—who returned home at the wrong moment—seemed to stand before me as if they were alive. While the story seemed ordinary, something about it clearly unsettled me. It was something that completely threw my soul off balance.

I took a few deep breaths to collect myself, but it didn't help much. So, I decided to seek support from my best friend.

Gladys must have been impressed by the story as well, since she immediately guessed the source of my worries. Unlike me, she was always rational and never easily discouraged, so she simply shrugged and said reassuringly, "Relax, it's just a legend."

Gladys's confidence somehow helped me regain my composure. "Yeah," I replied, "I know. Sometimes I hate how easily I get affected."

The lighting inside was dim, creating an uncomfortable, oppressive atmosphere. We wandered through the winding corridors for about an hour before finally entering a room. The room was more spacious than most we had visited, but the lighting was even dimmer. The walls were adorned with strange patterns, and sharp hooks were visible on the ceiling.

I shuddered and moved closer to Gladys. "It's so creepy here."

"Yeah, pretty much," she agreed, stepping closer to the guide to ensure we wouldn't lose sight of him. I readily followed her. Better safe than sorry; staying here alone if I fell behind the group would not be a pleasant experience.

"Earlier, we explored the newer part of the catacombs, constructed several centuries after Pilzernath's reign," Mr. Teudos continued. "While you can find many mysteries there, the older part holds many more. The old tunnels are narrower and more labyrinthine. In some areas, navigating—even with the signs—can be challenging. Moreover, due to the narrow passages, visibility in the tunnels is limited, and to be honest, there isn't much of interest to see. They lead to vaults and storage areas that are off-limits to tourists. Only one excursion route in the old part is recommended for visitors. This route leads to the famous Stone Halls. And that is where we are heading now. However, there is one thing I must warn you about. The route to the Stone Halls passes through the so-called Dark Isthmus. It's a tunnel approximately a hundred meters long and sixty centimeters wide. It connects the new and old parts of the catacombs and is called "dark" because, due to technical restrictions and safety reasons, lights are not allowed. So, if you're claustrophobic, nyctophobic, or have any other reason to believe you might struggle to make it through this passage, it's best to stay here. A museum worker will accompany you until we return to pick you up."

"Sounds like an offer for you," my best friend giggled.

"Very funny, Gladys," I snapped back. "And your eyes have a night vision mode."

"It would come in handy, though. I wonder how walking in complete darkness can be safer than using a flashlight."

"I'm thinking the same thing. But they must know better."

"Let's hope so."

As no one expressed a desire to stay, we moved from the spacious room to a dimly lit one with entrances to two corridors. The first corridor had dull lights, while the other was completely dark. The guide led us to the dark corridor and stopped at its entrance.

"Now we need to form a chain. Hold hands and move ahead."

When I heard the number sixty, I didn't realize how serious the situation was. It struck me only when I saw the narrow rectangle leading into complete darkness. Sixty centimeters is roughly the width of a standard refrigerator. Can you imagine walking inside a refrigerator in a human chain?

As soon as the guide told us to align, Dean, who had kept his distance from Gladys and me since the beginning of our excursion, approached me and reached out his hand. I accepted his offer without hesitation. Oddly enough, Gladys didn't comment or make a caustic sniff but simply took my other hand. To Caleb's delight, he turned out to be following Gladys, and she had no choice but to take his hand.

When the human chain was finally formed, we began to move slowly along the narrow corridor.

Aside from the generally unpleasant atmosphere, there was almost no air in the Dark Isthmus, and the smell was peculiar. I closed my eyes because there was no point in keeping them open. I gasped and squeezed Dean's hand tightly. Probably due to the lack of air, at some point, my head started spinning. I felt disoriented; my fingers weakened, and I released Dean's hand. In the blur, I touched a cold, solid surface—probably a stone wall. I leaned on it but lost my balance and fell. Or so it seemed to me, as I couldn't estimate it properly due to my dizziness. After that, I must have fainted, as the spinning in my head stopped.

I found myself lying face down on the floor. I wanted to say something, to call Dean or Gladys, but I couldn't pronounce a word. I vainly moved my lips and tongue, but no sound came out. It was as if someone had taken my voice. I tried to move and, surprisingly, was successful. I spread my arms and was even more surprised to realize there was enough space to make such a move. I stood up and took a deep breath.

Enough air and not that specific smell, I thought, shocked. *This means only one thing—I'm not in the Dark Isthmus anymore. Then where am I? And how do I get out of here?*

I extended my arms forward and turned around. There were no walls, and there seemed to be nothing above me, either.

I checked my jacket and felt my cell phone in the right pocket. There was no signal, and the battery was low, but it was still better than nothing.

I illuminated the space around me and discovered I was in a square room about 2x2 meters in size. There were three doors: one in front of me, one to the left, and one to the right. A solid wall was behind me. Before my phone died, I managed to examine the floor and ceiling. Both seemed trustworthy, with no signs of hidden traps. The ceiling was high enough for me to stand comfortably with my hands extended above my head, but if I jumped, I could probably touch it. I decided not to test the assumption, though, and it was probably one of the few wise decisions I'd made in my life.

When I found myself in complete darkness again, I tried to recall the image I'd just seen. The doors had no handles, but I thought I'd seen levers to the right of each one.

Well, I thought, *it seems like I've got no other choice. I should try the doors. Which one to start with? Hmm… we usually read and write from left to right, so I probably shouldn't be original here. The left door it is.*

I walked up to the door and touched it. The stone surface was rough and cold. I felt around where I thought the lever was. Finally, I grabbed it and pulled it down carefully. The lever moved in response, and I heard a quiet click. When I let go, the lever returned to its original position.

Sliding my hands along the wall at the same height as the first lever, I began moving to the right. After a few steps, I bumped into a corner, so I turned and continued along the front wall until I found another lever. I pulled it down as well and heard the same click in response. In the same way, I made my way to the third lever and pulled it down. To my disappointment, nothing happened after the third click. I was ready to despair when a thought struck me, *That sound seems familiar. Oh, maybe I shouldn't pull the levers randomly. There's probably a specific order to them. All I need is the right combination.*

To avoid getting lost in the darkness, I slid to the wall without a door and pressed my back against it. Mentally, I designated the left door as 1, the front as 2, and the right as 3. Back in school, I attended a math club where we often solved problems involving combinations. I remembered that for three items, the number of possible permutations was six, provided no item was used more than once. Otherwise, the number of permutations could reach twenty-seven.

Keeping track of my position while moving from lever to lever was difficult, and when I tried to estimate how much time and energy it would take to check every combination, I was terrified. Hoping the creator of this puzzle wasn't too into math and chose the version without repetitions, I decided to stop overthinking and take action.

At first, I planned to check the combinations in their natural order. I'd already tried "123" so that left "132," "213," "231," "312," and "321." But then I realized if the number of attempts wasn't limited, the task would be too easy. Based on fairy tales and myths, there had to be a limit, and three seemed like a fair number of tries. One attempt had already been wasted, leaving me with two tries and five options. I asked my intuition for advice, but it remained treacherously silent. I had no choice but to rely on luck—and maybe a little logic.

If I were protecting something with this kind of lock, what combination would I use? Most people would start from left to right, like I did. So, combinations like '123,' '132,' and '213' would be tried first. That makes them unlikely to be correct. I narrowed it down to the three remaining options.

I rubbed my forehead nervously, trying to focus. *Three options for two tries... Damn, it's still risky.*

I turned to my intuition again. To my surprise, it stirred, yawning lazily before suggesting "231."

I looked up at the ceiling, hoping God could still hear me through the thick layers of rock and earth above, and asked Him for help. Right after that I slid along the wall to the front door's lever.

After the third click, the room plunged into a deathly silence. *Looks like I was wrong*, I thought, as panic gripped me. I took a deep breath, trying to calm down, but before I could finish, I heard a strange noise and felt a slight vibration beneath my feet.

I caught the same smell as in the Dark Isthmus and saw a faint light coming from the front door. I stepped closer and felt the door. It slid back, revealing two grooves on either side, just wide enough for me to squeeze through. I squeezed through one of the grooves into a large, dimly lit room.

The smell was much stronger there. I felt dizzy again, the world spinning wildly. Then came a blindingly bright light. The last thing I saw was a pair of fierce, dark eyes and the sound of a distant, ominous laugh.

CHAPTER 4: EVASIVE SILENCE

The first thing I saw when I opened my eyes was Dean's tangled black hair. He was kneeling beside my bed, his head resting on the edge of my pillow, holding my hand as he slept.

I tried to turn my head, but as soon as I stirred, Dean lifted his head and looked at me intently. I blinked, taking a breath to say something. Realization hit Dean, and his eyes lit up with happiness. He let out a relieved sigh and said, "Thank God you woke up, babe!"

My brain frantically tried to process the situation, but I couldn't believe what I was seeing.

Dean? On his knees? By my bed? With that hopeless look on his face?

The harder I tried to make sense of what was happening, the more scared and confused I became. I clearly needed more information, and I wanted it immediately.

"Where am I, Dean?" I asked softly. My throat was dry, making it hard to speak.

"In the hospital," Dean said reassuringly, gently stroking my hair.

I swallowed, trying to moisten my dry throat, and asked with effort, "What happened?"

"Well…" Dean paused, as if deciding what to say, then winced and added, "You've been unconscious for three days. You scared us all to death."

"Three days?" I asked in shock, staring at Dean in disbelief.

Dean nodded slightly. I took a deep breath, glanced around, and asked, "Where's Gladys?"

"She's having coffee with Caleb. We've been taking shifts to watch over you."

Unconscious. Three days. Hospital. Gladys. Caleb. Shifts. I tried to piece together the puzzle of my hospitalization, but everything stayed hazy.

"Can I stand up?" I asked, attempting to sit up.

"I don't think you should," Dean replied, gently easing me back down.

Only then did I notice the IV in my arm and the wires connected to medical equipment. I sighed and complied. But the fact that I couldn't remember how I ended up in the hospital kept nagging at me. I looked at Dean, pleading. "Dean, please, tell me what happened."

Dean winced, clearly reluctant to talk about it. He was struggling with something inside. I kept staring at him, silently begging him to speak.

"What's the last thing you remember?" he asked, his voice calm and steady.

"We were in the Dark Isthmus. I felt dizzy from the lack of air. The rest is a blur. I might have been hallucinating. Then I fainted."

I gave him the vague version because I wasn't sure if what I remembered was real. The part I called "blurry" wasn't blurry at all. The three doors, the code lock, the grooves behind the front door—they were still vivid in my mind. And that ominous laugh echoed in my ears, making me cringe. But I didn't want Dean to think I was crazy. I needed to find out what happened, to decide for myself if it had been real—or just my imagination playing tricks while I was unconscious.

Dean rubbed his forehead and sighed, "Hmm..."

Growing impatient, I cut into his thoughts. "So what, Dean?"

Just then, a doctor and a nurse entered the room. The doctor addressed Dean in a calm but firm voice, "She needs to rest. You can talk later."

Relieved by the chance to avoid answering, Dean stood up and nodded quickly. "Get some rest, babe. I'll see you later," he said, disappearing through the door.

Gladys and Caleb, back from the hospital café, sat on a bench in the lobby. Gladys looked exhausted. She tried distracting herself by scrolling through the news on her phone, but it wasn't helping. When Dean appeared in the corridor, Gladys quickly put away her phone and walked toward him. Caleb got up from the bench and followed.

"How is she?" Gladys asked, hopeful.

"She's awake."

"Thank God!" Gladys breathed. "Can I see her?"

"Maybe later, she's with the doctor right now."

"Will she be okay?"

"Hopefully," Dean said with a shrug.

Gladys sighed, lowering her eyes. Caleb, standing behind her, gently placed his hand on her shoulder. Gladys covered Caleb's hand and nodded gratefully.

Seeing this moment, Dean, who had stayed calm until now, couldn't hold back his emotions any longer. He sat on the nearest bench, rested his elbows on his knees, and buried his face in his hands.

"Jeez, it's all my fault! Why did I let her go on that excursion?"

Gladys sat down beside Dean. "Calm down, Dean. It's no one's fault. This trip was her dream, and what happened was just an accident."

"I never should have let go of her hand!"

"There are plenty of things you shouldn't have done," Gladys said, irritated, but then softened her tone. "But I'm just as guilty. I was holding the other hand."

Dean lifted his head, about to speak, when Caleb interrupted, "Tayra's doctor is back!" He nodded toward the ward, where the doctor and nurse had just emerged. Dean and Gladys immediately got up and rushed after the doctor. Surprised by their reaction, Caleb hurried after them.

"Dr. Jones," Gladys called out as she hurried alongside the doctor, "please, tell us how she is."

"Surprisingly well, considering how long she was unconscious," the doctor replied. "We'll need to run a few more tests to make sure we haven't missed anything. If everything looks good, we should be able to discharge her in a couple of days."

The three of them let out a collective sigh of relief. The doctor smiled, then added with a gentle but firm tone, "Please try to avoid any stressful conversations with her."

The guys took the doctor's recommendation to avoid stress way too seriously. The entire time I was in the hospital, they treated me like a fragile vase, never leaving me alone for even a minute. Their care was both comforting and suspicious. They all seemed to feel guilty about what had happened to me, even Caleb, who I'd never been close with.

What made me most suspicious was how carefully they avoided talking about the excursion, especially how it ended. Whenever I asked direct questions, they dodged them with responses like, "It's not important right now—you're fine, and that's all that matters," or, "You shouldn't stress. It's not good for you. We'll talk later." But their strange behavior and silence about the incident only made me more anxious. I needed to know what had happened and why my mind kept clinging to strange memories of doors, painfully bright light, and chilling laughter. I didn't tell anyone about these memories and stuck to my original story—that I remembered nothing after feeling dizzy from the lack of air in the Dark Isthmus.

After countless failed attempts to get the truth from any of them, I stopped asking, pretending I didn't need to know. In reality, I was just waiting for the right moment to bring it up again.

CHAPTER 5: THE TRUTH

A few days later, I was discharged from the hospital, and we finally returned home.

"Well, that excursion sure turned into a long one," I said, breathing in the familiar scent of my dorm room.

"I couldn't agree more," Gladys said as she closed the door.

"I'm so sorry for everything that happened. I never imagined the excursion would take such a turn, even in my wildest dreams."

"Stop it, Tayra. The important thing is that everyone's alive and well."

"Yes, that's true," I sighed. "Well, they say every cloud has a silver lining, so I hope your nerves weren't completely shot."

"I believe we have enough left. But I wouldn't want to spend them on something like this again," Gladys giggled.

"I can imagine. By the way, am I imagining things, or are you actually giving Caleb a chance?"

"Well… it's a bit early to say, but… there, in the catacombs, and later at the hospital, Caleb really showed himself to be reliable, caring, and supportive. I'm starting to think I may have judged him unfairly. I mean, I've always found him attractive, but I avoided getting involved because of his friendship with Dean. Now, I'm not so sure I was right about Dean either. Honestly, he surprised me in Tiamon."

"Could you tell me more about that part?"

Gladys hesitated, rubbing her cheek nervously. "I… I'm not sure that's a good idea…"

"Gladys, please. I know you don't want me to worry, but this uncertainty is driving me crazy. I keep replaying that day in my mind, trying to piece everything together, but I can't. It's stressing me out so much. I **need** to know what happened in the Dark Isthmus. Please, I'm begging you."

Gladys shrugged and glanced at my bed, still looking unsure. Before she could change her mind, I quickly sat down, motioning for her to join me. She sat on the edge of the bed, taking a deep breath before starting her story.

"We were walking through the Dark Isthmus. For a moment, I felt your hand slip from mine. Then I heard something, like movement. I panicked and grabbed for your hand again, but realized it wasn't yours—it was Dean's. You had simply disappeared. Vanished into this narrow tunnel with no side passages. Saying we were horrified doesn't even begin to cover it.

Word about the emergency spread faster than we could have imagined, and chaos broke out. The guide did his best to keep everyone calm and somehow managed to lead us out of the tunnel. That's when he called for the rescue team.

The rescuers turned on the lights and began searching the Dark Isthmus. We went with them to show the spot where you disappeared. And that's when we realized why the Isthmus had to be crossed in darkness—because with the lights on, it was horrifying. It seemed impossible to avoid a full-blown panic attack."

Gladys cleared her throat, and I took the opportunity to ask, "What made it so scary?"

The memories seemed too unpleasant. Gladys cringed so hard, I immediately regretted asking. I couldn't remember ever seeing her like that. I was about to take back the question when, after swallowing hard,

Gladys finally replied, "There was dried blood everywhere and horrific depictions of ritual murders. It looked so realistic, it was terrifying. Brr… I'd rather not remember. Walking through that corridor in the dark was a genius idea..."

I kicked off my shoes and scooted further onto the bed, leaning back against the wall. "So, what happened next?"

"Then the rescue team scoured the Dark Isthmus multiple times, searching for any clue to solve the mystery of your disappearance. At first, they wouldn't let us join the search, but after some arguing, they eventually allowed us to help. For hours, we searched the awful walls and the equally horrible floor in that suffocatingly narrow tunnel. But there was no sign of you.

The rescuers were at a complete loss. They paused the search to discuss their next move. From what I gathered, they needed to check the corridor for hidden voids behind the walls, but they required special equipment they didn't have with them. Their discussion went on for a while; they were clearly hesitating over something. But then Dean spoke to the rescue team leader. After their conversation, the leader returned to his team, and after a brief discussion, they resumed the search."

"Really? What did Dean say to him?"

"I have no idea. He just pulled the team leader aside, and they talked for quite a while. Afterward, the team leader gave an order, and the rescuers brought out some extra equipment and went back to comb the tunnel.

You know my attitude to Dean, but I must admit in that situation he behaved more than adequately and your rescue might be partially his merit."

I took a deep breath and rubbed my forehead. Gladys immediately stopped her story and looked at me in concern. I nodded, letting her know that I was fine and that I was ready to listen further. So, she continued, "During the final round of searching, one of the rescuers noticed a pattern on the wall. It was an entrance to a small, square cell. Inside, we found you lying face down on the floor, unconscious."

"Wait... a swivel door in a corridor that's only sixty centimeters wide? How is that even possible?"

"Surprising, right? I was shocked too. I wouldn't have believed it if I hadn't seen it myself."

"Was it big?"

"Not really, just wide enough for an average person to fit through."

"Was it made of stone?"

"Yeah, and it had those creepy patterns on both sides. Who would've thought pictures could be such a good disguise?"

"So, you're telling me I accidentally opened a swivel door and fell into a square cell? And that's how I left the Dark Isthmus?"

"Pretty much, yeah."

"Okay, this is starting to make sense," I said thoughtfully, my mind drifting back to the moment I felt dizzy. Combining my own memories with what Gladys had told me, I pieced together the following.

I had been walking through the Dark Isthmus, holding Dean and Gladys by their hands when, suddenly, I felt dizzy. Instinctively, I reached out for support and accidentally pressed a hidden button in the wall's pattern, triggering the swivel door mechanism. The door swung open, creating a passage. Disoriented, I mistook the door for the wall and slid along it, stumbling into the cell instead of continuing down the tunnel. Then the door closed, locking me inside. Everything seemed to fit together.

Then I remembered lighting up the room with my phone, revealing three doors with levers in front of me. I was certain the central door wasn't a swivel door. Could it have been one of the side doors that led me to the cell?

Still hesitant to share my memories, I decided to test the waters with an unexpected question, "Was it possible to open that swivel door from inside the cell?"

Gladys raised an eyebrow in confusion and shrugged. "I don't know. The rescuers used some levers to keep it from closing."

"Was the door in front of me or behind me?"

"Behind you," Gladys said, frowning. She clearly didn't understand why that mattered.

"And what was behind the door in front of me, then?"

Gladys widened her eyes, no longer hiding her confusion. "There were no other doors, Tayra. It was a dead-end cell."

My eyebrows shot up. Refusing to trust my ears, I asked again, "Are you sure?"

"Absolutely," Gladys nodded. "I was standing right behind the rescuer while he was shining his light and checking the walls."

So, the rest was just hallucinations, I thought, still refusing to believe the obvious.

"Well, I get it," I muttered, disappointment washing over me. Then I remembered something else. "How did you handle the smell in the Dark Isthmus? Were you wearing respirators or something?"

Gladys shook her head. "No, nothing. Despite how terrible the place looked, I didn't notice any specific smell. And no one else mentioned it either."

Heat quickly built up inside me. My hands started trembling, and it became hard to breathe. Within seconds, the heat of frustration and indignation consumed me. Everything went dark and blurry. I tried to calm down and focus, but the same thought kept running through my mind over and over: *Could all my memories just be hallucinations*?!

Despite how much my mind and body resisted, I had to face the unpleasant truth: the mysterious images in my head had nothing to do with reality. Gathering the last of my strength, I swallowed hard and whispered, "Well, it's clear." As the heat began to fade, I sighed quietly.

"Maybe I should have stayed in the weak-nerves zone, so I wouldn't ruin your fun. Sorry."

I glanced at Gladys, guilt heavy in my chest, but she met my gaze with a faint smile, as if to say, "Stop it, Tayra, you're not to blame for any of this."

But I couldn't shake the guilt. I felt deeply responsible for all the stress and chaos I had caused—hours of searching through the dreadful Dark Isthmus, days my friends had spent in the hospital, the fear, the desperation, and the pain they had endured. Yes, I felt guilty—overwhelmingly so—but also endlessly grateful, because if it hadn't been for them, I wouldn't be alive.

I turned to Gladys and said, "Thank you. I couldn't ask for better friends."

Gladys smiled. "You're welcome. But I know you would've done the same for any of us. And... Don't forget to thank Dean. He really deserves it this time."

I nodded in agreement, unaware of just how much more complicated that task would be.

CHAPTER 6: PARTY

When Monday classes started, I dove headfirst into my studies. Having missed several labs and practicals, I needed to catch up on assignments quickly to avoid losing points. So, I stayed late at the university to access labs that were off-limits during regular hours.

Though I was working twice as hard, being busy felt more like a blessing than a burden. It left me with neither the time nor the energy to dwell on the memories of the Tiamon accident. Surprisingly, it also helped me avoid Dean.

Whenever he called or texted to meet, I'd refuse, claiming I was either busy or too tired. He never questioned or objected to my excuses, and knowing Dean, that felt strange. Still, his unexpected understanding worked in my favor. Sure, I was tired, but not so exhausted that I couldn't find time for a guy who lived one floor down and could be in my room in under a minute. Oddly enough, after the emotional shock and a few days of unconsciousness, I had more energy than ever, and my mind was sharper than before the accident.

I avoided Dean for a different reason altogether: I couldn't figure out how I felt about him, or how I should act around him. Just hours before the accident, I'd vowed to never let him pull me into his web of charm and desire again. When I promised Gladys, I meant it. But after Dean showed himself to be the most caring boyfriend, I wasn't so sure that breaking up was the only option. More and more, I caught myself wondering if this new side of Dean—the one I saw in Tiamon—was reason enough to give us another chance.

I knew avoiding Dean wasn't the best option and that this wouldn't resolve itself, but I couldn't muster the courage to make a move. So, I managed to avoid Dean all week—until Friday morning, when we ran into each other in the university lobby. For some reason, the auditorium where our lecture was scheduled was closed, and the teacher was running late.

Dean stood against the wall, phone in hand, glancing toward the entrance as if waiting for someone. With hardly anyone in the corridor, there was no way I could pretend I hadn't seen him. I had no choice but to walk over and say hi.

"Hi, babe!" Dean replied, slightly stumbling over the word "babe," making it clear he knew why I'd been avoiding him. Still, he looked genuinely happy to see me. His eyes were filled with tenderness, and he hesitated, unsure if it was appropriate to hug me.

I felt my cheeks flush. Fortunately, just as the tension peaked, a familiar voice broke through: "Hi, guys!"

I turned my head, breaking eye contact with Dean and spotting my classmate Jenny. She tossed her pigtail back and said, "I'm throwing a party at my place. You two are invited—oh, and invite Gladys too; I haven't seen her today."

"Thanks for the invite!" I replied. "Is it tonight?"

"Yep, as usual."

I glanced at Dean and saw doubt in his eyes. He'd always loved parties; even an earthquake would barely make him skip one, so I was confused. But then I recalled Dean's gaze before we were interrupted and guessed what the reason might be. In that moment, something shifted within me, and I said confidently, "Okay, we'll come."

"Great! See you then," Jenny said happily, walking away as quickly as she had appeared.

Dean looked at me and asked, "Are you sure? It's only been a week since… well…"

In that last sentence, he stammered and rubbed his cheek awkwardly. Both his gesture and the uncertainty in his voice made me doubt whether I was doing the right thing. But I decided to stand my ground. "Well, it's been almost two weeks, to be precise, and I'm absolutely fine, Dean. Besides, I really need a distraction."

"You said 'we'… Do you really want to go together?"

"Yeah, why not?" I shrugged. "We haven't officially broken up yet. And… I owe you."

Dean brushed his fingers gently along my cheek. For the first time, I saw a glimmer in his eyes and was surprised to realize they were tears he was trying to hold back.

"Babe… We've had a rough time lately, but when it all happened, I couldn't imagine…"

I pressed my finger to Dean's lips, silencing him.

"You don't have to continue," I said softly. "I know, and… I'm grateful."

Dean took a deep breath and closed his eyes for a moment. He stood there for several seconds, trying to gather himself. When he opened his eyes again, the glimmer of tears had faded. Dean smiled awkwardly, as if to excuse the vulnerability he had just shown. I smiled back, though I could feel a tension lingering in the air.

I needed to break the tension somehow, so I lowered my head and, playfully curling a lock of hair around my finger, asked, "So, what time do you have in mind to pick me up?"

"You decide," Dean shrugged, his eyes lighting up with genuine joy as his lips curved into a silly smile.

"How about half-past seven?"

"Got it."

***

Jenny lives with her parents in a spacious private house. Her family is wealthy, running their own business and spending two-thirds of the year on trips abroad. Thus, Jenny mostly occupies the house alone. Though very sociable, Jenny doesn't seem to be a big party lover, so I feel she arranges her gatherings out of boredom, wanting to fill the empty space of her house with joy. And she undoubtedly succeeds.

The student community greatly appreciates Jenny's kindness. After the parties, a few guys always stay to help Jenny clean up, keeping the house in decent condition. This is probably why Jenny's parents don't mind her hosting them.

The dress code at Jenny's events is very casual, prioritizing the comfort of guests. In other words, whether you choose an evening gown or baggy jeans and a loose T-shirt, others will treat you the same.

That day, however, my soul asked for something more than just casual, so I started getting ready two hours before the scheduled meeting with Dean. It felt special for several reasons. First, it was my first social event in a long time, and second, since I decided to reconcile with Dean and give our relationship another chance, I wanted him to feel proud of how beautiful and sexy his girlfriend was.

To execute my plan, I dug out my high-heeled boots from the far corner of the closet. I rarely wear them because they're not the most comfortable shoes. But that day, I was determined to endure the discomfort for the sake of looking irresistible. Next, I found a tight black skirt and a yellow top. I finished off my look with a leather belt and a black leather jacket.

I was naturally gifted with a striking appearance: dark brown, almost black hair, tan skin, brown eyes, and long black eyelashes. This means I usually wear little to no makeup in my everyday life. But that day, I decided a few strokes of eyeliner and mascara were necessary. This took another half-hour, but fortunately, I finished just as Dean arrived.

He was right on time. Wearing tight black pants and his signature leather jacket, he looked like the typical "bad boy," exuding vibes of danger and mystery. He was undeniably hot.

Dean's gaze undressed me instantly. "You look stunning, babe!" he whispered in my ear, barely restraining himself as his lips chastely brushed my cheek.

Dean's reaction flattered me, and I felt a sense of satisfaction wash over me. Those two hours of effort had not been wasted—my look had achieved exactly what I intended.

By the time we arrived at Jenny's, the place was already packed. My eyes scanned the crowd until they landed on Gladys, standing by the window with Caleb. They were deep in conversation, exchanging flirty smiles, so I decided to leave them undisturbed. Dean and I made our way deeper into the room, heading for the drinks table and searching for a comfortable spot to settle.

We danced more than I ever expected that night—so much, in fact, that by the end of the party, I could barely feel my feet. But the amount of alcohol we drank was even more surprising. Laughing, fooling around, and dancing, we downed drink after drink without a second thought. We felt good—almost as good as we did at the start of our relationship.

Lately, the only place where Dean and I connected was in bed. Outside of that, our time was filled with mutual blame and biting insults. Dean constantly demanded attention, grew jealous for no reason, and often treated me like I was something he owned.

As an independent person, I couldn't stand how he violated my personal space, and I never stayed silent about it. But I struggled to find the right words to express my frustration, which often led to conflict. Needless to say, things between us were tough.

Dean's shift in attitude after the accident was both pleasant and unsettling. As much as I wanted to believe it wasn't temporary, that things between us could stay this way, I doubted it was possible. Consumed by constant fears and doubts, I desperately needed to let go and relax. The party seemed like the perfect escape. It let me stop dwelling on all the negativity in my life, and the alcohol certainly helped with that.

I remembered the end of the party in fragmented flashes. At some point, we joined a group of dorm mates and called a taxi. There were eight of us, all crammed into a single sedan, ignoring the driver's unfiltered curses. We sang loudly the whole ride, probably making the poor driver curse his job. Everything after that was a blur. The last thing I remembered was Dean's hands undressing me, and I didn't mind.

CHAPTER 7: THE FIRST ALARM SOUND

The moment I cracked my eyes open, a sharp headache hit me in response. The sunlight was harsh and unbearable. I quickly squeezed my eyes shut again, and the pain eased slightly.

Great... I thought sarcastically, lying there with my eyes shut, analyzing my condition. Everything felt hazy—my head was heavy as a stone, and dizziness clouded my senses. My temples throbbed, and any movement only intensified the discomfort.

Welcome to hell, my inner voice muttered as I braced for death. Then, I reconsidered and began plotting how to get up. Step one: open my eyes. I focused all my energy on this monumental task. I managed it, but the second my eyes opened, the headache slammed even harder. Still, I refused to give up and forced myself to scan the room.

The first thing that caught my eye was my boots, carelessly tossed in the corner. They looked trampled and pathetic.

Serves you right, you torturers! I thought bitterly, but then reconsidered. Once I conquered the headache, I'd clean them up and put them away. After all, it wasn't the boots that were to blame for last night's booze-induced misery—it was me.

I tried to sit up, but immediately regretted it. The walls and furniture began to sway as if I were on a rocking boat. I collapsed back onto the bed, staring at the ceiling. That's when I heard Dean's footsteps. He moved carefully, but every step felt like a hammer pounding inside my skull.

"Morning, babe!" Dean's cheerful voice cut through the fog, his smile annoyingly tender.

How does he do it? I thought. *He drank as much as I did—maybe even more—yet here he is, fresh as a cucumber and bursting with energy.*

My head throbbed again, as if agreeing with me.

Well, at least this hangover from hell should keep me from becoming an alcoholic, I thought, finding a sliver of positivity. With that, I turned my head to greet Dean.

"Hi," I attempted, but all that escaped was a faint, raspy wheeze.

"Are you okay?" Dean asked, his voice tinged with unease.

Honestly, could he ask a more idiotic question? *Can't he see I'm not okay*? *I feel terrible*! *I can't move, and my head's about to explode*!

Despite my mental rant, I knew there was no way I could say all that out loud. So, I settled for a simple, "Still alive." Strangely, it came out clearer than "hi."

Dean stared at me, both alarmed and confused.

Oh God, Dean, now's not the time to panic! I thought, frustrated. Summoning all my remaining strength, I focused on speaking clearly and managed, "I've got a terrible headache. Please, bring the aspirin from my bag."

Nodding, Dean hurried to get the aspirin, which, of course, didn't bring instant relief but gave me hope the pain would ease soon.

Dean gave me a sympathetic look and asked, "Coffee?"

"I'm afraid I'm out," I said with a hint of disappointment. Then, encouraged by being able to speak clearly, I added, "I was planning to grab some today."

"How about tea, then?"

"No, tea won't cut it. I need coffee—the stronger, the better. But I'll manage. The pill will kick in soon, and I'll be okay."

"I'll head to the nearest coffee shop," Dean said, standing up.

I thought about stopping him, but then decided it wasn't worth ruining this rare moment where Dean actually wanted to take care of me. So, I just nodded and said, "Thank you."

After Dean slipped out the door, I lay back down and closed my eyes. I must have dozed off because, at some point, the throbbing pain in my head eased up. I returned to reality when I heard a dull click of the door lock.

Dean's probably back, I thought lazily as I opened my eyes. My headache was gone, but my mind still felt foggy.

Dean slipped off his shoes and approached the bed. Sitting on the edge, he handed me the precious cardboard cup, the rich aroma of espresso wafting from the lid. I sat up and gratefully accepted the cup from Dean. With the first sip, I felt life slowly returning to my body. After another, I looked at Dean and said, "We definitely drank too much last night."

"That's putting it mildly," Dean agreed.

"Do you even remember last night?"

"Bits and pieces."

I rolled my eyes, took another sip, and said, "Same here."

"Listen, babe..." Dean hesitated, rubbing his cheek. "You didn't enjoy it last night, did you?"

"What do you mean?"

"Well... we, uh, had sex..."

Big deal, I thought, but Dean's embarrassed expression stopped me from saying it or rolling my eyes. Dean has never been uncomfortable with talking about sex, thus, there must have been a respectful reason for his concern.

Dean rubbed his cheek again, blushing like a schoolboy, and said, "And... you acted a little strange..."

"What do you mean by 'strange?'"

Now the concern was creeping in. This conversation was getting way too weird.

“Well…” Dean said, “you barely reacted to my touch, like you didn’t feel a thing.”

“Seriously?”

“Yup.”

I sipped my coffee, trying to recall anything about what Dean was saying, but came up blank.

“Honestly, I don’t remember anything about it, so I can’t confirm or deny what you’re saying.”

“I get that, but still...” Dean looked down, clearly regretful he’d even started this conversation.

I felt a mix of discomfort and guilt. Putting my coffee on the bedside table, I moved closer and gently took Dean’s hand. “Dean, I’m really sorry, but I don’t think you need to worry about it. You’re an amazing lover, and sex with you is always incredible.”

Dean blushed a little, clearly relieved by the compliment. I lifted Dean’s hand to my lips and kissed it softly. “I was so drunk last night. I don’t think I’ve ever been that wasted.”

Dean pulled me into a hug. “You’re right, babe, we should’ve just gone straight to bed,” he said, kissing the top of my head. Then he pulled back slightly, looking into my eyes. “But you looked so beautiful, and I wanted you so much...”

I playfully tousled Dean’s curly hair and smiled. “I’m going to shower and try to look human again. Then we can have breakfast and maybe go for a walk if you’re up for it.”

“I’d love to,” Dean said, smiling and shifting aside to give me room to get out of bed.

“Great,” I said with a grin, getting up and heading for the shower.

We didn’t bring up the party, or what happened after, for the rest of the day.

CHAPTER 8: NOT A CURSE BUT A BLESSING

Two days later, another alarm went off.

I had a free evening, and Dean and I had planned to spend it together. I was sitting at the desk and reading a book when Dean entered the room. To tease him, I pretended not to notice him come in, keeping my eyes glued to the book with the most focused expression I could manage. Dean locked the door and came up behind me, gently kissing my bare shoulder. "I missed you," he whispered.

I intended to tease him a bit longer, but his lips were so hot and insistent that I decided to show mercy and let him have what he wanted.

I turned around and brushed my lips against Dean's cheek. "I missed you too," I whispered into his ear, and that was all the invitation he needed.

With his usual confident move, Dean lifted me from the chair, turned me around, and kissed me. His passionate lips devoured mine, and I could feel his arousal growing quickly. But I couldn't say the same for myself.

The sensations felt strange. It was just physical contact that could be compared to tasteless food. I could feel Dean's lips and the insistent movements of his tongue, but there was no pleasure, no excitement.

My body always reacted to Dean's closeness immediately.

Sometimes, I'd even get mad at myself for how easily his scent and touch excited me, making it hard to stay angry, prolonging the agony of our complicated relationship.

But despite the difficulties, there were advantages. For two years, Dean and I had come to know each other's bodies perfectly. We knew all the partner's sensitive spots and how to touch them just right to draw shivers and moans. We felt each other, and our sex would always be something more than just physical contact. It was a unity of energies emitted by our excited bodies, resulting in a powerful symphony of mutual pleasure.

But now, despite all of Dean's efforts, my energy was gone—like someone had flipped a switch. I only felt the physical sensations—pressure, temperature, friction, and vibration. There was no enjoyment, whether he was touching me or I was touching him. My hands and lips couldn't catch the waves of Dean's pleasure; all I could feel was pressure and heat. I wanted to at least make it enjoyable for Dean, so I used all my experience to try. I managed some success, but it was nowhere near the symphony we were used to.

After sex, Dean and I usually cuddled for a few minutes, savoring the sweet aftertaste of our recent storm. But this time, Dean got up as soon as we finished. He walked over to the open window and lit a cigarette.

I lay in bed, confused and unsatisfied. I tried to calm myself and think, but all I could do was loop the same thought in my head: *What the hell is going on*?!

In a minute, the smoke from Dean's cigarette drifted toward the bed. This annoyance was the last drop in my cup of patience. I couldn't stay silent any longer. I quickly got up, slipped on my dress, and walked over to Dean.

"I've asked you a hundred times not to smoke in here!" I said, my voice rising. Subconsciously, I was looking for a fight; the negative emotions building inside me needed an outlet.

To my disappointment, Dean didn't retaliate. He simply tossed his cigarette out the window and watched it fall to the ground. "Sorry," he mumbled, leaning against the edge of the desk. He looked lost and troubled.

His bleak expression made my irritation fade, so I asked in a softer tone, "What's wrong?"

"I'm the one who should be asking, Tayra! We're not drunk today."

I sighed and perched on the desk beside Dean. "I have no idea," I shrugged. "Maybe it's just the wrong moment."

Dean raised an incredulous eyebrow. "Tayra, even in our worst times, we had no 'wrong' moments."

"Yes, I know... and I'm just as surprised."

At a loss for words, I fell silent and gazed out the open window. I had never considered the concrete wall of the neighboring building and two half-dried maples a scenic view, but that evening, the landscape appeared even more dismal than usual. The ominous silhouettes of the trees against the cloudy night sky and the peeling plaster of the wall, visible even in the dim light of an old streetlamp, only deepened my already depressed mood. To calm myself, I took a deep breath of the cool autumn air drifting in from the window and turned my gaze to Dean.

Dean stared at the shabby wall as well. It was unusual to see him so detached and contemplative. I felt a pang of guilt and wanted to find a way to cheer him up. I moved closer and gently placed my hand on Dean's shoulder. "Dean, please don't take this personally. I don't know why this is happening, but I'm sure it's not your fault. I probably just haven't recovered from the stress yet."

Dean turned to me, sighed, and said, "Well, maybe..." He paused briefly before adding, "Sorry, babe, I should've been more patient. I think I should go." With that, he quickly gathered his clothes scattered around the room, got dressed, and left.

As Dean busied himself, I sat on the desk, silently watching him. Once he was gone, I stood up and locked the door. My emotions were in turmoil. I couldn't say I was sad or hurt, but I felt an unsettling confusion that gnawed at me for the rest of the night.

By morning, this uncertainty had morphed into irritability that seeped out of me like a crack in a dam. As I made my way through the lecture auditorium, I snapped at Emmett when he asked to borrow my laboratory report as an example and yelled at Lucas for accidentally bumping me with his backpack.

Seeing all this, Gladys looked genuinely concerned. "What's wrong?" she asked as I reached the desk and sat down on the bench beside her.

I exhaled, weary of my own hostility, and replied, trying to sound neutral, "I don't know yet. But something definitely is."

"You're scaring me," Gladys said, her voice laced with concern.

"Drop it," I said dismissively. "The lecture is about to start."

Gladys shrugged and turned to the blackboard.

I took another deep breath and followed her lead. *It's fine*, I told myself. *It's going to be alright.*

Yet, despite my desire to remain optimistic, things only worsened. Over the next two days, the situation repeated itself again and again. I couldn't find a reasonable explanation for it, which made me increasingly anxious. Dean was anxious too, as despite all my efforts, sex no longer brought him the satisfaction it once did. For Dean, sex was less about physical contact and more about having dominion over my body. He loved seeing me enjoy his touch and knowing he could either bring me to heaven or cast me into hell with a single move of his finger. This realization made Dean feel powerful, confident, and happy. But now, with that power gone, Dean felt lost and insecure.

Dean's dissatisfaction led to a depressed mood and irritability. The further we drifted apart, the tenser our relationship became, and this only added to my stress. Along with my own worries, I feared upsetting Dean and provoking a fight. This fear poisoned my already complicated life, even as conflicts arose regularly.

If I were honest and acted on my feelings, Dean was angry because he wasn't experiencing the satisfaction he desired. When I pretended to feel pleasure and faked an orgasm, Dean always sensed the lie and grew angry because I tried to deceive him. I didn't know how to respond, and as a result, I felt angry too. I was angry at my body for inexplicably behaving differently. I was angry at Dean, whose displeasure made me feel guilty, even though it wasn't my fault. Finally, I was angry at myself for not finding a way out of this vicious cycle.

In fact, a way out existed, and it was quite obvious, yet for some reason, I lacked the courage to admit it. I needed advice and support, and Gladys was the only person I could trust with such a delicate matter. However, I knew that discussing my sexual problems with Gladys would be akin to suicide, so I kept postponing the conversation, justifying my procrastination with the absence of a suitable moment. Fortunately, the perceptive Gladys noticed that something was off with me. One day, as we had lunch in the university cafeteria, she looked at me with concern and asked, "What's going on with you, Tayra? You seem so sad and irritated all the time."

"Well, it's probably just PMS. Don't pay attention."

"I thought so too and tried to ignore it, but this 'PMS' has lasted for about three weeks now."

I sighed and rubbed my forehead nervously. "Yes, Gladys, you're right. But it's personal, and I don't know how to explain."

"I'm your best friend, Tayra, and I just can't see you like this anymore. You know you can always count on me."

"Yes, Gladys, I know, but… em…"

I was about to say, "It's not that important, nothing to worry about," and change the subject, but my throat wouldn't let me lie, and I started coughing instead. Gladys watched me silently, her eyes full of concern and confusion. That's when I realized my need to share was stronger than my fear of being judged, so I dropped all my angst and said, "Something's wrong with me..."

Gladys raised an eyebrow. "What do you mean?"

"I mean... my relationship with Dean."

"Wow, what a shock," Gladys muttered, disappointed. "Your relationship with Dean has always been messed up. It's wrong at the core. I'm not even sure if there was ever any real love between you two. Sex is all that's left now, and I don't think it can last much longer."

"Yeah, sex has always been a big part of our relationship, maybe even the main part at times. But then Dean saved my life, and I thought it would bring us closer... but it did the opposite."

Gladys opened her mouth to ask something, but the confusion in her eyes said it all. I nodded. "I'll explain."

Nervously, I brushed my hair back and started, "You know Dean and I had problems, but our sex was always good. Always. Until now." I paused, looking into Gladys's wide eyes. She took a deep breath but said nothing.

"When Dean kisses or touches me, I feel nothing. No excitement, no pleasure. It's weird because he's doing everything I used to love, but now... nothing. I'm numb to his touch."

Gladys rested her chin on her hand, staring at the table. She sat silently for a few moments, digesting everything I'd said. Finally, she lifted her head and said, "Well, it's strange, sure, but it makes sense. Your feelings for Dean burned out long ago. Yeah, he saved your life, but maybe that's just his apology for all the misery he's caused over the last two years. That accident showed you life's too short to waste on toxic relationships. It's no secret that sex is partly mental, and your brain knows better than ever that Dean doesn't belong in your life. I know Dean has his good sides, but he's quick-tempered and jealous as hell, and you don't need me to tell you where that leads. Your numbness to Dean's touch isn't a curse, it's a blessing. It's your brain telling your body it's time to end this."

"You're right, Gladys," I said softly. "I think it's time to finally end things with him."

Dean was supposed to come that evening, and I decided I wouldn't procrastinate about the breakup. Though we'd had our share of arguments and separations before, I never got used to it. Each time left me feeling worse than the last. And now, I was freaking out again, struggling with how to tell Dean it was really over this time. I paced the room, trying to draft the right words in my head, but nothing felt right. I knew this would hurt him, no matter how carefully I said it. Despite his flaws and our constant fighting, I didn't want to cause him more pain than necessary.

The second half of the day crawled by, filled with dread over the upcoming conversation and a growing desire to just get it over with. Time seemed to stretch, and no matter how much I tried to distract myself, thoughts of the evening ahead gnawed at me. Finally, I heard the familiar sound of a key turning in the lock. Dean was here.

"Hi, babe!" His usual friendly tone only made the weight in my chest heavier. I felt even worse for what I was about to say.

"Hi," I responded, keeping my voice neutral, as I paused to watch him close the door. Once he did, I looked at him seriously and said coldly, "We need to talk, Dean."

"Has something happened?" Dean asked, his voice a mix of surprise and anxiety.

"No... Well, yes..." I stammered. In that moment, my plan to break up was on the verge of collapsing. Still, I clenched my fists and tried again. This time my voice was cold and clear, "I've thought a lot about us, and I've realized something. My body doesn't respond to your touch anymore because I don’t feel anything for you in my heart. And this is why I don’t see any sense in keeping our relationship.”

Dean sat on the edge of the bed and sighed, “Again, Tayra, really? We’ve been through this so many times. Admit that you didn’t mean what you just said and our feelings are alive. It’s just a phase, and it’s going to pass.”

“No, it’s not, Dean. It's different this time. This is a point of no return and I’m a hundred percent sure of it. We are done. I’m sorry.”

Without saying a word, Dean stood up and walked to the door. He paused for a second, took the keys from his pocket, and handed them to me.

“Keep it until you pack your things,” I said, forcing a chill into my voice.

Dean nodded, quickly turned away, and crossed the threshold.

CHAPTER 9: INKLING

After breaking up with Dean, I decided to make the most of being single and immerse myself in my studies. Dean and I didn't communicate and tried to avoid each other on campus and in the dormitory. If a meeting was unavoidable, we limited ourselves to a formal greeting and quickly went our separate ways.

Nevertheless, Gladys doubted my resolve and worried that I would give in to Dean again. To prevent that, she sought a new crush to set me up with. I had many male acquaintances in our faculty and dormitory, yet I wasn't interested in any of them. Thus, Gladys pulled out all the stops to find perfect places where I could meet decent guys. She hardly left me unattended, fearing that I would "do something I might regret" and filled all my free time with cultural programs.

Since I'm not a fan of clubs and discos, she almost daily hauled me to theaters, cinemas, museums, or exhibitions, leaving me only to prepare for serious tests and exams. Gladys's efforts were rewarded surprisingly quickly, and just a month after breaking up with Dean, she managed to introduce me to Nick. To be precise, Nick and I met by chance at the cinema, where Gladys dragged me on a Saturday night, claiming she had found "a movie that couldn't be missed."

To say the movie was bad would be a compliment. I was extremely bored and didn't know what to do with myself. I was afraid my jaw might dislocate from constant yawning, enduring only out of respect for Gladys. Also, because the weather was cold and walking outside seemed less appealing than sitting in a warm, soft chair.

When I counted the tiles on the ceiling for the fifth time, Gladys whispered in my ear, "Do you feel that guy's eyes on you?"

"Which guy?" I asked indifferently, more interested in Gladys's ability to spot guys behind the tall armchairs in the dark cinema.

"That one, to the left in the front row."

I scanned the lower row for male heads. Just then, a brightly lit scene began, and the light from the screen partially illuminated the audience. I saw a redhead hastily turn toward the screen. It must have been the guy Gladys was talking about.

"Red-haired?" I asked, maintaining the same indifference.

"Oh my God, Tayra! He has ginger hair!"

"Big difference!" I shrugged. "Especially in the darkness."

"Even in the dark, he finds you more attractive than the movie..."

"Nothing surprising," I cut in. "The movie is rubbish."

Gladys giggled and shrugged apologetically. "The trailer looked good, though."

After the movie, I noticed the ginger-haired guy standing in the lobby, not far from the exit, clearly waiting for someone. I assumed he was waiting for a friend or a girlfriend, feeling a slight twinge of disappointment, but my curiosity got the better of me, and I decided to study him anyway.

Slender and tall, he made a rather pleasant impression. He wore gray jeans and a green hoodie that matched his fair skin and slightly disheveled, wavy ginger hair perfectly. As Gladys and I got closer, I could take a better look at his face—almond-shaped eyes, slightly squinted as if in a smile, and light freckles scattered across his nose and cheekbones. Individually, the features of his face weren't remarkable, but together they created a surprisingly attractive picture.

Gladys caught my gaze in the guy's direction, and I could practically see a match-making plan forming in her head. She waited until we were just a few meters away from him, then casually slipped her bag into my hands with a quick, "Hold this, I'll be right back," and dashed off to the bathroom, leaving me stranded in the middle of the lobby.

The ginger-haired guy smiled and confidently approached me. "Hi, I'm Nick!" he said warmly, blushing slightly as he smiled again.

My usual response to attempts like this is caustic—making it clear the guy picked the wrong person to approach. But Nick's genuine embarrassment set him apart from the usual cocky pick-up artists, so I decided to keep the conversation going instead of shutting it down. So I smiled back and replied with a friendly, "Hi, I'm Tayra!"

Encouraged by my friendliness, Nick met my eyes and asked perhaps the most predictable question, "What do you think of the movie?"

Nick's almond-shaped eyes were striking emerald green, his eyebrows and lashes a shade darker than his hair, giving his face a sharper, more expressive look. It was one of those faces that you can look at forever and never get enough. My heart quickened, and I was surprised by how long it had been since I'd felt anything like this.

After two years with Dean, I knew him inside out. He was an open book, and even if I didn't know every twist in the story, I knew the general plot and could predict his reactions in almost any situation. But Nick was different. He was like a new book with an intriguing cover. I didn't know the story yet or if it would even hold my attention—but I knew I wanted to open it and read the first page.

Despite wanting to impress Nick, I also wanted to be myself—to show him that while I might seem like a soft fruit, I could still break someone's teeth. So instead of answering directly, I tilted my head and smiled playfully. "Do you want me to be sweet or honest?"

Nick grinned, showing off his perfect white teeth. "I saw you counting the lights and ceiling tiles, so I'm dying to hear the 'sweet' version. But I'd rather hear the truth."

His sharp wit and keen observation caught me off guard, instantly wiping away any of my playful pretense. I felt a wave of relief—I didn't need to play any games. Channeling my inner TV news anchor, I announced, "The movie was predictable and shallow. I figured out the villain in the first 15 minutes and was bored for the rest."

"You're so funny," Nick laughed. "But I totally agree, though it took me about twenty minutes to figure out the main villain." Nick paused, and after a brief hesitation, added, "Luckily, I could admire you. Though it was a little uncomfortable turning my head back the whole time, it was definitely worth it." Nick paused again, looking at me closely. His nose and cheeks flushed a bit more, and he nervously ran a hand through his tousled hair, as if trying to tame it. "You're really beautiful."

I felt heat rise from my chin to my forehead, so I tilted my head slightly, letting my hair fall to cover it a little. I felt flattered but confused, unsure of what to say next. Nick didn't seem to know either, but he wasn't ready to give up easily. He decided that saying something, even random, was better than staying silent and blurted out, "How about a cup of coffee?"

"It's already half-past nine, a bit late for coffee," I said, turning him down. "Besides, we both have company."

Nick smiled. "Yeah, I get it. I came with a friend, but he had some urgent stuff and left earlier. I was actually waiting for **you**. I knew my odds were one in ten to start a conversation, but I figured I'd try my luck."

I appreciated Nick's honesty and didn't want our conversation to end there. Since he'd already taken the first step, I decided to take the initiative. "Do you like walking?" I asked.

"Yeah, I do," he said.

"Tomorrow's Sunday, so we could go for a walk if you're free."

"I'd love to," Nick nodded. "How can I contact you?"

"Just text me tomorrow," I said with a smile, then gave Nick my number.

The next day, Nick and I met in the city center. Despite the cold, we wandered around the park for about an hour, visited a newly opened modern photography exhibition, and then warmed up in a cozy café.

Nick had recently defended his master's thesis and started working as a QA engineer at a small IT company. It was so far from my world of interests that, at first, I worried I wouldn't find anything we could talk about. But my worries were unfounded—talking with Nick was effortless. We chatted, laughed, and joked around.

As it started to get dark, we headed to the embankment to catch the last moments of the sunset. It was cold, and a strong wind whipped around near the water. Nick turned his back to the wind, shielding me from the cold gusts, and gently rested his hand on my shoulder. The red rays of the setting sun danced through Nick's ginger hair, and his green eyes glimmered in the glow of the streetlights. Nick gently brushed a stray lock of hair from my forehead and gazed into my eyes.

In that moment, I realized I badly wanted him to kiss me. Not just because Nick seemed like a great guy who'd made my Sunday wonderful, but because I was gripped by a simple curiosity—would I feel anything? For a few moments, I wrestled with the fear of being misunderstood or getting the answer I dreaded. But in the end, I decided knowing was better than wondering.

I closed my eyes and rose onto my tiptoes, tilting my face toward Nick, giving him a clear signal. Nick didn't hesitate—he gently pressed his lips to mine...

***

Fifteen minutes before the lecture, I walked into the auditorium. Gladys was in our usual spot, listening to music. When I approached, she paused her music and pulled out her earphones—clearly eager to hear all about yesterday's date.

"Hey," I said calmly, unzipping my bag to grab my workbook.

"Oh my God!" Gladys exclaimed, eyes wide. "What happened?"

"Nothing, everything's fine," I said, still calm, as I laid out my things on the desk.

But Gladys wasn't giving up that easily. Ignoring my evasiveness, she pressed on, "So, how did it go?"

"Good," I said flatly, sitting down next to Gladys.

Gladys crossed her arms, eyeing me skeptically. "That doesn't sound like a 'good.' Did he turn out to be a cocky jerk?"

"Oh no, Nick's not like that at all! He's great—charming, kind, funny. I really liked our date."

"Congrats!" Gladys said with a sarcastic grin. She leaned in, looking me right in the eyes. "So, what happened next?"

I sighed and shrugged. "He kissed me."

"And that's a reason to be upset? Didn't you want him to?"

"I did… I really did… but…"

"Was he a bad kisser?"

"No… yes… I don't know!"

"Now I'm completely lost," Gladys said, looking at me in confusion.

"You know, I really liked Nick. I really wanted him to kiss me, and he did. Technically, the kiss was perfect. I should've enjoyed it, but… I didn't feel anything!"

"Oh, here we go again, Tayra! After Dean, you're way too focused on the chemistry. Just enjoy talking to a nice guy. Give him a chance!"

"Yeah, you're probably right. I'm just overthinking it."

I pulled up a picture of Nick from yesterday's walk in the park and handed my phone to Gladys. "He's hot, right?"

"No doubt!" Gladys grinned.

***

Nick worked from 9 to 6, and his office was just two blocks from my dorm, so we saw each other pretty often. Nick was easygoing, understanding, and really caring. Sometimes I thought being a social worker would suit his personality better than his current job. But I had no idea how good Nick was at his job, since we barely talked about it.

Soon, our relationship progressed, and sometimes Nick would head to work straight from my place. Yet, even after months together, I didn't feel any excitement or pleasure when he kissed or touched me. It was strange, though, because otherwise, everything was perfect between us. I didn't tell Nick about my problem and just faked my reactions instead. It really started to take a toll on me, and I felt deeply depressed. I couldn't shake the feeling that maybe my body knew better than my head—if I didn't feel anything, maybe Nick just wasn't the one for me.

Breaking up with Nick was really hard because I didn't want to tell him the truth, and there wasn't even a real reason to leave. I ended up lying, saying I'd met someone else, making myself look awful. I felt terrible, but I was sure it was better for both of us.

As soon as I was single again, Gladys resumed her efforts to set me up with someone. With the weather warming up, we walked a lot and one day wandered into a pizzeria, where I met Xavier, a charming blonde with brown eyes—unusual for his coloring. Xavier was a fifth-year economics and management student who worked part-time as a waiter.

Things with Xavier followed a similar pattern as with Nick, except that after several kisses, I didn't take it further and just broke things off.

The day I broke up with Xavier, I sat on my bed thinking, *What's wrong with me? Why is this happening? It wasn't always like this!*

I mentally rewound the past few months and realized I hadn't had any issues with feeling anything until the trip to Tiamon. I remembered that sunny morning, and how Dean's touch almost made us miss the tour bus…

Suddenly, a terrible realization struck me. I saw the horrifying, fierce eyes and heard the sinister laughter ringing in my ears.

No, that can't be! I cried out, feeling the chilling horror fetter my body. The awful memories didn't just fade; they remained as clear and vivid as if they had happened only a minute ago.

It's impossible! I repeated to myself. *There must be another rational explanation.*

CHAPTER 10: FRIGHTENING DESIRE

The campus lobby was noisy and crowded. Gladys and I had our first classes on different floors, but I hoped to see her in the morning before lectures. Of course, I could text her, but I wanted to see Gladys in person.

Fortunately, my best friend's bright appearance and equally bright fashion choices always made her easy to spot, no matter how dense the crowd was. As soon as I spotted Gladys at the entrance, I rushed over to her.

"Hi!" I waved with unusual vigor for an early morning.

"Hi!" Gladys replied, waving back.

"I need to talk to you. It's important. Can we meet after lectures?"

"Yeah, sure," Gladys shrugged, "but we have that meeting about the expedition."

"Oh, right, I forgot."

Gladys looked at me with a mix of concern and mistrust and asked, "Have you applied?"

"Are you kidding? Of course, I did—two weeks ago! A chance to take part in real excavations under Professor Portonapoulos? I couldn't miss that."

"Yeah, well," Gladys nodded, "working with Portonapoulos must be an amazing experience. He's one of those rare professors who's not just great at his subject but also a genuinely good person."

"Exactly! Plus, it's near Amhitiemar. You can't even imagine how badly I want to visit that ancient city."

Gladys sighed, shaking her head. "Haven't you had enough of Tiamon?"

I gave her a conciliatory smile and replied, "I'll have my bachelor's degree in archaeology in a month. It's normal for me to be obsessed with ancient places..."

"Yeah, but there are plenty of ancient places that are less mysterious—and a lot safer. I'm just worried about you, Tayra."

"I know. But it's my passion. And we don't choose our passions—they choose us."

"I get it, Tayra, but... you can't follow your passion if something happens to you, right? Just... be careful. Please."

"I'll be fine. Don't worry. Besides, we don't even know if my entry will get picked, so there's nothing to stress about yet."

I glanced at my phone and saw we only had two minutes before class. I smiled and said, "We've got to go. We'll have time before the meeting, so see you in the cafeteria."

"Okay, see you," Gladys said quickly, hurrying upstairs.

***

Unlike the bustling morning lobby, the afternoon cafeteria was half-empty, giving me the freedom to choose a table. I picked one in the corner and was about to grab my phone when Gladys walked in, looking slightly disgruntled.

"Ouch, what's wrong?" I asked cautiously as she approached.

"Nothing new," she snapped. "That idiot Emmet sent Mrs. Lourens our lab report without any corrections, so I had to use all my diplomatic skills to convince her it was just a mistake—and beg for another chance to fix it." Gladys let out a sigh and sat down. "Why did I get stuck with him as my lab partner?! Seriously... out of all people!"

After venting her frustration, Gladys calmed down and quickly refocused on the reason for our meeting. "So, what did you want to talk about?" she asked casually, as if the storm from a moment ago had never even happened.

"Well... it's about my... insensitivity," I began awkwardly.

"Oh jeez! I thought it'd be something new," Gladys cut in, sounding disappointed. "It's already turned into your obsession."

"Maybe, but please, just hear me out before brushing it off, okay?"

"Okay..." Gladys shrugged, clearly not convinced.

"Do you remember the legend of Tiendal?"

"Tayra, aren't we too grown up to believe in fairy tales?"

"Yes or no?"

"Well, partly..."

"The women who experienced Tiendal's love became insensitive to other men's touch..."

"So what?" Gladys said with a yawn.

"The secret room. There was magic in it. Once they entered, the women were cursed, making them addicted to Tiendal."

"Sorry for them," Gladys said, clearly bored. "But what does that have to do with you?"

"I went into the room."

"Oh, dear," Gladys rolled her eyes. "I doubt the secret room of an all-powerful priest would look like a tiny 2x2 meter cell. And it would definitely be hidden better than behind a swivel door with a button disguised in some wall painting."

"You're right. But I'm not talking about that room."

"Which one, then?" Gladys asked, her voice tinged with irony and a hint of surprise.

"The cell had three doors, one in each wall, and each door had a lever beside it. The levers had to be pressed in the correct sequence to unlock the central door. When the right combination was entered, the central door slid forward, revealing two slits on either side. I stepped through one of the slits into the room. There was a powerful smell—so strong I could barely breathe. I felt dizzy, then saw a light... and heard something like sinister laughter... I saw something, but it was blurry. Then I must have fainted because I don't remember anything after that. But something happened to me there, Gladys. I'm sure of it."

To my surprise, Gladys didn't make a sarcastic comment this time. She paused, thinking for a moment before saying, "Okay, let's assume what you're saying is true. But if it was dark in the cell, how did you see the doors and levers?"

"I used my phone's light until it died. After that, I felt my way around."

"If you left the cell and blacked out in another room, how did you get back to the cell? And where did the doors go?"

"I have no idea. That's what puzzles me the most."

Gladys covered her face with her hands. "This is insane, Tayra," she said, sounding exhausted. "I'm certain there were no doors or levers in that cell. Just solid walls."

"What if you just couldn't see them, but I could? You didn't notice the smell either, but I did..."

"More likely, you were just hallucinating, but I wasn't. You're very susceptible and got caught up in the guide's legend. With the lack of air, you felt dizzy and stumbled into a hidden cell behind a swivel door. Before you passed out, your brain filled in the blanks with those images. It's nothing more than your rich imagination, Tayra. And your insensitivity is probably just a psychological block."

"I appreciate your rationality, and I wish I could be as convinced as you are. But I can't. I need to get to the bottom of this."

Gladys took a deep breath and rubbed her chin thoughtfully. "I honestly don't know, Tayra. I get that what you're going through is frustrating. It's hard for me to imagine how it feels, and I have no idea how I'd handle it in your shoes, but... you can't just dismiss rationality. Looking for answers in some old legend doesn't make sense. But... once you've set your mind on something, neither I nor anyone else has ever been able to stop you, so..."

Gladys sighed and shrugged. We sat there in silence, staring at each other, probably for the first time not knowing what to say. Finally, Gladys glanced at her phone and said, "It's time for the meeting."

"Yeah, let's go," I said, standing up. I looked at Gladys again and asked, "Where do you think I should start?"

Gladys shrugged. "Even though I doubt any of this is possible, I'd love to help you, Tayra. But I'm afraid I'm not much help. I'm the last person who'd know where to find info on legends and curses. You knew something about this legend before the guide in Tiamon mentioned it. Where did you read it?"

"Oh..." I said, heading for the exit. "I don't remember exactly. It must've been a book I read at my grandma's during summer vacation. Some collection of myths and legends. But it was a long time ago, so I'm not sure."

"Well, I'm out of ideas then," Gladys chuckled. "Except maybe hurrying up if we don't want to end up in the last row."

"Good point," I said, smiling as I quickened my pace.

***

The meeting was led by Professor Gregory Portonapoulos, an elderly yet still vigorous man who had not lost his former charm and attractiveness, despite the wrinkles and gray hair. Gladys and I arrived just in time for the start of the meeting, and as soon as we sat down, Mr. Portonapoulos began his speech.

"As you all know, the upcoming expedition is fast approaching. If you haven't applied yet, you have three more days until the deadline. At the moment, we have around a hundred applications, but we can only select ten participants. The selection process will be in two stages.

In the first stage, twenty participants will be chosen based on the information in your applications. The final ten will be chosen based on the results of the interview."

Mr. Portonapoulos nodded to the man standing by the right wall, signaling him to step forward. The man appeared to be in his early to mid-thirties. He had slightly tanned skin and slicked-back black hair. He wore a dark, elegant business-casual suit.

"I'd like to introduce Mr. Robert Jenkins, a well-known businessman and philanthropist," Portonapoulos continued. "Genuinely convinced of the importance of our research, he has graciously agreed to sponsor the expedition. However, Mr. Jenkins is invested in seeing meaningful results from our work, so we need the best team possible. That's why Mr. Jenkins will personally interview each of the second-stage participants and make the final decision. Now, I'll turn it over to Mr. Jenkins."

Portonapoulos stepped back, giving the floor to Jenkins, who immediately began his speech. "Dear future archaeologists, I share your passion for ancient history..."

Despite his attractive appearance and perfectly tailored outfit, I disliked Jenkins at first sight. Something devilish lurked beneath his impeccable shell. Although his speech was friendly and inspiring, even from the middle rows of the large lecture hall, I could feel the cold, negative energy radiating from him. But most horrifying were his black eyes, burning with a fierce fire even when he smiled. Fear gripped my heart, and my mind instantly willed me to stay far away from him.

However, my body's reaction was completely unexpected. With just one glance at Jenkins, a shiver of excitement ran through me. The longer I looked at him, the stronger the excitement grew. The attraction to Jenkins was powerful and difficult to control, and the discord between my body and mind was even more terrifying than his devilish appearance.

After the meeting, when Gladys and I stepped into the lobby, I still felt unsettled. To calm down and collect myself, I decided to go to the restroom and splash cold water on my face. I suggested that Gladys join me, but she refused.

"I need to make a call," she said. "I'll wait for you here, in the lobby."

"Okay, I'll be quick," I replied, heading off alone.

The restrooms were at the far end of a long corridor, nearly on the opposite side of the building. You could access the corridor from the lobby or from the upper floors by staircases on either side. Whoever designed this building clearly didn't think things through. The corridor was narrow, dark, and uncomfortably cramped.

Even though it was nearly 5 p.m., students still crowded the front of the corridor, likely waiting for their teacher. The far part of the corridor in the vicinity of the restrooms was almost empty.

About halfway down the corridor, I suddenly noticed Jenkins, standing with his back to me and talking on the phone. It was clear Jenkins was upset with the person on the other end—harsh, laced with icy cold, his voice conveyed so much threat that my skin got goosebumps. "What am I paying you for? You have a problem, so fix it—quickly. If you can't, you're not worth your position and will be replaced. You have two hours before you're fired!"

When I was about three meters away from Jenkins, I caught a faint, familiar scent. Before I could place it, Jenkins suddenly turned, and his eyes locked onto mine.

It hit me like a lightning strike. I froze, unable to move or tear my gaze away. A burning desire seized my body, growing stronger despite my efforts to suppress it.

At that moment, I heard Professor Portonapoulos's voice behind me: "Ah, Mr. Jenkins, there you are. Let's go, I'll show you our laboratories."

Portonapoulos's appearance snapped me back to reality. Movement returned to my limbs, and I continued down the corridor.

I turned on the tap, scooped water into my hands, and splashed it onto my face, drenching part of my hair. The cold water had the desired invigorating and sobering effect, but my heart still pounded faster than normal. I stared at my reflection in the mirror, thinking, *What is going on with me? From feeling nothing at a good guy's touch to this uncontrollable desire for someone clearly dangerous. What's next, Tayra?*

CHAPTER 11: DEATH AS A SPRINGBOARD

"I'm about to graduate with a bachelor's degree, but I still can't get used to the exam chaos," I said, slumping into a chair at the cafeteria table.

"Maybe you'll get used to it in your fifth or sixth year," Gladys said reassuringly, taking a sip of her coffee. Her eyes were half-closed and she looked like she was going to fall asleep right then and there.

"Doubt it," I muttered, sipping my coffee.

"Who knows," Gladys shrugged. "We'll see." She yawned and put her head on crossed arms lying on the table. Her pose and facial expression were saying, "Do not disturb!"

"Speaking of seeing... It's been two weeks since the submission deadline, and Portonapoulos should've posted the list of second-stage participants today. Let's go."

I quickly finished my coffee and stood, urging Gladys to join me. But she didn't budge.

"Can't you check it from here?" she asked, yawning lazily.

"How?"

"Like always—on your phone."

I chuckled. "That's impossible, Gladys. The list is either on his door or the bulletin board."

"It's the 21st century! What about emails or posting it on the website?"

"Stand up, you victim of information technology. It's Professor Portonapoulos—he prefers old-school methods of notification."

"Fine," Gladys sighed. "At least let me finish this coffee." She lifted her cup lazily and yawned again. "With all due respect to Professor Portonapoulos, I completely disagree with such an outdated way of spreading information."

As I predicted, the list was posted on the bulletin board beside Portonapoulos's office. I expected a crowd of people eager to see the results, but either we were the first or the last—there was no one but us.

As we walked, Gladys perked up and reached the board before I did, scanning the list while I paused to straighten my shoe. "Congratulations! You're the first," she said happily as I came up. "Looks like Portonapoulos was really impressed by your essay and achievements."

A wave of relief washed over me—I'd made it this far. Honestly, I wanted to get into the expedition group so badly, I had no idea what I'd do if I failed.

"Are you on the list?" I asked nervously.

"Thank God, no!" Gladys sighed. "I only applied because everyone else did. Honestly, I was praying they wouldn't pick me—I'd much rather spend my summer with Caleb than with shovels, tents, and ancient stones. I've already got another job lined up for the summer."

I snickered but didn't comment. "Who else made it?" I asked instead.

"Oscar Biddenrow, Louis Nelson, Jenny Popovsky, and Ahish Agirra. I don't know the others. Some of the names aren't from our university."

"Got it," I said, thinking. "By the way, who's Oscar Biddenrow? Is he that red-haired nerd?"

"Yeah, but he's not a nerd—just a redhead."

I giggled, and Gladys couldn't help but laugh along.

"So, when's the interview?" I asked, calming down and glancing back at the Bulletin board.

"It says interviews start in three days, but the exact time will be sent by email." Gladys paused and shot me a reproachful look. "See? And you said he prefers old-fashioned notifications!"

"The interviews are probably organized by Jenkins's assistant, not Portonapoulos."

Just thinking about Jenkins made me feel sick. "Brr... the thought of being interviewed by that guy freaks me out," I said, cringing.

"Yup. Irresistibly hot, but seriously creepy," Gladys said.

The words "irresistibly hot" caught my attention. Maybe I wasn't the only one dealing with this weird attraction to Jenkins. I decided to test my theory right away.

"Did you feel any attraction to him?" I asked, unsure.

"Are you kidding? Definitely not. The devil isn't my type."

"It's just... you called him 'irresistibly hot.'"

"Well, you can't deny he's handsome, but even someone blind could see through the insincerity in his friendliness. For me, that cancels out all his looks."

I nodded in agreement. Just then, Gladys's phone chimed with an incoming message, and she pulled it from her purse to check. I glanced at the list again. "Aren't businessmen supposed to be busy?" I said.

Gladys looked up from her phone. "They are. Why?"

"Doesn't Jenkins's obsession with this expedition seem a little... suspicious?"

Gladys rubbed her temple. "Well... maybe a bit."

"Think about it. It's just a chance for inexperienced students like us to learn about real excavations. Does anyone really expect a historical breakthrough from a group like that, and in only a month?"

"I don't know," Gladys shrugged. "Rich people have their whims.

Amhitiemar was only just discovered and it's not well explored. Maybe he hopes to find some hidden treasure."

"Even if there is treasure, it should only have historical value."

"Not everyone thinks like you."

While we were talking, Gladys replied to the message and unzipped her purse to put her phone away. Halfway through, she paused, looked at me, and said, "When you get there, you'll figure out what's really going on."

"**If** I go."

"I don't think there's any doubt," Gladys said with a reassuring smile.

"I wouldn't be so sure," I sighed. "Portonapoulos is a passionate scientist—he's looking for genuinely interested and inspired people. But what's Jenkins after?"

"Speak of the devil," Gladys murmured, glancing at something behind me.

I turned my head and saw Jenkins at the end of the corridor. He was heading straight for Portonapoulos's office, moving quickly toward us since we were standing nearby. As he came within a few meters, I felt a sudden heat flare inside me, spreading through my entire body in an instant. My knees weakened, and I gasped. Jenkins paused at the door and looked at me, now just a meter away. An overwhelming urge to reach out and touch him surged through me. My hand twitched involuntarily, but I gripped the edge of my skirt, forcing it to stay still. And then—"Hello, Mr. Jenkins!" Gladys's voice cut through the tension.

I glanced at Gladys, breaking eye contact with Jenkins for just a moment. It was enough to snap me back to reality. I inhaled sharply and whispered a quiet "Hello" on the exhale. Jenkins gave a barely noticeable nod, muttered a low "Hello," and slipped into Portonapoulos's office without knocking.

"Are you okay?" Gladys asked, concerned.

"Yeah, I'm fine," I said, still catching my breath.

"You've got to relax around him. If you keep reacting like this, you'll never make it through the interview."

"Well, I..." I rubbed my forehead, still trying to calm down and steady my heartbeat. "What did it look like?"

"You froze up. It looked like you were choking."

I took a deep breath and muttered to myself, *Why the hell is this happening? I need to get into this expedition group. I can't let this mess get in the way of my dream*!

The next evening, I noticed an email from an unknown address. It turned out to be the notification for my upcoming interview, scheduled for two days from now.

I decided to use the time to prepare for the it. I needed to know more about Jenkins. So, I started where it made the most sense—gathering and analyzing information on him.

I sat at my laptop, opened the search engine, and typed in: "Robert Jenkins, businessman." The search was popular, and the engine immediately flooded me with options. There were a surprising number of relevant results. Scanning the page, I was pleased to see that Jenkins even had a Wikipedia article. I decided to start my research on this mysterious man right there.

"Robert Jenkins, 30 years old, unmarried, no children. Owner of the 'BitterSweet' corporation." That's what I gleaned from a couple of paragraphs.

Confectionery? I thought, stunned. *Of all things*! *The owner of a candy corporation sponsoring an archaeological expedition... Could it get any weirder*?

After finishing the article, I didn't find anything else useful, but a link to another article titled "Death as a Springboard" caught my eye. Without hesitation, I clicked the link and started reading.

"Just six months ago, no one had heard of Robert Jenkins, and now his name is everywhere. No social event happens without him. He's a regular on TV, always in the headlines. He's earned many nicknames—Chocolate King, Phoenix, Golden Boy, Discovery of the Year. His meteoric rise keeps surprising, and it's certainly worth the attention.

Six months ago, 'BitterSweet' was just a small confectionery factory, producing three types of chocolate bars, known only in its hometown and surrounding areas—a traditional Jenkins family business.

A year ago, the elder Jenkins, Christopher, passed away, leaving the factory to his sons, Philip and Robert. As the brothers fought for control, the business teetered on the edge of bankruptcy.

A large corporation saw an opportunity to buy the factory at a bargain and began negotiating with the Jenkins brothers. Philip was ready to sell, but Robert fiercely defended their father's legacy. The disputes dragged on, but Robert refused to back down.

One evening, as Robert was returning home from the factory, he was attacked. He sustained several bullet wounds at point-blank range. The neighbors, hearing the commotion, called for an ambulance, and Robert was rushed to the hospital in critical condition.

All night, the doctors fought desperately for his life, but by morning, they had to surrender and confirm his death. However, the pathologist scheduled to perform the autopsy unexpectedly found a pulse. After a brief stay in the morgue, Jenkins was transferred back to the intensive care unit, where his condition stabilized following a successful operation. The doctors could only explain this mysterious resurrection as a miracle.

Jenkins recovered quickly. Within two weeks, he was back at work, but a week later, his brother Philip vanished without a trace. But the amazing events didn't stop there.

In just a month, Robert managed to transform a failing factory into a thriving enterprise with an expanded product line. A month later, the owner of a large confectionery factory died from an illness, leaving all his assets to Robert Jenkins. Soon, Jenkins made several successful marketing decisions that brought his company substantial profits. Within two months, 'BitterSweet' absorbed several small enterprises, and Jenkins finalized numerous lucrative contracts. In just six months, 'BitterSweet' transformed from a family-run factory into the largest industrial giant in the country.

But these are not the only mysteries surrounding Robert Jenkins. The Chocolate King is passionate about the history of the ancient world. He provides financial support to museums dedicated to ancient history and sponsors archaeological expeditions. He is handsome, successful, and famous, yet his heart remains free. Perhaps the country's most eligible bachelor has high standards, as no woman has ever been seen with him. Well, let's see if anyone can win the heart of a man who has proven to everyone that the impossible is possible..."

I glanced from the laptop screen to the wall and back again. *An interesting character; nothing else to say...* I sighed, *I don't even know what to do with this information.*

I rested my head in my hands and began to analyze what I had read. The information was so incredible that processing it logically seemed impossible, yet I tried to pinpoint the main point. While the miraculous resurrection of Jenkins and the dizzying success of his business were certainly entertaining, I was more intrigued by his passion for ancient history and archaeology. Despite my efforts, I couldn't find any connection between these interests and Jenkins's personality or his business.

I returned to the search engine and refined my query: "Robert Jenkins and archaeology." I received a link to a recording of his recent interview. I turned up the volume and played the video.

A pretty, fair-haired journalist appeared on the screen. Looking directly into the camera, she spoke in a smooth, clear voice,

"Philanthropy and charity are commonplace for successful businessmen. Their typical areas of interest include schools, orphanages, and hospitals; occasionally, they may support the arts. However, the most enigmatic man in the country has chosen an equally mysterious hobby: the history of the ancient world..."

She turned to her left and addressed her guest: "Mr. Jenkins, please tell our audience when you first became interested in the history of the ancient world."

The camera panned to show the entire studio before zooming in for a close-up of Jenkins.

Jenkins wore a casual gray suit and a white shirt. He looked just as flawless and equally unpleasant as on the day we met. I tuned into my body and, with immense relief, realized that I felt no excitement when I looked at Jenkins on the screen. This allowed me to fully focus on the content of his answers.

"I don't know—probably in childhood," he replied. "I loved reading historical books, but I was especially fascinated by myths and stories about explorers and archaeologists. For a time, I dreamed of becoming a historian or an archaeologist, but I was destined to work in the family business, so my childhood dreams remained just that."

"That is, you're saying that by supporting historians and archaeologists, you're touching your childhood dream," the journalist clarified.

"Yeah, I suppose..." Jenkins agreed.

I watched the video to the end and sighed thoughtfully. While the "childhood dream" explanation was undoubtedly appealing, it didn't clarify why he needed to personally select the expedition members. And it didn't bring me any closer to answering my question: *What should I say during the interview to secure the position*?

CHAPTER 12: INTERVIEW

On the day of the interview, I couldn't find a place for myself. I woke up at 5 a.m. and couldn't fall back asleep. After taking a shower, I started pondering the age-old question: *What should I wear*?

I pulled everything out of my closet and laid it on the bed. All the bright pieces were immediately set aside; restraint with a hint of sexuality seemed like the right approach for this situation.

No, I had no desire to charm Jenkins at all. I would rather avoid him completely. Yet I knew that in job matters, first impressions were crucial, so I wanted to make the most of this advantage.

After much consideration and trying on various outfits, I opted for dark gray tapered pants, a black blazer, and a white V-neck blouse. I completed the look with sleek black pump heels and a leather purse.

I cast a critical glance at my reflection in the mirror, wondering if I looked modest enough. To my liking, the restraint seemed to be overdone, but for obvious reasons, I didn't want to make any adjustments in favor of sexuality.

I decided against applying mascara because I have a bad habit of rubbing my eyes when I'm nervous, and this event promised to be quite stressful. Instead, I limited my makeup to just a matte brown lipstick, a shade slightly darker than my natural lip color.

It would take me about an hour to reach Jenkins's office, but I left two hours before my scheduled meeting. I walked to the subway, hoping that a stroll in the fresh air would help me calm down and collect my thoughts. I also wanted to avoid the chaos of a crowded minibus; exiting one often makes you look like a herd of horses just ran over you.

I arrived at the office 15 minutes early. In the waiting room, I noticed a young woman sitting at the desk, typing intently at the LCD screen.

I approached the desk and introduced myself. "Good morning, my name is Tayra Melfuri, and I received an invitation for today's interview."

"Hello, Ms. Melfuri," the young woman replied warmly, glancing at the schedule laid out on her desk. "You're a bit early. Mr. Jenkins is busy at the moment. Please take a seat; I'll call you when he's ready."

"Okay, thank you," I replied quietly as I sat in the nearest chair.

The office was large and bright, decorated in white and gray tones. It was as flawless and uninviting as Jenkins himself. The only warm spot in this cloister of discomfort was the secretary. Her brown hair, gathered in a low ponytail, shone beautifully under the LED lights, and she looked like an angel.

"How can such a sweet girl work for such a creepy boss?" I wondered, studying her. "I wonder if she knew Jenkins before he was wounded... Was he always this malicious?"

The girl glanced away from the monitor and stared at the ceiling, looking wistful. It didn't seem like I'd bother her if I asked a few questions, so I stood up and walked over to her desk.

"Excuse me."

"Yes?" The girl quickly shifted her gaze from the ceiling to me.

"Have you worked here long?" I asked cautiously.

"About two months. Why?"

"It's just… I'm nervous about the interview and thought maybe you could give me some advice on dealing with Mr. Jenkins."

"Honestly, I'd love to help, but I don't think there's a magic formula. Mr. Jenkins is really good at reading people, and he adjusts his approach depending on the situation."

"Thanks. Sorry to bother you."

"No problem."

So, she didn't know Jenkins before the resurrection, I thought, returning to my seat.

Ten minutes later, I was called in. The wait had calmed my nerves, and I felt confident as I opened the Jenkins's office door. But that all vanished the moment I saw Jenkins. My heart started racing, and I had to force myself to breathe as I managed to say, "Good morning, Mr. Jenkins. I'm Tayra Melfuri, here for the expedition position."

Jenkins's reply was flat, devoid of any emotion—neither friendly nor angry. "I know. Come in, have a seat."

I felt the growing excitement as I walked from the door to his desk. I'd expected this reaction and braced myself to suppress it. But the closer I got to Jenkins, the harder it became. Finally, I reached the chair and sat down.

Jenkins locked eyes with me and asked, "So, what are your expectations?"

"S-sorry?" I stammered, feeling awkward.

"What do you expect to gain from this expedition?" Jenkins repeated, his tone as neutral as before.

I had rehearsed answers to possible questions on my way here, and this was one of them. But, the proximity of Jenkins and his swirling gaze intensified the storm of inappropriate desires that had already been raging inside me. An overwhelming urge to reach out and touch him surged through me, but my tight grip on the armrests held my hands in check. I was struggling to breathe, completely unable to form words. Yet in that moment, I realized that if I didn't speak, I would fail the interview. That realization eclipsed the storm of excitement, replacing it with a wave of fear. Surprisingly, fear was easier to control. That shift in emotions helped me finally pull myself together and start speaking.

"For as long as I can remember, I've been fascinated by ancient history—starting with myths, then moving on to documentaries and literature. It's always been my passion. By the time I was a freshman in high school, I knew archaeology was the career I wanted. But after four years of studying, I haven't had much hands-on experience. That's why the chance to take part in real excavations near the ancient city of Amhitiemar excites me so much. I hope to gain new knowledge, skills, and experience. I understand the work might not be as romantic as it seems from the outside, but I believe the sooner you start learning, the quicker you master it."

My passionate speech didn't stir any emotion in Jenkins. He listened silently, his expression unchanged. Then he asked in the same neutral tone, "The ancient city can hide many dangers. How do you feel about risk?"

The question felt unclear rather than difficult. What kind of danger was Jenkins talking about, and what was the purpose behind it? After a moment of thought, I decided to play it safe and answered diplomatically, "Well, success is impossible without risk."

For the first time, I saw a flicker of emotion cross Jenkins's face. He raised an eyebrow ever so slightly and asked, with a hint of irony, "Indeed?"

The irony in his voice sent a jolt of electricity down my spine, and I realized that Jenkins, emotionless, had been less stressful.

As if reading my thoughts, Jenkins quickly resumed his poker face and asked in that same neutral tone, "Would you prefer never to take a risk, but always know the right decision?"

"No," I said confidently. "Risk is exciting, and that excitement can be a positive thing."

Jenkins's lips curled into a slight smirk, and an almost wicked light flickered in his eyes. As before, it disappeared in less than a second, but it was enough to send my heart racing.

"Well, now for the last question," Jenkins said, resting his elbows on the desk and leaning forward. He fixed his gaze on me and asked, "What are you willing to do to get this position?"

"Anything that doesn't harm others," I said without hesitation.

"Alright, you can go," he said negligently, leaning back in his chair.

I stood up, said goodbye, and headed for the door, relieved to finally be leaving that place.

***

The next three days passed in unbearable tension. Despite all my attempts to distract myself, the interview results consumed my every thought. I checked the bulletin board multiple times a day, hoping to see that longed-for list, but each time, it wasn't there. With classes and exams already over, I found myself going to the university just for this, but I didn't regret the time or effort.

At last, the long-awaited list appeared. From the far end of the corridor, I spotted a stark white sheet of paper and hurried to the board to read it.

I scanned the page from top to bottom, then again from bottom to top, and once more from top to bottom. But to my greatest horror, I couldn't find my name. I felt the ground sink beneath my feet, tears welling up in my eyes. For several seconds, I stared at the list, refusing to accept the awful reality. Then, something caught my eye. There were only nine names on the list, while line number ten was left blank. Driven by a flicker of hope and curiosity, I wiped away my tears and knocked on Portonapoulos's office door.

"Come in," came the familiar, pleasant voice, and I opened the door.

Portonapoulos was seated at his desk, writing something. I paused at the threshold and greeted him timidly, "Hello, I'm Tayra Melfuri, and..."

"Hello, Ms. Melfuri. Come in, have a seat," Portonapoulos said softly, gesturing toward the chair by his desk. "I think I know what you're going to ask."

I looked at Portonapoulos, feeling a mix of sadness and confusion.

"You see, Tayra," he sighed, "I believe you deserve to be on this expedition more than anyone, but Mr. Jenkins thinks differently. He's torn between you and Oscar Biddenrow, so he's scheduled an additional interview for you. It's tomorrow at 5 p.m. I was planning to send you an email, but I'm glad you stopped by."

"Okay, thank you," I said thoughtfully, then after a brief pause added, "Um... what do you think my chances are?"

Portonapoulos shrugged. "I don't know, Tayra. Honestly, I expected Jenkins to have doubts about anyone but you. For me, it wasn't even a question whether to choose you or not. I can't imagine what he could have against you. But, unfortunately, it's out of my hands. All I can do now is wish you good luck."

"Thank you, Mr. Portonapoulos. Luck will certainly come in handy."

***

The next morning, I woke with the unsettling thought that I'd have to visit the Devil's lair again. After that, sleep was out of the question. So, I got up, washed, showered, and started preparing.

Like last time, I laid out my clothes on the bed and began to contemplate them. Something told me it wasn't my modest outfit that caused Jenkins's doubts, but as they say, a drowning man will grasp at any straw—and I was no better off.

This time, I had no idea what my outfit should be. I tried various combinations, but none seemed quite right. Exhausted, I settled on a fitted black knee-length skirt and a turquoise blouse, pairing them with the same black pumps and familiar purse.

After studying my reflection in the mirror, I felt neither satisfaction nor disappointment. Since black and white with pants hadn't worked last time, I decided to take my chances with turquoise and a skirt. Once again, my makeup was just lipstick, this time a slightly brighter bronze shade.

I was anxious even as I opened the door. On my way to Jenkins's office, I replayed our last meeting in my mind, searching for where I might've said something wrong. Yet nothing stood out that could explain why I wasn't suited for the expedition.

I entered the room and pronounced the greeting, "Hello, Mr. Jenkins."

"Hello, Tayra, come in," the reply was.

The word "Tayra" cut my ear right away. *Tayra*?! *Not Ms. Melfuri*? I thought, my heart sinking. A bad feeling crept in. Still, I sat in the same chair as before.

"We didn't quite finish last time, did we?" Jenkins said in a velvety, muffled voice, his gaze trailing over me in a way that felt invasive.

A familiar shiver of excitement ran through me as I caught a faint scent, something oddly familiar, though I couldn't place where I'd smelled it before.

"Possibly. You'd know better," I replied neutrally, masking my fear and irritation with forced humility.

"I like your obedience," Jenkins remarked. "Why do you think I've called you back?"

"I have no idea," I shrugged.

"Let me give you a hint. Last time, you said you'd do anything to get this position..."

"Yes, anything harmless for other people," I confirmed.

"Well, yeah..." Jenkins said, rolling his eyes, "I want you to prove it."

"How?" I asked anxiously, still not understanding what he was driving at.

"You want a spot on the expedition, and I have a desire of my own. Let's make a deal."

"And what do you want?" I asked cautiously, my voice trembling despite my efforts to steady it.

"You."

"What do you mean?" I swallowed hard, my heartbeat quickening with each second.

Jenkins leaned over the desk, his face close—too close—his breath hot against my skin. "Isn't it clear?" he breathed, voice low. "No harm will come to anyone. It's just you and me."

The heat of his presence sent a wave of discomfort through me, but beneath it, cold realization twisted in my gut. Sex with Jenkins in exchange for a position in the expedition. The unfairness, the humiliation, made my blood boil.

But Jenkins knew exactly what he was doing. He circled behind me, slow and deliberate. He bent close to my ear and whispered, "You're offended, but I see it in your eyes. Desire is burning you up inside. You want me as much as I want you. Maybe more. I suggest you stop fighting what your body already knows. If you feel this way when I'm near, just think what you'll feel when I touch you. You can have both pleasure and your dream, or just your pride. It's your choice, Tayra."

Oh my God! *Oh my God*! My thoughts spun wildly, my breath coming in shallow gasps. Jenkins was still behind me, his scent, his heat, overwhelming. Rational thought was impossible. And yet, a decision had to be made.

I took a deep breath, exhaling slowly through my mouth, trying to calm my nerves and buy myself a little time. It wasn't enough to truly calm me, but at least my thoughts began to stir.

My desire for this man is abnormal, but irresistible. Maybe if I give in, this obsession will pass. But no—he's a poison. This desire is nothing but a sickness, and I can't let it grow. This expedition isn't my last chance. What should I do?

Despair and panic churned inside me, one after the other. But despite the overwhelming tension, I saw the only clear solution.

"I'm not for sale," I said, standing tall as I turned to face Jenkins. "And you're wrong about how I feel."

I turned and headed for the door, not looking back as I reached for the handle. "Goodbye, Mr. Jenkins."

I could feel his eyes burning into my back as he whispered, "See you, Tayra."

CHAPTER 13: STRENGTH TEST

I bolted from the building and rushed to the subway, not daring to slow down. Shock numbed everything else—no fear, no sorrow—just the single, urgent need to escape.

I sat through all five stops of the metro, staring blankly, incapable of thought or analysis. It was like sleeping with my eyes open. As I stepped out of the subway and onto the street, a rush of fresh wind brushed my face. Only then did my mind begin to lift from its stupor.

As I walked from the subway to the dormitory, the wind pushed my hair back, leaving a coolness on my skin. Everything around me felt hazy, but I kept moving, guided by an inner autopilot.

It wasn't until I crossed the threshold of my room that I began to feel how exhausted I was. I noticed my right shoe had rubbed my foot raw, but I hadn't felt a single pinch of pain.

I undressed, took a shower, and went to the window. Rays from the setting sun painted pink stripes on the shabby wall and across the tops of withering maples. With each passing moment, the stripes narrowed, fading into the grayness of twilight—just like my dream had, only two hours ago.

A lump formed in my throat as tears filled my eyes, building until they finally spilled down my cheeks and chin. I couldn't take it anymore. My feet carried me from the window to the bed. Covering my face with my hands, I cried aloud, no longer holding back, not caring who heard. The emptiness inside me gave way to pain, and I desperately needed to let it out.

I cried almost all night, only settling down at dawn—not from calm, but from sheer exhaustion. My face was swollen, and my temples throbbed.

It's not the end of my life, I thought wearily. Closing my eyes, I finally fell asleep.

A beam of sunlight tickled my nose, waking me up. Yawning, I reached for my phone to check the time.

Wow, I thought, surprised to see it was already eleven. I was about to set my phone down when a call from Gladys flashed on the screen.

Sitting up in bed, I cleared my throat and answered, "Hello!"

"Oh my God, Tayra! Are you alright?" Gladys blurted anxiously.

"Yeah, I'm fine. Why?"

"I sent you a bunch of messages, but you didn't respond. You always get up early, so I got worried."

"What's the point of getting up early? We're on vacation. About the messages... Sorry, I muted my phone for yesterday's interview and forgot to turn it back on."

"Oh, right, the additional interview. How did it go?"

How it went... The last thing I wanted to talk about, especially in detail. So, I decided to stick to the bare facts.

"Jenkins was torn between me and Oscar Biddenrow. In the end, he picked Oscar after the extra interview."

I tried to sound calm, like it wasn't a big deal, but I was barely holding back tears.

"Oh my God, Tayra! I'm so sorry. That's so unfair. What a jerk!"

You have no idea, Gladys. 'Jerk' doesn't even cover it, I thought, but kept silent.

"Don't worry," Gladys said after a brief pause. "Maybe it's for the best. After what happened in Tiamon, it's probably safer for you to avoid dangerous terrains."

I sighed. "Thanks for your concern, Gladys, but I think I just need to be alone for a while."

"I get it. Just don't stay sad for too long, okay?"

"Okay."

"Done," Gladys said with approval before hanging up.

I set the phone down. Life goes on...

***

The next two days passed smoothly enough. Though my mood stayed low, I began to accept that the excavations near Amhitiemar would go on without me. I started thinking about how to spend the unexpected free time this summer.

After some thought, I decided that once I passed my fifth-year entrance exams, I'd head home to visit my parents, then come back and look for a temporary job. I couldn't stay home for more than a week anyway—I'd grown too used to living on my own during my university years.

I picked up my phone to check train schedules and book a ticket, but it rang just as I was about to start. The number was unfamiliar.

I answered, and a familiar voice came through: "Hello, Tayra. This is Gregory Portonapoulos. Can you come to my office today?"

"Hello, Mr. Portonapoulos. I can be there in fifteen minutes if that works for you."

"That works perfectly."

"Great, see you soon."

Portonapoulos's call both intrigued and puzzled me, but with only fifteen minutes to spare, I had no time to dwell on it. Instead, I focused on getting ready. I quickly grabbed the first outfit that came to hand: a yellow button-down skirt and a black T-shirt with a cut-out back. Slipping into my white wedge sandals, I grabbed my phone and bag and rushed out to the university.

“Hello again, Mr. Portonapoulos. Why did you call me?” I asked, a trace of worry in my voice as I stepped into the office.

“Hello, Tayra. Come in,” Portonapoulos nodded, gesturing toward the chair by his desk. "I have two pieces of news: one good, one bad. Which would you like to hear first?”

“The good one,” I said confidently, thinking to myself that I’d had more than enough bad news these past few days.

“Well, congratulations—you’ve been selected as a member of our expedition team,” Portonapoulos said with a smile.

“Um...” I forced out, swallowing hard as a wave of heat pierced down my spine. “There must be some mistake. Jenkins picked Oscar, not me.”

“Well, yes,” Portonapoulos sighed. “But here’s the bad news. Oscar was attacked by two hooligans a few days ago. They beat him badly—he has a severe head injury and multiple fractures. He's in the hospital now, and it'll be quite some time before he recovers. Since you were next in line, you’ve been enlisted to take his place in the group.”

“Oh my God! What a tragedy! Poor Oscar!” I gasped, completely stunned.

“Yeah...” Portonapoulos sighed again. “But I’m hopeful he’ll be okay once he recovers.”

“I hope so too,” I said quietly, falling into silence.

I didn’t know what to say. The news was so shocking that I wasn’t sure whether to feel relief or grief. Sure, the sudden resurrection of my dream—one I’d already buried just two days ago—was a pleasant shock. But the senseless accident that landed Oscar in a hospital bed wasn’t something to celebrate.

What puzzled me most was that they’d targeted Oscar. He was a red-haired, nerdy guy—quiet, non-confrontational, always modestly dressed. Sure, he was thin and unsportsmanlike, an easy target on the surface. But except for his old smartphone and some books, there wasn't much to steal. If I were a robber, I'd have picked someone more polished, but then again, what do I know about crime?

My thoughts were interrupted by Portonapoulos's voice. "Mr. Jenkins had all the participants sign contracts. I've already contacted his assistant, and she's prepared one for you. You should head to their office and sign it."

"When should I do that?"

"The sooner, the better. Today, if possible, would be perfect."

"Alright, I'll head over there now."

"Thank you," Portonapoulos said, then added after a brief pause, "There will be a meeting for all the expedition members soon. I'll email you the exact date and time. Honestly, it would be easier for me to just post a note on the bulletin board, but since the group has people from different universities and many of you have already started your summer break, I'm worried it might get overlooked if I use my usual methods. Just make sure to check your email regularly, okay?"

"Sure, Mr. Portonapoulos. Thanks again."

"You're welcome, Tayra."

After speaking with Portonapoulos, I went straight to the bus stop. The thought of having to visit Jenkins's office didn't thrill me, so I wanted to get the task over with as quickly as possible. Deep down, I really hoped I could sign the contract without running into Jenkins himself, and that sliver of optimism gave me a small sense of relief.

Aside from that, my feelings were far from positive. Despite the favorable outcome of the expedition situation, I felt no joy. My heart was a muddled mix of sadness and fear, though I couldn't pinpoint what exactly I was afraid of.

As I entered Jenkins's waiting room, I headed straight for the secretary's desk.

"Hello, madam!" I said briskly, making it obvious I didn't plan to linger. "Mr. Gregory Portonapoulos mentioned you've prepared a contract for me to sign."

"Hello, miss. You must be Tayra Melfuri?" the brown-haired girl replied with the same friendliness as before.

"Yes, that's me."

"Your contract is ready, but Mr. Jenkins insists you sign it in his presence. I'll check if he's available to see you."

"Sure," I replied, struggling to sound calm while everything inside me churned. *Oh God, no! No, no, no, no! Meet this devil again?! Lord, what did I do to deserve this?*

While I was mentally lamenting, the secretary slipped behind the door to Jenkins's office. As soon as I noticed, my already frazzled nerves took it as a bad sign. Surely, having an expedition member sign a contract wasn't something that required a personal report—couldn't she have just asked on the speakerphone? Still, I tried to keep my panic in check, though it didn't help much. I'd been on edge ever since I learned I had to come here.

Finally, the girl returned, her practiced politeness as sharp as before. "Mr. Jenkins is busy at the moment. You'll have to wait until he's free. Please, take a seat. I'll call you."

I nodded and sank into the nearest chair. Deep inside, I was oddly relieved by the delay. First, it postponed my meeting with Jenkins. Second, I could feel my fear shifting into something darker—hatred and irritation. I hoped the wait would help me suppress those feelings.

Twenty minutes later, the secretary invited me in, and I stepped into Jenkins's office. After a cold greeting, I crossed the room quickly, the distance to the chair feeling like miles. My body reacted with tension, and it took twice the effort to suppress my growing frustration. I was furious with myself for losing control of feelings that had no place here.

Jenkins must have sensed my struggle because he smirked, his voice dripping with malice. "Hello, Tayra. As I promised, we meet again."

"I hope this will be the last time," I replied, matching his spite.

"Nice hope, but pointless," Jenkins said, smirking. His gaze was so intense, I felt goosebumps crawl up my skin.

I refused to show weakness. Gathering all my will, I said coldly, "Just give me the contract."

"Here it is," Jenkins said, handing me the papers. "But I suggest you read it carefully before signing."

His voice was neutral, and his face as expressionless as always, but I could still feel the venom in every word he spoke.

Trying to ignore the negativity as much as possible, despite the excitement building inside me, I took the contract and began reading. Normally, I'd just scan the page for key elements, but this time, I read carefully. I wouldn't trust that man with a single strand of my hair.

As I read, Jenkins stood and walked to the door. The click of the lock made my heart stop, and icy horror spread through my entire being. I could feel his lustful gaze on my back. Worse still, the thought of his desire for me only heightened my excitement.

Fighting the urge to panic, I kept reading. *Lust is lust*, I reminded myself, *but as long as I can resist and keep thinking, I need to make sure I'm not signing away my soul.*

Jenkins seemed to know exactly how I felt. His eyes bore into me with desire, but he kept his distance. But as soon as I finished and signed the contract, he approached me quickly. The heat inside me surged, barely contained, but I still found the strength to stand.

"I signed it. Can I go now?"

"Try," Jenkins shrugged, his voice dripping with sarcasm.

"Open the door, please," I said, locking eyes with him. Only God knows how I managed to hold his gaze for even two seconds, but it was worth it.

Jenkins grinned, appreciating the gesture. He stepped back and leaned against the edge of his desk, crossing his arms and tilting his head slightly. "I always get what I want, and you know exactly what I want right now. Don't you think you were lucky to get this position without paying for it?"

My entire body began to tremble, from my head to my heels. I couldn't tell if it was from anger or excitement—both were raging inside me—but one thing was clear: last time, Jenkins had offered me a choice. This time, he was merely stating the hopelessness of my situation and savoring his inevitable victory.

Every second of holding my defenses required more effort, and I knew it was only a matter of time before they broke. Still, I resolved to delay surrender for as long as I could.

I took a breath and kept my gaze locked on his. "Honestly, I thought luck was real," I said, adding as much defiance as I could.

Jenkins seemed to find my futile resistance amusing. He didn't rush but kept playing our verbal game.

"So naive," he said calmly, though with a hint of irony. "Unlike you, I never rely on luck. Some things could've been avoided if you'd just listened to your body."

That's when it hit me. *Oscar*! *Those hooligans—Jenkins's men*! *Oh my God, it's all my fault.*

Jenkins cut through my thoughts. "Figured it out, haven't you? So, what now? Regret? Guilt? Don't you see your mind is just causing you and everyone else pain? Turn it off for a while. Let your body take over."

With those final words, he stepped closer. So close I could feel his breath on my face. He leaned into my ear, his lips barely grazing it, and whispered, "The best way to defeat temptation is to give in. Let it happen, Tayra. Let the flame out."

Jenkins stood so close, but our bodies never touched. He didn't kiss me, didn't lay a hand on me. He was teasing me, stoking the fire raging inside. He relished watching me struggle to suppress it. If he'd touched me then, I would've surrendered instantly, but he kept me on the edge.

For some reason, he needed me to admit I couldn't resist. Maybe it wasn't his lust for me that drove him, but the satisfaction of knowing I wanted him.

At some point, his seductive whisper made me lose control. With an unrestrained moan, I wrapped my arms around Jenkins and pressed my lips to his. Driven by raw passion, our bodies intertwined in a single impulse. Everything else became a blur...

CHAPTER 14: PSYCHOLOGICAL PROBLEM

Everything stayed hazy until I returned home, and even then, the fog lingered. Clarity only returned under the warm streams of the shower, and even then, it carried no comfort.

Wrapping myself in a towel, I stepped out of the shower and sank onto my bed.

Lord! The thought hit me like a slap. *My lust for Jenkins completely shut off my brain. Unsafe sex with a stranger*! *What was I thinking*? *My period is due in two days. In theory, those days are safe, but accidents happen. And I definitely don't need that kind of accident now.*

I'd never waited for a period so impatiently. Two days stretched endlessly, like an eternity hanging by a thread. When my period finally started, relief washed over me in waves. Still, my intuition whispered that my "meeting" with Jenkins wouldn't be the last, and the thought of enduring that kind of stress again made my stomach twist.

It was clear—I needed to take care of contraception. That meant a trip to my gynecologist. Without hesitation, I scheduled a consultation and prayed desperately that I wouldn't see Jenkins until I was ready.

Fortunately, my prayers were answered, and the days leading up to my appointment were calm. I focused on preparing for my entrance exams, grateful for the lack of distractions. I avoided thinking about Jenkins; any thought of him or what had happened threw me completely off balance—something I couldn't afford. After all, failing the exams would shatter the future I'd worked so hard to build, forcing me to prioritize wisely.

The doctor listened carefully to my concerns. After weighing my situation, she recommended an IUD, and I agreed without hesitation. After the procedure, I took the opportunity to ask a few lingering questions.

"I have a delicate problem, doctor," I began hesitantly. "I feel nothing from men's touch—except for one."

"That's normal," the doctor replied. "You're often more sensitive to someone you're emotionally connected to."

"That's the problem," I confessed. "There's no emotional connection. It's purely physical. I don't even like him—I'm afraid of him. But my desire for him is... overwhelming. And when men I actually like touch me, I feel nothing."

The doctor shrugged lightly. "I've examined you thoroughly, Tayra, and everything looks fine. I'll know more once your test results come in, but I'm confident it's nothing physical. It's likely a psychological issue."

The doctor's words echoed in my mind all the way home.

Psychological problem... Psychological problem... What does that even mean? I liked Dean, Nick, and Xavier, but felt nothing for them. Jenkins, though—I hated him, yet my body burned for him. What if I need fear and hate to feel attracted to someone? If so, things are really bad. Looks like therapy is inevitable. But first, I need to test my theory. Jenkins can't be the only man I respond to. I'll have to find a bad boy, kiss him, and see if I feel... anything.

The idea was utterly stupid at its core, but I couldn't bring myself to care. I needed answers immediately; even waiting until the next day felt unbearable. So, the moment I got home, I called Gladys.

"Hey, girl! Are you free tonight?"

"Well, yeah... Why?"

"I need your help. Can you go to a club with me?"

From the clatter on the other end, I guessed Gladys had dropped her phone. The string of curses that followed confirmed it. The drop must have been soft, sparing her screen—otherwise, her swearing would've been much louder. Finally, Gladys came back on the line. "Hey, are you okay? What have you done with my friend?"

"I'm fine, Gladys. Just tired of the same old routine. I want to try something different—shake things up a bit."

"You don't actually expect me to believe that, do you? Come on, you're clearly up to something you're not telling me."

"Uh... okay, fine. You're right. I lied. Sorry."

"All right, now that you've confessed... Gladys is on her way!"

Gladys arrived hours before the clubs opened, but we dove straight into getting ready without wasting a second. We pulled together an outfit: a short black leather skirt, lace-up sandals with twelve-centimeter heels, and a black-and-white blouse tied at the waist. To give the look an edge, Gladys pulled my hair into a sleek high ponytail. We finished the look with smoky black eyeshadow, glossy lips, and silver hoop earrings.

When I looked in the mirror, I barely recognized myself. It took everything I had to step outside in that attire. But the experiment was worth a sacrifice.

By the time Gladys and I arrived at the club, it was already buzzing with people. We settled midway between the exit and the bar, perfectly positioned to take in the entire room. As I danced, my eyes continuously scanned the crowd, searching for a suitable target. I know this sounds psychopathic—maybe it was—but I had to test my hypothesis, no matter what.

Most of the men I noticed were with dates and, naturally, off-limits. Among the seemingly single, the first to catch my eye was a long-haired blond in a gray T-shirt with a dark blue cross stripe. He probably wasn't a regular in clubs—like me—his movements slightly stiff and awkward. Next, my gaze landed on a short, chubby, dark-haired guy who, despite his build, moved with surprising energy and skill. Then I noticed a red-haired guy in a green shirt. He reminded me of Nick, though he seemed less restrained and polished.

You're wasting time, Tayra, I scolded myself after an hour of ogling decent guys. *Focus on the mission—find someone you* ***don't*** *like.*

Maybe the guys at the club that night were genuinely decent, or maybe my intuition wasn't sharp enough to sense the right kind of "badness" from afar. Either way, one thing was clear. None of the men stirred even the faintest hint of negative emotion in me—let alone the storm I was looking for.

After another hour of fruitless searching, exhaustion started to set in. My twelve-centimeter heels, though steady, had begun to remind me of their presence, persistently begging for a break. The suffocating stuffiness, heavy tobacco smoke, and pounding music had me teetering on the edge of a headache, making me seriously consider calling it a night.

Then, suddenly, *he* appeared at the club's entrance. A tattoo-covered, disheveled, and thoroughly drunk figure stumbled toward the center of the dancefloor. Along the way, he shoved and cursed at people three times, even attempting to start two fights. Unfortunately for him, his would-be opponents were wiser and refused to take the bait.

The moment I spotted him, a shiver of fear and disgust crawled down my spine—but I knew I'd hit the jackpot. Once he planted himself in the middle of the dancefloor, I positioned myself where he'd have a clear view of me. Then I started dancing, making sure to showcase my figure in the best possible light. As I danced, I gradually moved closer to my target. When a slow song started, I boldly approached him with a playful, "Hello!"

"What do you want?" he snapped, his eyes shamelessly glued to my cleavage.

"Bad boys like you are so sexy... I just couldn't resist getting to know you better. You know what I mean?" I purred, adding a sly wink.

He stared at me, dumbfounded—the exact reaction I was hoping for. "Let's dance," I said, grabbing his hand and leading him onto the floor.

He immediately placed one hand on my bottom, giving it a light squeeze, while the other hand snaked around my waist, pulling me closer. We started to dance, his stench of tobacco and alcohol nearly making me gag. I decided I didn't need to wait for the song to end to finish what I'd started. I leaned in, clasping my hands around his shaggy head before decisively pressing my lips to his. Though clearly drunk, he wasted no time taking control, shoving his tongue into my mouth and moving it energetically.

As I pulled back for air, I opened my eyes to find Gladys staring at me, her expression screaming, *What the hell are you doing*?

I leaned in close, pressing my face to his cheek, and subtly winked at Gladys, signaling her to head for the exit. Once I was sure Gladys understood and had reached the door, I abruptly pulled away from the guy. "You know what? I've changed my mind—you're not bad enough for me," I said. Without waiting for his reaction, I slipped into the crowd and caught up with Gladys.

We bolted out into the street and raced toward the subway, praying to catch the last train. We dove into the departing car, and as the doors slid shut, relief washed over us.

"What was that?" Gladys asked, her eyes flashing with a mix of surprise and disapproval.

"Forget it," I said, waving dismissively. "I just needed to test a theory."

A storm brewed in Gladys's eyes, but, oddly enough, she only said one word: "Proved?"

"Not really," I admitted with a guilty shrug. I felt stupid and ashamed—it had been selfish to drag Gladys into this without even explaining why. She couldn't imagine how grateful I was that she'd agreed to help me without asking too many questions.

Gladys sighed but said nothing. She stayed silent the whole way back, but I could tell she wasn't truly mad at me.

Once home, I took a shower, washing away the traces of the night's adventure. Wrapped in a towel, as usual, I sat on my bed, replaying the night in my head. *Negative emotions toward a bad boy didn't work.*

I couldn't think of another explanation for this "psychological problem" except that it might be tied to Tiendal's curse. I needed to learn more about the legend. But where should I even start?

CHAPTER 15: ACQUAINTANCE

I entered the lecture room fifteen minutes before the meeting. Scanning the rows, I counted nine people and thought, *Wow, these guys are really responsible. I came early, but I'm still the last one here.*

I glanced around the auditorium again, deciding where to sit. After a moment of hesitation, I chose a seat in the second row next to Jenny.

"Hey!" I greeted her. "Have you seen Portonapoulos?"

"Hey," Jenny replied. "He was here earlier. Opened the room, then left."

"Okay," I nodded and glanced around the room again. "Why does he need such a big auditorium for just ten people?"

"I don't know," Jenny shrugged. "He seems to like this room for some reason."

Well, I guess it makes sense. It's comfortable here, I thought, turning my attention to the rest of our expedition group.

Jenny, Louis, and Ahish were in the same row. We'd had plenty of classes together, so we knew each other well. The other six, however, were more interesting.

Two guys sat in the front row. I didn't know their names, but they looked like third-year students, probably in the same specialty as me.

In the third row sat two girls and a guy whose faces were familiar. The plump girl with curly blond hair was a graduate student of Portonapoulos. Her name was Chiara. She sometimes helped him with newsletters, so I'd exchanged a few emails with her. I'd spoken to her a couple of times, and she seemed pretty sweet. The other two were fifth-year students. I'd seen them around the dorm but never really talked to them.

The guy in the fourth row, though, was someone I hadn't seen before. Luckily, this slightly tanned, brown-haired athlete was staring thoughtfully at the empty blackboard, allowing me to study him without drawing any attention.

He had short, slightly curly hair that framed his strong features. His blue cotton shirt complemented his dark blue eyes. He was really handsome, and I would've liked to admire him a bit longer, but the sound of the door slamming as Portonapoulos entered made me quickly look away.

Portonapoulos strode energetically from the door to the center of the room and began, "Hello, everyone! I'm really glad you could all make it today, as this meeting is very important. During the expedition, you'll be spending days and nights together, so it's important to get familiar with one another now. Let's start with introductions. My name is Gregory Portonapoulos, though I hope you've all memorized that by now."

The room filled with smiles and chuckles. Portonapoulos grinned and continued, "Now, I'd like each of you to stand up, say a few words about yourself, and tell us why you're interested in this expedition. Let's start from the front row, Miles, you go first."

Dark-skinned Miles and fair-skinned Jacob, seated beside him, turned out to be third-year students. They had recently started scientific work under Professor Cowen, a colleague and longtime friend of Portonapoulos. Cowen had informed them about the expedition and encouraged them to apply.

Fifth-year students Alicia and Peter were diploma students under Associate Professor Drekston from a different department. They'd discovered the expedition by chance after spotting an announcement on the bulletin board.

Louis, Jenny, and Ahish, like me, were enthusiastic fanatics, drawn in by Portonapoulos's passionate tales of his past expeditions. He often used those stories to entertain us during lectures, especially when the course material got too difficult to absorb. It seemed to me that half the people attended Portonapoulos's lectures more for his stories than the actual course material—though he taught that pretty well too.

Finally, it was the unknown blue-eyed guy's turn. He stood up, smiled slightly embarrassed, and began, "Well... My name is Tony Weiler, and I seem to be the only alien here. I'm a postgraduate student in the historical faculty at the Pedagogical University. My PhD thesis focuses on the symbols of Amhitiemar, so this expedition seems like a great opportunity to engage with some subjects of my research, not just in literature, but in real life."

Wow... symbols of Amhitiemar! I thought, impressed. *That sounds intriguing*! *It would be great to talk to him about it. Plus, he seems cute.*

Before I had time to ponder, Portonapoulos announced the end of our meeting: "Well, everyone, I think that's enough for today. You can continue socializing after the meeting, but you'll need to find a different place. I expect to see you all tomorrow at 11 a.m.; I'll brief you on Amhitiemar and our expedition tasks."

The students quickly stood and flowed into the corridor, dispersing to continue their business. Exchanging a few words with Jenny and Louis, I was about to head to the exit too, but then I paused in the lobby and pulled out my phone to check the time. It was five minutes past twelve.

It's still early, I thought. *I could go to the library, but searching for keywords and subject catalogs might take forever. Portonapoulos may know something about the legend; I should ask him for advice on some literature.*

I turned, and instead of going out, I headed to the stairs leading to the second floor, where Portonapoulos's office was located. The office door stood ajar. After hesitating for a moment, I approached and peered through the gap.

What I saw displeased me completely: a familiar figure in a dark business suit. Jenkins stood with his back to the door, examining a document alongside Portonapoulos.

Honestly, as soon as I recognized Jenkins, I lost all interest in what they were doing and just wanted to leave, especially before my body betrayed me again.

I stepped onto the threshold of the educational building, and to my horror, I spotted a man nearby. Pale-skinned, black-haired, and dressed entirely in black, he looked ominous—almost like a vampire. I had seen him before in Jenkins's office; he seemed to be Jenkins's driver. While his presence near the building made sense, it gave me a bad feeling, so I decided to take a different route to the dorm.

I seized the opportunity to go shopping, and after spending about half an hour on the road instead of my usual seven minutes, I arrived at the dormitory feeling calm and in a good mood. At the entrance, I paused to retrieve my pass and keys. Unfortunately, the room key had fallen to the bottom of my bag, and I had to fish it out from under my wallet and phone. While this was a standard annoyance, it slightly dampened my mood.

Finally, I fished out the coveted key, hung it on my finger, zipped my bag, and sighed with relief, ready to take the last two steps to the entrance when a familiar velvet voice called from behind me, "Hello, Tayra!"

A wave of annoyance washed over me; all my efforts to avoid this encounter had been in vain. Out of irritation, I disregarded basic politeness and turned to Jenkins with an angry question: "What do you want?"

Jenkins folded his arms and grinned maliciously. "It seems you'll never tire of asking that stupid question."

I rolled my eyes and grunted in annoyance. "Don't you think sneaking around a student dorm is a bit suspicious for a Golden Boy?"

"Only if someone spots me."

"The dorm is bustling with people."

"It's nearly empty because it's summer. Plus, the concierge isn't at her post right now," Jenkins protested, his icy calm scalding me worse than boiling water.

"How do you know?" I asked, doing my best to hide my concern.

"My guy is taking care of her."

Oh no, poor Mrs. Hudson! I thought with horror, and my expression clearly reflected it.

Jenkins stepped closer, looked me in the eye, and said earnestly, "She'll be fine if you obey. So, will you invite me in?"

"You're just a monster!" I hissed furiously, maintaining my gaze on his black eyes.

Jenkins grinned again, seemingly unfazed by my rage. Slowly, he leaned in, his hot breath brushing my ear as he whispered, "But I'm the monster you want, right?"

I clenched my teeth and didn't reply. We walked upstairs in silence, unlocked the door, and stepped inside. Jenkins followed me in and closed the door. He cast a quick glance at the lock, then at me. Unceremoniously, he took the key from my hand and locked the door.

Jenkins turned around, scanning the room quickly. Without removing his shoes, he approached the window and drew the curtains. Next, he walked to my roommate's bed, took off his jacket and shirt, and carefully folded them on the bedspread.

He acted so freely that it felt as if I were his guest instead of the other way around, but the thought of Mrs. Hudson kept me from commenting.

I slipped off my sandals, placed my bag and package on the nightstand, and froze at the entrance, confusion washing over me as I involuntarily stared at Jenkins's flawless, slightly toned body.

Heck! I thought, feeling waves of excitement rapidly swell within me.

Mentally conceding that escape was impossible, I slipped behind the bathroom door to wash my hands and delay the inevitable moment of intimacy. I turned on the tap and, feeling conditionally alone, frantically brainstormed wild "rescue" plans in my head.

Action movies immediately sprang to mind, where tough guys always escaped through the ventilation system. I glanced sadly at the exhaust vent in the ceiling. It was so high that I could only reach it with a jump, and even if I somehow managed that, I couldn't squeeze through a rectangle measuring just 15 by 20 centimeters. This option was definitely out.

Next, I thought of the story of Odysseus, specifically the episode where he had himself tied to the mast to resist the Sirens' enchanting song. I scanned the bathroom for something that might help me emulate the legendary hero. Strapping myself to the shower with a hose would be ineffective, and while locking myself in the bathroom seemed like a viable option, two significant obstacles stopped me.

First, the lock on my bathroom door was broken. Since my roommate had moved in with her boyfriend back in our sophomore year and only technically still resided in the dorm, I lived alone and had no one to hide from. As a result, I never bothered the dormitory commandant about getting it fixed. Now, that oversight felt like a serious mistake.

Second, that conniving bastard had anticipated my resistance and threatened me with Mrs. Hudson. Deep down, I hoped he was bluffing, but after the tragedy with Oscar, I didn't want to tempt fate.

I sighed, turned off the water, wiped my hands, and returned to the room. In my absence, Jenkins had completely undressed. Seeing him sitting on my bed like that made my cheeks flush. I dropped my gaze and covered my eyes with my hand.

Jenkins rose, circled around me, and pressed himself against my back, making me acutely aware of his growing arousal. He whispered in my ear with his velvety, hypnotic voice, "Why be shy when it's just the two of us?"

He slowly unfastened the top two buttons of my skirt and slid it down, deliberately brushing his hand over my thigh. The warmth of his touch ignited my skin, heat radiating through my body. I groaned as my hands instinctively rose, giving Jenkins the chance to pull off my T-shirt. With every passing second, my thoughts became hazier, and the sensation of Jenkins's lips on my neck enveloped my mind in a thick fog. What happened next is best left undescribed.

***

Once he was finished, Jenkins got up, dressed, unlocked the door, and quickly disappeared behind it without a word. I lay in bed, utterly bewildered, looping through the same question in my head: *What just happened*?

Gradually, my body returned to normal after the hurricane that had swept through it, and my thoughts began to clear.

Hmmm, I pondered, *this situation... and most importantly, it's completely incomprehensible what to do about it. The only silver lining is that Jenkins doesn't seek publicity, so he will likely try to hide our 'relationship'—whatever I should call it. I sincerely hope he will succeed, because if the guys from the expedition group found out, it would be a real nightmare. They wouldn't trust me, and I'd become an outcast. Lord, please explain how I got involved in this mess—and why*?

Having finished feeling sorry for myself, I remembered Mrs. Hudson and decided to check on her. I took a quick shower, slipped into a house dress, and hurried downstairs, relieved to find the lovely old woman at her desk. She seemed to be okay, though she looked a bit unwell.

I stepped closer and greeted her, "Hello, Mrs. Hudson. Is everything alright?"

"Hello, Tayra. Yes, I hope so. I must have fallen asleep and just woke up. My head feels cloudy, and I'm a bit dizzy."

"Yes, you look pale. It's probably a bit stuffy in your room. Perhaps you should go outside."

"Oh, I don't know. It's hotter outside than in here. I'd better turn on the fan."

"Well, look how convenient it is for you. The main thing is to take care of yourself. Summer can be an insidious time of year."

"Oh, don't tell me that."

I smiled and prepared to leave when Mrs. Hudson asked, "Did you need anything?"

"No, nothing special. The light in my bathroom started blinking, so I thought I'd ask if it's happening everywhere or just for me."

"It's probably the bulb. I'll tell the electrician tomorrow; he'll replace it for you."

"Okay, thanks a bunch."

I wonder if they drugged her with something or just hit her on the head, I thought as I walked back upstairs. *Either way, the important thing is that she's okay.*

When I returned to the room and glanced at the clock, I saw it was already half past two.

What a crazy day! *So many impressions, and it's nowhere near sunset yet. By the way, I need to eat something*, I thought, finally heading to sort through my purchases and cook.

After a meal and a cup of aromatic tea, all the impressions from the first half of the day transformed into monstrous fatigue—both mental and physical. I tried to cheer myself up by pacing around the room, but alas, it didn't help.

Well, fine, ten minutes, and then I'll get to work, I said to myself, lying on the edge of the bed. The soft pillow joyfully accepted me in its embrace, and I thought that happiness really exists. However, this happiness was short-lived. The bedding still held the scent of Jenkins's body and his perfume. Although this scent was faint, washed out by the air, it still irritated me greatly.

Damn, I thought angrily as I stood up. *No, I can't just leave it like this.*

I turned on my computer, opened a search engine, and typed in the most obvious query: "The Legend of Tiendal."

In response, the search engine returned several bus excursions to Tiamon, along with reviews of the historical monuments in our region.

Great, thanks. I've already been there, and I don't want to do that again, I thought as I scrolled down the search results.

Around the twentieth line, sites containing the legend's content began to appear. Most of them contained the same text; some had minor differences, but none provided anything beyond what I already knew.

A general request isn't working; I need something more specific, I concluded, stifling a yawn. I yawned again and realized I could see the laptop screen with great difficulty.

Okay, I decided. *Tomorrow, I'll consult Portonapoulos and continue the search. Hopefully, I'll be lucky enough to find some answers.*

CHAPTER 16: EXPEDITION MISSIONS

I walked into the auditorium at a quarter to eleven and was surprised to find only Tony. He sat in the second row, studying the ceiling with genuine curiosity.

I wonder what he finds so interesting in the white stucco? I thought, looking up at the ceiling again to ensure I didn't miss anything. Right after this, I walked over to Tony and interrupted his fascinating activity. "Hi!"

"Hi!" Tony replied amiably.

"May I sit here with you?"

"Sure," he nodded, moving a bit to the side.

I thanked him, sat down, and asked, "Do you always come this early?"

"Well, you know, whoever lives the farthest, comes the earliest."

"Yeah, true," I chuckled. "But I'm a bit of an exception. Despite living in a dorm, I usually compete with those who travel from the other end of the city."

Tony smiled. "Punctuality is a good thing," he agreed, "but it's a bit unusual for a girl."

I giggled and retorted, "The lack of punctuality in women is just a cliché."

"I agree," Tony nodded, "but clichés don't just grow on trees."

I shrugged and smiled. Tony's irony was exceptionally good-natured, and I didn't mind it at all. Still, I decided to change the topic and asked, "Are you excited about going to Amhitiemar?"

"You bet! I've read so much about its symbols and architecture, but seeing even a small part of it in person will be different."

"Yeah, can't deny that. What do you think of our team? You're the only one who isn't local here..."

"I haven't had a chance to talk to everyone yet, but the guys seem fine. Portonapoulos is just awesome—such a great scientist and a good person. But Jenkins... he may be a philanthropist, but that doesn't make him any less creepy. His constant roaming around is extremely irritating. I wonder, will he be going on the expedition with us?"

"Jeez," I cringed. "Do you think that's possible?"

"Who knows?" Tony shrugged. "But you couldn't help but notice how much attention he pays to its organization."

"Yep, that's true," I nodded, looking at Portonapoulos standing in the middle of the room. I was so immersed in my chat with Tony that I didn't even notice everyone gathering.

Portonapoulos cleared his throat and began, "Hello, everyone! As promised, today I'll tell you about Amhitiemar.

Amhitiemar was the cultural and scientific center of its time, renowned for its stunning temples and gardens. The architecture of Amhitiemar was marked by an abundance of symbols on the walls of its buildings.

The site where our expedition is headed is the location of one of Amhitiemar's temples. According to historical records, a vast library is hidden in its dungeon.

A large portion of the temple has already been excavated. Despite its age, much of the structure remains remarkably well-preserved. Previous expeditions cleared the entrance of blockages, but the door remains locked.

The lock is typical of Amhitiemar's designs, featuring five

depressions shaped like different symbols. To unlock the door, each depression must be filled with items matching the corresponding symbols. According to legends and historical accounts, these items are hidden within the temple's walls, and the symbols on the walls point to the location of hidden caches.

The walls are still covered in dust, sand, and clay. Our task is to clean them, locate the caches, and unlock the entrance. It's a labor-intensive task, and I'm not sure we'll complete it within the month, but we must give it our best effort.

Also, remember that all of your findings hold immense historical value. That's why you must take photographs or make drawings of every new symbol and document them thoroughly."

"So, what do you think?" I asked Tony as soon as Portonapoulos finished the lecture.

"Cleaning walls seems like the typical grunt work of field archaeology. Everything else sounds more interesting."

"That's exactly what I was thinking."

I headed to the lobby but stopped in my tracks. I needed to talk to Portonapoulos, yet yesterday's unpleasant encounter filled me with dread.

What if Jenkins is there again? I wondered anxiously. *But what does it matter*? *If Jenkins wants to run into me, nothing's going to stop him. There's no use being afraid.* With that, I strode energetically toward the stairs.

I approached Portonapoulos's door and, after making sure everything seemed normal, knocked. I heard a friendly "Yeah, yeah" from inside, so I opened the door and stepped through.

"Mr. Portonapoulos, do you have a moment?"

Portonapoulos nodded warmly. "Yes, come in. What's going on?"

I stepped into the room and gently closed the door behind me. "I just wanted to ask... do you know anything about the Tiendal legend?"

"Well, not much, to be honest. Why do you ask?"

"You mentioned Amhitiemar today, and it's from the same era as

Tiamon. That made me think of the Tiendal legend, and I got curious."

"I've heard of the legend, but I've always been more interested in facts than myths. However, there's someone who spent most of his life researching it—Paulo Cognitio. His team collected an impressive amount of data over the decades. You'll find plenty of journal and conference papers under their names. A few years ago, Paulo and his colleagues even published a monograph, *Tiendal Legend: Facts and Fallacies*. I'm not sure if there's a digital version, but there's a hard copy in the library. I tried reading it once—it's fascinating, but enormous. I'll admit, I didn't get through even a quarter of it. But in my defense, it's a bit outside my research field."

"That's more than I expected! Thank you so much, Mr. Portonapoulos."

I took a breath, about to say goodbye, when a knock sounded at the door. A moment later, Tony appeared in the doorway. Seeing me, he gave a shy smile. "Oh, sorry. I'll come back later."

"No, no, I was just leaving," I said quickly, taking a step toward the door, but Portonapoulos stopped me.

"Tayra, hold on a second. Come in, Tony. I've been thinking about your question, and here's the name of a book that might help." He handed Tony a small slip of paper.

Tony glanced at the note and nodded happily. "Thanks a lot! I'll head to the library right away. But... could you tell me how to get there?"

"Of course, but it's easy to get lost around here. Tayra, could you show Tony the way to the library?"

"Sure, I'm heading there anyway."

"Great, then. Good luck, guys."

The library was in a separate building, a little distance from the main educational blocks. It took about fifteen minutes to get there from our faculty, with the path winding through narrow alleys. In summer, though, this was a blessing, as most of the route was shaded, making the walk much cooler.

"So, why did you choose the symbols of Amhitiemar for your research?" I asked as we turned into the first alley.

"Don't you find it fascinating?" Tony asked, raising his eyebrows in playful surprise.

"Of course I do," I said with a nod, "but there are so many other fascinating areas..."

"I don't even know, really," he shrugged. "Honestly, I'm so tired of all these symbols. I'd rather talk about something neutral."

"For example?" I asked.

"Weather," Tony said, smiling as he glanced up at the immaculate blue sky.

"Okay," I giggled. "Don't you think today's weather is perfect?"

"Oh, undoubtedly!" Tony said theatrically, chuckling.

I looked at Tony, raising an eyebrow. "Well, what's next?"

Tony shrugged, glancing around. "I don't know. Propose a topic and I'll generate a question."

"Okay... So... nature."

"That's unfair!" Tony pretended to be offended. "My topic was easier."

"Sorry," I giggled, shrugging. "It was the first thing that came to mind."

"Well..." Tony sighed. "Don't you think those trees look mysterious?"

"Yeah, and the one on the right looks like a head with curly hair."

I felt completely at ease in Tony's company. It was that special kind of connection where the spirit mattered more than the words, and though our talk was pure nonsense, I didn't want it to end. But the path to the library wasn't long, and soon we were sitting in the reading room, where every extra sound earned an angry glance from the strict librarian...

CHAPTER 17: FACTS AND FALLACIES

Paulo Cognitio's book left me in awe. Portonapoulos put it mildly when he called it big. It had over a thousand pages of small print, and the volume was nearly ten centimeters thick.

Oh my God, I thought. *Even if I camped out in the library and read day and night, I'd never finish it in two weeks.*

Suppressing my rising panic, I opened the book and skimmed the contents. It was divided into chapters covering different aspects of the legend. A large part of the book described historical finds that helped scholars draw conclusions about the legend and the halo of myths surrounding it.

Okay... I thought with relief. *Maybe I don't need to read everything. For now, it's enough to skim the chapters that focus on the most interesting aspects of the legend. Then we'll see.*

I decided to begin with the chapter about Tiendal's bodies.

"After each reincarnation, Tiendal appeared in the body of a young, handsome man around 30 years old. The body belonged to someone killed on the day of the reincarnation rite, and there are documented facts that support this theory."

The murdered man—but not just any dead body... Why? Probably because Tiendal needed a young, healthy, attractive vessel, not that of a sick old man.

"Over the years, Tiendal's appearance barely changed. He aged very slowly, remaining attractive for a long time. Many believed that this was nothing but the merit of magic.

Each of Tiendal's lives was long, lasting two or three times longer than the average person's. He always died of old age, except in his final life, when he was poisoned by one of Pharaoh Pilzernath's mercenaries.

Tiendal returned to Pharaoh's palace sometime after the reincarnation rite. The time varied from days to months, likely depending on the severity of the donor's wound and how far they had died from Tiamon."

I wonder how the Pharaoh recognized Tiendal if he was in a new body. For some reason, there's nothing about this here. Maybe there was a password or something.

My thoughts were interrupted by the librarian's voice. "Excuse me, miss, it's time for us to close."

"Oh, sorry! I lost track of time."

My brain was overloaded with information, and I struggled to process it all. Plus, my eyes were aching after hours of reading tiny print. So, once I stepped outside, I paused at the doorstep, gazing at the distant green trees. Someone once told me it helped relieve eye strain.

Before I could test whether it worked, Jenkins's vampire-like driver appeared in my field of vision.

Oh, God, not again, I thought, my breath quickening as my heartbeat sped up.

"Tayra, are you okay?" Tony's worried voice broke through. He stepped closer, placing a hand on my shoulder. Studying my face, he added, "Have you seen a ghost? You look so pale."

"Tony, I... Yeah, I'm fine. I probably just over-studied and gave myself a headache."

I glanced at the spot where Jenkins's driver had stood just moments ago, but he was gone. Based on yesterday's experience, I knew this didn't mean I was safe from an unpleasant encounter, so I wasn't keen on being alone.

I looked up at Tony and asked, "Could you walk me to the dorm? Please?"

"Sure, let's go."

"Thanks."

We walked in silence for a few minutes before Tony asked, "Feeling better?"

"Yeah, much better. Sorry for the trouble, Tony. This isn't like me."

"Oh, stop. It's no trouble. By the way, what were you reading? If it's not a secret... that book looked huge."

"It's about the Tiendal legend."

"Wow, that's unexpected. Why do you need it?"

"I'm planning my master's thesis on Tiamon, and I thought I might find something valuable in the legend."

"Okay, got it. Was it Paulo Cognitio's book?"

"Yeah... Have you read it?"

"No, but don't tell him. Paulo Cognitio is my supervisor."

"Wow, I'm speechless. But didn't you say your thesis was about the symbols of Amhitiemar?"

"Yeah, after the book was published, Paulo switched to a different research focus."

"Well, that's understandable. After decades of Tiendal, he probably got tired of it."

"Yup, probably."

We quietly made our way to the dormitory and stopped a few meters from the entrance. Jenkins's car and his driver were nowhere in sight. I listened to my body, and to my great relief, I didn't feel any waves of excitement. Still, something felt uneasy.

What if Jenkins is waiting for me inside? Maybe I should ask Tony to walk me to my door. But... I've only met him twice. What will he think if I start acting paranoid? Better not drag him into my problems. Besides, I don't even understand what's happening in my life right now.

Pushing aside my doubts, I turned to Tony and said, "Well, here we are. Thanks for walking me."

"Not at all," Tony smiled. "Hey... wave to me from the window, so I know you didn't faint on the stairs."

"Oh, come on, Tony! I'm not that fragile, and I've never fainted."

"Well, that didn't work," Tony chuckled. "Maybe I just wanted to know where your window is."

"Why do you need to know? Planning to rob me at night? I don't have anything worth stealing."

"Rob you? Maybe I just wanted to sing you a serenade..."

"Ah, a serenade... that's possible. But just so you know, Mrs. Hudson, our concierge, has zero tolerance for night singers. I'll show you the window if you want, but it's on the other side of the building."

"Alright, let's go."

We walked around the building and stopped near one of the semi-dry maples I often stare at from my window.

"Second from the left, third floor."

"Got it, thanks. Now go upstairs and wave so I know you're not pulling one over on me."

"Wow, so distrustful," I chuckled, heading back to the dorm entrance.

Thankfully, no one was waiting for me in the stairwell or the hallway. I unlocked my door, kicked off my shoes, and went to the window. Tony was still standing where I'd left him. I waved, and he smiled, waved back, then turned and headed toward the bus stop.

He's actually really cute, I thought, watching him go, and then went to change.

Over the next week, I read Paulo Cognitio's book whenever I had the chance. Tony stayed late in the library too, working until closing, and then he'd walk me home. I never asked him to, but it was entirely his choice. I didn't mind; I enjoyed spending time with Tony. Our carefree conversations helped me unwind after hours of reading and forget the problems hanging over me. Those problems only seemed to grow the deeper I delved into the facts about Tiendal.

I wonder how soon after Tiendal's death his reincarnation rite was usually conducted. Pharaohs must've wanted their valuable advisor back as soon as possible.

"The time between Tiendal's death and his reincarnation rite could range from a few days to several years, depending on how quickly the Pharaoh's servants could find a suitable woman to unlock the secret room."

Hmm… I thought any woman could do it. Oh, here's a whole chapter on this...

"The entrance to the secret room was protected by a series of puzzle locks and powerful magic. The ancient spell of disguise rendered the coveted door invisible to all but the elect. So, to conduct the rite of reincarnation, they needed a woman with special abilities, able to see the door through the spell and open it. It was likely hard to find such a woman, so the search often lasted years, sometimes beginning even during Tiendal's lifetime. There's no documentary evidence describing this woman's features. But since she was destined to become Tiendal's first mistress after his resurrection, these women were always young, beautiful, and shared a similar appearance—likely one preferred by Tiendal."

Gladys didn't see any doors in the cell, but I did. Could the ancient spell of disguise still be in effect? And if I could open the door… does that make me the Chosen One? Great to be chosen, nothing to say... What sins could've earned me such a 'blessing'?

"Tiendal was notorious for his passion for women. He had countless mistresses, changing them frequently. Yet he was only ever married once—to the beautiful Ilze, whose betrayal drove him to resort to magic to prevent it from happening again."

Hmm... so Ilze wasn't just a mistress, she was his wife. But that doesn't really change things, since it wasn't a consensual marriage.

"In none of his lives did Tiendal have children."

Weird... He had plenty of women, so was magic involved? But what about the curse?

"Every woman Tiendal set his sights on was subjected to a special ritual. Afterward, she became numb to the touch of other men, but burned with desire for Tiendal alone. Ilze's betrayal didn't break Tiendal's heart as much as it wounded his vanity. His curse was designed to ensure he wasn't just a woman's lover, but her best and most unforgettable one.

The cursed woman could be with other men, but only Tiendal's touch and caresses brought her true pleasure. If a woman had sexual experience before Tiendal, all previous sensations faded during their time together, leaving only the memory of Tiendal's touch.

Tiendal likely chose women who valued pleasure above all else, as there isn't a single account of an abandoned mistress finding another relationship or living a normal life afterward. Sex with Tiendal was addictive, and once they could no longer have him, the women either went mad or met an untimely end soon after the affair ended."

Nothing reassuring here. Not a word about breaking the love curse. But then again, there's also no mention of anyone even trying.

"Tiendal's magic wasn't just for enchanting women—it also maintained his other special abilities. Unwilling to believe in the full extent of Tiendal's magic, people spread rumors that if he lost access to the source of his power, his abilities would weaken.

It was believed the source of Tiendal's power was hidden in his secret room. However, since the pharaohs relied on Tiendal's magic, he always had access to his source of power during his lifetime, so this theory was never tested."

It offers a glimmer of hope. But I have no idea how this could apply to my situation.

CHAPTER 18: STALKING

Besides reading Paulo Cognitio's book, I had another important task to finish before the expedition—passing the final entrance exam for the fifth year.

The exam wasn't hard for me—it was one of my favorite subjects, and I'd prepared for it ages ago—but the day itself was still stressful. We wrote the exam in a tightly closed classroom (probably to prevent a bird from flying in with the right answers), so when I finally stepped out, it felt like I was reborn, breathing fresh air for the first time. There was only one thing I needed to feel completely happy—go to the bathroom and splash cold water on my face. I decided to make that dream come true right away.

On the stairs, I bumped into Tony.

"Hey! How are you?" he asked with a smile.

"Hey! I'm fine, thanks. I just finished my entrance exam."

"Wow! How'd it go?"

"I'll get the results in a few days, but I think I did well enough to get into the fifth year."

"That's great! But I'll wait to congratulate you once you get the result."

"Yep, makes sense."

"I'm really happy to see you, but I've got to run. I've got some stuff to finish at my university and need to be there in under an hour."

"Yeah, sure. See you."

"See you."

I went to the bathroom, turned on the tap, and held my hand under the stream. The cool, life-giving water flowed over my palm, bringing a feeling of instant refreshment.

Mmm... I thought. *Just what I needed*!

I lifted my other hand to the water and bent over the sink to wash my face when the door suddenly clicked open, and Jenkins stood in the doorway.

"Hey! Miss me?" he said, stepping closer.

I turned off the water and glared at him. "What the hell, Jenkins? This is the women's bathroom!"

"Yes, and it's a place where we can be alone."

"Someone could walk in any minute."

"Not while my guy's standing outside. It's closed for now."

Damn! I thought, frantically running through possible escape routes in my head. A week without Jenkins had almost made me forget about him.

But Jenkins hadn't forgotten his ways. He stepped closer, unbuttoning his jacket as he moved. A warmth spread through my lower abdomen, quickly turning into heat. Instinctively, I touched the cold sink, trying to cool down, but it was clear I wasn't winning this battle.

I looked up at Jenkins, my voice earnest. "Please, stop. Let me go."

"I'm not holding you, am I? It's your body that's drawn to me, that won't let you leave. You know you can't fight this, so why try?"

As he spoke, Jenkins teasingly ran a finger along my neck, leaving a burning trail in its wake. I felt the urge to tear off Jenkins's clothes and press myself against his bare skin, the desire overpowering my thoughts. The feeling was much stronger than before. Fighting it now caused me physical pain. Unable to take it any longer, I collapsed into

Jenkins's arms...

***

A couple of days later, Portonapoulos called us for another meeting. This time, he covered aspects of field archaeology, the nuances of camp life, safety measures, and other things he thought would be useful. At the end of the lecture, feeling sorry for our heat-melted brains, he decided to give us a challenge—to think about a solution and present it at the next meeting.

Here was the task: While exploring the dungeon of an ancient temple, an archaeologist accidentally gets locked in a room. The room has three doors. Behind one is poisonous gas, behind another is a river full of crocodiles, and behind the third is a corridor with devices that continuously shoot sharp arrows. Which door should the archaeologist choose to escape?

The variety of options intrigued everyone, so after the meeting, we gathered in the lobby to debate the possibilities.

For some reason, third-year students Miles and Jacob immediately decided that the corridor with arrows was the most realistic escape route. The guys had probably played a lot of action games because they were convinced that weapons without reloading didn't exist. Practically foaming at the mouth, they tried to convince everyone that if the archaeologist opened the door and waited long enough, the arrows would eventually run out, allowing him to pass safely. Tony's argument that an automatic reloading system could exist, perhaps with arrows coming from the opposite direction, didn't convince them. They stuck to their theory.

The girls banded together in support of the gas theory. Chiara suggested the archaeologist close his eyes and hold his breath, while Alicia recommended wrapping his head in a T-shirt for extra protection. The ever-optimistic Jenny claimed that a smart archaeologist would already be wearing a respirator, solving the problem automatically. However, she didn't have a plan for what to do if the archaeologist wasn't quite that smart.

Louis and Peter, the animal lovers of the group, opted for the crocodile route, reasoning it might be the best way out. They claimed that if the crocodiles weren't too hungry, they could probably strike some kind of deal with them.

The inventive Ahish proposed a combined theory: the archaeologist should cover his head with clothes, hold his breath, and stroll through the gas-filled corridor to get soaked in poison. Then, he could calmly walk along the crocodile river, since clever crocodiles wouldn't eat a poisoned archaeologist.

Tony and I didn't propose any theories ourselves, we just rationally debunked the ideas of others. I wasn't sure what drove Tony's behavior, but for me, it was partly my own unpleasant experience and partly not wanting to ruin the general cheer. After all, debating these absurd theories was incredibly fun, and our laughter echoed through the lobby.

I knew from experience that if an archaeologist somehow ended up in a room with three doors, then there was clearly a fourth door he had come through. Whether above, below, or on the opposite wall, it certainly existed. My experience made it clear that the focus should be on finding that fourth door, rather than wasting time and energy on the other hopeless escape routes. More importantly, I knew that unfamiliar doors should never be opened. After all, an ancient sorcerer with fiery eyes could be waiting behind one.

In the middle of the discussion, my phone rang. The number was hidden.

Probably just another advertisement, I thought, but I stepped aside and answered anyway.

"Nice guys, aren't they? Especially that boy in the blue T-shirt..." I heard a familiar, velvet voice through the receiver. "It'd be a shame if something happened to him... Life is so unpredictable."

"You wouldn't dare!"

"Tayra, don't make me laugh. Haven't I already proven how serious I am?"

"Fine. What do you want?"

"Parking lot behind the building. You've got 1 minute."

Luckily, the guys were too engrossed in the discussion to notice my absence. I darted out of the building and sprinted to the parking lot. There were always so few cars there, it was impossible to miss Jenkins's sedan. I approached, the door swung open, I climbed in, and the car took off.

Jenkins glanced at his watch and calmly said, "Right on time. Well done."

At that moment, I wanted to kill him—grab his flawless neck and choke him with all the hatred I could muster. I stared at Jenkins, weighing the reality of this plan.

Jenkins caught my gaze and grinned. "Relax," he said. "Trust me, it's a bad idea."

I snorted, not even realizing he'd somehow read my mind. But honestly, it didn't take a mind reader to guess what I was thinking.

Gradually, my anger shifted to a sense of hopelessness. Since there was no way out, I figured we might as well talk. I looked into Jenkins's black eyes and asked, "Where are we going?"

"To a place where we can finally enjoy each other's company," he replied.

"I never said I enjoyed your company!" I snapped.

"Your body did. And it's ready to prove it right now, but the surroundings aren't suitable. You'll just have to wait, my dear. But trust me, it'll be worth it."

"Jenkins, you're handsome, rich, and famous. Why me?"

"You're asking too many questions."

"This is the longest conversation we've had since we met."

"I prefer hearing you moan, not talk. So shut up. Or I'll make you."

I rolled my eyes and turned defiantly toward the window. It was darkened with something, making it impossible to see through. Still, I stayed in that position for the rest of the ride, pretending to be deeply interested.

Jenkins's mansion was surprisingly small for someone of his wealth. We entered quickly, so I didn't get a good look at the outside. Oddly enough, the inside was quite cozy. The decor was elegant minimalism, lacking the cold, impeccable precision that characterized Jenkins and everything about him.

Probably left by the previous owners, I thought sarcastically but kept the comment to myself—just in case.

We went upstairs and entered a spacious room. The large bed in the center made it obvious this was a bedroom. There were several windows, but all except one had the curtains drawn, leaving the room dimly lit. Still, it was enough light for me to take in everything.

The room felt more like a museum than a living space. It was the size of four of my dorm rooms—you could probably ride a bike or even a horse in here. The room was bathed in light colors, but unlike Jenkins's office, warm shades of beige, ivory, and champagne dominated, creating a surprisingly pleasant atmosphere.

He definitely didn't renovate when he moved in, I concluded, mentally acknowledging the harmony and elegance of the space.

"Yes, true," Jenkins said as he closed the door.

"What's true?" I asked, confused.

"I didn't change a thing when I moved in. The interior's all from the previous owners."

I was dumbfounded, my eyes widening like walnuts. "How the hell...?"

"I just know," Jenkins said with a grin.

A sudden wave of fear hit me. *Is he really reading my mind*?!

"To some extent," Jenkins said, smirking smugly. "But with you, it's easy. Poker face isn't really your thing. Everything you think is written right there on your forehead."

So what? I thought. *I just don't like lying.*

"You shouldn't," Jenkins agreed. "I can always sense a lie, so don't bother wasting your energy."

Devil, I thought. But since my thoughts had no privacy anyway, I asked aloud, "What else do you know?"

"I know you feel the attraction between us. In the car, it was under control, so you could put on a brave face. But it's growing now... getting stronger."

Jenkins spoke as he slowly moved toward me, his last words coming when he was already standing inches away. His lips hovered just above my neck, his hot breath on my skin as he whispered, "We have plenty of time... I know you're dying to rip off your clothes, but I'll take my time. I want to make every inch of your body shiver, anticipating what's to come. I love watching you struggle, but seeing you surrender—oh, that's even better."

He slipped my blouse off, his lips trailing down my neck, lingering on my breast, then moving lower to my belly. His hands unzipped my pants, caressing my skin as he undressed me slowly.

The heat inside me surged to a boiling point as Jenkins returned to my face, pressing his lips against mine. Every move he made was filled with confidence, as if he knew exactly what feelings each would evoke.

In contrast to Jenkins's deliberate, slow movements, my hands moved uncontrollably. Overcome with passion, I tore Jenkins's shirt off and greedily pressed my fingers against the bare skin of his strong back. I felt Jenkins's heart racing, a clear sign that maintaining slow, controlled movements required considerable effort.

Seized by desire, Jenkins finally let go, shifting from the controlling

Master to a fellow Slave in the storm of passion raging between us.

***

When the storm reached its climax, Jenkins rolled to the other side of the bed and lay back, staring silently at the ceiling. Even after a game of tennis, people shake hands in gratitude; surely our passionate encounter deserved at least a brief appreciative kiss on the forehead or cheek, yet Jenkins seemed unconcerned with such nuances.

To be fair, I behaved no better. Even though I could hardly move, my body still trembling from the powerful orgasm, I offered Jenkins no words of praise, like “Oh, that was divine!” Instead, I lay in proud silence, staring at the ceiling just like Jenkins.

Once I realized I could move normally, I quickly got up, collected my things from the floor, and dressed. During this time, Jenkins managed to pull on his underwear and pants.

I shot him a bold look, accompanying it with an equally bold question, “Well, how can I get out of here?”

Jenkins grinned and countered, “Don’t you like my house?”

“Not really,” I said with a shrug.

“What exactly don’t you like?”

“You.”

Jenkins laughed, but not with his usual venom—it was more genuine. It was the first real emotion I’d ever seen on him, and it felt strange. It must have felt strange for Jenkins too, because he quickly masked it with his usual neutral expression and said, “That was rude. Aren't you afraid to be rude to me?”

“No, I prefer honesty. You make my body lie, but luckily, my mind stays clear. It’s easy to be honest with you.”

“Really? Why’s that?”

“Because I’m not afraid of hurting you. You don’t have a heart to feel pain.”

Jenkins laughed again, this time with his usual sarcastic edge. “It’s a blessing, not a curse," he smirked, "to always get what you want and never feel pity or regret."

"You'd know better," I shrugged. Then I sniffed and shot Jenkins a questioning look, reminding him he still hadn't answered my first question.

"Peterson will drive you home," Jenkins said with a nod, walking toward the door.

"Thanks," I muttered, quickly following him, afraid he might change his mind.

The ride with vampire-looking Peterson passed in eerie silence, broken only by the hum of the engine. I didn't mind, though—I had no desire to talk to that creepy guy.

By the time I got back to my dorm, it was already getting dark. I kicked off my shoes, collapsed onto the bed, too tired to even undress. I leaned forward, elbows on my knees, cradling my head in my hands.

Damn Jenkins... Why is he stalking me? There are plenty of women dying to jump into his bed and enjoy his so-called 'skills,' but he focuses all his lust on me, threatening and blackmailing along the way.

Even if I hypothetically assume he's the reincarnation of Tiendal, his behavior still doesn't add up. Is that even possible? Or have I just lost touch with reality, digging too deep into the legend?

Either way, something is definitely wrong with him. The expedition is in two days, and it promises a month-long break from Jenkins. That alone makes it worth going.

CHAPTER 19: CAMP

We arrived at the Amhitemar temple at dawn—or rather, at our campsite in the nearby forest, about three hundred meters from the excavation site.

The camp was already buzzing with activity. We were just a small part of the expedition team, alongside Jenkins's men, who had arrived a few days earlier and already set up part of the tent city, built canopies, and started the generators.

Clearly, the success of this venture was crucial to Jenkins, given the comfortable conditions he arranged for us. The camp's logistics—food, water, and other essentials—were handled mostly by his people, leaving us to focus entirely on our work.

The head of the expedition, Carlo Rodriguez, greeted us. He was a swarthy, dark-haired man around forty-five, wearing a brown plaid shirt with rolled-up sleeves that revealed strong, tattooed arms—either snakes or dragons inked across his skin. At first glance, Carlo reminded me of a villain from an Indiana Jones movie. But I quickly dismissed the thought—partly because I was biased against anything linked to Jenkins, and partly because Carlo seemed friendly enough.

Carlo led us to the site where we'd be setting up camp and gestured toward a neat pyramid of tubes holding rolled-up tents. "We had trouble with the generators, and the terrain here is tricky—lots of ravines and gullies," he explained to Portonapoulos. "We had to level the soil in some spots just to set anything up. Your tents should've been ready by now, but we couldn't get here in time, and I doubt my crew will be free anytime soon. You'll have to start setting up on your own. The tents are small, doubles, and there seem to be enough flat spots here, so it shouldn't be too difficult."

Carlo glanced around our group, as if sizing us up, then smiled. "I'll be nearby, so feel free to call if you need help. The reception is terrible here—out of range in most spots. If you need to call, you'll have to find a hill. Honestly, it's easier to just find me in person. Oh, and one more thing... You might want to see the temple itself. You can leave your gear here and walk over to the excavation site, then come back to set up."

Portonapoulos nodded but glanced hesitantly toward the tents. Carlo caught the look right away and reassured him before he could voice his concern. "Don't worry, nothing will happen to your gear. Aside from you and my crew, there's not a soul around. Even birds don't come here often. It's a pretty secluded spot."

Portonapoulos smiled, thanked Carlo, and motioned for us to drop our bags and follow him to the excavation site.

The excavation site was large and open-air. Besides the temple, there were remnants of other buildings, though they were far less preserved and still in the early stages of being cleared.

In a few years, a museum complex like the 'Tiamon Catacombs' will probably be built here, I thought, gazing at the ancient ruins with awe and respect. *And there really will be something worth seeing.*

Contrary to my expectations, the temple left me with mixed feelings. By Amhitemar's standards, where temples could soar to a hundred meters tall, this was merely a small chapel. This "baby," however, covered about two hundred square meters and stood roughly fifteen meters tall, judging by the upper edge of the partially ruined decorative structure on the roof. In fact, this was just the upper level; most of the temple lay underground, still waiting to be uncovered. Estimates suggested that the underground portion was several times larger than the visible part, both in area and height.

The visible structure was a massive foundation shaped like a truncated prism, with a wide staircase in the center. I estimated the staircase to be about two meters tall. A gap of about one and a half meters ran along the edges of the prism. In the center stood a rectangular structure with a roof, also shaped like a truncated prism, topped by a decorative stone feature resembling either a honeycomb or a lattice. The walls stood about five or six meters tall, with the remaining height split evenly between the roof and the decorative structure. The walls were made of stone blocks, each etched with countless symbols. Much of the stone was still smeared with clay, hiding most of the carvings, but even the small part that was visible left me in awe.

Huge walls, entirely covered in intricate patterns, partially obscured by thick layers of clay and dust... I thought skeptically. *How are we supposed to make sense of this, let alone find any hidden caches*?

The most striking part of the temple was its entrance. The doors were huge, roughly three meters high, with a doorway about one and a half meters wide. The doors were slightly recessed into the wall, flanked by wide rectangular columns, each adorned with intricate patterns.

The doors were made up of two massive leaves, likely very heavy, their surfaces covered in ornate patterns. At eye level, in the center of the door, was a large circle, just over a meter in diameter. Inside the circle were five slots, just as Portonapoulos had described during one of our pre-expedition meetings.

I glanced at Tony, standing to my left, and asked, “What do you think?”

“I’m not sure,” Tony shook his head. “It’s impressive, no doubt.”

He took another look at the temple and added, "Especially with all the work we have ahead of us."

"True enough," Portonapoulos agreed, overhearing our whispers nearby.

Tony and I exchanged a slightly embarrassed glance, but Portonapoulos offered an encouraging smile. Then, in a louder voice to the whole team, he said, "I get it, guys. It's jaw-dropping, but we can't stand around staring. Tomorrow, we start clearing, and we've got a lot to do before then. Let's head back to camp and get unpacked."

But before we could start, we were called to breakfast, where Carlo introduced us to our chef, José. In my cliché-driven imagination, I pictured the chef as a plump, rosy-cheeked man in a white cap and apron. So, it took me a moment to process that our chef was a broad-shouldered, six-foot-tall man with jet-black hair pulled into a ponytail, looking more like a thug from a Colombian drug cartel movie than a chef.

What does appearance have to do with cooking? I reminded myself. *Come on, Tayra, don't be biased, be above stereotypes.*

Surprisingly, the food José prepared was not just edible but actually tasty. After a sleepless night and two hours on my feet in the fresh air, though, the fact that there was food at all mattered more than its quality. I wasn't picky analyzing the flavors.

Finally, we went back to our gear and started unpacking. As it turned out, Tony was the only guy who knew how to set up tents. He took Louis and Peter under his wing, while Ahish, Miles, and Jacob set off to learn the ropes under Portonapoulos's strict supervision.

Meanwhile, the girls were busy dismantling, sorting, and distributing the equipment. Out of all of us, only Chiara had seen this in action before, since she had already participated in an excavation once. Alicia, Jenny, and I, much to our shame, were pure theorists—sure, we'd seen all this, but only in textbooks and long ago. Of course, we'd had labs with real equipment, but what we used then and what lay on the grass in front of me now were worlds apart. So, as we sorted, Chiara helped align our theoretical knowledge with the practical tools we'd be using.

I was especially impressed by the diamond-shaped trowel. It seemed like such an inconspicuous tool, yet it was the most essential in a field archaeologist's kit. It had endless uses—from carefully removing soil from fragile finds to handling stratigraphic fixation tasks.

I looked at Chiara in amazement and said, "I had no idea archaeologists used such a variety of tools. For some reason, I feel like if you asked the average person about an archaeologist's main tool, they'd confidently say, 'a shovel.'"

Chiara laughed. "Well, they wouldn't be entirely wrong. Just look," she said, pointing to a neat row of shovels nearby, "standing tall and proud, like guards on duty."

Compared to the small trowels and brushes scattered on the ground, the shovels looked like giants—serious and intimidating. I couldn't help but laugh too. "Well," I said, "I see. The shovel clearly isn't giving up its throne."

Once the guys finished with the tents, we started settling in and making them cozy. There were six tents, which we divided by the simple rule: boys on the left, girls on the right. Jenny became my tent neighbor, Alicia paired with Chiara, and the guys formed pairs: Miles with Jacob, Ahish with Peter, and Louis with Tony. Portonapoulos, of course, got his own tent.

Even though we were exhausted from the journey and the hectic day, that evening we gathered around the campfire. Despite Portonapoulos advising us to pack light, practical Louis had brought a guitar, which turned out to be quite handy.

I knew Louis was a big music lover, and Jenny had told me he played guitar really well. But I'd never heard him play, so I was more than curious. The warm summer night and the steady crackle of the fire practically begged for a soulful song.

Louis wasn't just a talented guitarist—he had a rich baritone voice, too. And his taste in music matched mine so perfectly, I could've listened to him all night. But after a few songs, Louis paused and offered the guitar to someone else.

The guys exchanged hesitant glances. No one dared to pick up the guitar—Louis had set the bar too high, and no one wanted to risk embarrassment. But without music, things quickly got dull, and we desperately needed someone to break the silence.

To my surprise, Tony stepped up to save the night. With a shy smile, he took the guitar from Louis and said, "Well, guys, I haven't done this in ages, so go easy on me."

Wow! I thought, freezing in anticipation. *Not only can he put up a tent, but he can also play the guitar. Isn't he the perfect travel companion*? *I've got to ask where he learned all this. Was he a Boy Scout*?

In the seconds before Tony touched the strings, my heart raced from zero to a hundred. Heat rose up my spine, my head spun, and it became harder to breathe. I'd never been this nervous, not even before an exam. It was strange—scary, yet oddly pleasant.

As soon as Tony started playing, I recognized the first chords of "Nothing Else Matters" by Metallica and melted like butter. It was so perfect, so sweet, that a tear slipped down my cheek. Night. Forest. Campfire. Tony. Guitar. I watched him, spellbound, and softly whispered along, "And nothing else matters..."

As great as it was sitting around the fire, fatigue eventually caught up with us. So, we decided to put it out and head to our tents. After all, we had to get up early.

Jenny and I had the tent furthest from the fire, so we were the last to reach it. As soon as we got there, Jenny yawned, glanced at the starry sky, and said, "I think it's time to call it a night. I'm dead tired. I'd better get inside before I fall asleep standing." With that, she ducked into the tent and seemed to fall asleep instantly.

I lingered outside. The night was warm and nearly windless, and even the mosquitoes seemed well-behaved, not spoiling the mood. I didn't want to hide in the stuffy tent. I was still emotional for reasons I couldn't quite understand, and I thought maybe some fresh air would help me calm down.

I looked around and realized I wasn't the only one still awake. Miles and Jacob were outside smoking, while Tony and Louis stood nearby. The four of them seemed to be talking, but they were too quiet and I couldn't make out their words.

Soon, Tony noticed me and walked over. "Everything okay?" he asked.

"Yep, it's fine," I said with a nod.

"Why aren't you heading to bed then?"

"Well," I shrugged, "I don't know. I just don't feel like sleeping."

"Fancy going for a walk?"

"Um… It's so dark. Won't we get lost?"

"Nope, we won't go far."

"Okay," I shrugged, still unsure if it was a good idea.

Tony took my hand, and we left the glade, heading deeper into the forest. To be honest, I could barely tell where we were going, let alone find my way back, so I relied entirely on Tony. Whether it was because I'd mentally enrolled him in the Boy Scouts, or because Tony's presence itself made me feel secure, I had no doubt everything would be alright. Which surprised me, since I couldn't remember ever feeling comfortable with having zero control over a situation.

I had no idea how long we'd been walking—I didn't check the time, and my internal clock wasn't even working—before we finally reached a small clearing. From there, the night sky opened up before us, offering a breathtaking view.

I've always been a city dweller, so I've only ever seen the night sky with city lights in the background. Even then, I always thought it was beautiful. But the sight before me now was incomparable to anything I'd ever seen. Bright stars were scattered across the night sky like diamond dust, their radiance simply magical. The atmosphere was completed by the moonlight, which cast a soft bluish glow on the treetops.

I froze, mouth open, unable to look away from the incredible sight. I was utterly lost in the dizzying depth of the sky above until Tony's voice snapped me out of my daze.

"Beautiful, isn't it?" he said, gazing up at the sky.

"It is," I said, still standing with my head tilted back, staring at the stars like I was bewitched.

"Still can't compare to you, though."

I turned to Tony, surprised. My face flushed, and though it was too dark for him to see, I still tried to hide behind my hand.

"I… uh…"

Tony moved closer and gently brushed a stray strand of hair from my forehead. I couldn't see his eyes in the darkness, but I felt the warmth radiating from his face and knew he was blushing too.

In that moment, confusion and panic hit me. Friendship—that's how I'd always seen my relationship with Tony. Easy conversations and nothing more. I'd built this barrier between us, convinced it had to be there, even though it often made me wrestle with my own feelings.

My unresolved issues with Jenkins, my sensual numbness—it made sense that I needed to sort that out before letting anyone else in. But life seemed to challenge that belief when Tony came into my world.

I have to admit, Tony never crossed the friend zone boundaries. Up until now, we'd masked our flirting as goofing around, turning it all into a joke, pretending not to notice the attraction between us.

But Tony wasn't joking now. It was both comforting and terrifying.

I was terrified of hurting Tony. Whether it was now, by rejecting him, or later, when—God forbid—he learned about my secrets. The situations with Nick and Xavier didn't offer much reassurance, even though Jenkins wasn't part of my life back then.

It was late, but the air was still warm. Due to my internal worries, a chill ran through me, and I shuddered.

"What's wrong?" Tony asked gently, his hand resting on my shoulder.

"I… uh…" I mumbled.

Tony smiled and stroked my arm. "Relax," he said softly, "it's okay."

I took a deep breath and nodded, giving him an apologetic look. His palm still rested on my shoulder, and before he could pull away, I covered it with my hand, letting him know I wanted it to stay. Tony smiled, stepped behind me, and wrapped both arms around my shoulders. I nodded, letting him know he understood me perfectly. Tony kissed the top of my head gently, then looked up at the sky.

"It's amazing," he said, "it really does seem endless."

"Yes," I agreed, "an endless path into the unknown..."

My back pressed against Tony's chest, and I could feel his heartbeat—steady, but just a little faster than normal. The warmth of his hands on my shoulders chased away all my fears and worries, replacing them with a calm sense of confidence. In that moment, I knew exactly what I wanted. I wanted this feeling to last forever. I wanted to stand there, under the stars with Tony, in the peaceful silence of the summer night.

But as much as I wished it could last, we had to get back to camp and sleep if we wanted to be ready for tomorrow.

CHAPTER 20: BONDING

For the next several days, we rose with the first light of dawn and worked until darkness set in. It was only during these days that I truly understood why people say field archaeology is one of the hardest and most tedious jobs.

Under the scorching sun, dirty, thirsty, and exhausted, we painstakingly cleared the walls of dust, sand, and soil. This routine could have driven anyone crazy, but the warm, friendly atmosphere in our team kept our spirits high.

Tony's work area was close to mine, so we had plenty of chances to talk during breaks. In the evenings, we'd gather around the campfire to sing songs with the guitar. After lights out, Tony and I would visit our clearing to admire the starry sky for a little while.

One night, on our way back to camp, we heard a strange noise—the sound of a car engine running. We stopped behind the trees, searching for the source of the sound. Soon, we spotted a trailer parked not far from our camp.

"Hmm... Who could this be at such a late hour?" Tony asked. "Let's get closer."

Staying hidden behind the trees, we moved closer to the trailer. A few meters away, I caught a faint, familiar smell, and the familiar wave of excitement surged inside me.

Oh, come on, why? I thought bitterly and then muttered aloud, "It's

Jenkins."

"How can you be sure?"

"I've got a feeling in my gut."

Tony raised an eyebrow, skeptical but silent.

"So, what do we do now?" I asked, feeling confused.

"We could just walk over and say hi," Tony suggested.

"Absolutely not!" I blurted, feeling a surge of panic.

"Relax, I'm just messing with you," Tony said with a grin, then added, "I do want to know why he's here, though. But we can't just stand here hiding behind the trees all night."

"Why not?" I asked, feeling unsure.

"It's a trailer, a house on wheels. He's probably staying inside until morning."

"Maybe he's just here to relive some childhood dream," I said sarcastically.

"Yup," Tony nodded, "because nighttime is clearly the best time for that."

I'm not sure why Jenkins abandoned the civilized world to disappear into the middle of nowhere, but he never missed a chance to kill two birds with one stone—and shamelessly exploited my constant availability. Yet, smart and calculating, he made sure our interactions didn't attract any unwanted attention. Which, I must admit, was the only thing I agreed with him on.

On Jenkins's very first evening with us, I was sitting with the others by the fire when a sudden wave of excitement hit me. Guessing the reason, I turned my head, searching for the source. I spotted movement behind the distant trees and headed straight for it. Of course, it was Jenkins.

"Don't you have more important tasks than tormenting me?" I snapped the moment I reached him.

"They might be more important, but far less enjoyable," he replied in his usual seductive tone, which was infuriating.

"They'll notice I'm gone soon," I said coldly, reminding him he wasn't the only one in control.

"I know," Jenkins said calmly. "That's why you'll come to my trailer after everyone's asleep—and make sure no one sees you."

"And what if I don't?" I asked, defiant.

"You will," Jenkins said with absolute confidence. "And there are many reasons for that—both internal..." He paused, leaning in closer. His hot breath seared my neck, sending a surge of excitement through my body. Jenkins held the pose for a few seconds, savoring his power and my inner struggle, before pulling back with a devilish grin. "And external."

As Jenkins stepped back, the tension inside me eased slightly. I took a deep breath, trying to steady my voice. "And what are the external ones?"

"Well, the work of a field archaeologist is dangerous... anything can happen. A collapse, poisonous vapors from a newly formed hole in the wall... Or, say, if you're far from camp, it's dark, and you don't see a pit or a cliff..."

"You won't harm anyone," I said firmly. "You wouldn't want that kind of attention on the expedition you're sponsoring."

"You're smart, which makes you an even more valuable trophy. But it'll just be an accident, and I won't be around when it happens. Of course, I'll be deeply upset, publicly devastated. But believe me, I'll turn the tragedy into an advantage. So don't provoke my dark side, Tayra. You can have the pleasure your body craves... and none of those innocent men will get hurt. Doesn't that sound like a fair deal?"

Jenkins's threats shattered my remaining confidence. I couldn't think of a reply. All I could do was sigh, feeling utterly defeated.

Jenkins seemed quite satisfied with my reaction. He stepped closer, locking his gaze with mine. "You know if I so much as touch you, you won't be able to fight the storm of desire inside. Yet you make me convince you every time. Stop this vain stubbornness, Tayra. I'll see you later tonight."

Thankfully, I didn't encounter Jenkins during the day—no trace of that unsettling "connection." He was probably nowhere near the camp, which came as a huge relief, though it contradicted his talk of "touching the childhood dream."

I'd had enough of Jenkins at night; during the day, I didn't want to waste my dwindling energy digging into his life or his motives.

On the third day after Jenkins's arrival, Tony didn't show up at breakfast, and my heart froze with fear.

Oh my God! *If something's happened to Tony, I'll never forgive myself*, I thought in panic, rushing to find Louis. "Have you seen Tony today?" I asked breathlessly when I found him.

"Yeah, he slept in the tent, but he left before I even washed my face."

"Do you know where he went?"

"Nope," Louis shrugged. "Ask Portonapoulos—he should know."

Please, *Tony*, *be okay*, I pleaded silently as I ran toward Portonapoulos. *Please*!

I spotted Portonapoulos talking to Carlo. It felt rude to interrupt, and I definitely didn't want Jenkins's people paying attention to my business, so I decided to wait until they finished. Even though I knew waiting was the right thing to do, every second felt like an eternity.

I silently cursed Portonapoulos's endless chatter several times before they finally finished, and my dear professor headed toward the excavation site. Without wasting a second, I rushed toward him, practically blocking his path like a bullet. "Mr. Portonapoulos, have you seen Tony today?" I blurted.

"Yes, he came by early and asked for a day off," Portonapoulos replied, still looking a bit startled by my sudden appearance.

Relieved, I asked my next question more calmly, "Do you know how he planned to spend it?"

"I'm not sure," Portonapoulos shrugged. "He probably wanted to check out some other historical sites nearby."

Really? I thought skeptically. "Which ones exactly?" I asked aloud.

"Well, Amhitiemar was a big city, and this temple isn't the only structure that remains. There's a ruined mansion a few kilometers from here. It's in much worse shape than the temple, but you can still find symbols on its walls. Tony might've gone there to study them."

What the heck? I thought. *Why would he need to study other ruins when we've got these giant walls covered in symbols right here*? *It makes no sense.*

I kept my doubts to myself and only asked, "When was he supposed to be back?"

"By dark."

I rubbed my forehead, deep in thought. Portonapoulos's explanation didn't make sense—too many pieces just didn't add up. Trying to gather more information, I asked, "Was he nervous when he left?"

"Well, he seemed a bit agitated and in a hurry."

"Do you think he'll come back?" I asked, my voice uncertain as I fought to keep a tear from slipping down my cheek.

Portonapoulos looked into my eyes, his voice carrying an almost exaggerated confidence. "Of course, he will. Believe me."

His words only deepened my distrust of the whole mansion story. It felt like a lie, something made up to cover the real reason for Tony's disappearance. Portonapoulos obviously knew more than he was letting on, but for some reason, he couldn't tell me. All he could offer was a reassuring look, as if silently saying, *Don't worry, he'll be okay.*

Out loud, however, Portonapoulos kept it neutral. "Please, go back to work. We have a lot to do." It left me with no choice but to obey.

"Okay. Thank you, Mr. Portonapoulos," I nodded, trailing sadly back to the excavation site.

Although I listened and went back to work, I could barely focus. My hands worked mechanically, clearing the stone wall with its spirally entwined circles, but my thoughts kept drifting back to Tony.

Last night, he didn't mention taking a day off or planning to go anywhere. Doesn't he trust me? Why did he leave so suddenly? What does Portonapoulos know, and why won't he just tell me? Could Tony's disappearance be connected to Jenkins?

My head spun with questions, but the one that haunted me most was: *Is he okay?*

Each time I glanced at Tony's empty workspace, tears welled up. Only now, in his absence, did I realize just how much I missed him. The thought that something might've happened to him was driving me insane.

Anything but this… I begged silently. *Please*!

I didn't eat at lunch or dinner. Just one glance at Tony's empty seat was enough to drain my appetite, along with any desire to do anything at all.

For the first time in my life, I found myself looking forward to sunset.

Jenkins hadn't appeared at the camp, and I couldn't tell if that was a good sign or a bad one.

After dinner, instead of joining the usual fun at the campfire, I sat near Tony's tent. It was dark and cool there, but I didn't care. I sat motionless on the grass, arms wrapped around my knees. I didn't think—I couldn't. I just prayed.

I wasn't sure how long I had been sitting there, but eventually, I felt the familiar stir of excitement.

Jenkins, I thought, disappointed, clenching my fist in anger, ready to pounce on him with accusations about Tony's disappearance. But then I realized, if Jenkins were involved, he wouldn't be able to resist gloating.

Determined not to let him relish my pain, I mustered the strength to stand and walked resolutely toward where I expected him to appear.

"Good evening," I said when I saw him. "Nice weather, don't you think?" I added theatrically, trying to fill my voice with icy indifference.

Jenkins looked confused. "Uh... What happened?" he asked, slightly bewildered.

For the first time, I saw a flicker of concern cross Jenkins's face, but I was too upset to care.

"Just thrilled to see you. Isn't that what you want?" I said coldly, shooting him a withering look.

Jenkins raised an eyebrow, remaining silent, though his eyes clearly asked, *What's gotten into her*?

Ignoring Jenkins's questioning look, I continued pouring out my irritation, "Well, I know what you want... and sure, you'll get it, like always. Can I go now, or is there something else?"

Jenkins swallowed, hesitated, and asked in a neutral tone, "Why are you alone out here?"

"I don't feel like being around people," I snapped. "But you're not human, so you can stay—though I'd prefer you didn't."

"Where's this aggression coming from?" Jenkins asked, clearly perplexed.

"From deep inside," I replied, my voice so full of hatred it could have destroyed an entire army.

Despite maintaining a calm exterior, Jenkins was clearly confused, and this confusion stripped him of his usual devilishness. Perhaps now, he was more human than ever before, and this unfamiliar feeling unsettled him. But I was too consumed by my own sorrow to notice.

Jenkins lingered for a few more seconds, then shrugged and vanished into the darkness. Relieved to have rid myself of him, I was about to sink back into my grief when I suddenly noticed a silhouette behind the trees.

"Tony!" I exclaimed, rushing toward him.

I reached Tony in a flash, wrapping him in my arms. I hugged him so tightly, as if I would never let him go. Happy tears streamed down my cheeks.

Tony clearly hadn't expected such a reaction. Though he embraced me back immediately, his expression was one of confusion.

Once I calmed down and felt certain that Tony had no intention of leaving again, I loosened my grip and looked into his eyes. At that moment, I realized it was now or never.

I leaned in and softly pressed my lips to his. Tony's lips responded with equal gentleness. My body didn't react, but it didn't matter, because my heart was overflowing with indescribable happiness.

Kissing Tony felt like being a blind person wandering through a flower garden. I couldn't see the beauty, but I could feel the fragrance and the soft touch of petals, crafting my own image of the garden in my mind.

The movements of my lips and tongue were blind, but the sensation was still amazing, even in its detachment. My body couldn't sense or gauge Tony's response, but my heart could. The warmth and tenderness it felt made it blossom.

After our kiss, I pressed my head to Tony's shoulder. Tony kissed my head softly and whispered, "Let's go."

Hand in hand, we silently walked to our usual spot.

It was only as we walked that I noticed Tony looked tired, puzzled, and upset. All day, I'd been dying to ask where he had been and what he had been doing, but now it felt best to stay silent. Tony seemed to appreciate that.

We sat on the grass, cuddling in the quiet of a beautiful summer night, gazing at the endless, starry sky for about an hour.

CHAPTER 21: CARE

The camp was already asleep when Tony and I returned. We wished each other goodnight and went to our tents.

I sat on my mat and yawned. After two sleepless nights and a hectic day, exhaustion weighed on me. But I couldn't sleep; an unsettling feeling gnawed at me—the need to visit Jenkins.

When Jenkins and I were separated by several dozen meters, I felt no attraction to him. The feeling that kept me awake had nothing to do with desire or excitement. It was a sense of duty mixed with the fear that someone might get hurt if I disobeyed.

I had no idea how Jenkins had lodged this thought in my mind, but I knew I had to go. I couldn't resist it, just as I couldn't resist the desire for Jenkins when he was near.

So, I quietly sneaked out of the tent and made my way through the summer night's darkness to my tormentor's trailer.

The tempting serpent awaited me, having left the trailer door open.

The bastard's not even afraid of mosquitoes, I thought wearily. *If I were a mosquito, I'd fly as far away from this trailer as possible. Wish I were one. At least mosquitoes have a choice.*

I climbed the steps and entered the trailer. "Well, I'm here," I said, my voice flat. I was so exhausted, I couldn't bring myself to care. Fear, anger, curiosity, irritation—none of it mattered. All I felt was an all-encompassing fatigue. I doubted I could be of any use as a sex partner in my current state, but I couldn't be bothered. I just wanted to get through this moment and secure my freedom from Jenkins for the next

24 hours.

Yet, Jenkins's damn charm worked flawlessly. Despite barely feeling alive, the moment I saw him, it was like a spare battery clicked on inside me. Fatigue vanished, replaced by a surge of strong sexual arousal.

Anger swirled within me, both at Jenkins—who was doing God knows what to my body—and at my own body for betraying me to this incomprehensible force. Though my energy was running low and I should've conserved it, I used the last of it to shoot Jenkins a glare full of hatred before defiantly turning my head away.

Jenkins grinned. "Well, well, my passionate, recalcitrant beauty. First you make me wait, and now you're showing contempt."

I sniffed in disdain, but Jenkins remained unphased. With his unshakable calm, the bastard stood up and moved closer to me. He placed his thumb and forefinger under my chin, forcing me to face him, and, locking eyes with mine, said, "But I must admit, it makes me desire you even more."

I shut my eyes in protest. Jenkins chuckled. "Stop it, Tayra. You surrendered the moment you walked through that door. There's no need to struggle anymore." He wrapped his arms around my waist, leaned in close to my ear, and whispered, "You've made the right decision. I'll give you your reward."

And then, everything unfolded as usual.

***

The next day, I barely managed to drag myself out of bed, and even then, I felt like a zombie. Whatever I did, I struggled against the urge to lean my head somewhere and just fall asleep.

I cleaned the wall stones slowly, barely able to see the symbols etched on them because my eyes were half-closed.

After a lunch where I ate almost nothing, I could barely hold the trowel, let alone do anything with it. The sun burned relentlessly, and the stone wall, heated by its rays, was too hot to lean against. I tried to fight through my state, but soon the symbols on the wall began to blur. Moments later, the world plunged into darkness.

I woke up in my tent, feeling rested with a clear head. The fresh coolness and birdsong told me it was morning. I reached for my phone to check the time, only to realize something was unusual. I turned my head and understood why I felt so comfortable: Tony was sleeping beside me, his arm wrapped around my waist.

I tried to piece together yesterday's events after lunch, but I couldn't. Carefully, so as not to disturb Tony, I reached for my phone.

4:30. Half an hour before wake-up. I wonder, where's Jenny?

Yet, Tony's presence reassured me that everything was fine, so I decided to enjoy the moment instead of overloading myself with questions.

I slowly turned to face Tony. He was sleeping peacefully and looked so cute… I leaned in and softly kissed his cheek. Tony purred softly, smiled, and opened his eyes.

"Sorry, I didn't mean to wake you," I whispered.

"I don't mind if you wake me up like that," Tony replied with a smile. He gently brushed the hair away from my face and asked, "How are you?"

"Better than ever," I said, catching Tony's hand and pressing it to my cheek. "But what happened?"

"You fainted. Probably from the heat and lack of sleep. I carried you here."

"Oh my God," I covered my flushed face with a hand, "that's so embarrassing."

"It's not embarrassing at all. But you really scared me."

"Sorry, it wasn't on purpose. That's only the second time I've ever fainted."

"Really? When was the first time?"

"It's a long story," I said, brushing it off with a smile.

Tony gently slid his thumb above my eyebrow and said, "I'd love to hear it. I think you have a lot to tell me."

An arrow of anxiety pierced my mind. *What does he mean*?

"Tony, I..." I began awkwardly, but Tony didn't let me finish.

"Later, Tayra," he said calmly, "we need to get up and head to work now."

I sat up on my mat and rubbed my face. "Okay, but where's Jenny?"

Tony sat up too and replied, "Ah, that. I have some suspicions about why you haven't been sleeping well. So, to prevent this from happening again, I decided to take your safety into my own hands. I'm your new roommate—or tentmate, to be precise."

"Uh..." I mumbled, thinking in horror, *Does he know about Jenkins*?! *This is a disaster*!

"Relax," Tony said reassuringly. "I won't jump to any conclusions before you tell me yourself. And yeah, Jenny's Louis's tentmate now. They like each other, so it's kind of a win-win."

"If you know... why don't you hate or despise me?" I asked cautiously.

"Because I have no reason to—at least, not yet," Tony replied. "Besides, I've got something to tell you too. So between the two of us, you're not the only one with secrets."

"Come on," he said, standing up. "Work's waiting."

After breakfast, we headed to the excavation site. As we walked, I tried to recall the last stone I had worked on before fainting. I vaguely remembered it being the one with the snail-like spiral.

Alright, I thought, *I need to find it and continue. I had several more stones planned for yesterday, so today I'll have to work twice as hard to catch up*.

But when we reached the temple, I found the stone—it had already been cleaned, along with several others nearby.

Wow, I thought, surprised, as I looked at Tony questioningly.

"Well," Tony waved dismissively, "I helped out a little. I know you usually plan out your work for the day, so I figured you'd push yourself harder to stick to it. But after seeing you faint once, I don't want you overworking again."

"Oh my God, Tony!" I said, hugging him. "Thank you so much. That's really sweet of you."

Tony smiled shyly. "It's nothing, Tayra. Think of it as my apology for making you worry while I was gone."

The rest of the morning passed calmly, but when I returned to the site after lunch, I noticed that Jenkins's trailer was gone.

What a relief, I thought. *It's good he's not around, at least until I figure things out with Tony. He was probably upset that I ditched him last night. I just hope this doesn't cause any trouble for anyone. What's really going on here? Why was Jenkins even here? Where was Tony? And what does Portonapoulos know about their business?*

Well, I sighed, *I'd better get back to work before my head explodes from all these questions.*

CHAPTER 22: REVELATION

That evening, Tony and I skipped the campfire and went straight to our clearing. The sky, endless and dotted with silver stars, stretched above us, but even their beauty couldn't ease my worry about the conversation ahead.

Tony seemed agitated too, but while I preferred to avoid the unpleasantness as long as I could, he cut straight to the point. As soon as we stopped, he fixed his gaze on me and asked, "What do you know about Jenkins?"

"Not much," I shrugged. "I read an article about him before the interview. It had an intriguing title—'Death as a Springboard'—and the content was just as interesting." I briefly summarized what I remembered, then added, "I also saw an interview where he talked about his interest in ancient history—something about fulfilling a childhood dream. That's about it."

"Not much indeed. Don't you think it's all a bit suspicious?"

"I'm not sure what you mean," I replied, trying to keep my voice neutral, though inside I was trembling. "If you mean his resurrection and the rapid rise of his business, then yeah, it's pretty weird. His obsession with ancient history too."

Tony winced and rubbed the bridge of his nose. In that moment, I knew exactly what his next question would be, but every cell in my body silently prayed it would never be spoken. Apparently, my prayers weren't diligent enough.

"What kind of relationship do you have with Jenkins?" Tony asked, looking at me so intently I could feel it physically.

Tony's voice, however, was neutral—no jealousy, offense, or sarcasm. Just a straightforward question, seeking information. It was both reassuring and unnerving. I tried to sound confident, keeping my emotions in check as I said, "It's complicated, but I swear it's not what it looks like."

Tony clearly expected my evasiveness. He just nodded and, in that same neutral tone, said, "Okay, I'll tell you something, and I hope after that, you'll be honest with me too."

I took a deep breath and listened.

"Jenkins's dizzying success attracted the attention not only of the press, but also the secret service. Several aspects of his story raise questions. Even with his successful business in two factories, Jenkins couldn't have amassed enough money to purchase new plants in such a short time. This led us to suspect he obtained the money through less-than-legal means. Jenkins's sudden passion for ancient history was particularly intriguing.

The stories about his childhood dream were, of course, for the press. According to his school teachers, Robert had little interest in ancient history. There isn't a single history book in the Jenkins family library. Yet, over the past eight months, Jenkins has financed five expeditions to ancient cities, all from roughly the same historical period.

Around the time of the first expedition, a new drug appeared on the market. Its composition was entirely unknown. The drug is potent, causes instant addiction, and even the slightest overdose is fatal.

Our investigation has revealed the origin of these drug consignments. We discovered a laboratory near the excavation site where the drugs were being produced. It's likely Jenkins transported both lab supplies and finished drugs disguised as equipment and materials for the expedition.

However, the most surprising detail is that the capture team found only an empty warehouse where the lab had been. Similar situations occurred with other expeditions. Jenkins somehow uncovered our agents' locations and acted swiftly.

Although there are many links between Jenkins's expeditions and the drug trade, we still lack direct evidence. That's why I was sent undercover as a researcher—to gather more intel on the expedition's organization and how drugs were being transported.

But once again, Jenkins was one step ahead of us. The lab we recently found had been relocated, and the drug consignment was shipped right under our noses."

"So, this is what you discovered during your absence..." I said, sighing thoughtfully. Tony's story began to connect the dots, but it was still too much to process all at once.

"Now you understand why I couldn't tell you," Tony said, his voice apologetic, though I could barely hear him. I sank onto the grass, burying my head in my hands. I was overwhelmed by the weight of the information I'd just received. Jenkins's involvement in drug trafficking didn't surprise me, but Tony... that was something I hadn't expected. The one man I thought I could trust wasn't who I believed him to be. I felt completely shattered because of it.

I sat on the grass, motionless and speechless. Shock hit me so hard I couldn't even cry. The venom of frustration coursed through my veins, making the inner pain unbearable. I wanted nothing more than to wake up and realize this was just a nightmare. But no, I was more awake than ever.

It took a moment before I could speak again. Swallowing hard, I looked up at Tony. "So, you're one of the agents, huh?"

"Yeah," Tony muttered, dropping his eyes in shame.

I nodded, sighed, feeling the sting of tears welling up. But I was still too tense to let them fall.

"And what's your real name?" I asked. "Or am I not allowed to know?"

"Um..." Tony knelt down beside me. "You probably won't believe it, but Tony Weiler is my real name. Turns out the real PhD student of Paulo Cognitio just happens to have the same name as me."

"Does Portonapoulos know who you really are?"

"He does. He's been helping me."

And this was where I lost it, and tears finally streamed down my cheeks. "Tony, I… I trusted you so much. You were the best thing in my life for the past several months. I thought you were my blessing for all the mess I had to endure, but that blessing turned out to be fake. Well, I admit I wasn't completely honest with you. Maybe I even deserve this, but I just wasn't ready for something like this—not now, not ever. You knew about Jenkins and me all this time and used me to get closer to him. Believe me, your efforts were in vain. I know nothing about Jenkins, his drug business, or his legal business. All I know about him is that he's been poisoning my life since the first moment I saw him, and I have no idea how to escape this mess."

"Tayra, please calm down. I beg you. You're a clever girl, so think for yourself. If I were just using you, would I share any of this?"

I stopped crying and tried to brush the tears away, but only ended up smearing them across my face. "What is it, then?"

"Your role in this story is also quite strange. Jenkins is an attractive man, yet for the eight months I'd been observing him, he hadn't been involved with a single woman. And then you appeared.

I suspected something was off when Jenkins appointed you for an additional interview. Portonapoulos said that among all the applicants, you were the most qualified candidate, and Jenkins's doubts about you were simply ridiculous.

My suspicions deepened when you asked me to walk you home for the first time. That day, I noticed Jenkins's people near the university, and they seemed to be watching you. After that, I saw them watching you multiple times, and it made me really worried.

I conducted a background check on you but found nothing—nothing that could connect you with someone like Jenkins. You're beautiful, no doubt, but there are many beautiful girls, so that wasn't the answer to my question. I decided to get to know you better to understand what you and Jenkins could have in common.

But the more I learned about you, the more I fell for you, and the more questions arose."

Tony stopped, sighed, and rubbed his forehead as if he had a headache. "I need to know what's going on between you two. I'm pretty sure Jenkins is forcing you into a relationship with him because your reaction on the day of my absence left me in no doubt about the sincerity of your feelings for me. Yet the number of questions hasn't diminished."

Tony looked at me intently and said, his voice tinged with genuine tiredness, "Sometimes I wish October 16 had never happened."

"What's wrong with October 16?"

"It's the date of Jenkins's damn resurrection," Tony said, frustration evident in his voice.

In that moment, I realized I had finally received the last piece of the puzzle to my assumptions.

"Oh, Tony..." I sighed. "You've just killed the last germ of doubt about the correctness of my theory. All this time, I've tried to fight off these thoughts as fiercely as possible, but now it's clear: Jenkins's resurrection is my fault."

Tony dropped his jaw and gave me a look full of mistrust, questioning my sanity. I met his gaze and said, "I know it sounds insane. What I'll tell you next will sound even more insane, but please don't interrupt me and try to believe me as much as you can."

Tony rubbed his eyes and looked at me attentively, ready to listen.

"The Tiendal Legend," I began, "Do you know what it's about?"

"The one thoroughly studied by Paulo Cognitio?"

"Yeah, exactly."

"Generally, yes."

"Okay, I'll tell you," I said calmly, sharing the version of the legend I heard from the guide near the Tiamon catacombs.

"Well, that's fascinating," Tony said after I finished, "but what does it have to do with you?"

"Patience, Tony. This is where my story truly begins. On October 15, my friends and I went on an excursion to the Tiamon catacombs..." I then told Tony everything that happened to me that day, including what my friends had told me afterward.

"Well, Tayra, it's a tragic story," he said once I finished, "I'm really sorry you had to go through that, but it's nothing more than a coincidence."

"No, Tony, unfortunately, it's not, and I can prove it. What do you know about Jenkins before he was shot?"

"Well... his neighbors said he changed a lot after the tragedy. He became cold, haughty, and calculating, whereas before he'd been friendly and kind-hearted."

"What color were his eyes?"

"Green or hazel, something like that."

"In Paulo's book, I read that Tiendal migrated into the body of a young, handsome man, around thirty years old, who was killed on the day of the reincarnation ritual. Robert fits all these descriptions. And now, his eyes are black. They're the same fierce eyes I saw in that room before I fainted.

You said Jenkins was always a step ahead. Tiendal was prized by the pharaohs for his ability to see the future.

But there's more. The door to the secret room was protected by a powerful spell of concealment. It could only be opened by the Chosen woman, the one able to see the door through the spell. I'm the Chosen—that's why I saw the door, but my friend Gladys didn't.

The last part is the most embarrassing, but well… there's no going back now, so listen. After that day in the catacombs, I found myself completely numb to men's touch. I had a boyfriend, but after that trip to Tiamon, I stopped feeling anything when he touched me. Things between us were rocky, so at first, I thought it was just because my feelings for him had faded. Later, I tried dating other guys, but I still felt nothing when they kissed me.

And then Jenkins appeared. I disliked him instantly, but my body felt this irresistible pull toward him. The closer we are, the stronger it gets, and if he touches me—or if I touch him—it's overwhelming. I have no idea how it works, but it's real. He pulls me in like a magnet, and when I try to fight it, it causes actual physical pain. But I only feel that pull when we're close, and to make sure I don't stay away, he threatens to hurt the people I care about—my friends, the team, and especially you.

I want to break free from this, but I don't know how. I've looked for answers in the legend, but I haven't found any yet. I know after this, you probably won't see me as a woman anymore, but whatever. My feelings don't matter compared to the need to stop this monster."

Tony grabbed his head and took a deep breath, massaging his temples and rubbing his forehead and the bridge of his nose. But it probably didn't help.

"I don't know what to say, Tayra," he said, his voice thick with uncertainty. "I just... I really don't know."

"Please, don't hate me," I asked, lowering my gaze. Saying I felt bad would be an understatement.

CHAPTER 23: VERSION

Of course, I couldn't sleep. I tossed and turned on my mat, trying to find a comfortable position, or just lay on my back, staring at the dark roof of the tent. My head felt like it was about to explode from the endless questions, while my heart ached, torn apart by the pain.

By morning, I was certain I had found true love and that my curse was the only thing standing between me and happiness with Tony. But the new knowledge made me realize just how wrong I'd been.

I sensed Tony wasn't sleeping either, but I didn't dare speak to him—I didn't even know what to say.

The next day, we didn't speak either, and it felt strange—unnatural. I decided to use this forced silence to think, not to grieve.

What I already knew about the legend helped explain some of the unclear moments in Robert Jenkins's story, but many questions still had no answers. I replayed parts of the legend and facts from Jenkins's biography in my head, again and again, but the pieces didn't add up.

The secret service agents and I viewed the Jenkins-Tiendal story from different angles, but clearly, we were both missing something. No matter how hard I tried to make sense of it, that something continued to elude me.

Immediately after dinner, Tony disappeared. I had a hunch about where to find him, but I decided not to rush the check. If Tony needed space, then I needed it just as much.

Driven by an inexplicable inner force, I walked to the temple. It wasn't very dark yet, so I could see it clearly.

Okay, if I were an evil ancient genius, what would I do? I wondered, walking around the building and inspecting the walls.

I studied the temple entrance. In the dim light of twilight, it looked majestic and mysterious. I admired it for a few minutes before a realization struck me.

Sorry, Tony, I said quietly, *I know you need space, but I have to disturb you*. I turned and rushed into the darkness of the dense forest without hesitation.

My hypothesis was confirmed when I found Tony sitting under a tree in our clearing. I approached him and said, "Tony, we need to talk."

"Sorry, Tayra, I..." Tony began awkwardly, waving his hand to signal his reluctance to talk.

"I get it, and I can't blame you, but just listen to me. This isn't about us; it's about Jenkins. I'm not well-versed in crime, but I'm sure there are many ways to mask drug production, and placing labs near ancient ruins isn't the most typical approach."

Tony stood up and fixed his gaze on me. "Okay, continue."

"Imagine you're an ancient evil genius capable of magic. When you suddenly find yourself in an unfamiliar world, what's the first thing you would do?"

Tony shrugged. "I have no idea."

"Come on, Tony, think like him. Using magic to solve your problems is something you're familiar with. When you find yourself in a new environment, you realize that even though the world has changed significantly, magic can still be useful. Clearly, you've retained some of your special skills, like hypnosis and your ability to see the future, but it's minimal compared to what you could do before. However, to regain your former power, you need to find its source. But you don't know where it might be in this world. So, you look for something familiar to understand how this new world connects with your old one."

"Okay," Tony said, rubbing his forehead. "That explains Jenkins's interest in ancient history."

"But that's not all. He's searching for something. This something is hidden in one of the ancient cities where excavations have taken place. Either he doesn't know exactly where it is, or the necessary parts of those cities have been destroyed, but he keeps searching. I have no idea what it is, but it's valuable. That's why the expedition team includes not just creepy thug-like guys, but also true archaeology enthusiasts.

Please gather the names of the cities where previous expeditions took place, along with as much information about the historical artifacts found there as possible. Perhaps involve professors who have researched in that area; it might help predict his next move.

And one last thing: he's the Chocolate King. Isn't it easier to conceal drug production somewhere in his confectionery factories? Have you looked into them?"

"Of course. All his businesses are clean, and the quality of his confectionery meets the required standards."

"I think the drugs are prepared using some ancient recipe. It probably requires components that are only found in the vicinity of those ancient cities. Perhaps some rare plant, something in the soil, or possibly even some kind of energy. I don't know exactly what it could be, but it explains why they need to build laboratories in such unusual locations."

"Well, that makes sense," Tony said, nodding.

I hesitated for a few seconds, debating whether or not to say the next sentence. But curiosity got the better of me, and I finally spoke. "Since the mission with the Amhitiemar laboratory failed, there's probably no need for your undercover stay here anymore..."

“Yes, that’s true,” Tony confirmed. “I’ve already received the corresponding order. But now, I'm not so sure there’s nothing left to investigate here. It’s unbelievable how, in just one day, you managed to come up with a version none of us, not even I, had thought of. So, I’ll probably discuss extending my stay here.”

“You know better,” I nodded. “But there’s more to this. I’ve spent all my time thinking over the version I just told you, leaving me almost no time to reflect on other things, like Tiendal and me. I don’t know why, but I’m pretty sure he’ll be back soon, and he’ll contact me again, no matter what. Maybe I can be of use to you and your people. Just know that I’m ready to help.”

“Well, I’m afraid it might be necessary, but I’d rather not put you in harm’s way.”

“Danger..." I rolled my eyes. "Tony, I’m the Chosen one, the one who released evil imprisoned for centuries. I’m tied to the ancient devil, and yesterday, I severed the only thread to happiness with the man I love by telling him all of this. Tell me—what worse could happen to me?”

“Tayra, human life means nothing to him.”

“True, but mine matters for now. He needs me for some reason, and while I’m useful to him, he won't harm me. Yet he can hurt the people I care about, and I’ll try my hardest to prevent that.”

I sighed and, despite the pain and shame, looked into Tony’s eyes. “Just forgive me, if you can,” I said earnestly. “I understand that you may never be able to love me, but we can still be allies.”

Tony lowered his gaze and said nothing. I swallowed hard and said, “Sorry for disturbing you, Tony. Good night.” Then I quickly walked away without looking back.

When I woke up the next morning, Tony was gone. I had some ideas about why he was absent, so I decided not to ask anyone about him to avoid attracting extra attention.

As I worked, I couldn't stop thinking.

Unbelievable! Without Jenkins, it's even easier to breathe. I should find answers to as many questions as possible while my mind is sharp. I think I should focus first on solving the problem of drug laboratories, and only then address my relationship with Jenkins or... Tiendal. I wonder how soon he'll be back. How much time do I have left? Maybe Portonapoulos knows. I'll wait until he takes a break, then I'll go and chat with him.

Despite his age and high status, Portonapoulos worked alongside the students, scrubbing stones and documenting the results. This behavior was yet another coin in the bank of his merits.

Fortunately, the wait for a break didn't take long—the heat was relentless, and people often felt thirsty. As soon as Portonapoulos put down the trowel and headed to the water tank, I "happened" to walk nearby.

"This building is incredible, isn't it?" I said, nodding toward the temple wall.

"Not that word!" Portonapoulos agreed enthusiastically. "And it's so majestic, even despite its age. Imagine how beautiful it must have been in its prime."

"Yeah, indeed. I wonder what's hidden inside."

"According to literary sources, there should be a large chamber and several smaller ones. From each of them, there's a passage that leads underground. In general, there must be a complex system of underground passages beneath this temple. One of them leads to the library, while the others lead to various repositories."

"Wow! Do you think all of this could survive?"

"Perhaps," Portonapoulos shrugged, "these old buildings are incredibly durable."

"So, which of these passages is our area of interest?"

"What do you mean?"

"Well, this building speaks to history only for you, for me, and a few others on our team... I don't think Mr. Jenkins came to you and said, 'Mr. Portonapoulos, you're a great scientist. I'm a huge fan of yours, and that's why I've decided to give you a chance to discover something of great importance. I'll fund an expedition to Amhitiemar.'"

Portonapoulos chuckled. "It sounds fantastic, indeed. But the funny thing is, it's quite similar to what he actually said."

"Seriously?!" I exclaimed, surprised.

"Yes. According to our agreement, if we manage to open the door, I'm obligated to ensure that Mr. Jenkins is the first to enter this temple."

"Why?"

Portonapoulos shrugged. "The rest of the money we received is for not asking unnecessary questions."

"Well, fair enough. So, he needs something from this temple, and the rest we can take for scientific advancement."

"Exactly."

"Wow! Looks like an offer too good to refuse," I giggled.

"Yeah," Portonapoulos nodded. "Nevertheless, I hesitated for a while, but in the end, I surrendered to curiosity."

"Do you know anything about other expeditions funded by Jenkins?"

"Only one. Its goal was to find an entrance to the underground temple in Enskriyar city."

"Wow. Did they succeed?"

"Partly. The entrance was found, but the descent into the dungeon was badly damaged. Clearing it took much more time than Jenkins initially stated. As a result, once the allotted time was up, all excavations at the site were suspended. However, it's now under protection as a historical site, awaiting new researchers."

"And how do you assess our chances of solving the task?"

Portonapoulos waved his hand. "So-so. We're moving much slower than originally planned. Certainly, we've found many things valuable for science, but half of the expedition time has already passed, and not a single recess has been found."

"And what if we don't open the door?"

"We're not obligated to open it. To my surprise, the terms of our agreement are rather flexible. So, it seemed like a dream proposal for a scientist like me."

"Why did you hesitate?"

"Well... You know how it is. Older people tend to be less trusting. So, I was looking for a catch. But, seeing as we're here, I guess I didn't find one."

"Does Mr. Jenkins monitor our progress?"

"He asks for a report every three days."

"So, will he be back the day after tomorrow?"

"Very likely. If not, I'll just pass it on to Carlo. Despite his young age, Mr. Jenkins is even more distrustful than I am, so he likes to oversee everything personally."

"I understand. It was a pleasure chatting with you, Mr. Portonapoulos, but it's time we get back to work."

"Yeah, you're right. Let's go."

I returned to my wall and thought, *Portonapoulos's talkativeness is a treasure. I learned everything I needed. The underground temple in Enskriyar... and those surprisingly lenient terms of the agreement. You keep puzzling me, Tiendal.*

CHAPTER 24: ALLIANCE

Tony didn't return until late in the evening. Despite the tension between us, I was incredibly relieved to see him, knowing he was safe. I wanted to hug him, but after hesitating, I decided it wouldn't be appropriate.

Tony looked exhausted. He sat on his mat and yawned, then rubbed his face, trying to shake off the fatigue. "Is he here?" he asked.

"Not yet. He's supposed to come the day after tomorrow for the report."

"Fine," Tony exhaled, holding his hands near his face. He sat like that for a few moments, then stood up and said, "Talking here is still too risky. Let's go."

"Tony, you're tired. Are you sure you want to go anywhere?"

"Yeah, I'm fine. Don't worry."

"Okay," I said quietly, following Tony outside.

We walked to the clearing in complete silence. When we got there, Tony sat down on the grass beneath a tree and motioned for me to sit beside him. I did.

Tony looked at me intently and said, "It wasn't easy to get my superiors to buy into your version."

"Understandable," I said. "Did you tell them everything?"

"Are you kidding? Of course not. I just gave them a general overview of the events. Even that was enough for them to think I was crazy."

"Ouch," I said, wincing, resisting the urge to pat Tony on the shoulder.

"It wasn't easy convincing them to give it a shot," Tony said, rubbing his forehead.

"So… does that mean you did it?"

"Yeah, but honestly, even though I convinced them, I still haven't fully wrapped my head around it."

"Why?" I asked, surprised. "I thought my explanation made sense."

"We never focused on the research side of those expeditions. They had all the proper permits and didn't raise any suspicion. We only saw them as potential drug routes. But your perspective is so unconventional, it was hard to explain why I'd even consider something so crazy."

I smiled, shrugging. "What else?"

"We had our lab do a more thorough analysis of the drug content. We also sent a team to survey the area around the old lab. It'll take a few days to get results."

"Good. I hope they find something."

"I'm screwed if they don't." Tony gave a tight smile.

"They will, don't worry," I said, trying to reassure him. "I'm confident. My intuition hasn't let me down lately."

"It better not," Tony sighed. He rubbed his forehead again, trying to fight off the fatigue. Then, dropping his hand, he continued, "We've contacted the leaders of the research groups that were part of Jenkins's expeditions. Our team is going out to question them about their goals and findings."

Tony reached into his jacket's breast pocket and pulled out a folded sheet of paper. "Here's what you asked for—the list of sites explored by the expeditions. I based it on the official permits, but it's the best I could do with the time I had."

I unfolded the paper and scanned the list. "This is great. Thanks."

Tony gave me a tired smile, as if saying, *You're welcome.*

Even after a crazy day, he still found time to help me. Now he's smiling, pushing through the exhaustion. Does he really believe my help could make a difference? Or… does he still care about me?

Tony interrupted my thoughts with more news. "One last thing—I'm staying until the end of the expedition."

I was about to shout with joy but held back. "Oh… that's great news."

An awkward silence settled between us. I'd spent the whole day thinking, gathering information, and I had so many questions. But Tony looked exhausted, and I wasn't sure if I should overwhelm him with it all now. But we only had one day before Jenkins returned, so everything needed to be handled soon. After some internal struggle, I chose duty over pity and broke the silence.

"Tony, I… I've been thinking about the drug labs..." I began hesitantly, then paused.

"Seriously, Tayra? Maybe you should stop thinking. Your last crazy theory was more than enough."

"Fine," I snapped. "I'll keep it to myself then—it's even crazier than the last one." I sighed, staring at the ground. I was tired too, and my frustration was starting to show.

Tony patted me on the shoulder. "Sorry," he said, his tone softer. "Bad joke. I'm listening."

I lifted my head, checking if he was serious this time. Tony's eyes were full of genuine interest, so I continued, "There are a few things I need to clarify first."

"Go on."

"You mentioned they found an empty storage facility where the lab was supposed to be. How can you be sure there was ever anything inside?"

"Well, we calculated the likely location of the lab. An old storage facility near some ruins seemed like the best fit, so we kept it under surveillance. Two agents monitored it around the clock. They saw trucks coming and going, and estimated the number of people working there. When our agents finally snuck inside, they took photos—solid proof that confirmed our suspicions. They called for backup, but then... all contact was lost."

"How much time passed between their call and when the capture team arrived?"

"The location's pretty remote, so it took about an hour to get there."

"An hour... Is the storage that big? Could they really pack up all the equipment and people in that time?"

"An hour's not short, so it's possible, in theory. But the storage is pretty big. It's not like they could've packed everything ahead of time and just tossed it into the trucks. The loading would've taken a while. And even if we ignore that—there's something else. The storage is out in a field, and there's a two-kilometer stretch of unpaved road leading from the highway.

First of all, to move everything, they'd need a few trucks, and a group like that would be hard to miss on the highway. Plus, loaded trucks couldn't reach high speeds, especially on a dirt road. There would've been traces, too... Checkpoints were set up on the highway in both directions; they checked every passing truck and even some cars during the day—but found nothing. We even considered the possibility they didn't drive along the road but cut straight across the field instead, though it seemed completely far-fetched. In that case, they'd move very slowly, and we'd definitely spot them. In the end, there are more questions than answers in this story."

"Yeah, exactly. Was Jenkins around the storage at the time? Did your agents report anything about it?"

"Yeah, they spotted him entering."

"Oh!" I exclaimed, my excitement clear. "I think that's the explanation."

"Ehm..." Tony mumbled, eyeing me curiously, but I ignored his look and kept pulling at the missing pieces of the puzzle.

"What happened to the agents?"

"They vanished. Still haven't been found."

"When they called for reinforcements, were they inside the building or outside?"

"I don't know," Tony shrugged. "What difference does it make?"

"Huge," I said, my voice firm.

"Tayra, my brain just can't process your riddles right now. Please explain what you're getting at, in the simplest way possible."

"Of course, Tony, just give me a second. You see... Let's assume Jenkins knew about your agents. In that case, he could just 'take care' of them and then have his people move the laboratory. It would've been smart for him to keep the agents from getting inside. Obviously, someone connected to the drug business wouldn't help 'BitterSweet' succeed, so it makes sense if all of this happened without Jenkins around."

"Yeah, exactly. I've thought about it a thousand times."

"Yes, but you didn't know Jenkins was a reincarnation of Tiendal back then."

If Tony weren't so tired, he'd probably be really surprised by that. But since he had no energy for strong emotions, he just rubbed his forehead with both hands and looked at me intently. "Do you think he turned to magic for help?"

"Why not? Wouldn't you do the same if you were him?"

Tony rolled his eyes. "I've never imagined myself as an ancient sorcerer, so it's hard for me to say." Then he looked down and added, "But it's true—when you can jump over a fence, you don't need to climb it."

"Exactly. And I know him a bit. He loves theatrics. Loves showing off his power. That's exactly what he's doing with you. He's playing with you, enjoying the game, convinced you won't be able to prove a thing."

"Heck," Tony muttered, running his hands over his face for the hundredth time. "Do you think it's that spell of disguise?"

"Possibly," I shrugged. "Were there any new drug shipments after you found those empty storages at the old lab sites?"

"Yeah, but we thought they were coming from the relocated labs."

"It's very likely you were wrong. You weren't keeping an eye on those empty storages, right?"

"Yeah, and now it feels like we were careless for nothing. Our agents... Do you think they're inside?"

"Most likely. I think you should send teams to the old labs. I'm sure you'll find something interesting this time. But it needs to happen at all the labs at once, so he doesn't have time to prepare. I doubt he's powerful enough to be in four places at once."

"Yeah, exactly. It's genius, really. But how do we explain the need to watch empty storages? And what if we're wrong?"

"We can check it out. Take me to the storage. I saw the door in the cell—maybe I'll spot a hidden lab. Tomorrow, since it's the only day we have before Jenkins comes back."

"Do you know how this disguise spell works?"

"Tony, you're overestimating me. Tiendal's the wizard, not me. I honestly have no idea."

"You know better than I do what happened when you opened that door. Who knows what could happen this time."

"Oh well, this is just a regular storage, not the Secret Room, so he probably didn't put as much into it. Anyway, it's our best shot. Let's give it a try."

"Alright, let's head back. I'll ask Portonapoulos to give you the day off. Hopefully, it's not too late and he's still awake."

CHAPTER 25: CHECK

We got up at dawn, while the camp was still asleep, and headed straight to the warehouse. It was about five kilometers away, but luckily, most of the road cut through a forest belt, so even when the sun got high, it was still a comfortable walk.

At first, we walked in silence, and I used the quiet to think about something I hadn't had time to dwell on before. Something important, but pushed to the background while I focused on Jenkins and his drug operation. My feelings toward Tony.

Until just the other day, Tony was someone who walked the same path as me, only several years ahead. I, too, had planned to stay in graduate school after my sixth year and pursue science. That Tony had been an example for me. But who was this Tony now?

I mentally replayed all my moments with Tony. It became clear why we hardly ever talked about my studies, his work, or our future plans. All the things I used to question now had a logical explanation. The distance he kept, the way he avoided my questions about his research...

But now it was clear that Tony didn't win me over with his knowledge of history or archeology, or even his scientific achievements. It was the way I felt around him—how good and comfortable it was just to hear his voice, his laughter, even his breathing. His presence alone made my days better...

Did that change when I found out he wasn't a graduate student in history, but a secret service agent? Something definitely changed, but my feelings stayed the same—no doubt about that.

I turned my head, glanced at Tony, and thought, *Here I am, walking across a field in some unknown direction with someone I don't even really know. How old is he? When's his birthday? Where's he from? Who are his parents?…*

But... does any of this even matter? I don't know anything about him, and I'm heading off with him to who knows where, yet I don't feel the slightest bit of fear or anxiety.

I feel calm just knowing he's walking beside me, hearing the crunch of branches beneath his feet. And if someone asked me right now if I love him, I'd say 'yes' without hesitation. This is probably the first time in my life that I've been so sure of anything. And it doesn't matter that there's an impassable wall between us now. I still want to be close to him, even if it's only as an ally.

At some point, I wondered how things would've turned out if a real graduate student from Paulo Cognitio had gone on this expedition. I thought of the poor guy who missed the chance to gather valuable material for his PhD thesis and publications, and decided to break the silence.

"Tony," I asked, a bit timidly, "How old are you?"

Tony turned to me with a small smile, "Almost 28. Why?"

"Oh, nothing... I was just curious. Thought you wouldn't answer."

"Not exactly a big secret," Tony shrugged.

"And you… I mean, agents... are you allowed to have personal lives?"

Tony chuckled. "You think agents aren't human?"

"Well, judging by the movies, not really," I said with a shy shrug.

Tony shook his head and chuckled. "You really pick some interesting movies, don't you!"

"Um... actually... that's not really what I wanted to ask."

Tony smirked, his voice full of playful irony. “Then why’d you ask?”

“Well... I guess I was curious about that too,” I confessed, feeling my face flush.

Tony glanced at my flushed face and smiled. “Oh, your curiosity!”

“I actually wanted to ask about the Paulo Cognitio’s student. Is his dissertation really about the symbols of Amhitemar?”

“Yeah, something like that. I can’t remember the exact title—it’s too tangled for me.”

“Still, he needed this expedition like air, didn’t he?”

Tony’s expression grew serious. “Yeah, that’s true. You think we screwed over the poor guy just for the mission?”

“I have no idea how these things are organized, so yeah, I’m curious,” I replied defensively.

“We chose him for a reason. And not just because he’s my namesake. Antonio Weiler has serious health issues that would’ve made it nearly impossible for him to join the expedition. He didn’t submit an application—I did. You saw I did my part honestly as a member of the team. I’ll hand over all the material to Antonio, and he’ll use it for his publications. It was a unique opportunity for both of us.”

“Wow, that’s really great—and noble,” I said, genuinely impressed. “But what if Jenkins noticed the switch? A medical record is easy to check.”

“Did anyone ask for your medical record when you joined the expedition?”

I shook my head, a touch of resentment creeping into my voice. “You don’t even want to know how I got into the team.”

Tony lowered his eyes. “Yeah, I’m sorry.”

“Whatever… If I knew back then what I know now, maybe I could’ve kept Oscar safe. I still can’t forgive myself for that.”

“Hey...” Tony said, trying to soothe me, “It’s not your fault. You couldn’t have known.”

"Yeah, but still... There's one more thing I don't get. Jenkins can sense lies—how'd you pass the interview?"

"I didn't lie," Tony smiled. "My name really is Tony Weiler, and I truly wanted to join the expeditionary group. And everything I said about loving to analyze facts, connect details, and solve riddles—that was pure truth."

"Wow!" I said, truly admiring him. "That's genius!"

"No applause, please," Tony joked, giving a theatrical bow.

"What if you hadn't passed?"

"I don't know for sure, but it probably wouldn't have been anything good. So yeah, I guess I was lucky. Maybe it was fate."

"Fate..." I echoed with a soft, sad sigh.

Tony glanced at me and, for some reason, grinned. "We're almost there," he said, pointing toward a lone rectangular structure about two hundred meters away.

"Really?" I said, following Tony's gaze. "I'm kind of disappointed. I expected something more mysterious."

"For places like this, the plainer the better. Less unwanted attention that way."

A few minutes later, we reached the warehouse and found the front door locked. It seemed to be the only door, and the fact that it was shut really puzzled me.

"Uh-oh," I muttered. "How are we supposed to get inside?"

"It's not like it's the tricky Amhitemar temple lock—this one's easy," Tony said, pulling a lock pick from his backpack with a confident grin.

"Uh... what?" I stammered, dumbfounded.

Tony smiled at my reaction and, as he opened the door, said, "Yeah, I know—in some ways, agents aren't much better than criminals."

Before we stepped inside, Tony took my hand and, looking me in the eye, said, "I hope I won't regret this."

I shrugged in response. I hoped so too, but how could I guarantee anything?

"Jesus Christ!" I gasped the moment we stepped inside.

"Well, I don't think a shabby, empty storage room warrants invoking the full name of our God, so I suppose we hit the jackpot."

I moved further in, walking between the neatly arranged rows of laboratory desks.

"Feels like I'm back in my old school chemistry lab—though I've never seen this many flasks, test tubes, and bottles, or whatever else they are."

Tony stood in the doorway for a moment, looking confused, before walking in and following me, scratching his head.

I kept describing what I saw as I moved further in. "Stands, some kind of heating devices... lots of tables with this stuff. And many cabinets with packages and containers."

As I wandered between tables, examining their contents, I got so caught up in it that for a moment, I forgot I wasn't alone. At some point, I turned around and saw Tony... standing in the middle of a desk. Like a ghost. Despite how creepy it looked, the scene was oddly funny, so I couldn't help giggling. Seeing me laugh, Tony walked straight toward me, ignoring all the furniture in his path, which was absolutely hilarious.

"What's so funny?" he asked when he reached me.

"It's just... you're walking through the furniture," I said, smiling.

Tony raised his eyebrows and turned around. Clearly, not seeing anything I was talking about made him uneasy.

"Please, Tayra, be serious," he said earnestly. "This isn't the time or place."

"I know, I know," I said, calming down. "Stay right there."

I approached the table next to the one Tony had just walked across a few seconds ago and tried to lean on it. My hands went straight through the countertop, and I nearly lost my balance.

"I see, it's transparent for you too," Tony said.

"Yeah, it is," I confirmed. "It's such a strange feeling. It looks so real, yet somehow it feels like a hallucination."

I wondered if it would show up in a photo, so I pulled my phone out of my pocket to check. To my surprise, the phone was off. I tried to turn it on, but it didn't work.

Strange, I thought. *I just disconnected it from the power bank this morning and didn't even use it. Could it really have discharged this quickly*?

"Tony," I called. "Is your phone working?"

"Let me check," Tony said, pulling out his smartphone. "Nope, it's off."

"Can you turn it on?"

"Nope, seems dead."

"You charged it last night, didn't you?"

"Sure, even though the connection here is a pain in the ass. Without my phone, I feel like I'm without hands."

"Same here," I agreed. "This is so weird. In the cell, I touched the walls and pulled the levers—they felt real. But now... it's all like a dream. Do you think disguise spells have variations? Or is this just my imagination?"

"I'm not exactly an expert on disguise spells," Tony said thoughtfully. "But maybe I can help rule out the 'hallucination' theory."

"Okay, how?"

"The agents sent a report before we lost contact. I have excerpts on my phone, and I've gone over them like a hundred times, trying to figure out how it all happened. It hasn't helped much, but I pretty much know them by heart now. So, we can compare your experiences with the report."

"Good idea. Give me a second."

I turned, trying to figure out the best way to get back to Tony. We weren't far, but a long row of lab desks stood between us. For some reason, walking straight through the furniture didn't appeal to me, so I took the longer route around.

I reached the end of the row and screamed. Tony rushed over. "What happened?"

"Two men. The first looks around 40, tall, average build, red hair combed back. The second is younger, Asian, with medium-length black hair."

"Dumfley and Zyong!" Tony exclaimed, looking shaken. "Are they dead?"

"Unconscious. No signs of breathing."

I knelt beside the Asian man and studied him closely. He looked like he was just sleeping. After a moment of hesitation, I reached out and touched his neck where I should have felt a pulse. But, as expected, my hand passed through his body like it was made of air.

I stood up, giving Tony a guilty shrug. "They're transparent, just like the furniture. I can't check their pulse."

"Alright, that's enough," Tony said. "Let's get out of here. We'll talk about it on the way back."

We left the warehouse, and Tony locked the door with his miraculous tool. As we walked away, Tony quizzed me on the details he remembered from Dumfley and Zyong's report. All my answers matched what the agents had reported.

"Well, now we know you were right, but we've got no evidence to prove it," Tony summarized. "Any ideas on how we fix that?"

"You'll need to convince your authorities to check the other labs, and keep a close watch on this one. Jenkins is probably the only one who can remove the spell, so he'll need to be there in person. Plus, I suspect Jenkins handles the drug shipments himself."

"Do you think the drugs are disguised by the spell, too?"

"Why not? It's incredibly effective. Even if someone saw through it, they wouldn't be able to prove a thing."

"True," Tony nodded. He looked up at me and added, "Thank you, Tayra. What you've done is priceless. Now it's up to me to handle the rest." He paused, sighed, and scratched his forehead again—his go-to move today. "Now, I just have to convince my boss that monitoring the empty warehouses is crucial... but honestly, I have no clue what argument to use without bringing up all this magic stuff."

"How about your keen intuition?" I suggested.

"Yeah," Tony sighed. "Looks like that's my only option."

"Maybe I could help?"

"No way, Tayra. You don't know what you'd be getting into. Once they find out about your connection to Jenkins or your abilities... I don't even want to think about what could happen."

"I don't have any special abilities."

"Sure, except for a few little things—like understanding the mind of an ancient sorcerer and seeing through his disguise spell."

I giggled and shrugged.

"Well, I'll take you back to camp and then head to see my boss."

"How do you even get back to civilization from here?"

"By helicopter."

"Seriously?!"

"Of course not. You really think it's possible to land a helicopter unnoticed?"

"Who knows," I shrugged. "I'm not exactly an expert on flying vehicles."

Tony chuckled and smiled. "I'll walk to where there's reception, call my colleague, and he'll come pick me up and drive me back."

"Got it. By the way, does your phone even work out here?"

"I hope it does. Let's check." Tony pulled out his phone, pressed the power button, and the screen lit up. "There we go."

"Will you be back tonight?"

"I'll try, but no promises."

CHAPTER 26: PLAYING WITH FIRE

When I returned to camp, the whole place buzzed with excitement. High spirits filled the air, and naturally, I was curious about the cause.

The first person I saw was Jenny, so I asked her what was going on.

"Oh, it's such great news!" Jenny exclaimed. "Louis found a cache!"

"Seriously? That's amazing!" I said, my excitement rising. "How did he do it?"

"You should ask him yourself," Jenny said, smiling. "There he is," she added, nodding toward Louis, who had just finished smoking with Ahish. "Our superstar will love telling the story again."

I laughed at Jenny's sarcasm and rushed over to Louis for the details.

"Louis!" I called out as I approached. "Congratulations!"

"Thanks, Tayra!" he grinned.

"Well, don't leave me hanging! How did it happen? I can't believe I missed it."

"Yeah... too bad you weren't there," Louis said with mock sympathy, but his grin quickly returned. "So, here's what happened. I'd cleaned up a major section of my wall region when I noticed something odd. A few symbols looked almost identical, except for these tiny differences. I studied them closer and found three like that. The key was in the details—once I figured out the right order to push the stones, the cache opened."

"Wow, well done!" I said, genuinely impressed. "What was in the cache?"

"As we thought—one of the door keys."

"Cool! What does it look like?"

"Uh, you can see for yourself. Just ask Portonapoulos to show you."

"Yep, for sure," I giggled. "I'll ask him. But Louis, were those stones with symbols far from the cache?"

"Not really. But it's interesting—they were at the tops of an equilateral triangle, and the cache was right in the center."

"Woohoo! That's something. Do you think the rest of the caches are organized the same way?"

"I wish. At least then we'd know what to look for."

"Yep, true. Hopefully now, thanks to you, things will move faster."

"We'll see," Louis said, flushing with pride.

Unbelievable, I thought as I headed to Portonapoulos's tent. *I was almost certain those caches were impossible to find, but here we are with our first success. Will we really be able to open the door*?

But I decided thinking about it could wait. Solving ancient puzzles to save the world from some long-lost evil was exhausting, and I badly needed a break from my life as the Chosen One. So I pushed aside all the questions filling my head and let the young archaeologist inside me take over. All she wanted was to revel in the excitement of this important discovery, made by the research group she belonged to.

The next day, though, the questions came flooding back, and Tony was still nowhere to be found. As I worked, I replayed those questions in my mind, over and over.

What are you hiding, temple? *How dangerous is this thing*? *What happens if Tiendal gets his hands on it*? *Is he certain it's even there, or is it just a guess*? *Could it help lift my curse*?

I was so lost in thought that I didn't notice the growing excitement building inside me. I only realized it when it became overwhelming. I frantically tried to plan my next move, but it was already too late—I heard that familiar, velvety, hypnotic voice behind me: "Missed me, dear?"

I gathered the last of my strength, ready to snap back with something sassy, when an idea hit me. *Confusion. I need to throw him off to buy some time. He's expecting me to be defiant, so I should do the opposite.*

To catch Jenkins off guard, I spun around and exclaimed with as much enthusiasm as I could muster, "Good morning, Mr. Jenkins! What a surprise! Have you come to celebrate our success?"

My plan worked. The tension eased a little, and I felt myself regaining control.

"Oh... well... yes," Jenkins mumbled awkwardly. "The cache... it's great news."

"Not just 'great news,' Mr. Jenkins! We're all so inspired! You can't imagine how excited we are right now! This first step has made us believe we can uncover something truly important!"

Jenkins took a breath to respond, but I didn't give him the chance to gather his thoughts. I kept talking non-stop: "Honestly, I'm dying to know what's inside! Mr. Jenkins, we're all so grateful you gave us this chance to explore these echoes of ancient history!"

At that moment, I saw the strangest thing. Jenkins's fierce black eyes shifted color—now there was a hint of green in them. Fear gripped me, but curiosity won out, much stronger than my fear.

It seems there's more of Robert in him than Tiendal now, I thought. *Maybe if I touch him, I can resist the desire... There are people around, so if this doesn't work, I'm screwed, but... I'd give anything to know if it's possible.*

Wasting no more time doubting, I leaned forward and exclaimed, "Thank you, Mr. Jenkins! You're the best person I've ever known!" I hugged him and kissed his cheek, then quickly stepped back.

My loud proclamation caught the attention of the other expedition members, especially Mr. Portonapoulos. He approached us and joined the conversation.

"Oh, Mr. Jenkins, Tayra just voiced what we all feel! We don't even know how to thank you!"

He then offered to show Jenkins the first key we'd found, and to my great relief, led him away.

I didn't know how my performance looked to the others, but it didn't matter. The only thing on my mind was, *I touched Jenkins and resisted! I controlled my desire while hugging him! I've won this battle! Oh my God, I'm so happy!*

It took me about an hour to calm down and regain my rational thoughts.

It's great, but this is only one battle, not the war. I hadn't thought about it before, but Tiendal didn't just take Robert's body—he also needed his knowledge and experience, especially since the modern world is so different from the one Tiendal last knew. I wonder how much of Jenkins is still Robert, and how much is Tiendal… I need to learn more about who Robert was, and I definitely need more information about Tiendal. Tony could help with Robert's background, and maybe Paulo Cognitio's book has something about Tiendal I haven't discovered yet. But neither of those options is available right now. So what do I do? I can't just sit here waiting! Tony, where are you? I need to talk to you so badly. What's taking you so long?

The sun went down, the working day was over, yet I couldn't rest. Annoying questions boiled inside me, threatening to tear me apart. Too agitated to enjoy the campfire gathering, I slipped away to my tent, where it was quieter, a place to think.

I pressed my forehead against the cool tent roof and muttered, *Think, Tayra. Everything is connected. You just need to find the missing pieces...*

Suddenly, the universe answered, though for some reason in Jenkins's voice: "Alone again?"

Damn it, I thought, clenching my fists. Crossing my arms, I turned toward the voice and asked, sarcastic, "Want to keep me company?"

"Actually, yes," Jenkins replied in his usual flat tone. "Though, we probably mean different things."

"One doesn't exclude the other. Let's go somewhere less crowded."

"I see zero people," Jenkins said, shrugging.

"That could change any moment, and I don't want anyone seeing us together."

Jenkins raised a brow, lips curving into a smirk. "Ashamed of the country's most enviable bachelor?"

"You've only ever offered me sex—on your terms. Nothing to envy."

Jenkins smirked again, about to say something, but changed his mind and simply offered, "Let's go to my trailer."

Of course, the bastard would get what he wanted anyway, so moving the conversation to his trailer worked to my advantage. Parked just outside the campsite, the trailer was a safe enough spot. No one ever came out that far except for Tony and me. I followed Jenkins in silence, using the walk to plot new ways to annoy him.

When we reached the trailer, I stopped by the entrance and said, "Let's stay outside for a while... if you don't mind."

"I mind," Jenkins said, coldly.

"Come on, the evening is perfect! It's not like you're in a hurry. We've got the whole night."

"You won't buy me with that," Jenkins said, apathetic. "What's your angle?"

I softened my voice, mimicking Jenkins's usual tone. "Robert, you're good at reading people. You'd sense a lie instantly..."

Jenkins raised an eyebrow. "Robert?"

"What's the problem?" I asked, feigning confusion. "I've seen you naked. Why can't I use your name?"

Jenkins started to get irked, and though he tried to sound calm, irritation seeped into his voice. "I hope you realize you're playing with fire..."

Encouraged by his reaction, I pressed on with more enthusiasm. "Your fire's brought me nothing but pleasure lately, so why should that change? Or is it my resistance that excites you—the thrill of breaking it? So many women would drop their panties if you just beckoned... but you don't want them. You, the Chocolate King, chose me, a regular student. Isn't that strange? At first, I thought maybe you just wanted some variety... but it wasn't a one-time thing, was it? Now I don't even know what to think, Robert."

I'd probably pushed too far, giving Jenkins time to regain his composure. "Women are for sex, not for thinking," he said coldly.

Shit, I thought, frustrated, but I wasn't giving up. "What about love?"

"Love doesn't exist. It's just a fairytale for wimps who can't get sex with whoever they want."

"So you'll stay with me until you get bored, right?"

"Something like that."

"And when you do get tired of me? Will you leave me alone or...?"

"Enough talk for today. Get inside," Jenkins ordered, but I had the audacity to ignore him.

Jenkins's patience snapped. He stepped closer, leaned into my ear, and whispered in that devilishly sexy voice that made me shiver, "I've always known talking to women is a waste of time."

I wanted to retort but gasped, unable to speak. Jenkins used the pause to shove me into the trailer. Once inside, he pressed me against the wall and started undressing me hungrily.

Back in my tent, I sat on the mat, analyzing the results of my research.

He's a tough nut to crack. Getting him into a heart-to-heart won't be easy, but teasing him is fun, and I'll probably try it again. At least now I know he can control both his and my desire. Who knows... maybe he can break the curse.

CHAPTER 27: TEASING

The next two days were busy for our team, but fortunately, productive. We spent them actively searching for similar symbols arranged in specific patterns, and finally, our hard work paid off when we found two more caches.

Tony was still absent, but he contacted Portonapoulos, asking him to spread the word that he'd injured his hand and needed medical help.

In an attempt to crack the code of my irresistible attraction to Jenkins, I experimented with different ways to pester him.

On the first day, I skipped the campfire after dinner and decided to wait for Jenkins by my tent. I had a gut feeling that bastard would come to remind me of his presence, and he didn't disappoint. Soon, I sensed Jenkins approaching and prepared for the show.

I waited until he was just a couple of meters away, then turned sharply and said, "Bicycle."

"Sorry?" said Jenkins, stopping.

"Bicycle," I repeated. "Do you like riding bikes?"

"Well, I..." Jenkins mumbled. It was unusual to see the all-controlling Master at a loss for words. The best part was that his confusion instantly eased the tension in me, and I could think as quickly as the situation demanded.

"You come from a wealthy family, Robert. I can't believe you didn't have a bicycle growing up."

Jenkins stared at me so intensely, it felt like his eyes might burn a hole in my chest. I realized I was toeing the line, but decided to go all in anyway.

"Tell me about your childhood, Robert!" I said playfully, ignoring the adrenaline pumping through my veins.

The clever bastard saw through my game, of course, but for some reason, he decided to play along. Probably curious to see where it would lead.

"Nothing special to tell," he replied in his usual, unemotional way, instead of striking me down with a bolt of lightning.

Woohoo, I'm still alive, I thought, continuing the performance. "Really? And how did you spend time with your brother... Philip, right?"

Jenkins gave me a wistful, suspicious look but only said, "Let's go, Tayra. I don't have time for chatting."

I couldn't help but admire his consistency and determination. This man saw his goals so clearly that even a meteor shower probably wouldn't make him turn aside. But I was more cunning than a meteor shower. So, I didn't argue, just dutifully followed Jenkins, resuming my pestering a few seconds later as we walked.

"Please, Robert! No matter how much we want each other, sex can wait. You're so mysterious. Just tell me a little about yourself. I'm sure it'll make me want you even more. Just a bit... please."

"Are you always this annoying?" Jenkins asked in a neutral tone, but I caught hints of fatigue in his voice.

Even though Jenkins wasn't an ordinary person, it turned out he could have difficult days too, and he could get tired just like anyone else. Somewhere deep in my soul, I felt a tiny bit of human pity for him. But it was buried so deep, I could easily ignore it and keep teasing him.

"Oh no. I'm usually much worse."

"Disaster," Jenkins sighed, and I took it as his consent to answer a few questions.

"So, was Philip your older or younger brother?"

"Older."

"Do you miss him?"

Jenkins raised an eyebrow and slowly turned his head toward me, a silent question in his eyes. Clearly, I'd hit a nerve, which was exactly what I needed, so I didn't waste a second before explaining.

"I read in the paper that he disappeared. Such a tragedy. I really sympathize."

Jenkins stared at me for several seconds, then blinked. He seemed to be considering something but decided not to voice it. "What else have you read?" he asked.

I laced my voice with fake respect. "That you fought desperately for your old confectionery factory, because it was a memory of your father."

Jenkins smirked and turned his gaze to the path ahead. I realized I wasn't getting anywhere this way and decided to try a different angle.

"You know what I think? You can't be that bad. You just hide your insecurities behind your villainy. Honestly, it's a bit embarrassing to admit, but for a gorgeous man like you, you don't seem to have much experience with women."

Jenkins laughed. "Tayra, that's the most ridiculous thing I've ever heard. I can turn you on in a second. I can make you moan, scream with pleasure, and beg for more. How could I be inexperienced?"

"Your perspective is narrow. It's not just about sex. Normal people date, spend time together..."

"Finally," Jenkins said, unlocking the trailer door. He looked at me with a smirk. "Consider that walk our date. Come in."

As I climbed the steps, a rush of arousal hit me. *Damn, another failure,* I thought, frustrated. *But at least I stalled him longer this time.*

Next time, I'll get under his skin.

I spent the entire next day thinking of a new way to get to him. I couldn't repeat myself—I needed something fresh. After cycling through countless ideas, I realized the only thing I hadn't tried was flirting and seduction.

Seducing someone who constantly forces sex on you seemed illogical, but when did logic ever apply here? If you can't swim against the current, shift course. Maybe the goal isn't upstream, but ashore. Sometimes even the craziest ideas work, so I figured, why not try?

Once I settled on my plan, I started thinking about execution. It's hard to look seductive when all you've got is a couple of T-shirts and shorts, both caked in dust from days spent scrubbing ancient stones. On top of that, you're lucky if you get 30 seconds in the shower.

Okay, I've got that black strappy top and jeans I only wear in the evenings—so, less dust. I'll wash my hair despite the water restrictions. It'll probably still be wet, but that's even sexier. What else? Nothing. My acting will handle the rest.

I headed to Jenkins's place without waiting for an invitation. I didn't knock, just opened the trailer door and slipped inside. I turned to face Jenkins with a flirtatious smile as I playfully hooked a strap of my top with my finger, letting it slip off my shoulder. "Hi, Robert," I purred in a low, velvety voice.

Jenkins gave me a slow once-over, his eyes lingering on the fallen strap. "What brings you here so early?" he asked calmly.

I twirled a lock of hair around my finger, just as playfully. "Maybe boredom... Maybe desire..."

"And which is it?" Jenkins asked, his voice icy.

"I just couldn't wait any longer. I had to see you," I said, biting my lip, still twirling the curl.

Jenkins stepped closer, crossing his arms. His eyes swept over me again before he smirked. "Flattering, no doubt. Except it's all a lie."

"Guilty as charged," I replied, still flirty but with a bite in my voice. "Even if it's not convincing, it's still annoying, isn't it?"

Jenkins raised an eyebrow, hellfire flashing briefly in his eyes, though his voice stayed disturbingly calm. "Don't you think I'm dangerous when I'm annoyed?"

"Most likely," I nodded, "but you can't hurt me physically."

"Really?" Jenkins drawled, lips curling into a devilish grin. A sharp pain suddenly tore through me, as if an invisible hand was crushing me from the inside.

I shut my eyes, hiding my fear, and clenched my teeth, refusing to let a moan escape. As the pain peaked, one thought flashed in my mind: ***Anger won't work. Confusion will.*** After a few agonizing seconds, the pain faded, and I gasped for air.

"Still so sure?" Jenkins asked, his gaze smug and triumphant.

I was terrified, of course, but I'd gone too far to back down now. Fear morphed into something stronger—defiance. I straightened up, meeting my tormentor's black eyes. "Impressive," I said, my voice steady. "But now I'm even more curious about you."

Jenkins gave me another incinerating glare, his voice still eerily calm. "Shall I repeat my warning?"

The power balance was obvious. I knew the game was dangerous, and I should've stopped—but I couldn't. My self-preservation instinct had shut off completely, leaving me reckless. Even though I was as defenseless as an insect beneath a hippo's foot, I stood firm, proud, unmoving, showing no hint of fear.

"As you wish," I said calmly, "It hurts, but I think it's harmless."

It was clear Jenkins had no intention of killing me, but he couldn't show weakness either. Yet, being a wise and perceptive man, driven by his goals above all else, he chose to compromise—though in his own, unique way.

He stepped closer, locking his gaze with mine. "Don't make me prove otherwise," he said.

Despite the coldness in his voice, I could tell it was a request, not an order. There was a word he wouldn't say out loud, but I could feel it hovering in the silence. That word was **please**.

Something inside me thawed. The wall of my stubbornness crumbled, and I could feel my emotions flooding back. I took a deep breath, swallowed, and asked, "Jenkins, explain one thing to me. I'm not the most beautiful, I'm not the smartest. I don't have anything valuable you'd need. I'm not irresistibly sexy. I'm... ordinary. So, why me? What am I missing?"

As I spoke the last sentence, a tear rolled down my cheek. Without breaking eye contact, Jenkins dried it with his scorching hot lips and whispered, "You're everything you claim you're not, but also blessed."

"Or cursed?" I whispered in reply.

"Same difference," said Jenkins, before passionately covering my lips with his.

CHAPTER 28: CONFESSION

The next morning, I learned Jenkins had left. Surprisingly, I felt more frustrated than relieved, as I still had so many ideas for pestering him. On the other hand, his absence gave me a chance to focus on my work.

Over the next two days, we finished cleaning the stones. By the evening of the third day, the whole camp exulted, as our combined efforts had led to finding the fourth cache.

We had almost a week ahead, and only one cache remained undiscovered. Finding it seemed easy, so everyone was energized. We felt like we were standing on the threshold of a great discovery, our souls united in a shared gust of curiosity. The excitement was palpable, and the guys made bold assumptions...

But since I knew more about our benefactor, Robert Jenkins, than the others, my feelings about opening the door were ambiguous. I still didn't know which outcome would be better for mankind: success or failure. An evening without Tony and Jenkins left me no choice but to turn these questions over in my mind, again and again.

What's behind that door? I wondered, staring at the closed temple. *What will Tiendal do when he receives this*? *Why is it hidden here, not in Tiamon*? *How much of the ancient temple still survives inside*?

But no matter how hard I tried, I couldn't answer any of these questions. So, I fell asleep feeling unsatisfied.

When I woke up, something felt off. I couldn't believe my eyes when I saw Tony sleeping nearby. His arms were gently wrapped around my waist, which was even more surprising. My heart began to pound like a drum. Sleep was no longer an option.

As soon as Tony felt me stir, he opened his eyes. "Morning, dear! I'm glad you're okay. I missed you so much."

"Tony... I thought... that you... we..." I stumbled awkwardly, but Tony gently pressed his forefinger to my lips, stopping me from finishing.

"I know," he said earnestly. "I know what you thought, and I'm really sorry for making you feel this way. Let me explain. What you told me was completely unexpected. I've dealt with criminals and crimes before, but I never imagined that wizards and ancient magic were real, or that the people around me could be affected. I was shocked, dumbfounded, and I needed time to process this new information and fit it into my old beliefs.

I didn't know how to tell you the truth about myself—the truth that could easily be justified by errands, duty, and necessity. Yet, despite that, I was terrified by the thought that you might not understand or forgive me.

But your story... It's so incredible that the mere fact you dared to share it deserves admiration. You could've invented any lie to justify your connection with Jenkins, you could've refused to reply, or you could've hidden the most embarrassing parts. But you told me everything, despite how difficult it was. You showed me your unconditional trust, and I truly appreciate it.

Look, Tayra. None of what happened was your fault. You're just a victim of senseless randomness. Stop blaming yourself. I never hated or despised you. I had doubts and fears, but I never stopped loving you. I never had the chance to say it before, but I love you, Tayra. More than anything in this world, I want you to be with me."

My cheeks were wet with tears. What I'd just heard should've made me the happiest person in the world, but instead, I was overcome with confusion. I sat up on my mat, sighed, and said, "Tony, I... I love you too. I'd love to be with you, but... How do you see our relationship? My insensitivity and my connection with Jenkins are still here. I'd love to rid myself of these 'gifts of fate,' but I have no idea how. I can't even control my body around this devil. I suppose it must feel awful knowing that every moment I'm not with you, I could be with him."

Tony sat down beside me, gently turning my face towards him as he wiped away my tears. "Well," he said, "I must confess, at first, the very thought of you being with Jenkins drove me crazy. I thought I wasn't really jealous, but it was probably just because I had never found myself in the middle of something like this. I thought about it again and again, yet I couldn't believe there was a force that could make lust this uncontrollable. I did have those doubts, and I'm truly sorry for them now.

I know you were hurt when I kept my distance. I saw how happy you were to see me, how you refrained from hugs, and how fully you trusted me while I kept doubting. I needed something exceptionally convincing to rid myself of those doubts, and I finally received it after our visit to the warehouse. **It was a breaking point.** The moment I realized we were dealing with someone capable of turning physical matter into air. It was when I understood the full power of the force you tried to resist—alone, with no one to rely on. My doubts died, replaced by admiration.

I was terrified when I imagined what he could do to you if you didn't play by his rules. I was terrified when I thought about how scared you probably feel every time you have this uncontrollable urge. At that point, I understood my doubts were nothing but the voice of selfishness.

Finally, I told myself I could cope with this, as long as I was sure it was due to the curse, not because you changed your mind and chose him over me. I hope, together, we'll find a way out of this mess."

Tony smiled, looked into my eyes, and added, "I'm ready to fight for you—even against the ancient wizard."

"And what if we lose?"

"Why should we? From what I understand, you don't feel any connection with Jenkins when he's far enough away. So, I just need to make sure he never gets close to you again. And I've got some ideas on how to make that happen."

"And what about my insensitivity... What if I stay this way forever?"

Tony smiled, pulled me close, and gently kissed my head. "You know... we haven't been intimate yet, but I can honestly say that the time I spend with you is the best of my life. It would be amazing if we could find a way to lift your curse. You deserve to feel everything, both with your heart and your body. Those feelings might be simple or intense, but they should be real, not restricted by some mysterious force. But even if we don't... life has plenty of other joys, and I'll do everything I can to make you happy."

I lifted my head and pressed my lips to Tony's temple. I felt grateful—genuinely grateful and happy. Tony smiled, closing his eyes for a brief moment. I used that moment to lean in and kiss him—softly at first, then with more boldness and vigor. Tony's lips responded to my touch with boundless tenderness, every movement full of care and affection. And it was beautiful, despite the ancient magic and its wretched curse that kept my body from feeling excitement.

Tony paused, taking a breath, his face flushing with a hint of embarrassment. He smiled and said, "When you kiss me like that, it's hard to believe in your insensitivity."

I smiled back, saying, "My insensitivity will never make your kisses any less desirable."

We sat in silence for a few minutes, just holding each other. It felt so unusual, so unexpected, and yet so perfect. In Tony's arms, I didn't have to struggle or hide my weakness or fear. It was a place where I didn't have to be a hero—I could just be a woman, fragile and vulnerable. But instead of savoring our long-awaited union, listening to the rhythm of our hearts beating together, I let my restless thoughts ruin the moment. I broke the silence with a question, "Have you got any news? What about the laboratories?"

Tony nodded, replying quietly, "I've got plenty of news, but this isn't the place to talk about it. We've already said too much today, and I can only hope no one overheard us. So, we'll discuss it later."

"Fine, I'll wait," I said with a sigh. "But I might just die of curiosity."

Tony patted my head, smiling affectionately. "There are so many mysteries around you... what's one more secret?"

"Can't argue with that," I sighed, shrugging. "But still."

Tony kissed my cheek softly. "Be patient."

CHAPTER 29: NEWS

"Wow, you guys made a lot of progress while I was gone," Tony exclaimed as we arrived at the excavation site.

"Yeah, that's right," Louis agreed. "How's your hand, by the way?"

"Seems fine," Tony said, waving his hand energetically to prove it.

"How'd you even manage to hurt it, buddy?" Louis asked.

"I'm not really sure," Tony shrugged. "Probably just inexperience with your tools."

"Yeah, that's true," Louis laughed. "Those six-inch nails give me goosebumps every time I see them—so intimidating."

Tony glanced at the temple, then back at Louis. "So, what's our task for today?"

"We're putting all our effort into finding the last cache."

"Alright," Tony nodded. "What's the catch?"

"Tayra didn't tell you?" Louis asked, surprised.

"Not yet," Tony shrugged. "So, you tell me."

"Well," Louis began, "it's all about the symbols. They have different numbers of small details—like short strokes or tiny circles. You need to press the stones in order, from the fewest to the most details."

Tony looked at the wall, scratching his head. "Wow, that's interesting. Any other features?"

"Yeah. The stones with the right symbols form a geometric figure, and the cache is at its center."

"Cool," Tony said. "What shapes have you found so far?"

"Triangle, square, diamond, pentagon."

"Okay," Tony said, rubbing his chin thoughtfully. "Any thoughts?"

"Maybe a hexagon or a circle," Louis shrugged. "I'm not sure what else it could be."

"Well, I doubt it's anything else. A hexagon seems like a solid guess."

"Then we need to find six matching symbols," Louis concluded.

"How many have you found so far?"

"If you mean the last six, then zero. They're messing with us. I've been circling that temple all morning, and I can't find a single matching pair, let alone more."

"Well, it's okay, buddy. Not everything works on the first try. We just need to work harder. Let's start now. By the way, where's Tayra?"

Louis glanced around and saw me staring at the wall. "There she is," he said, nodding toward me.

Tony turned and saw me as well. I was standing by the wall, staring intently at a single spot. To be honest, with my personal life taking an unexpected turn just an hour ago, my head was full of thoughts that had nothing to do with temple stones or their patterns. Still, my expression was intensely focused. That's probably why Tony said, "Oh… maybe I shouldn't distract her…" and the guys laughed.

***

Finding the last cache seemed easy, but for some reason, it refused to reveal itself. We'd been studying the temple walls from every angle all day, but found nothing. There were no matching symbols or distinct patterns.

By evening, everyone was tired and puzzled, and even the bonfire didn't have its usual uplifting effect. Louis didn't even bring his guitar, figuring no one was in the mood for singing.

The ten of us sat around the bonfire in silence, watching the flames dance and listening to the steady crackle of burning logs, each lost in our own thoughts. It was both unusual and depressing. After a while, Louis broke the silence.

"So, any ideas?" he asked, trying to sound encouraging.

Nine pairs of eyes turned to Louis, and nine shoulders shrugged in unison.

Louis glanced around at the group and muttered, "Is it really that bad?"

But when all he got was a collective sigh, Louis sighed too and stared into the fire.

After a few more minutes of silence, Jenny spoke up. "Guys, what if our assumption about the circle or hexagon is wrong?"

"Who knows," Alicia shrugged. "Those were just the most obvious guesses."

"What if the person who designed the lock had some trick up their sleeve?" Miles chimed in.

"Yeah, clearly this guy had a twisted sense of humor," Ahish replied.

The atmosphere around the fire grew less tense, and people began sharing their ideas instead of keeping them to themselves.

"So, if you were the lock designer, what would you prepare for the final test, Miles?" Chiara asked with a smile.

Miles hadn't expected such a question, but he didn't miss a beat. "I'd be hospitable and wouldn't lock anything at all."

Laughter greeted Miles's clever answer. Though it didn't help solve the puzzle, at least the mood was lighter than it had been earlier.

I decided to share my idea. "What if the secret of the final cache isn't in the pattern, but in the meanings of the symbols?" I said after the laughter died down.

"So, we should take photos of different symbol groups, and Tony can try reading them," Louis said, glancing at Tony for his opinion.

Tony started coughing, and since I knew why, I couldn't help but giggle. "Is something wrong?" I asked, trying to stifle my laughter.

“Uh... no, it’s a good idea,” Tony began awkwardly. He swallowed, then continued with more confidence, “But there are so many symbols... deciphering them could take forever.”

“So, what’s the solution?” Jenny asked.

“I like the idea of taking pictures of the walls,” I said after a brief pause. “It’ll give us a chance to analyze the patterns in comfort, instead of wandering around the temple in the scorching sun.”

“Yeah, I agree with Tayra,” Jenny nodded. “This way, we can think about it individually, then discuss our ideas.”

“And worst case, we could just try all the possible combinations,” Louis added, his remark sparking a burst of laughter. Louis smiled and continued, “Why are you laughing? Life is long...”

“I’m afraid Jenkins won’t appreciate your sense of humor,” Jenny said dryly.

“Do you think he’ll be upset if we fail to open the door?” I asked, directing the question at Jenny.

“Maybe,” Jenny shrugged. “He organized this expedition for a reason. No one believes it was purely for the love of science.”

A brief silence followed, broken by a loud yawn. All eyes turned toward the source of the sound—Tony.

“Sorry, guys,” he said, yawning again. “I’m so tired. I’ll keep thinking about this stuff while I sleep. Pretty sure I’ll see all those symbols in my dreams. Good night. See you tomorrow.”

People giggled, and I quickly joined in. I yawned too and said, “Well, yeah, I feel like I’ve already dreamed a couple of times during this discussion. So, good night, guys! We’ll pick this back up in the morning.”

The others wished us good night, and we left. But instead of heading to our tent, we made our way to the clearing. Even though we were tired, we had plenty left to discuss, so sleep had to wait.

Once we reached the clearing and stopped, I looked at Tony, smiled, and said, “You could’ve won an Oscar for acting and an audience award for resourcefulness.”

“And you would’ve been kicked out of spy school,” Tony replied. “You’re going to blow my cover laughing like that.”

“Sorry, I couldn’t help it,” I said, smiling and shrugging apologetically.

“I’m not as hopeless as you think,” Tony said defensively. “I prepared for this mission and learned a bit about those symbols too. When I spent two weeks in the library, you weren’t the only reason I was there.”

“Whoa,” I said, trying to soothe him, “Big guy but acting offended like a kid.”

“I’m not offended,” Tony said stubbornly. “Just saying.”

“Relax, I believe you,” I said softly. “And I don’t doubt your knowledge or responsibility.”

I patted Tony on the head. For some reason, his hair was tousled, which made him look a bit funny.

“Did you bring a book about those symbols?” I asked, looking at Tony with a hint of irony.

Tony stopped pouting and smiled. “Honestly, I brought one. Just in case. Do you think it’ll really be useful?”

“Unlikely,” I shrugged. “But I can't be completely sure. The puzzle with the last cache is tougher than we expected.”

“Yeah, true,” Tony agreed. Then he sighed and added, “Do you think opening this temple is worth it?”

“For science, definitely. For Tiendal... I’m not sure. But it’s better to know how to open it and not use that knowledge until we’re sure of the consequences than to stay in the dark.”

“Yeah, you’re making sense,” Tony said thoughtfully. “But we’ll see.”

A pause was about to hang in the air, but I cut it off with a quick suggestion, "Tell me the news already."

"I don't even know where to start," Tony said slowly, deliberately dragging it out.

"Just start somewhere, stop stalling!" I said impatiently, and Tony chuckled.

"Okay, okay, listen," he said with a smile, taking a deep breath as if preparing for a long story.

"Well, most of your assumptions were right. First, about the drug's composition and the location of the labs. The analysis showed that the pollen of an unknown flower is one of its key ingredients. This pollen was found on the stones of ancient ruins and in the soil around them. Interestingly, the pollen changes its properties over long distances. That's likely why the labs are located so close to the ancient ruins."

Wow! I was right. Am I really this clever, or just lucky? I thought, smiling to myself, but I didn't interrupt Tony, staying silent.

"The second thing is about the expeditions," Tony continued. "They all explored ancient temple ruins in cities from the same period as Tiamon and Amhitiemar. You looked through the list I gave you, didn't you?"

"Yeah, but I only recognized two names."

"Which ones?"

"Amhitiemar and Enskriyar."

"Only those two cities have well-preserved buildings. The others are mostly in ruins. The entrance to the underground temple in Enskriyar is blocked by debris and huge stones, so it'll take time to clear. But Jenkins is running out of time, so Amhitiemar is really his only chance to get what he needs—if it's even there."

"Are there any other options? Besides the five Jenkins already checked?"

"We've involved many scientists, and they're studying all the relevant sources. But as of now, there's no trace of any other cities from that period."

"Yeah... but that period lasted long enough. He had many lives."

"True," Tony shrugged. "But that's all I've got for now."

"Okay. What about the labs?"

"You were absolutely right—they're still operational. But, of course, my gut feeling wasn't enough to convince my boss, so I had to go there myself to gather evidence."

"Still operational..." I echoed uncertainly. "Does that mean you haven't closed them?"

"Yes, it does."

"But why?!" I asked, frustration rising. "The drugs are still hitting the market—more people could get addicted!"

"True," Tony agreed, "but that's only one side of the situation. I prefer to look at it from a different angle."

Surprised and bewildered, I stared at Tony, silently demanding an explanation. I didn't understand any of this.

"Yeah, I know it might seem illogical at first," Tony said, nodding, "but there are reasons. First, drug consignments aren't sent that often, so if we're lucky, we'll finish the operation before a new batch hits the market. Second, if we shut down the labs now, we'll lose our chance to prove Jenkins's involvement in all of this. I need him behind bars to make sure he never comes near you again."

"So, what's your plan?"

"I need more information to decide if my plan can actually work. Our people are undercover in some of the labs, gathering what we need. It'll take time, but I'm confident it's worth the wait."

"Aren't you worried Jenkins might detect your agents with his abilities?"

"I think his ability to see the future and present is selective. He can see possible outcomes based on different choices, but he has to focus on it. So, if he doesn't suspect anything, we should be in the clear."

"Still not convincing..." I said, shaking my head.

"Well, I remember you telling me how he missed his wife's betrayal. That gives my theory a chance."

It felt like I got scalded with boiling water. I dropped my jaw and could barely breathe. Did I really hear it or did it seem to me? How did Tony know that? Did that mean he wasn't as honest with me as I thought?

I gathered all my strength, took a deep breath, and slowly exhaled. It helped a little. I could speak again, but slowly, as a lump formed in my throat and my eyes stung with tears.

"Tony, I..." I paused, taking another breath. "I never told you that Ilze was Tiendal's wife. And I never mentioned Tiendal's time limits either. How do you explain that?"

Tony, who had noticed my panic attack and watched it with genuine concern, breathed a sigh of relief and broke into a wide smile. "Easily," he said reassuringly, gently pulling my hair back from my shoulder.

Tony's reaction helped me relax a little, but doubt still gnawed at me. Sensing this, Tony decided not to delay the explanation.

"Paulo Cognitio is one of our partner scientists who helps locate other ancient temples. Apparently, I asked him a few questions about the legend."

"Phew," I exhaled in relief. "Thank God! I was already thinking... Well, never mind. I'm sorry. It's just... if you ever betrayed me, it would be too much to handle."

Tony placed his hands on my shoulders, looked into my eyes, and said, "Tayra, there are at least two reasons why betrayal would never benefit me. First, I love you—even though you're stubborn as hell and unbearable at times. Second, we make the perfect team. I believe only together can we defeat our common enemy."

I gave Tony a guilty smile and shrugged, embarrassed. After a moment, I added, "Okay, I'll believe you, but only if you tell me about the time limits."

Tony shook his head and laughed, "Told you, stubborn as hell." Then, looking at me again, he said, "If you don't want me to fall asleep right here, let's finally get some rest. We both need clear heads tomorrow. I'll tell you next time."

"Do you promise to hug me?"

"Yes, yes, yes! I'll hug you so tight, I won't even let you go to the bathroom in the morning!"

"Deal," I laughed. "Let's go then."

CHAPTER 30: SYMBOLS

As morning broke, we returned to the search. Despite combing the walls up and down several times, we found nothing encouraging. We concluded that perhaps the meanings of those symbols mattered, and that we couldn't dismiss the possibility.

Between searches, the others gathered in small groups to share their thoughts, but there was no real progress.

After a couple of hours of this, I began to feel a sincere hatred for the temple and its walls, wanting to send it all to hell. Only my ardor and curiosity kept me coming back to solve the problem, despite my growing frustration.

So, as I looked up at the wall once more, I began sorting through the information again. *Triangle, square, diamond, pentagon... What else? What are we missing?*

"Have you come up with anything?" a voice sounded behind me.

I jumped in place, my heart nearly leaping out of my chest. "Lord, Jenkins, you scared me to death!"

"You should have felt me approaching," he said, his voice calm as ever.

I was so stressed I didn't even feel the usual excitement. "Maybe, but I was too lost in my thoughts," I said, catching my breath.

"Yeah, I see," Jenkins said calmly, giving me a moment to settle.

A few moments later, I felt better, my voice nearly steady. I nodded toward the wall. "What's inside?"

"What's usually inside ancient temples?" Jenkins shrugged, still calm.

"It's not like I've ever been to one."

"Don't disappoint me, Tayra. You're an archaeologist. You should know."

"Let's say I do. But what do you need from it?"

"Don't you think that's none of your business?"

"Maybe, but curiosity makes people bold."

Jenkins smirked. "Well, that sass suits you. Makes you sexier."

Maybe that was a compliment, and maybe I should have blushed, but not for Jenkins. I just rolled my eyes and moved on. "Do you know how to open it?"

"Why would I need you if I did?"

"We both know you don't need me for thinking."

"Lucky for me, you can do both."

"Maybe if I knew what's inside, I'd think better. Motivation's a powerful thing."

"So, you need motivation..."

"Something like that."

"Well, then..."

"Tayra!" Tony suddenly called from around the corner. He quickly approached Jenkins and me, adding, "Oh, good morning, Mr. Jenkins. Sorry for the interruption. Tayra, Louis has an idea, and we'd like your opinion. Come up and join the discussion."

"Okay, I'll be there in a minute," I said with a friendly nod. Then I turned back to Jenkins. "Sorry, Jenkins, I'd love to chat, but I've got work to do."

Jenkins watched Tony leave and muttered, "I haven't seen this guy around for a while..."

"He hurt his hand and needed a few days to recover."

Jenkins raised an eyebrow, wincing in suspicion, but quickly returned to his blank expression. "So, he could be injured again if you don't think carefully enough."

"I'm no genius, Jenkins. Even if I thought day and night, I might come up with nothing. It's a creative process. And if you want results, you won't touch him—he's the only one of us who knows what those damn symbols mean."

Jenkins chuckled coldly. "No one is indispensable."

"Oh, really? Then replace me in your bed."

Jenkins shot me a withering glare, and goosebumps prickled my skin. But then, he seemed to change his mind, softening his gaze unexpectedly fast. "You'd be the one losing out if I did."

"Why?"

"Because you know better than anyone who the only man that can give you pleasure is..."

"Yes, that's true. But it's not you."

My sass must have crossed the line, because Jenkins's poker face shifted to genuine curiosity.

"Oh, really? And who have you slept with since me? That injured loser?"

At that moment, I felt the advantage in this verbal badminton finally shift to my side. I decided to finish Jenkins off before the situation shifted again. Smirking, I repeated his own words back at him, "Don't you think that's none of your business?"

"Whatever," Jenkins muttered, determined to get the last word. "I'm not jealous. And you're lying. Even if you had something with him, you felt nothing. That's why you'll always come back to me. Oh, and by the way, I'm expecting you tonight. Be smart—don't make me drag you there unwillingly."

"I've never been with you willingly."

"Keep lying to yourself if it helps you sleep at night."

With that, Jenkins left, and I pretended to head toward the guys, but instead, I slipped around the corner and stopped. Tony waited until Jenkins was far enough away, then rushed over to me.

"At last," he exhaled. "Are you okay?"

"Yup, I'm fine," I said, nodding.

"What's the outcome of your talk?"

"A threat to injure you and an invitation for tonight," I said, indifferently.

"Lustful jerk," Tony snorted, clenching his fists angrily.

"Tony!"

"Well, well, okay. I'm sorry. I promised, I remember. I know you're his charger and so on, but... Look... May I kill him?"

"No. Not yet."

"Glad you liked the idea itself," Tony said, letting out a sigh of relief.

I waited until he calmed down and seemed ready to continue. Then I asked, "What should I do, Tony?"

Tony obviously knew the answer right away, but since he didn't like it, he spent a few seconds frantically considering alternatives. Those few seconds of silence felt like an eternity, but I waited patiently for Tony's verdict, afraid to interrupt his thoughts in any way. Somewhere deep inside, I hoped Tony would come up with a way out, but he just shook his head. "I'm afraid there's no better option," he said, spreading his arms. "You have to do it. He can't suspect anything."

"Are you sure?" I asked awkwardly, still hoping some last-minute idea would pierce Tony's mind and save me from the worst situation ever.

"Yes, I am," Tony said, nodding. "Don't worry, I'll pretend to be asleep and not notice. I'll try, anyway."

"Okay," I said, swallowing hard and dropping my eyes. *Heck*! I thought. *Heck*!

Tony moved closer and stroked my shoulder, trying to comfort and cheer me up. "Relax," he said softly. "The evening is far off, and before that, we've got a tricky lock puzzle to solve. So, let's focus on this door."

"Yes, yes, you're right," I whispered. "I need to concentrate. Because it's important. It's so important."

I looked up at the wall, and in my mind, I saw a smug grin on Jenkins's face.

Well, yeah, I thought. *Despite how important this is, with my concentration like this, I have no chance of opening the door. I need a break, and I need it now.*

I turned to Tony and said, "I'll go sit in the shade for a few minutes, if you don't mind. Could you bring me some water, please?"

"Sure," Tony said, then left.

I walked to the shadowy side of the temple, sat on the ground, and leaned my back against the wall. Resting my elbows on my bent knees, I wrapped my hands around my head. A lump formed in my throat, and my eyes welled with tears.

This isn't the first time, so why am I so scared? Jeez, I'm so ashamed and terrified! I hate this temple, these symbols, these walls, Jenkins, and this entire expedition! I'm so tired of it all! I just want to go home. Please, let me go home.

I sighed, looking up. *But... going home won't solve my problems, while the open door of this fucking temple might. Pull yourself together, Tayra, and think. Damn triangle, square, diamond, and pentagon... It's not as simple as it looks. There's something we missed. Focus and think! You need that key—at any cost! At any cost!*

CHAPTER 31: BREAK DOWN

The way back after visiting Jenkins was always a happy time for me. I don't know if it was the sense of accomplishment or the anticipation of a few hours of freedom, but I always felt relieved, even a bit uplifted. Until today—or tonight, to be precise.

It was that night when everything turned upside down. The fear that usually gripped me before meeting Jenkins hit me afterward, as I made my way back to the tent where Tony was waiting. Tony... He was the reason I felt so awful.

When I thought Tony didn't know about my relationship with Jenkins, I felt guilty, but I could still make excuses. I justified it with the curse, telling myself I had to protect Tony and our friends. It worked—it was soothing.

After I told Tony about the curse and thought he hated me, I felt even less guilty. If Tony and I were no longer together, then what I was doing couldn't be called infidelity.

But now, I had no justification. The curse and my need to lull Jenkins's vigilance to help Tony's investigation didn't seem like good enough reasons anymore. What I was doing was cheating. And in my opinion, the fact that Tony knew made everything worse.

For the first time, I didn't want to go back to the tent. I just wanted to sink into the ground along the way, so I wouldn't have to look Tony in the eye. I knew he was awake, even though he promised he wouldn't be. I tried to imagine how he must've felt, and it only deepened my pain.

I trudged at a snail's pace, but eventually, the moment came. I pushed the tent flap aside and slipped through, trying not to make any noise.

I sat down on the mat and sighed quietly. Suddenly, a voice rang out from the darkness, "Successful?"

This was the last straw for my patience. I knew I needed to restrain myself and stay silent, but I couldn't.

"Please, Tony, don't be sarcastic. You promised to sleep and ignore everything, so do it," I said, barely managing to hide my irritation.

"Well, sorry," Tony said coldly before falling silent.

It would've been wise of me to stop talking too. I planned to just take a deep breath and go to bed, but as soon as my lungs filled with air, the words slipped out on their own. Even though I knew I'd regret it, I couldn't stop the flow.

"Tony, I know you're feeling awful. Honestly, I have no idea how you're handling this. I've tried to imagine myself in your shoes, but it's beyond me. If I were you, I couldn't stand seeing you cheat on me right before my eyes. No matter what kind of curse it was, I wouldn't accept it. It's just gross, plain and simple. And do you know what the worst part is? Sex with him is fucking pleasant. And I enjoy it as much as I don't want it. I know talking about this with you is inhuman. I'm sorry for saying it, but I can't keep it inside anymore, and you're the only person I can open up to. It's like being forced to eat chocolates. You don't want to because you're on a diet or something, but deep down, you don't mind because the chocolate tastes great."

I covered my face with my hands, smearing the hot, salty tears, and whispered, "God, my life's a theater of absurdity. I can't live like this anymore... I'm sorry."

I stood up and bolted outside. I ran as fast as I could, not caring about direction or where I'd end up. I just wanted to run—far, fast, without stopping. To feel the cool wind of a warm summer night on my flushed face, wet with tears.

I didn't stop because I was tired, but because my tears were choking me, and I needed to cry them out. I sank to the ground and started to weep—bitterly, loudly, without holding back. I lost track of time, so I don't know how long it lasted. Eventually, I took a breath and looked up at the sky. The moon shone brightly, almost full, and its light made it not so dark.

I got up and looked around. It turned out I hadn't wandered far—only to the opposite side of the temple, away from its door. I looked at the dark, bulky silhouette of the temple, its edges outlined by the moonlight, and said, "Why do you pull me to you like a magnet? Why don't you leave me alone? Damn you, fucking stone structure!"

I bent down, took a breath, and counted to ten as I exhaled. It helped me calm down a little, and I looked around again, feeling lost. I had no idea what to do next. That's when I noticed a man's silhouette emerging from behind the right wall of the temple. It was Tony—no doubt about it—and he was walking toward me.

How long has he been standing there? Has he been watching me cry this whole time? I thought as he approached. *Shit! This is so embarrassing.*

When Tony came close enough, he placed his hand gently, yet firmly, on my shoulder, as if to stop me from running away again, and said, "I'm happy you're okay."

"I'm not okay. You can't even imagine how much I'm not okay! I hope he leaves tomorrow, so I can finally breathe. Tony, my heart is about to tear apart from shame, fear, and pain. Your presence makes it even worse. I'm hurting you... and it's the last thing I want. I need to do something about it, and the sooner, the better. And these fucking walls. Three days have passed. Eleven people have been racking their brains for three days... And nothing. We still have nothing. Oh, God!

I must disappear. Yeah, really—it's the solution. Without me, everyone's life will be better. Tony, I never wanted any of this. If I'd only known, I would've never gone on that excursion to Tiamon... And though it was my dream, I'd rather it had never come true."

Tony placed his other hand on my shoulder, looked at me intently, and said, "Tayra, calm down. Or cry if it helps, but stop saying all this scary nonsense about disappearing. Look at the situation from a different perspective. If none of this had happened, we never would've met. And I don't know about you, but I'm glad we did."

"If we'd never met, you would've found a normal girl and been happy with her. And honestly, that's what I'd advise you to do as soon as you finish your mission with Jenkins and the drugs. I'm nothing but trouble. Leave me to him. Let him use me as much as he wants, then throw me away like trash. I feel like my life is over. Don't torture yourself. Leave me, please."

Tony took his hands off my shoulders and said in a calm, steady voice, "Well, I'm giving you ten minutes to pull yourself together. And keep in mind that I'm watching you. So don't even think about doing something stupid." Afterward, he took a few steps toward the temple wall, giving me some space.

I was surprised and puzzled by Tony's calmness. How could someone stay this calm after hearing everything I'd told him? Was it because he didn't care? But if that were the case, why would he follow me and then wait for God knows how long while I struggled with my emotions? Obviously, he did care. So how could he maintain that composure? And why hadn't he revealed himself earlier and come to comfort me?

I spent a few minutes reflecting on this and realized that, despite the new questions forming in my mind, Tony's calmness was contagious. And although I was still far from emotional balance, I felt much better and was ready to talk more constructively.

"Tony, just listen to me, please. I can't live like this anymore."

"Just wait a bit longer, everything will settle somehow."

"How, Tony, how? I don't understand anything. I need answers. I have a feeling I can only get them from him. But he won't talk to me. He's just teasing me, showing me how much power he has over me."

"Tayra, relax. He certainly can't let you find out the truth."

"Which truth, Tony?"

"No matter how much he tries to convince you of his power, you can live without his 'attention,' but he can't live without you."

I rubbed my eyes, wiping away the last of my tears, and looked at Tony. "Continue."

"According to the legend, Tiendal had many women, but Jenkins had none before you and has no other relationships, except with you, at the moment. This means only one thing. While you can have relationships with other men and stay indifferent to their caresses, he can, for some reason, only have sex with you."

"I thought about it too. But how can we use this information?"

"How often does he 'contact' you?"

"Well, during the expedition, he comes once a week and stays for about three days."

"Probably, he gets energy from sex with you. After several encounters, the amount of energy he receives is enough for him to stay apart from you for a few days. Then, a new recharge is needed."

Tony's words made me recall our conversation from the morning. The charger. That's what Tony meant when he said it. And as unpleasant as it was to admit the truth of that assumption, I couldn't find any argument to deny it.

"Yes, it looks very much like that," I agreed. "And how long will it last?"

"I have no idea. But I suppose it'll last until he finds another source of energy. Possibly that mysterious Source of Force."

"What about the time limits?"

"In Paulo's book, there was something about rumors regarding 'Tiendal's year.'"

"Yeah, I remember. But they had no rational confirmation."

"Where there's smoke, there's fire. I'm not sure about the 'year,' but it's obvious his time to find the Source of Force is limited, which is why he's in a hurry. I think that's why he started all this stuff with drugs—because it was the fastest way to earn big money and gain the corresponding power. That's also why he abandoned the excavations in the first four cities and switched to Amhitiemar."

"What do you think will happen to me once he finds the Source of Force?"

"I don't know exactly," Tony shrugged. "I think he'll be able to use other women, and you'll be free from him. According to the legend, your insensitivity will remain. But the main question is how powerful he'll become with this Source of Force. How dangerous is it to let him get to it?"

"Well, at least this scenario is described in the legend. But what happens if **he doesn't find** the Source of Force?"

"Yeah, that's the question. He might die."

"And what will happen to me?"

"I'd prefer to think the spell will be broken and you'll be free."

"And what if you're wrong?"

"We're screwed."

"Great. Very reassuring."

"At least it's honest. Let's go; I'll think about it later. The sunrise is coming soon, and we haven't even slept yet."

"I'm not sleepy."

"You'll be soon. Otherwise, you'll just lie there, silently."

Tony extended his hand to me, inviting me to follow him, and I was about to accept it when I noticed a strange shine on the temple wall. Glare flashed in several spots, then disappeared.

"Did you see that?" I asked, nodding toward the wall.

"What?"

"Something glittered there."

"Really? I didn't notice."

We moved closer to the wall and started examining it carefully, but the glitter didn't appear again.

"Maybe it just seemed that way," Tony shrugged. "I don't see anything unusual. Just a dark wall."

"I'm pretty sure it was real. We need something to light up the wall."

Tony pulled the phone from his pocket. I was genuinely surprised.

"Seriously?" I asked. "You ran out of the tent after me and somehow managed to bring the phone with you? How is that even possible?"

"Unconditioned reflex," Tony smiled, shrugging.

He turned on the flashlight, directing its beam at the wall. He moved the phone side to side, up and down, but the glitter didn't reappear. Tony switched off the light and glanced at me. "Do you remember the exact spot where you saw it?"

"Nope. Just the wall area. Let's head back to the tent. I'll check it out in the daylight."

"Are we done with tantrums for today?"

"Looks like it," I said, lowering my eyes.

"Good then. Let's get some sleep."

"You're not mad at me for what I said, are you?"

"Nope. Well, maybe a little," Tony said with a smile. "Honestly, I wondered how you held on under so much pressure for so long. I started to think you were a robot, not human."

"I'm gonna kill you."

"Too late. You should've done it earlier, in a state of passion," Tony said with a grin, offering me his hand. "Alright, I'm glad you're feeling better. Let's go."

I took his hand, and together we finally headed back to the tent.

CHAPTER 32: FAILURE

The next day, right after breakfast, Tony and I headed to the back wall of the temple to investigate where I had seen the shine last night. We carefully examined every stone in the area, but couldn't find any pattern in the symbols.

Puzzled, we sat down on the ground near the temple, staring at the wall, trying to make sense of the phenomenon. Soon, Jenny and Louis approached us, looking both perplexed and somewhat down.

Louis rubbed his forehead with both hands and said, "I've been thinking about those symbols all night, but I have no idea how to crack the code."

"Yeah," Jenny sighed. "I couldn't sleep either. I was staring at the photos of these damn walls, studying them from every angle, but it didn't bring me any closer to an answer."

If they were awake, they might've heard our argument last night, I thought, worried. *If so, that's not good. Not good at all.*

The thought worried me so much that I almost asked if they'd heard anything last night, but since they didn't mention it, I decided not to draw attention to the incident.

Louis usually keeps his headphones on, I thought, relaxing a little. *I hope he got Jenny into the music too, so there's a chance they were too absorbed in their own stuff to hear our late-night conversations.*

Tony joined the discussion, his voice interrupting my thoughts.

"Tayra and I tried to find any regularity in the locations of the symbols and their meanings, but we've had no results yet."

"It's a real mystery," Louis uttered, rubbing his forehead in confusion. "The first cache was so easy. I arrived at the site in the morning, and it just revealed itself to me. I saw those same symbols, forming a triangle."

"Who found the second cache?" I asked.

"I did," Jenny said.

"Was it also in the morning?" I asked.

"I don't remember exactly, but it wasn't early. It must've been around noon—the sun was scorching mercilessly."

I winced as I processed the information, my eyebrows rising. Jenny seemed to notice and asked, "The time—do you think it's important?"

"Oh," I smiled. "I have no idea. Probably not. I just don't know how else to tune my brain into solving this riddle."

Jenny and Louis started laughing, and Tony and I couldn't help but giggle too. Later, the others joined our discussion, and we went through tons of theories and hypotheses again, but none of them proved true.

After a whole day of fruitless searching and equally pointless discussions, by evening, everyone was really upset. The spirit of failure poisoned what had once been a warm, positive atmosphere. Portonapoulos came to the bonfire to encourage his team, who were ready to give up.

"It's such a strange feeling," Louis said sadly. "We're so close to the solution, but success keeps slipping away."

"That's true," Portonapoulos agreed. "But who knows? Maybe fate is trying to show us that opening the door is a bad idea."

"Still, I feel disappointed," Jenny said with a shrug. "At some point, I really thought we could do it."

"You shouldn't be disappointed," Portonapoulos said, his tone reassuring. "I understand how you all feel, but failure is still a result. In fact, I wouldn't call our expedition a failure at all. We've gathered plenty of valuable materials for future analysis and publication. And you've gained equally valuable experience in fieldwork and camp life. Honestly, I'm very pleased with what we've achieved."

"And what about Jenkins?" I asked. "What does he think of the result?"

"Fortunately, I don't know what he's thinking, and it's unlikely to be anything good," Portonapoulos said with a smile. "But according to the agreement, we owe him nothing."

"Well...," I continued, "is it possible he'll ask to continue the research on this object?"

"We haven't discussed that possibility yet. But with classes about to start, involving students will be impossible until the holidays. After that, the season won't be suitable for an expedition. We could probably gather PhD students and young researchers for an expedition, but that'll take time too."

"Especially considering how picky he is about choosing team members," Miles commented. From the number of giggles, I realized the interview was challenging for everyone, not just me.

"We still have two days," I said thoughtfully. "Do you think it'll be good if we manage to open the door?"

"I'm curious about what's hidden behind it, I won't deny," said Portonapoulos with a shrug. "But honestly, I have mixed feelings about opening it."

"Does that mean we should stop trying?" Jenny asked, uncertainty in her voice.

"No, not at all," Portonapoulos retorted. "Keep trying. Who knows... maybe we'll get lucky and my worries will be for nothing."

And what if they aren't? I thought, a sinking feeling in my chest. *What if they aren't*?

I turned to Tony for support, only to realize he wasn't there. After hesitating for a few seconds, I asked, "Has anyone seen Tony?"

"I'm pretty sure I saw him here just a few minutes ago," Louis said in surprise. "How did he manage to disappear?"

"Yeah, true. Well, I'll go and try to find him."

I went to our tent, but Tony wasn't there. I wasn't particularly surprised; the tent had never been his favorite place to think. For that, he'd more likely go to our clearing. I was about to head there, but then it dawned on me, and I rushed to the temple. As I expected, Tony stood by the back wall, staring at it.

I walked up to him and asked softly, "What are you doing?"

"Checking your theory," Tony replied, eyes still on the wall.

"Um... Are you serious?"

"Absolutely."

"Any luck?"

"Not yet. But I think I know why."

I turned my head to the temple wall and stared at it too. The stone structure was hopelessly dark, offering no sign of hidden knowledge to be found. Tony, however, remained determined and hopeful.

I shrugged. "And what do you think it is?" I asked.

Tony nodded toward the sky. "Cloudy."

"Okay," I said. "So, what shall we do?"

"Wait," Tony said, shrugging, his eyes still fixed on the wall as if they were glued to it.

"How long?" I asked, glancing back at the wall. The idea of spending the whole night near it, waiting for whatever Tony hoped to find, didn't seem appealing.

Tony glanced at the sky, then back at the wall. "I hope not too long. But I'll wait anyway."

I glanced at the sky too, then stepped closer to Tony and kissed him. Tony smiled. "What's that supposed to mean?" he asked.

"It's my offer to make waiting more... enjoyable," I said, smiling back.

"I seem to recall someone begging me last night to leave her and find another girl."

"Well, I changed my mind. Besides, you turned me down yesterday."

"True. But this offer seems impossible to resist. Only... aren't you afraid I might lose control and devour you?"

"Whatever," I giggled. "You know, I won't feel anything anyway."

"You've been warned," said Tony, brushing my hair back from my face and leaning in for a kiss.

We stood by the temple wall, kissing in the quiet of a warm summer night, until the clouds cleared and the moon shone bright in the sky, almost as big and luminous as the night before...

When we returned to the tent, the camp was already asleep—or so it seemed. We slipped inside, sat on the mat, and looked at each other.

"Hold me," I whispered, moving closer.

Tony wrapped his arms around me and sighed softly. "Don't let me get used to your closeness. I'll miss it once this expedition is over."

"With your crazy work, I'm the one who shouldn't get used to it," I said with a sad smile.

"Well, my work... I hope it won't be much of an obstacle. But it's better not to get ahead of ourselves."

"Do you think it's even possible? Are we possible?"

"We're already a fact, Tayra. There are just a few minor issues left to solve."

I sighed, and the tent plunged into tense silence. It lasted for several long minutes until Tony finally spoke up.

"Listen..." he said earnestly, "if I were a PhD student in history, would you be asking this?"

"I don't know, maybe. But it would be for a different reason."

"Exactly, Tayra. So what's the difference? What are you afraid of?"

I pressed closer to Tony, burrowing deeper into his arms. A tear rolled down my cheek as I whispered, "Losing you."

Tony kissed my head tenderly. "I hope that doesn't happen. I'll do everything I can to prevent it. Anyway, let's not invent new worries until we deal with the ones we already have, okay?"

"Okay," I said quietly, feeling my eyes begin to close on their own. I looked up at Tony and offered, "Sleep?"

"Sleep," Tony nodded with a smile.

***

Two days later, our expedition was officially over. We rolled up the tents, gathered all the equipment, and loaded it onto the bus. The campsite now felt empty and sad.

Even though everything was ready for departure, no one was in a hurry to board the bus. The group lingered around it in indecision—clearly, no one wanted to leave.

Portonapoulos scanned the somber crowd and said, "Well, everyone, I think we can all agree that we've spent an incredible month on this expedition. I hope many of you will look back on it with warmth in your hearts. Sure, we didn't open the door, but I believe we should be proud of ourselves. We accomplished far more than anyone could've expected from a student team with practically no hands-on experience. It's been a pleasure working with you all, and I hope to collaborate with some of you again in the future."

His words were so touching that the girls' eyes welled with tears. The guys were probably on the verge of crying too, but they kept their emotions in check.

"Well..." Portonapoulos continued, "We still have a little time before the bus leaves, so do some final checks to make sure nothing's been left behind. Then, you can go say your goodbyes to the main site of our excavation."

Everyone obediently dispersed toward the site of our former camp, and I seized the moment to approach Portonapoulos.

"Mr. Portonapoulos..." I began hesitantly. "I know this might not be the best moment, but would you be so kind as to be my master's thesis supervisor?"

"Well," Portonapoulos said kindly, "if you're interested in the history of Amhitiemar, we can continue researching in that direction."

"Does that mean you agree?" I asked, excitement rising in my voice.

"Yes," Portonapoulos nodded, "but please remind me at the university after we return."

"Certainly! Thank you so much, Mr. Portonapoulos!"

"You're welcome, Tayra."

Just then, Tony approached. "I checked everything; it seems like nothing's left," he said, addressing Portonapoulos. He then turned to me and added, "Are you going to say goodbye to the temple?"

"Sure, let's go," I said with a nod.

We walked to the temple and stopped near its entrance. Despite the many unpleasant moments tied to this stone structure, it still inspired respect and admiration in me. Proud, majestic, and mysterious, it towered above the everyday bustle, reaching upward, toward something new and unknown.

"It's become a part of me this past month," I said, admiring the beautiful, ancient building.

"Yeah," Tony agreed. "I can't deny I have some warm feelings for this temple too." He looked at me and asked, "You haven't changed your mind, have you?"

"No, I haven't," I said confidently. "I'm more sure than ever."

"Okay," Tony nodded. He turned back to the building and added, "Well, goodbye, temple."

"Or who knows..." I said with a smile. "Maybe one day we'll discover your secret. So it's not a goodbye, but a see you later..."

CHAPTER 33: BARRIER

As soon as I stepped into my dorm room and breathed in the familiar scent, a feeling of calm and comfort washed over me, like it always does when you come home.

Tony, however, paused at the entrance, looking a little confused. At first, I didn't understand why, but then I realized what it might be about. Before the expedition, Tony had walked me to the dorm almost every day. I always waved to him from the window, but I never invited him in, which must have seemed strange. I had my reasons, but he didn't know them, so he probably came up with his own explanation. So, I hurried to fix the situation and ease Tony's worries.

"Come in, Tony," I said with a smile. "The threshold won't bite if you cross it. It's not bewitched—at least I hope not. Make yourself at home. I wasn't very hospitable back then… I hope you understand. But I'm still sorry about that."

Tony shrugged and finally stepped inside. He still looked a bit unsettled, maybe even embarrassed, which surprised me. The man who stayed calm and cool-headed in far more stressful situations was now emotional over something so trivial. But maybe, to him, it wasn't as insignificant as it seemed to me.

"The bathroom's over there if you want to wash your hands. I'll put the kettle on."

"Okay," Tony said, taking off his shoes.

While I tinkered with the tea, Tony looked around the room.

"So, this is how you live?" he said, smiling.

"Well, yeah. I still remember the day I moved in. Hard to believe it's been four years already."

"Do you like it here?"

"It's a dormitory, so I can't say I'm thrilled. Living in a student dorm is like living in a fishbowl—everyone knows everything before it even happens, so you have to be extra careful. It's a real swamp of gossip. Other than that, it's fine. These days, I feel more comfortable here than at home."

"Do you have a difficult relationship with your parents?"

"No, it's not that. I'm just an only child, and they've always been a bit overprotective. Life in the dorm gave me the freedom and independence I've always craved."

"Oh yeah, I get that. You have no idea how much."

"Really? Are you an only child too?"

"Nope. But that's a long story. I'll tell you another time. By the way, I don't see any sign of your neighbor. Do you live alone?"

"Yeah, I do. My neighbor moved in with her boyfriend back in our second year, but she kept her dorm registration and pays rent, so no one's been placed in her spot. So, I've been living alone since then."

"Isn't it boring being alone all the time?"

"Oh Tony, I see you've never lived in a student dorm. You have to be really lucky to stay alone here. There are always people around, whether you want them or not. You can't even lock the door—they'll just break it. Sometimes you have to pretend you're dead just to get some quiet time to study."

Tony laughed. "How often have you had to do that?"

"More often than you'd think. I'm a diligent student, after all."

"I know you are. Okay, may I open the window?"

"Sure, that's a good idea. This room could definitely use some fresh air."

I went to grab the cups of tea, while Tony walked to the window and stared down thoughtfully. The embarrassment that seemed to disappear when we talked about the room crept back onto Tony's face.

I set the cups on the windowsill and asked, "Is something wrong?"

"No, it's fine," Tony said, blushing slightly. "It's just... it's a bit unusual. I was more used to seeing this room from the other side, looking up."

I shrugged, blushing too. "I've already apologized for that, Tony. I thought keeping my distance was the right thing to do."

"No, no, Tayra. It's okay, you don't have to apologize," Tony said, then paused, hesitating. He was clearly worried, and there was obviously a question on the tip of his tongue. It was a question he was embarrassed to ask, yet for some reason, the answer seemed important to him. I had a feeling I knew what it was about, but since I knew Tony wouldn't like the answer, and because I didn't want to discuss it either, I pretended not to notice his concern and changed the subject.

"The tea must be cold by now. You should drink it before it evaporates. Sorry, all I can offer is tea for now. I haven't been home in a month, so there won't be food until tomorrow."

Tony smiled, took the cup in his hands, and sat down on my bed. "No problem. Tea's fine."

I sat down next to Tony, looked at him, and asked, "So, what's next?"

Tony took a sip of tea and said, "Let's stick to the plan. Unfortunately, I haven't heard anything about the laboratories yet, but I'm hoping to get news soon."

I took a sip too. The tea wasn't cold, but it wasn't hot enough to taste good either, so I set my cup down and sighed. "It's been three days. He'll probably show up any day now."

"Yeah, I know," Tony said quietly, his voice heavy with guilt and uncertainty. "Honestly, I'd prefer you stayed at my place, just to make sure you're safe. But that would look suspicious and make him angry. I have no choice but to let him use you a bit longer."

I didn't say anything. We both knew it was the right thing to do for our ultimate goal. As unpleasant as it was for both of us, there was little we could do at this point. I just looked at Tony and nodded, letting him know I understood and accepted it all. Tony gently stroked my hand and sighed softly.

"My classes start in a couple of days. Maybe I could visit the library and look through Paulo's book again," I said, trying to ease the rising tension.

"Fine," Tony nodded. By now, he had finished his tea, and after setting the cup aside, he stood up and glanced toward the door. "Thanks. I've got to go."

I stood up too, stepping in his way, and asked softly, "Are you going to work early tomorrow?"

"Not too early," Tony shrugged. "But I've got some things to take care of. You know what I mean."

"Yeah, I get it..." I nodded, forcing a smile, trying to hide my anxiety.

The awkward tension lingered in the air again. The situation felt utterly ridiculous. I didn't want Tony to leave, but I couldn't muster the courage to ask him to stay. I had no idea how he'd react, and that terrified me.

I felt my face flush with embarrassment as my hands began to tremble with nerves. I took a deep breath, trying to calm myself, but it didn't help much.

"Tony..." I began, but paused, unsure if I should say it. I knew I'd regret it if I didn't try. If I did, there was at least a 50 percent chance of not getting rejected, and that was enough for me to give it a shot. So I took another breath and finished the sentence I'd started. "Maybe you... could stay... with me... tonight..."

Tony looked just as embarrassed as I felt. "Tayra, I..." he stammered, his voice trembling with uncertainty, "Of course I'd like to, but... I'm not sure it's a good idea."

Well... I thought, *I landed in the wrong 50 percent. But it was worth a shot anyway.*

The awkward question seemed settled, but the tension lingered, growing no better. There was an unspoken issue between us, and I decided it was better to address it than to stay silent and suffer.

I looked Tony in the eye and asked, "It's because of him, isn't it?"

"Partly," Tony said, rubbing his face nervously. "You see..." he continued, dropping his hand, "It's hard to compete in bed with a man who has centuries of experience. I'm doomed to lose, knowing my touch won't bring you any pleasure."

"You're wrong, Tony," I said, trying to steady my voice and sound more confident. "If you think that, then he's already won. Chances are, I'll always be... numb. I have to live with that. And you promised to accept it. What I have with him... it's not real... It's... I don't know how to explain it... But it's a sensation without feeling and pleasure without joy. I miss warmth and tenderness—things he's incapable of giving me. I genuinely want to be with you—to give you pleasure, to feel your response to my touch. I know this will feel infinitely better than anything he could ever make me feel with his devilish tricks. I don't care how many women you've had before me, or how skillful they were. Maybe you're right—this moment isn't right. I'm not insisting. But I want you to know, I crave this to happen."

Tony listened intently, not even interrupting with the sound of his breathing. When I finished, he sighed, looked at me closely, and said, "I love you, Tayra. Believe me, I find you incredibly attractive, and you are deeply desired by me... But today just isn't the right time."

He kissed me on the cheek, wished me good night, and left.

I closed the door behind Tony, walked into the room, and sat on the bed—my favorite place to think. I felt foolish. No, I didn't regret telling Tony how I felt—not in the least. It was important to me, and I needed him to know.

Even though our feelings were strong and sincere, there was still some kind of barrier between us. Maybe it was my curse, or maybe it was our inner fears and insecurities, but one thing was clear. For our relationship to continue, we had to overcome this barrier. But I wasn't sure we could do it. And, unfortunately, I couldn't see a way out of this vicious cycle of uncertainty.

CHAPTER 34: ULTIMATUM

As Tony and I had agreed, I went to the library the next day. The university was already waking up after the summer holidays, and many more people could be seen around campus than a month ago. On autopilot, lost in my thoughts, I walked along the cozy, well-maintained paths, enjoying the soft warmth of the last days of summer. I was about to turn a corner when I suddenly heard a voice behind me: "Tayra!"

I turned and saw Gladys, waving happily as she quickly approached. I smiled and stopped. Within seconds, Gladys wrapped me in a tight embrace. "How are you, my dear? I missed you so much!"

"Oh my God, Gladys! What a surprise!" I said, hugging her back. "What are you doing here?"

"Same as you, I suppose. I came to check my schedule."

"Wait... You weren't planning on continuing for the fifth year. Did I miss something?"

"Oh, yes, a lot," Gladys giggled. "My uncle got me a job, but it requires a master's degree. They agreed to take me part-time if I continued into the fifth year, so I had to change my plans. Luckily, I passed the exams just in case and applied for admission. So, instead of withdrawing like I was planning to, I had to let them enroll me. So, dear, it looks like we'll be sharing a desk for another year and a half."

"This is great news, Gladys! I mean, I'm sorry you had to change your plans, but I hope it's for the best. Anyway, I'm happy to have you around and share our university days again. I missed you too. So, what kind of job do I have to thank for bringing my bestie back?"

"Oh, it's a long story. I'll tell you later. Let's go."

"Where?"

"Uh, Tayra, are you okay? Don't you remember where we usually get our schedules?"

"Oh, of course I know that. But honestly, I totally forgot we even needed to get the schedule. If it weren't for you, I probably wouldn't have remembered."

Gladys's jaw dropped as she looked at me with a mix of concern and disbelief. "Tayra, you've always been a model student. Something serious must've happened to make you forget. What did they do to you on that expedition?"

Oh, Gladys, believe me, you're better off not knowing, I thought, but smiled and waved it off. "Don't worry. I only got back last night, and I'll need a few days to get back into my usual routine."

"Okay, fine. Wait… where were you heading then?"

"To the library."

Gladys winced hesitantly, and from her expression, I realized I needed to change the topic fast if I wanted to avoid an interrogation about my insensitivity. So before she could even take a breath to respond, I quickly added, "Portonapoulos agreed to be my master's thesis supervisor. He told me to study a few historical documents about Amhitiemar. I figured I could get a head start while I've got some free time."

"Okay, got it," Gladys said, still eyeing me with slight disbelief. "So, about Amhitiemar... How was your expedition? Was it worth all the nerves you spent fighting for the spot?"

"Well, in some ways, the expedition exceeded my expectations. There were plenty of surprises, though. Still, I think it was a valuable experience, and I can definitely say it changed my life."

"Could you explain that last part in a little more detail?" Gladys asked, smiling and giving me that "I know you're hiding something" look.

"Of course," I said, smiling mysteriously. "But I can't do it now. Maybe some other time."

Gladys shrugged, staying silent. What I love about her is that, despite being terribly curious, she always senses the boundary where it's not worth digging. That shrug, paired with a sigh through slightly pouty lips, was her eloquent way of showing that, though reluctantly, she respected my right to stay silent for as long as I needed.

I nodded, and we headed to the dean's office to get our schedules. Our university has a tradition that has always seemed a bit strange to me. The new semester's schedule first appears on the bulletin board near the dean's office, and only a few days later—after classes have already started—does it show up on the university's official website. In my opinion, the reverse would be more logical, but who knows. There must be a reason behind this tradition, though students aren't privy to it. So, we had no choice but to take photos of our schedules at the start of every semester and use them until they could be replaced by more user-friendly digital versions.

Standing by the bulletin board, I scanned my schedule up and down several times. *Too many classes for a fifth-year, and too many professors I don't know*, I thought with some disappointment as I pointed my camera and took a picture. Suddenly, a sharp pain shot through my stomach. It was so sudden and intense that I screamed and doubled over.

"Oh my God, Tayra, what happened? Are you okay?" Through the haze, I heard Gladys's terrified voice.

Barely able to breathe through the pain, I started thinking feverishly, *He's somewhere near. God, it's not just excitement—it's pain, and it's strong. I'm not sure I can take this much longer. He must want something urgent. Lord, what should I do*?

The pain eased slightly, and I managed to straighten up. Trying to sound as confident as possible, I said, “I'm fine, Gladys, don't worry. I don't know what it was, but it's gone now. Let's meet later, okay? I'll text you. Right now, I really need to wash my face.”

With that, I rushed to the bathroom, leaving Gladys dumbfounded in the middle of the corridor. As I expected, Jenkins was already there, clearly waiting for me.

“What now?” I snapped as the door slammed behind me.

“Is that your idea of a hello?”

“Your hello wasn't very pleasant either.”

“Was it that painful?” Jenkins asked with mock sympathy.

“Oh, I loved it,” I retorted, giving him a contemptuous glare.

“Shall I repeat it?” Jenkins said in an icy tone, menace clear in his voice.

“Do as you like. But the sooner you're done, the better.”

“Tayra, you've learned nothing from our time together...”

“You're wrong, Jenkins. I've learned plenty.”

His incinerating glare burned through me as he uttered a low, threatening, “Never play with me, Tayra.”

According to his calculations, I should've been terrified here, yet to his great surprise, I shrugged off his threat with a sarcastic, “I'd prefer not to deal with you at all.”

Jenkins snorted furiously. I'd never seen him like this before, not even when I pestered him on the expedition. His eyes burned with a destructive fire, ready to crash down on me and erase every trace of my existence. It was both terrifying and amusing. I didn't know exactly what had pushed him to this emotional state, but I felt oddly honored to be part of it. Knowing how well Jenkins usually kept his composure, I saw his seething anger as a personal victory, and I couldn't help but rejoice over every nerve cell fried by the heat of his boiling blood. Jenkins, however, apparently valued his nerve cells, so his fury didn't last long. Soon, he continued in a calmer voice, "Maybe I'll arrange that one day. But for now, I need something. And you know I always get what I want."

"Since you've replaced excitement with pain, I assume we're not talking about sex."

"It's always a pleasure dealing with someone clever."

"What do you want?" I asked, weary but calm. My voice sounded even, though it was brimming with rage and irritation, making it clear I was no longer afraid of him.

Though clearly impressed by my audacity, Jenkins had no doubt he could break it. "The door," he demanded, "I need you to open the temple door."

I snorted with disdain and rolled my eyes. "Ten people, personally chosen by you, spent a week trying to solve that riddle and got nowhere. What could I possibly do alone?"

Jenkins tried once again to pierce me with his glare and said, "You've already solved the task, I know. Just give me the last key."

His ridiculous sense of superiority started to piss me off, so I let my insolence run free. "If I knew how to open it, I'd have done it during the expedition. Who could resist the temptation to explore an ancient temple? So it could only be in your dreams that I found that cache and didn't use the key from it. And by the way... if you know so much, why don't you get it yourself? Why do you need me for this?"

"Three days, Tayra."

"Are you deaf?" I shot back, meeting his drilling stare with a glare just as lethal. "I couldn't find the right pattern, even after walking around that temple all day. Nothing will change in three days. So if you're going to kill me for failing, go ahead and do it now."

Jenkins grinned. "It's amusing how little you value your own life.

But there are people you care about far more than you admit. And their lives... they matter, don't they?"

"Jenkins, my life has no value because it's poisoned by your constant presence. And if you touch any of my friends, I'll do something drastic. Yes, Jenkins, and that disbelief in your eyes is completely unnecessary. You need me, so keep in mind, I'm not kidding."

"Ridiculous threats," he said, with that arrogant smirk still on his lips. "There's at least one person who'd be devastated if something happened to you, and you won't let that happen."

"Jenkins, if you're done, can I go?" I said, defiantly turning away. But the devil quickly grabbed my wrist and slammed me against the wall, his fierce black eyes locking onto mine.

"Tayra, no one can lie to me."

His fury grew, and my blood surged with adrenaline. Recklessness blurred my mind, making me desperately brave. Like Yvaine in Neil Gaiman's *Stardust*, I decided to shine and finish him off with my brightness. I raised an eyebrow, looking him straight in the eyes with brazen defiance, and said, "Jenkins, you want the truth? Fine. I don't have the last key, and I don't know where it's hidden. Are you satisfied?"

For a moment, genuine amazement flickered in Jenkins's eyes as he stepped back, releasing my hand. But in the next instant, he recovered, his haughty expression returning.

"Impressive," he said indifferently. "I'll deal with that later. Now, my unruly beauty, it's my turn to satisfy you—and I'm sure you won't mind."

With those final words, he stepped closer and pressed his hot lips to my neck. A flame ignited inside me, one I couldn't resist, no matter how fiercely I fought.

CHAPTER 35: SHOWDOWN

When Jenkins let me go, I decided to finally finish what I had come to campus for in the first place. It's amazing how much I've adapted to Jenkins over the course of our acquaintance. At first, after sex with him, I felt dirty, insignificant, and guilty. But oddly enough, the moment I left the ladies' bathroom, I didn't feel anything. Well, maybe except for the freedom and relief of not seeing him again for at least a few hours.

I indifferently straightened my clothes, smoothed my hair, opened the door with pride, and calmly headed to the library. To the library! Just minutes after sex with a powerful genius wielding ancient magic. Adaptation is truly an incredible thing, with unexplored horizons.

But I must admit, I came to the library in vain. After several hours of leafing through Paulo Cognitio's book, I concluded it couldn't tell me anything beyond what I already knew. Worse yet, there wasn't a word about the possibility of removing the curse, let alone any hint of how to do it.

I returned the book to the librarian and headed home. As I walked, I went over the information in my head, trying to make sure I hadn't missed anything. I really hadn't, so there was no choice but to draw one disappointing conclusion. *This book won't help me remove the curse, while Tiendal might. But how can I convince him to do it? How?*

By the time I reached the dorm, I still hadn't answered any of my questions. I entered my room, changed my clothes, and went about my daily activities, which had piled up during my time on the expedition. Soon, I heard a knock on the door. It was Tony, beaming with happiness.

"Hi, dear!" he said, his radiant smile lighting up the room brighter than the summer sun. Before I could process what was happening, Tony's lips firmly pressed against mine.

I didn't hesitate to return his kiss, though considering how Tony and I parted yesterday, his confidence today was more than surprising. But since Tony's lips were tender and loving as always, I decided to enjoy the moment, rather than worry prematurely about something that might not even be real.

When Tony finally pulled away, I took a moment to ask, "Has something good happened?"

"Yeah, I've got great news," Tony whispered, his smile never fading as he looked into my eyes fondly.

"Can't wait to hear it," I said, smiling back. "Just let me close the door, and I'm all ears."

We moved into the room and sat down on the bed.

"Everything's ready to put my plan into action," Tony said, "But there's one thing I need your help with."

"Okay, what is it?"

"We need to plant recording equipment in Jenkins's office, but he has to be out of there, and he can't suspect a thing. That's where I need your help. I've gone through a lot of options, but considering how sharp his intuition is, no one can pull it off better than you."

"Uh," I sighed, a mix of surprise and confusion in my voice. "But what about the other staff? His office is always full of people."

"Don't worry about them, we'll handle that. Just get Jenkins out, and we'll take care of the rest."

I rubbed my forehead in confusion. "And how exactly am I

supposed to get him out of the office?"

Tony shrugged. "I don't know how, but the farther you take him, the better."

"How long does he need to be gone?"

"Half an hour would be ideal, but ten minutes should be enough to clean up and cover the tracks. If Jenkins weren't Jenkins, the guys could manage in 20 seconds, but with him, better safe than sorry."

"Okay, I got it," I said, standing up and walking to the window. I looked down, then glanced at the maple trees outside before sighing and returning to the bed. You see, Tony, I'd be happy to help, but I'm not sure I'm good bait. Jenkins minds his own business and just uses my body to solve his problems. I have zero influence on him. I don't think there's anything I can do to make him change his plans, let alone play by my rules."

"I think you're underestimating yourself and your influence on this bastard. Whatever hook you throw, he'll bite, I'm sure of it. Your connection works both ways, even if he's the main stakeholder."

"True, but... he might not be that interested in me right now, since we already saw each other today."

"Damn!" Tony said, dropping his head in frustration. "Where did he get you?"

"In the ladies' bathroom at the university."

"Shit!" Tony hissed, rubbing his face. "I should've seen this coming."

I shrugged, trying to reassure him. "Honestly, our knowing wouldn't have changed anything. If we want to keep him from suspecting, we just need to act natural. He was furious today. I can't even imagine how much worse it would've been if he couldn't find me. But it's okay, I can handle it."

"Mad, huh? Did he hurt you?"

"Uh... I don't think it's something you should worry about. He can hurt me, but he can't kill me. If he could, trust me, he would've done it today. Now I'm sure he can't. He needs me... for sex. Dead or injured, I wouldn't be very useful to him for that."

"Tayra, I'm so sorry you're going through this. I promise, I'll do everything I can to end it. Just a little more to get through."

"It's okay, Tony, don't worry. Just tell me—how reliable is your plan? How sure are you that it's going to work?"

"Ninety-eight percent guarantee."

"Well, not bad," I said, rubbing my chin. "That means I can say whatever I want to him."

"Tayra, please, be careful," Tony said, his eyes full of concern. "Don't provoke him anymore, I'm begging you. Be safe."

"Oh Tony, you have no idea how fun it is watching him lose it. I don't even mind the pain—it's worth every bit of it."

"Oh my God, Tayra. I never realized your dark side was this... dark."

"Who knows, maybe I haven't even reached my limit yet. You might want to think about backing down before it's too late."

"I hope you're joking. Anyway, don't get too carried away, and remember—he's sensitive to lies."

I smiled and nodded. "I know that better than anyone. So, Tony, when do you plan to put it in motion?"

"Tonight."

"Mmm... So you need me to distract him tomorrow morning?"

"Yes, but not too early. Probably around lunchtime. I'll text you the exact time later."

"Aren't you worried you'll be late with the recording equipment?"

"Trust me."

"Well, you know best," I said, smiling in agreement. Then, I let my smile twist into something more devilish as I added, "I'll try to do my best."

I started thinking through my plan as soon as Tony left. After carefully analyzing everything I already knew, I drew some key conclusions.

He's easier to handle when he's confused. I've tried different ways to put him in that state. Now it's time to disarm him with a breathtaking look. I tried something similar during the expedition, but back then, my plan lacked preparation and resources. This time, I'll give it everything I've got.

The next day I started to collect my outfit. It wasn't difficult, since the experience of seducing the bad boy in the club came in handy. This time, though, I decided to do without a blouse and threw the leather jacket right over my bra. The summer heat continued raging, but it didn't matter—Jenkins's office had air conditioners, while the jacket had a short role in my performance.

Like last time, I pulled my hair into a high ponytail and did my make-up, catchy, but not too defiant. I needed to look gorgeous and sexy, not cheap.

I went to the mirror and carefully examined the result of my efforts.

If only it worked, I told myself. *Good luck, Tayra*!

I stormed into Jenkins's waiting room like a hurricane, brushing off the secretary's attempts to stop me with, "It's personal. I'll take full responsibility." Without hesitation, I marched into his office, deliberately leaving the door slightly ajar behind me.

Standing in the doorway, I slowly unzipped my jacket, letting it slip off my shoulders and fall to the floor.

The look on Jenkins's face when he saw me was worth every bit of effort. His jaw dropped, and his eyes practically shot up to his forehead. He stood up, planting his hands on the edge of the desk, and took a deep breath.

"Does this mean you're happy to see me?" I asked, a flirtatious lilt in my voice, as I took a few steps toward Jenkins, swaying my hips seductively.

Jenkins let out a loud exhale, mixing it with a bewildered question, "What the fuck, Tayra?"

"Despite your attempts yesterday, I still made it to the library... I came across an amazing book... And suddenly, I had an unbelievable realization..." I said theatrically, sliding my hands slowly along my body, making him ache with desire. "This realization made me rush over... to discuss it with you..."

Jenkins narrowed his eyes in disbelief. "Indeed?"

"Yes..." I continued, approaching the desk slowly. "But there's a problem... While walking here, I ran into those guys..." I said, nodding toward the window and inviting Jenkins to look outside.

Jenkins gave me another mistrustful look but still walked to the window and glanced outside, where a crowd of frenzied journalists raged near the entrance of the office building.

"Recognized, I suppose," I said in a deliberately calm voice, defiantly ignoring Jenkins's furious glare. "You know, they're so intrusive, and they'll stop at nothing to get their sensation... They got very interested in a half-naked girl who entered your office... So, I think they'll break in here any minute... And they'll be thrilled to uncover the mystery of Robert Jenkins's resurrection... So, it's probably better if we talk somewhere more private, **Tiendal**..."

"You'll regret this," Jenkins hissed with such rage that I was surprised steam didn't erupt from his ears.

"I regret every time I meet you," I said with a sarcastic smile. "One more regret won't change a thing." Then I looked up and said dreamily, "Just imagine the headlines..."

"Okay, let's go," Jenkins said, heading for the door. "And put something on."

"No problem," I said, smirking as I picked up my jacket from the floor.

We left the office building through the back door and got into a car that was already waiting. We didn't talk on the way, which, in general, was understandable—who would want to discuss such things in front of their driver?

Soon, we arrived at Jenkins's mansion and, like last time, went up to his bedroom. Jenkins closed the door and nodded toward the bed. I took it as an invitation to enter, so I walked over to the bed and sat on the edge. Jenkins approached the bed as well and sat down a meter away from me.

For several minutes, we sat in silence, just staring at each other. Of course, I was torn apart by the questions I wanted to ask, but I didn't want to be the first to break the silence. I wanted Jenkins to speak up first, but for some reason, he wasn't in any hurry to do so. He just sat there, thinking, probably deciding what to do with me.

And this question was far from simple. What should be done with someone as reckless as me, who, moreover, knew too much? The answer seemed obvious, and though I should have been horrified by its clarity, I wasn't afraid at all. It was either due to my recklessness or my deep conviction that he still needed me for something, but that was a fact. I wasn't scared, and I was even a little bored because I desperately wanted to talk, while he stubbornly remained silent.

Finally, Jenkins made a decision and said, "It took you some time to guess..."

I was relieved that he finally spoke up, so I rushed to keep the conversation going. "It wasn't so hard to guess, but it was hard to believe that this was even possible. I'm a rational person. I don't believe in magic."

"So, what's changed?"

I shrugged. "Too many facts have converged."

Jenkins chuckled. "And what does that change for you?"

"Everything."

Jenkins chuckled again and said nothing, but it was obvious he was curious to hear the explanation, so I continued without waiting for a question.

"You see... Robert Jenkins is just an eccentric businessman. Handsome, rich, successful, but nothing extraordinary. Tiendal, on the other hand, is undoubtedly special. A genius who remained an indispensable adviser to many pharaohs. A man whose history has been studied by scholars for most of their lives. A passionate lover whose account contains the ruined lives of thousands of women. And this extraordinary person turned out to be sexually attached to me, a typical 21st-century student. Certainly, this is a tremendous honor... But I'm dying of curiosity. What's so special about me, **Tiendal**?"

"I don't know, **Ilze**."

If I hadn't been sitting, I definitely would've fallen. But since there was nowhere for me to fall, I just coughed. When I finished, I swallowed and, just to be sure, asked again, "Sorry, what did you say?!"

Jenkins was clearly pleased with the effect his words had, so he confirmed them with equal satisfaction. "Yes, you heard me right. You are the reincarnation of Ilze."

The instinct to reject this information kicked in, so I clarified again, but phrased it slightly differently. "How do you know this?"

"It's simple," he said calmly. "There was something special about her. I don't know exactly what, but even after her betrayal, no woman could outshine her memory. We were connected, and magic allowed me to use that connection for my own purposes. Only a woman containing a part of Ilze could unlock the secret room for my reincarnation ritual. Sometimes it took a considerable amount of time to find her, but I was always successful."

I sighed. It was hard to argue with the logic of this explanation, but I still refused to believe it. So, I decided to ask for more information and started with, "How could you be sure that part of her soul would move into a human, a woman, but not into an animal?"

"I took care of this," Jenkins said confidently, and his certainty somehow made me mentally accept the information, despite its incredibility.

I lowered my gaze and rubbed my forehead thoughtfully. Being the Chosen meant being Ilze's reincarnation. But if this were true, it meant Ilze had lived as many lives as Tiendal himself and, in theory, like him, she should remember something from her past. But I only remembered 21 years of my life, nothing beyond that, which made me question the truth of Tiendal's words again.

I took a deep breath and asked, "Why don't I remember anything from my previous lives?"

"I retained a part of her soul, but not the memories or past experiences. Every woman she relocates to receives a piece of her beauty. You don't remember anything from previous lives, but the connection with them is preserved. Why do you think you've always been passionate about ancient history? Why did you decide to become an archaeologist?"

Yes, indeed, I thought. *I have good logic and, generally, a mathematical mindset, but I've never seen myself as a mathematician or a programmer. Since childhood, though, I've been obsessed with historical literature and the scent of dust on old things.*

Yet one thing remained unclear to me, so I asked, "But how did you find those women?"

"The scent. Only these women could sense the specific fragrance that others couldn't. I used this ability to find them."

That's it, I thought. *This peculiar scent in the Dark Isthmus, the one no one else could sense except me. The scent I detect when Jenkins approaches, which grows stronger when he's angry or excited. Who would've thought this was the password?*

I looked up and stared at Jenkins, unsure of what to say.

Jenkins caught my stare and grinned. "Funny, isn't it?" he said thoughtfully. "I always had to spend a lot of time and energy searching for those women. Only one came to me herself. And although I had to wait a long time for her... it was definitely worth it."

"Oh my God!" I whispered, covering my face in frustration. "So, none of what happened in Tiamon was an accident."

"Yeah, true," he nodded. "I sent you the signals that led you to the ancient door. And, fortunately, you were smart enough to open the puzzle lock."

"God, it's all my fault," I exhaled, grabbing my head with both hands. "I shouldn't have gone to Tiamon. I'm a victim of senseless randomness."

"Your trip to Tiamon wasn't random," Jenkins objected reassuringly. "That was your dream for several years, don't you remember?"

"How the hell do you know that?"

"Sorry," he shrugged. "I couldn't resist the temptation to dig around in your head a bit while you were my guest in the secret room."

"But how did that part of Ilze end up inside me?"

"That was random. Think of it as a blessing."

A blessing? *Damn, what a blessing*! I thought, rolling my eyes. But after taking another breath and calming down a bit, I asked neutrally, "How many lives have you had?"

"Ten. This one's the eleventh."

"Do you remember all of your previous lives and experiences?"

"Of course."

"Wow. That's truly incredible," I said, my voice filled with genuine respect and amazement. "But what about me? What happens to me now?"

"You're doomed. That's why I told you all this."

"What do you mean, doomed?"

"Just what it means."

I took a breath, preparing to ask a clarifying question, but Jenkins didn't give me a chance to speak. "Enough talking," he said in a tone that left no room for objection. "You've pleased my eyes with that sexy outfit. I think it's time you took it off."

"Seriously, Jenkins? I was really hoping we'd stick to talking today."

"Well, no. Only a complete idiot would pass up this opportunity," he said with a grin, confidently reaching for the fastener of my bra. I managed to take just one breath before the flame of passion inside me grew uncontrollably...

***

Jenkins had to get back to work, so he dropped me off at the dorm on his way to the office. It was a kind and noble gesture. Nothing was stopping him from leaving me on the side of the road and letting me deal with this on my own, but he didn't. I decided not to test his patience, kept quiet during the ride, and even thanked him when I got out of the car.

As soon as I got to my room, I texted Tony to let him know I was fine, back home, and that Jenkins was on his way back. Jenkins had been gone for a couple of hours instead of the half hour Tony had asked for, so I figured Tony's colleagues were done at the office. I let Tony know about Jenkins, just in case.

Tony responded instantly: "Thank goodness! Thanks! Kiss you!"

I set my phone aside, undressed, and stepped into the shower. I stood under the warm streams for a long time, trying to wash away the exhaustion and stress of the day. The water eased my physical fatigue, but my mind remained restless.

I got out of the shower and made myself some tea. While the tea brewed, I changed into my house dress and combed my hair. Taking the cup, I sat on the windowsill. Cool air drifted in from the open window, a reminder that autumn was approaching. I wrapped my hands around the warm cup and took a sip, savoring the fragrance. For a moment, my anxiety receded, but just as quickly, the thought that haunted me returned and shattered the peace. I set the cup down and gazed up at the sky.

Doomed... What did he mean by that? I don't remember anything in the legend hinting at the inevitability of my death. Could he have been bluffing? But if not... how much time do I have left?

CHAPTER 36: CUNNING PLAN

Two days later, the academic semester began, and I plunged into a sea of new faces and impressions. Unlike many students, I always enjoyed returning to classes after vacation. Over the summer, I missed my friends, classmates, and the time we spent together. Plus, it was always exciting to see what we'd learn and who would teach us.

But this summer was so intense that I barely noticed it ending, let alone missed anyone. The new semester caught me by surprise, leaving me no time to mentally prepare. I had to jump into work mode on the fly while juggling my equally hectic social life. It drained a lot of my energy, often leaving me exhausted, which was a blessing in disguise, as it stopped me from constantly reflecting on Tiendal's words.

Still, the nagging question found its way through the university bustle. Whenever I wasn't busy with friends or caught up in discussions with professors, the question would creep back into my mind, poisoning my thoughts and drilling holes in my positivity with sharp doubt. No matter how hard I tried to distract myself, his words still echoed in my mind, forcing me to ask for the hundredth time, *What did he mean by 'doomed?'*

I wasn't good at hiding my concern, and Gladys noticed. Several times, she asked if I was okay and offered help, but I brushed it off with a forced smile every time.

Despite trying to appear strong, I wasn't fine, and I did need help.

More than anything, however, I needed an answer to the nagging question that kept me from breathing easy or living in peace. But with no hope of ever getting another Q&A session with Tiendal, I saw no way out of the darkness my mind was dragging me into.

I hadn't seen Tony in days. I missed him a lot, but knowing he was busy, I never called or texted him first. Tony, on the other hand, texted me at every opportunity, which, I must admit, he found quite often. Tony's texts were mostly just emojis or short phrases like "love you," "hug you," or "miss you"—typical couple talk. But Tony wasn't the type to express his feelings like that. I sensed it was his way of checking if I was okay, and it wasn't my reply's content that mattered to him, but the fact that I responded. That's why I made sure to reply right away, no matter where I was or who I was with when his message came through. Although nothing bad might have happened if I hadn't replied immediately, I didn't want to stress Tony out. I was afraid that if he got nervous, he might overlook something important. I wanted him to focus on his work without worrying about me.

One evening, however, Tony sent me a text that was very different from all the others. It was an actual question: "Is it okay if I come in 10 minutes?"

For some reason, I felt confused when I saw it, and instead of replying right away, I hesitated for half a minute before finally typing "Sure."

It's hard to say what exactly confused me about his message. I guess I didn't entirely understand why he asked if I would mind him coming. Well, how could I be against it? All these days I died to see him and to hear his voice. Why ask, seriously? He could've just stopped by without notification—in our dorm no one bothers about this at all. Well, yes, maybe that was the reason. When you live in an environment where everything is decided in the moment, you involuntarily become part of it too. That's why, maybe, when Jenkins stormed into my days and adjusted my plans without asking for my opinion, despite how bad it was, it felt less unusual for me than normal social behavior.

Before Tony showed up at my door, I kept overthinking, looking at the situation from every angle. One moment, the message seemed like a bad sign, and the next, it felt like a sign of mistrust. Then I tried convincing myself it was just a sign of respect, but my mind kept searching for some hidden trick. Only Tony's happy smile and the gentle touch of his lips made me realize how pointless my doubts had been.

"I hope I didn't ruin your plans for the evening," Tony said, pulling back slightly and stroking my hair.

"Of course not," I said, smiling. "You're my most desired guest, and I'm happy to change my plans for you anytime."

"Glad to hear that. Still, I'll try to let you know about my visits earlier in the future. The news came unexpectedly, and I had to act fast."

"Honestly, if you'd just dropped by, I'd have been less nervous than when I got your text. I didn't know what to think."

"Ouch, sorry about that. I just really needed to see you and talk to you in private. But I figured since your classes had started, your 'always surrounded by people' mode might be on. So I decided that it would be better to notify you beforehand than to appear in the middle of something and make you explain to everyone who I am."

"Do you think the girls would die of envy if I told them you were my boyfriend?"

"I don't know. But I'm against people dying, so it's probably best they're unaware. Boyfriend, huh? You've never called me that before. I like it," Tony said, smiling as he blushed slightly and kissed me again.

Seeing Tony happy and confident was a pleasure. Watching him slowly overcome his embarrassment and insecurities, no longer afraid to show his feelings for me, was both inspiring and reassuring. I especially needed it now, after several days of futile struggle with the annoying worms of doubt.

After we finished kissing, we went inside and sat on the bed. Tony looked at me, smiled, and said, "I don't even know how to put this, but I think we have something to celebrate."

"Wow, really?"

"Yes. These guys worked even quicker than I expected. It took just a few days to gather the evidence. Now I have enough to put Jenkins behind bars for good. And it wouldn't have been possible without your help!"

"Oh, it's just... great," I said, unsure, still not believing my ears.

Tony nodded, confirming that I'd heard him correctly.

"Well, so... how did you pull it off? What was your cunning plan?" I asked with a smile, hoping the details would fill the gaps and help me finally believe what I'd just heard.

"I don't know how cunning it was, but it worked. The plan was this:

We sent our people undercover to two labs. Their job was to find out how the drug shipments were disguised. Turns out, with four labs running, Jenkins no longer had the ability to personally send and receive the goods using his disguise spell. Plus, he was sure we weren't watching him anymore, so he came up with an easier way. The drugs were transported as medicine, with fake paperwork.

That's when I had a crazy idea. To get the evidence, I decided not to go after Jenkins, but his customers. Our agents hid timed explosive devices in the boxes of fake medicine. The devices went off as soon as the goods were loaded onto the customer's truck, and Jenkins's people got their money and left for a safe distance. Preliminary analysis showed Jenkins's drugs burned fast. So after the explosions, the truck's contents went up in flames almost instantly. So, the customers found their trucks empty.

Since kings prefer to deal with kings, not pawns, some serious people came to Jenkins in a frenzy to sort things out. They were so emotional they forgot to be cautious and came straight to Jenkins's office, where we were able to record their conversation.

Jenkins, unaware of the problem, rushed to the lab to figure out what happened, and we caught him there too. As soon as Jenkins left, we raided all the labs. So now, we have more than enough evidence to prove his involvement in the drug trade. But with the people he's angered, getting arrested might actually be a reward for him."

"Wow! You really know your stuff."

"Thanks, I try."

"What's next?"

"Well, with all the evidence we have, it'll take a few days to get the order for Jenkins's arrest."

"Do you think I can consider myself free now?"

"Not yet, but soon, you will be."

I covered my mouth with both hands and looked up at the ceiling. It was hard to put into words—a mix of gratitude, happiness, and stubborn disbelief.

Tony gave me a minute to digest the information before continuing, "The next few days could be dangerous. I suppose Jenkins will try to escape, and he'll most likely take his recharger with him. We've already notified airports, railway stations, and the road police, but to ensure your safety, I'd like you to move to my place."

"Well, but... I still need to attend classes."

"Tayra, dear, nothing will happen if you miss a few days. Believe me, if he gets to you, there'll be no attending classes anyway."

"Um... okay, but Tony, this seems like too much. I don't want to be a bother..."

"Tayra, what are you talking about? Having you around is nothing but a pleasure. So, grab your essentials, and let's go."

"Now?"

"Yep, and the sooner, the better."

Every minute, my life just gets more interesting... I thought, rushing to get ready.

CHAPTER 37: RUINING THE BARRIERS

To Tony's surprise, I was ready in under fifteen minutes, and we left the dormitory before it even got dark. Within half an hour, we reached a cozy residential area. After parking under a tall apartment building, we took the elevator to the 14th floor, where Tony's apartment was.

Tony unlocked the door, and we stepped into a small hallway with three doors: one to a living room, another to a bedroom, and probably the last to a bathroom. I paused at the doorstep, glanced around, and smiled.

Tony noticed and asked, "Does this remind you of something?"

"Um... Yep, it reminded me of Portonapoulos's puzzle about the three doors."

"Exactly," Tony chuckled. "It was the first thing I thought of when I got home after that meeting. But fear not, no crocodiles, poison gas, or arrows here—so come in and make yourself at home."

"Okay," I said shyly, and after taking off my shoes, I walked into the living room.

The room was more spacious than it seemed from the hallway, combining a kitchen and an office area. The furnishings were modest and minimalistic, but nice. What really caught my attention, though, was the perfect cleanliness—completely contrary to the bachelor pad cliché.

I turned to Tony and asked, "Do you even spend time here?"

"It happens. Why?" he shrugged.

"It can't be this clean where people actually live."

"Oh, that," Tony laughed. "Well, I like order, and I don't really have time to make a mess. But I'll admit, it's not always like this. I cleaned up for your visit, so consider this the demo version."

I sighed in relief and chuckled. "Well, thank God, because I was already thinking... Um... Never mind, it doesn't matter."

"It does matter, Tayra," Tony said, coming up from behind, wrapping an arm around my waist, and kissing my shoulder. "But you don't have to tell me if you don't want to."

I brushed Tony's hand and smiled, though I felt tense and a bit embarrassed, unsure of how to act. Everything felt so surreal. Deep down, I feared waking up to find it was nothing but a mirage from my overactive imagination. So, I clung to anything that could prove otherwise, and nothing convinced me more than the warmth of Tony's embrace.

Tony leaned close, kissed the top of my ear, and said, "Let's go. I'll cook dinner."

My eyebrows shot up as I turned, not bothering to hide my surprise. "You can cook? I mean... aren't you too good to be real?"

Tony laughed. "You're overestimating me. My cooking skills are pretty inconsistent, and the results are usually unpredictable. But I'll do my best, I promise."

"Can I help?"

"Sure, if you'd like."

Cooking together was fun and enlightening. Once we started, I realized Tony had been modest about his cooking skills. So, I took on the role of apprentice and followed his instructions closely.

My embarrassment from the unfamiliar situation faded soon. We chatted, joked, and messed around like we had before the expedition, but now there was no need to hide our feelings. It was one of those rare moments when Tony let go of his fears and worries and was simply happy. He didn't waste a single chance to kiss or hug me, and it felt incredible.

We devoured the meal quickly, laughing and chatting about meaningless nonsense, which created a unique, relaxed atmosphere. Being a team felt natural for us, even in the smallest things. After dinner, we washed the dishes and cleaned the kitchen. To my surprise, we did it so effortlessly as if we'd been living together for years. Once we finished, we moved to the large window in the living room. By then, night had fallen, and countless stars filled the sky.

Tony gently wrapped his arms around my shoulders and said, "The sky here isn't the same as in the clearing, but it's still beautiful, even with the city lights."

"Do you often admire the stars?" I asked, nestling into his arms, pressing my back tighter against his chest.

"Well, probably not. To be honest, when I get home, I'm usually too tired or lost in thought to even look at the sky, let alone admire it. But I do find it beautiful. And you're the one who helped me see that."

"In my dorm room, I often sit on the windowsill and stare at the sky. It helps me relax, clear my mind. I'd invite you to join me one day, but I don't think you'd be interested, since the view here is much better."

"I wouldn't say it's better—maybe I'm just biased. I associate everything about your dorm room with you, which makes me like it by default. My home, though... it's more about loneliness and the constant crap going on around me."

"I'm sure you're exaggerating. Your place is lovely—you must've had plenty of happy moments here."

"Maybe," Tony said, gently turning me around, brushing my hair from my forehead. "But I hope to have more, with you. Here or anywhere. Because the place doesn't matter—it's the company that does."

There was something about the way he said it that made me nervous—spoken in one breath, almost a whisper, and his words seemed to come straight from his heart. He meant every word, and I got the sense he'd already had a few backup plans for our happy-ever-after if something went wrong with Jenkins's arrest. Tony was determined to stay with me, no matter what. And it scared me—how much he was invested and how little I could give in return.

My cheeks flushed, and I shyly dropped my gaze, trying to hide it. Tony smiled, gently sliding his fingers along my burning cheek, coaxing me to look at him. Hesitantly, I glanced up and drowned in the adoration of his bottomless blue eyes. In that moment, Tony's lips found mine, confident and sure, as his hands pulled me closer. My heart raced, and my cheeks burned even more. Tony had never kissed me like this before. His touch was tender, as always, but his lips were more passionate, more demanding.

If my boyfriend had kissed me like this before the curse, I would've caught the hint right away and responded with all the passion I had, no questions asked. But now, my body was no help, and I could only rely on my brain—though it was a notorious overthinker and full of doubt. I wasn't sure of anything—starting with my interpretation of Tony's intentions and ending with how I should act to avoid messing it up. With every passing moment, I grew more confused, so I decided to clear things up—at least a little—before my mind exploded from the whirlwind of thoughts.

I gently broke the kiss and whispered, "Tony, what are you... I mean, what are we doing?"

Tony smiled and said, "Isn't it obvious? I'm accepting the offer you made a few days ago. Or have you changed your mind?"

"Um... No, I haven't. It's just... Are you sure?"

"Of course I am. More than ever."

Tony cupped my face and pressed his warm lips to my temple. I was about to kiss him back, but with the tension building inside me, I tilted my head so awkwardly it seemed like I was dodging his lips instead of meeting them.

Still holding my cheeks, Tony pulled back slightly and, looking into my eyes, asked, "Is something wrong?"

"No, nothing. It's just... it's such a strange feeling. I've imagined this so many times, but now that it's actually happening, I'm embarrassed. It's so stupid."

Tony ran his hand through my hair and smiled. "Believe me, I'm as nervous as a first-grader on his first day of school, and your embarrassment only makes it worse."

"You don't look stressed at all. You seem pretty calm to me."

"I'm trained to hide it, and I'm naturally reserved. Expressing my feelings is harder for me than keeping a neutral expression. But that doesn't mean I don't feel anything."

"I get it, and I respect that, but I like it when you show me how you feel. I especially need that during moments of intimacy since, because of the curse, I'm physically numb. I can't feel physical pleasure from your touch or gauge your response to mine. It's like we're on different wavelengths. Or rather... I don't vibrate at all. It's like I'm a pilot trying to land on a night runway. The equipment's malfunctioning, so I have to rely on visuals. But if the runway's dark, there's nothing to rely on, and only a miracle could stop the plane from crashing. So, give me those 'runway lights' if you can. I don't know exactly how, but just make it clear what feels good and what doesn't. I need to know—it's important."

"Okay, I'll try," Tony said, smiling again. "Is there anything else bothering you?"

I shook my head, crossing my arms playfully and grabbing the edges of my T-shirt, ready to pull it off, but Tony gently covered my hands, stopping them before they moved higher.

"Not here," he said softly. "I don't want to share your beauty with the neighbors—they've probably already claimed front-row seats. I want you all to myself, so let's go somewhere more private."

"Isn't there a window in the bedroom?"

"There are curtains."

I smiled, giving Tony my hand, inviting him to lead me. In moments, we were standing by the bed in a cozy, minimalist bedroom. The soft glow from a modern LED chandelier set the perfect romantic mood.

I took a few steps back, making sure Tony could see me clearly, and began to undress. This time, I moved slowly and gracefully, giving him the chance to admire my curves.

In just my lingerie, I moved closer to Tony, teasing his lips with a flick of my tongue before sliding my hands under his T-shirt. I pulled it up, and Tony's hands lifted too, helping me reveal his perfectly sculpted chest and broad shoulders. Slowly sliding my hands up Tony's back, I brushed my lips against his chest, then trailed them down his torso, covering every inch with gentle kisses. Tony seemed a little confused, his body slow to respond, so I moved on intuition and past experience, hoping I was heading in the right direction. The sensation was strange, even a little frightening, but my genuine desire to please Tony pushed me to continue.

When I knelt down and lowered Tony's jeans, caressing the base of his stomach, he seemed to come to his senses. With a faint moan, he gently but firmly lifted me up and pulled me close. Tony's palms stroked my back affectionately as his lips trailed down my neck with the same tenderness. Reaching my bra fastener, Tony skillfully unhooked it, letting the garment fall to the floor before fondling my breasts.

Despite his obvious arousal, Tony remained in strict control of every move. He seemed afraid to do anything that might cause me discomfort, handling me like I was fragile. His touches were exceptionally light, full of tenderness and care. No one had ever treated me like this before—it was unusual and made me feel shy. With every move and glance, Tony showed me I was his queen. Deep down, I worried I wasn't worthy of the title. But the adoration in Tony's eyes was so flattering, and he seemed to enjoy the touch of my skin so much that my heart filled with a warm, involuntary glow.

I wrapped my arms around Tony's neck and pressed my lips to his, pushing my chest against his. Tony moaned again, his fingers caressing my back and thighs, pressing harder into my skin. With each moment, Tony's hands and lips grew more passionate, yet held onto a boundless tenderness I couldn't explain. Tony's love was fiery, yet soft, gentle, and caring. I couldn't compare this feeling to anything. I knew without a doubt that if it weren't for the curse, this would have been the best feeling in the world. But despite my physical insensitivity, knowing I could give pleasure to the man I love made me insanely happy.

After reaching climax, Tony pulled me close, pressing his lips to my temple in a tender gesture of gratitude. He stayed like that for a few seconds before rolling to the side. After catching his breath, Tony hugged me.

We lay in silence for several minutes, tightly cuddled. Then Tony looked into my eyes and whispered, "I love you, Tayra. I love you so much. I'm so lucky to have you."

I pressed myself closer to Tony, sinking deeper into his arms, and whispered, "I love you too."

CHAPTER 38: OBSESSIVE THOUGHT

The next morning we got up early, because Tony had to go to work.

"I'll be back as soon as I can," he said, kissing me by the door.

"Should I stay here all day?" I asked, sheepish.

"Yes, and please be good. Don't open the door for anyone, and try not to get too bored."

"Okay," I sighed, "I'll miss you."

I closed the door behind Tony and went to the kitchen. A few dirty plates were left from breakfast. I washed them in under a minute and looked around, lost.

Well... I thought, *this is the downside of dating a neat guy. There's nothing to clean in his apartment. I feel completely useless. What should I do with myself?*

I wandered around the kitchen, peeking into cupboards and opening the refrigerator.

Well, thank God, I thought, *there's enough to make dinner with, so at least I'll have something to do.*

I left the kitchen and wandered through the rooms. Even though I carefully examined every corner and studied the view from each window, the whole tour took me no more than half an hour.

Okay, take it easy, I told myself. *Everyone needs a lazy day sometimes. You never worry about what to do when you get a free day in the dorm, so what's the difference?*

I turned on the kettle, brewed some tea, grabbed a cup, and went into the living room. I walked over to the window and looked down.

Yeah, I thought, *the fourteenth floor isn't the third. It's great for stargazing, but looking down... it's kind of creepy. I'm already feeling dizzy. Anyone who falls from this height is doomed.*

It felt like a gunshot went off in my head. My vision darkened, and it became hard to breathe. Struggling to keep my balance, I placed the cup on the floor and sat down beside it.

"Doomed..." echoed through my mind, over and over.

I took several deep breaths, trying to calm myself and steady my racing heartbeat.

It's just a panic attack, I told myself. *Nothing bad happened, you just need to calm down and focus on something else.*

I picked up the cup and took a sip of tea, fixing my gaze on the surface of the liquid. The smooth, rippling movement was hypnotic, soothing.

Everything's fine, I told myself, but when I looked into the cup again, horror gripped me. Jenkins's black, fiery eyes stared back at me, and his voice echoed in my mind: "You're doomed. That's why I told you all this."

Heck! Heck! Heck! I screamed. *Please, just disappear! I don't want to think about it anymore. I don't want it! I just don't want to!*

I went back to the kitchen, poured the tea down the sink, washed the cup, and returned to the living room. Grabbing my phone, I found a movie I'd been meaning to watch and pressed play. The plot captivated me right away. I was completely immersed, genuinely feeling the struggles of the characters as they fought desperately for their love, overcoming every obstacle. No wonder I was so hooked—the story felt all too familiar.

Everything was fine until a certain moment. In the last quarter of the film, the main female character was diagnosed with a fatal illness.

That's when everything went downhill. The rest of the film focused on her shift in worldview and her growing acceptance of her fate. I hit the stop button several times, debating whether to finish it, but my optimism kept me going. I sincerely hoped for a miracle—a happy ending despite everything. But alas, the director and screenwriter were fucking realists. Not only did they let the heroine die, but they made sure to show every vivid detail of her loved ones mourning her loss.

Great, I thought, closing the movie, *Just what I needed. How in the world did I end up choosing this one out of all the options*?

I set the phone aside, slid off the couch onto the floor, covered my head with both hands, and thought. '*Doomed...*' *He must have said that just to scare me. He sensed he was losing his power over me. A frightened person is easier to control, so this is nothing more than an attempt to subdue me.*

I started flipping through the knowledge I'd gained from Paulo's book, remembering how it said the lives of Tiendal's abandoned mistresses were usually cut short.

Okay, I thought, *just calm down and think rationally. What's written in the book has nothing to do with you. It's talking about suicide. These women couldn't come to terms with their insensitivity or rebuild their personal lives. They went mad or took their own lives. I can rebuild my life; I'm already well on my way. I don't think I've ever been this happy. I'm finally doing well. So why, why does this stupid thought keep creeping into my head and refusing to leave me alone*? *Why*?!

I tried to sleep, read a book, surf the Internet, but no matter what I did, I saw Jenkins's black eyes everywhere, and I kept hearing his voice uttering that single phrase.

Finally, I went back to the kitchen and started cooking. I was determined to forget Jenkins, to block him and his words from my mind. But as soon as I picked up the knife, his black eyes stared back at me from its mirrored surface, and his cold, indifferent voice echoed in my ears again.

Okay, I said, setting the knife aside, *you win. I can't hide from my fears—I need to face them. No matter how well Tony and I planned everything, there's something we might've missed. That means the plan needs adjusting. I hope Tony gets back soon. There's something we need to discuss.*

Fortunately, I didn't have to wait long. I'd just finished fiddling around in the kitchen when I heard the rattle of a key in the lock. I went to the hallway and stood near the door, waiting for it to open. As soon as Tony appeared in the doorway, I threw my arms around his neck.

Tony caught me by the waist and, smiling, asked, "How was your day?"

"Boring as hell."

"My poor girl," Tony chuckled, stroking my head.

I inhaled his scent deeply and hugged him tighter.

"Okay, okay," Tony said, gently stroking my back, "let me come in at least."

"Fine," I said, releasing him from my tight embrace. I nodded toward the living room and added, "Come join me there."

Tony gave me a "roger that" smile and headed for the bathroom, while I went to serve dinner. By that moment, I'd already had everything ready, so I just scanned the table with an appraising look, making sure I hadn't forgotten anything. This is when Tony entered the kitchen and noticed the results of my efforts.

"Wow!" he said, surprised. "This is unexpected. I mean, it's probably the first time in my independent life I've come home to food waiting for me."

I laughed. "What else can a prisoner do to fight boredom? I hope it's okay that I took over your kitchen a bit."

"Oh, I don't mind at all. You're free to do whatever you want," Tony said, coming closer and kissing me on the cheek. "But be careful, these benefits might make me want to keep you as a prisoner forever."

"Sit down and try it before you start praising me. I don't even know if it turned out well."

"Even if it didn't, I'd never admit it."

"In vain. Maybe I'd make a note for the future if you told me the truth."

"Or maybe you'd take offense and never cook for me again."

"You make a lot of sense. Did you learn that the hard way?"

"Trust me, you don't want to know. By the way, it's marvelous. I love it!"

"Flatterer!"

"Nope, it's heartfelt."

"Great, bon appétit then."

At first, I was going to bring up my obsessive thoughts during dinner, but Tony was eating with such pleasure, looking so relaxed and happy, that I didn't want to ruin his mood. Besides, I didn't know how to phrase it in a way that Tony would take it with understanding, rather than hostility. So, I decided to postpone the conversation until a more appropriate moment.

Choosing the right moment, however, proved difficult, because right after dinner, Tony got a call and went into another room to answer it. He made a few more calls, constantly shuttling between the bedroom and living room, until he finally sat down at his laptop to answer messages. He looked serious and focused, so I decided to wait patiently until he was free, avoiding unnecessary questions.

Quietly, I took a seat by the living room window and gazed up at the sky. It wasn't quite dark outside yet, so there were hardly any stars. Still, the remnants of sunset colors, complemented by the deepening blue gradient, looked truly beautiful. As I contemplated the sky, I began to doubt the reasonableness of my request to Tony, one I still didn't know how to voice. My resolve faded almost as quickly as the night's darkness overtook the fading daylight. At some point, I decided there was no need to raise the issue and stress out my boyfriend with problems that might not even exist.

I felt relieved to finally make up my mind on a matter I was so tired of, and my decision felt right—until I accidentally looked down. As soon as I saw the ground fourteen floors below, my head began to spin, and the voice that had been pestering me all day echoed louder in my ears.

I sank onto the couch, burying my head in my hands. *No*, I thought, *I can't just ignore this. I need to tell Tony and convince him to help me with what's on my mind. But what if he doesn't agree*?

I don't know how long I sat there, sorting through every possible pro and con. If overthinking were a profession, I'd be an expert, thanks to my outstanding natural talent. I was so lost in thought that I didn't even notice Tony approaching. When he put his hand on my shoulder, I flinched as if from a burn.

"Ouch," Tony said. "I didn't mean to scare you. Are you okay?"

"Yeah, I'm fine. Don't worry about it."

"Sorry for leaving you alone. I shouldn't have done that. It's just that some work stuff came up unexpectedly, and I had to deal with it right away. I thought it would take less time."

"It's okay, I understand. You don't need to apologize. You seemed a bit tense while you were on the phone. Did something happen?"

"No, nothing serious. Just a regular work issue, but it couldn't be postponed. It's normal for us, but it can be frustrating sometimes."

"I get it. Um... Look, Tony... I don't want to spend our time on more unpleasant stuff, but I'm afraid I have no choice. I really need to tell you something."

"Okay, I'm all ears."

"Well, it's been bothering me for a few days. I tried to push the thoughts away, but I couldn't. I can't stop thinking about it. You see... the day I had to get Jenkins out of the office, I told him I knew who he really was. That got him to talk, and I learned something. He told me that to open the secret room, a woman had to be Ilze's reincarnation. They detected these women by their sensitivity to a specific smell. It means I carry a part of Ilze, and my trip to Tiamon and everything that happened afterward wasn't just an accident. It was meant to happen. But that's not even the main part. At the end of our conversation, Tiendal said he told me all this because I was doomed. I asked him to explain, but he wouldn't tell me what he meant. I'm scared, Tony. I'm really scared. There are so many questions, and he seems like the only one with the answers."

Tony sighed and shrugged. "Well, the fact that you're Ilze's reincarnation is interesting, but it doesn't really change anything. As for 'doomed,' I'm pretty sure he was bluffing. Don't worry about it."

"And what if he isn't lying? What if it's true? I can't dwell in this uncertainty any longer. It's driving me crazy. I need to find out. But only he has the answers I need, so there's no other option but to ask him myself."

Tony sighed and rubbed his forehead. "You have no idea what you're asking of me..."

"I know, it's insane... but if we let him kidnap me, I'll have a chance to get the information we need."

Tony winced and shook his head. "He's cornered, Tayra. He's got nothing to lose, and that makes him dangerous."

"But we know he'll need me until he reaches the Source of Force."

"But what if we're wrong, and he can reach the Source of Force without the last key? What will he do to you then?"

"And what if he dies from not reaching the source, and I die with him because we're tied?"

"Well," Tony sighed, "let's think through possible solutions."

"I see only one solution. I go back to the dorm and start attending classes as usual. He'll grab me soon enough and take me somewhere. He's short on time, and he needs the last key, so he'll probably head to the Amhitiemar temple. That's where you can meet us. I hope by then I'll have gotten all the information we need."

Tony's eyes froze. He stared at me for so long without blinking that I started worrying about his eyeballs. When his eyelids finally moved, I sighed in mental relief. That blink seemed to start a chain reaction—the rest of the muscles in Tony's face slowly waking up. Tony's expression shifted, indicating he was deep in thought. Judging by his intense focus, he was probably calculating every possible outcome of this crazy plan I'd come up with. Finally, Tony shook his head and whispered, "Lord, am I seriously saying yes to this?"

I gave a slight smile and nodded. "Thank you."

"We need to hide a tracer on you to monitor your location. There's still a chance we're wrong and Amhitiemar isn't his destination, so I'll need to know where to find you if that's the case."

"Yeah, you're right, but..."

"But where can we hide it to make sure it won't be noticed or lost when this bastard undresses you? That's the real question."

I shrugged, staying silent. Tony knew exactly what I wanted to say, and it was as tricky as it was embarrassing. To my surprise, Tony spoke without a hint of jealousy. All I heard in his voice was genuine concern and the desire to find a solution. Obviously, I was no help, so I just sat silently, trying not to attract any attention, afraid to make a sound, even with a breath or a blink.

Tony looked me over thoughtfully, then winced. "Okay, I hope I'll have figured it out by tomorrow. You'll spend one more night here, okay? I'll drive you to the dorm early in the morning, so you can make it to your first lecture."

"O-okay," I nodded.

"Don't take anything valuable to the university, and leave your phone in the dorm. It'll be the first thing they get rid of, and I know it has things you care about."

"They? Do you think he'll send a team of thugs after me?"

"I'd guess two, but he might think differently. Anyway, you don't expect him to come himself, do you? Dirty jobs like kidnapping are way beneath him."

"Yeah, I get it. Um… okay, so what do we do now?"

"Now I'm going to imprison you in my arms and keep you captive until you beg me to let you go," Tony said, pulling me close.

"You know that might never happen, right?"

"I do, and that's exactly what I'm counting on—because holding you is such a pleasure. But the next few nights, you might not get much sleep, so tonight you need to rest. I'll guard your peace and make sure nothing disturbs you."

Believe me, I thought, hugging Tony back and sinking deeper into his embrace, *the only reason I'm doing this is so I can stay in your arms longer than just tonight.*

CHAPTER 39: THE MISSING LINKS

It didn't take long for Jenkins's signal to arrive. When I got back from class, I spotted a piece of paper on the floor near my dorm room door. As soon as I bent down to pick it up, someone attacked me from behind, and within seconds, the world plunged into pitch darkness.

I woke up in a dark room. The smell of wood and dampness filled the air. I tried to move and realized I was tied up, probably to a chair.

Wow, I thought, *it worked as planned. But where am I*?

I kept my eyes open, hoping they'd adjust to the darkness, but it didn't help much.

Alright, I decided, *vision's no help. Let's rely on my other senses.*

I took a few deep breaths, trying to analyze the scents around me, but nothing gave me even a hint of where I was or what my surroundings might be. Then I listened to my body, surprised to feel none of the usual excitement I got when Jenkins was near. That worried me.

If he's not here, then why am I? *Kidnapping me makes no sense—he's the only one who needs me. Or is there something I don't know*? *Did I miscalculate his goals*? *His motives*? *If I did, I'm so screwed.*

Despite the lack of information, I tried to think of a plan. It felt like I'd spent hours tied to that damn chair, my hands bound tightly behind me, my wrists and shoulders aching. The pain, combined with my foggy mind, kept me from coming up with anything workable. So, task number one became escaping the chair.

I tried to move my hands to loosen the knot, but the ropes only dug deeper into my skin. Ignoring the pain, I tried to free one hand from the knot, but it was no use. I tried spinning in the chair, sliding down, even standing up, but none of it worked. I stopped struggling with the ropes and the stubborn chair, deciding to look around again.

By now, my eyes had finally adjusted to the darkness, and I could make out the fuzzy contours of the objects around me. The room I was in seemed like some kind of forest cabin. The windows were covered with curtains, but as the sky lightened outside, faint beams began slipping through the gaps.

So, I summarized, *it's night outside. I'm tied to a chair in a cabin in the middle of God knows where, and I seem to be alone. That's as stressful as it is perplexing. If he wanted to kill me, he'd choose a more effective way than dragging me into the forest to let me die. So, his plan must be different. I wonder when he's going to show up. He has to; otherwise, I don't even know what to think. I hope the tracer's working and Tony knows where I am. He'll find me. If not... Well, no panic. Nothing bad has happened yet. I just need to be patient.*

It took a great deal of patience, but when I finally felt the familiar waves of excitement, I could make out not only the shapes of the objects but also glimpses of their colors. By now, my hands were so numb I could barely feel them. Obviously, this was one of those rare moments when the thought of meeting Jenkins felt almost uplifting.

With a nasty creak that sent a jolt through my teeth, the cabin door opened, and the 'hero of my novel' appeared in the doorway.

"Good morning," he said coldly, stepping inside.

"Not that I'm happy to see you, but... hello."

"Happy? Even death wouldn't be enough to pay for what you've done."

"Seriously? And what exactly have I done that's worth that much?"

"Betrayed me. Again."

He spoke in his usual cold tone, but there were extra notes in it—surprisingly, it was fatigue, not anger or frustration, which would've been more appropriate for his situation. He looked so tired and indifferent that his usual gloss seemed to have faded. In black jeans and a green Henley with rolled-up sleeves, instead of his usual suit, he didn't look as demonic or powerful as he used to. He looked more like the guy next door who'd had a shitty week. The only thing connecting the man before me to the one who always stirred my darkest feelings was his eyes. The same pitch-black, scalding with that hellish flame. The moment I looked into them, the tiny crumbs of pity that had formed in my heart burned to ash, and I went on the offensive again.

"Come on, Tiendal, let's sort things out. I never betrayed you, just like Ilze never did. Betrayal implies breaking a promise of loyalty. I never promised you anything, and the poor girl was forced to make her vow. So, where's the betrayal?"

Tiendal arrogantly ignored my question, his spine-chilling gaze drilling into me, as he said thoughtfully, "I underestimated you. I was too soft on you—and that Weiler boy."

It was probably a threat, but my numb hands were causing so much discomfort that I was immune to it. Besides, I'm a quick learner, and my time with Jenkins had taught me a few tricks. So instead of pursuing the "too soft" remark, I decided to steer the conversation in a more interesting direction.

"Can you untie me, please? It's not like I can run away—I don't even know where we are. And just so you know, I had a chance to hide, but I chose to let you catch me. I need some answers, Tiendal."

"Don't you think you're not the one who can dictate the rules here?"

"Maybe. But it seems like you're out of options. Mafia on one side, secret service on the other, and your energy running low. Use your super abilities and look into the future—you'll see you're screwed no matter which path you choose."

"Do you promise to shut up if I untie you?"

"No, but I can try to be less rude."

"At least that's something," Jenkins muttered, coming up to my chair and untying the ropes.

Relieved to move again, I got up, stretched, and walked around the room. "Thanks. So, what's next?"

"We could die here," he said with an indifference that looked oddly out of place on him.

I stopped and turned to Jenkins, a grimace of disagreement on my face. "Are there any other options?"

"We can reach the Source of Force."

"Am I just your charger, or do I have another purpose?"

"Are you always this blunt and direct?"

"I'm just saving you time. From what I hear, you're running low on it."

"Same goes for you."

"So?"

"I need you to open the temple door in Amhitiemar."

"Why can't you do it yourself?"

"Nothing's free in this life. I have plenty of special abilities, but I can't read those symbols, and without that, I can't find the right pattern."

"Poor boy."

"Tayra, don't push me. I can't kill you—yet—but I have enough power to make your life a living hell."

"Just curious—when you torture me, do you feed off my suffering? Or is it purely for your moral satisfaction?"

"Tayra."

"Fine. So, what's hidden in there?"

"The key to the Source of Force."

"You know I'm going to barrage you with questions, so just tell me the whole story now."

"Alright, listen. The source of the Force is in an ancient book stored in a hidden room. To access it, you need a seal, which is protected by a specific magic that only I can use. At first, there was only one seal, hidden in a secret cache in the room. But then I developed a system for conducting reincarnation rituals.

The participants of the ritual were the Pharaoh, a woman to open the room, and several priests. The Pharaoh had to read the spell from the book, which meant he needed access to its contents. But since I trusted no one but myself, I made a replica of the seal for the Pharaoh. Outwardly, they looked identical, but my seal gave full access to the book, while the Pharaoh's only unlocked the spell for the ritual. The seals were linked so that if one was destroyed, the other would be ruined as well.

With each life, I trusted the pharaohs less and less. That's why, in each life, I created a new copy of the seal and hid it in a temple in a nearby city. The copies held the same power as the original, but they weren't tied to the pharaoh's seal and could survive even if he destroyed it.

In fact, that's exactly what happened after my argument with Pilzernath. Judging by what you know, I assume you're familiar with the story."

"Yeah, more or less."

"So, one of the seal's copies should be hidden in Amhitiemar."

I sighed, genuine bewilderment crossing my face. "You never cease to surprise me, Tiendal. Couldn't you have come up with a simpler reincarnation scheme? This one seems a bit too tangled to me."

"Yes, it's quite tricky, I won't deny that," he nodded. "But ancient magic isn't simple—it comes with a lot of technical restrictions."

"I'm not sure the Source of Force can get you out of the mess you're in. But I'm willing to help you with the door to the Amhitiemar temple—if you remove my curse."

"Tayra, you're clever, but incredibly naive. I can't remove your curse."

"Why not? I know you can control the attraction. Look at us now—we're standing here talking, and it's not a problem."

"We both know it's not your attraction to me that concerns you—it's your insensitivity."

"Well..." I shrugged, uncertain, and was about to say something, but Tiendal continued before I could respond.

"Look, Tayra," he said, his voice unusually soft, sending chills down my spine. "Maybe creating this curse was inhuman, and maybe I would've regretted it if I could feel things like pity or remorse. But what's done is done. Unfortunately for you, ancient magic can't be undone. If I die from a lack of vital energy, you'll die with me. But if I reach the Source of Force, this connection will break. You'll be able to live apart from me, but I'll remain the only man you desire, the only one who can give you pleasure. You'll be numb to any other man's touch. Forever. So, just accept it."

The ground seemed to disappear beneath my feet, and the room started spinning. I felt like I was about to fall, but I refused to show how deeply his words hit me. A lump formed in my throat, and when I spoke, the words came out painfully slow. All I could manage was, "Can I go outside?"

"You're welcome," Tiendal said with his usual calm, stepping aside to let me pass.

I left the cabin and stepped away from the entrance. The sun hadn't fully risen, but it was already light outside. My mood, however, wasn't suited to admiring the beauty of the morning forest. Everything seemed wrapped in fog, though not from tears, but from the ache in my heart. I wanted to cry, but the tears wouldn't come. The heavy pain just lingered inside, trapped with no way out.

I took a deep breath, filling my lungs with the cool morning air.

Accept... I whispered sadly. *I thought I'd **already** accepted it, but it turns out I was still clinging to the desperate hope that the curse could be broken. It was that hope that kept me fighting. But now that it's gone, my strength is gone too.*

I just wanted to lie down right there in the middle of the forest and die. I didn't want to go anywhere, worry about anything, solve any puzzles, or pretend to be a hero. The entire journey felt meaningless. I lost the last battle. I lost the war. And now, I had to admit it. I had to accept it.

I looked up at the sky, still not fully blue, and felt a drop slide down, tickling the side of my nose.

Well, finally, I thought. *Now you can cry, Tayra. No need to hide your weakness anymore.*

CHAPTER 40: CHANGE OF WORLDVIEW

Tears streamed down my cheeks, each one heavier than the last. In the early morning, I stood beside a shabby cabin in the middle of an unfamiliar forest, sobbing as if I needed to pour every bit of myself into those tears, leaving nothing behind.

But contrary to my hopes, the tears brought no relief, only a dull headache. I took a deep breath, filling my lungs with the invigorating coolness of the autumn morning, when suddenly, a voice came from behind me, "Tayra..."

"Leave me alone, Tiendal," I said through tears, not bothering to turn around. "Just for a few minutes. Let me mourn my grief without you here."

"You can cry while we walk. We need to go."

Once again shocked by his impenetrable callousness, I lifted my tear-streaked face and asked, "To Amhitiemar?"

"Yes," Tiendal replied with his usual equanimity, so outrageously inappropriate that the tears instantly dried in my eyes, and the urge to cry vanished as if it had never existed.

Can't you show some sympathy? Is it really that hard to express normal human emotions just once in your life? raced through my mind, but strangely, the words stayed unspoken. Prudence stepped in just in time, reminding me that appealing to Jenkins's emotions was about as effective as talking to a brick wall. So, I chose a more constructive question instead: "Is it far from here?"

"About twenty kilometers."

"Wow, that's really close. How did you find this place and manage to get here, considering how many people were chasing you?"

Jenkins raised his brows and rolled his eyes, which I took to mean the task wasn't easy. It was clear he didn't want to talk about it, so I changed the subject.

"Are we going to walk there?"

"Do you see any transport?"

"Who knows," I shrugged. "You're a wizard, maybe you could open a portal or something. Or fly on a broom, like Harry Potter. I think I saw one behind that cabin."

"Do you think it's funny?"

"I don't, but you're so hard to deal with, I'm running out of ideas. So, do you think we can get there in like four hours?"

"More like five or six, if we're lucky. The path won't be easy."

I didn't quite understand what he meant, but it became clear as soon as we set off. I'm not good at orienteering, so if someone asked me to explain exactly how we went, I'd have no idea. But I can tell you, it definitely wasn't a road meant for walking. First, we wriggled through the forest, weaving between trees and bushes. Then, we waded across a stream and climbed uphill until my feet were ready to quit their job. Finally, we reached a flat area with a path wide enough for two. Walking there was much more comfortable than the earlier parts of our journey, so I decided to spill everything that had built up inside me.

"I've thought a lot about your situation, Tiendal, and here's what I think: She never would've cheated on you if she loved you. If you hadn't forced her to be with you but tried to win her love like normal people do, everything could've been different. I'm sure your chances weren't zero. Any woman would've been flattered by the attention of a man with your intelligence and authority. Respect was the least you could've earned, but you chose fear and hatred, and that led to the outcome you deserved. It's Newton's Third Law: every action has an equal and opposite reaction. You get back exactly what you give.

Making others happy is happiness in itself. But to you, this simple truth is incomprehensible. Just imagine how things could've been. Instead of hating you, she could've loved you. Imagine her meeting you at home with a smile, gently wrapping her arms around your neck. She could've truly been yours, caressing you at night, her every cell savoring your closeness and touch.

Tiendal, you've lived ten lives in vain. You had power, money, women... you even prolonged your youth, edging closer to immortality. But you've never been happy, because no one ever loved you.

I've thought a lot about why you had so many women and no children. Now I understand. Children are love, and love is something that's out of reach for you. Because there's nothing in you to love."

"I've always considered love unimportant. And that's why I became who I am."

"Unimportant? Tiendal, you're a genius, but an idiot. Love rules the world—only love! Not money, not power, not lust! Love drives people to do incredible things. If it weren't for love, I wouldn't be standing here next to you. I would've died in that cell in Tiamon if my boyfriend hadn't convinced the rescuers to check the corridor again. You're cursed, Tiendal. Cursed with the inability to love.

You know, I don't care that the curse can't be broken. Even cursed, I can still make the person I love happy. But you can't bring happiness to anyone. You talk about pleasure, so know: with him, my heart feels what my body will never feel with you.

I should've hated you. For Ilze, for all the women who died because of you, for myself. But I pity you. And pity is a kind of love too."

The impenetrability of this man's emotional shield was almost enviable. He listened to the end of my philosophical tirade without moving a single muscle, keeping his pace steady and not even glancing in my direction, as if I weren't there. Somewhat bewildered by his lack of reaction, I sighed and turned away, determined to digest my disappointment in proud silence.

The view along our path hadn't changed much, and by then, I was already bored of admiring the trees. So, once my frustration subsided, I began thinking of other ways to stir up my traveling companion. I ran through the results of all my previous "research projects," but it seemed like I'd already tested every possible option, and new ideas weren't exactly rushing to find me. I was almost desperate to come up with something workable when Tiendal suddenly broke the silence. He turned his head toward me and asked, "Would you like to hear a story?"

The enthusiasm that filled me the moment he spoke immediately lit up my face, but I tried to play it cool and said, "Why not? The way is long."

Tiendal smirked and began, "In a small village, there lived an old man. One morning, he woke to the sound of a baby crying. The man stepped outside and found a basket on his doorstep with a baby boy inside. The old man was baffled. He had never had a wife or children and had no idea how to care for an infant. After some hesitation, however, he decided to keep the foundling. The old man was a magic wielder, so he decided the boy could become his apprentice and continue his craft.

As time passed, the boy grew. The old man made his apprentice work hard and study often, but the boy didn't mind. He was smart, diligent, and made great strides. However, he was very different from other children, and it became more obvious as he grew older. He never had a friend, a pet, or even a plant to care for. He never bonded with anyone or anything, viewing people and objects only as tools for potential use. He seemed incapable of bonding or forming relationships. It was no surprise his personality was surrounded by rumors, and he was eschewed, even feared, in the village. Yet, the boy wasn't bothered by it, and his loneliness never burdened him. He was perfectly content with himself and didn't need anyone to feel whole.

When the boy turned fifteen, the old man told him, 'I know of a source of valuable knowledge. It can help you become a great man. You'll be able to get almost anything you want, but it comes with a very high price.'

'What's the price?' the boy asked.

'Your heart will turn to stone. You'll be unable to love, and you won't feel pain or pity.'

'Wait...' the boy said in surprise, 'if you possess this knowledge, then your heart must be stone too. But you've always been kind to me.'

'Having something doesn't mean using it,' the old man shrugged. 'When I faced the same choice, I made a different decision. That's why I'm neither rich nor famous, but I'm happy. And I think my life's gotten better since I found you. But that's my life—we're talking about yours. What I know is nothing compared to what you could master. But remember, there's a price you'll have to pay.'

'I don't see any price, let alone a high one. Of course, I agree.'

'Think again. There's no turning back.'

'There's nothing to think about. Love is for the weak.'

'As you wish. Tomorrow at dawn, we set off.'"

"Oh my God, Tiendal," I sighed in shock, "I'm even sorrier for you than before. Everyone makes mistakes, but not realizing one after ten wasted lives? That's a record. Don't you see how wrong you were?"

He drew in a breath, about to respond, when his face suddenly went pale. Tiendal fell to one knee, and a few drops of blood appeared on the ground beside him. It took me a moment to realize where the blood was coming from, and when I did, terror gripped me. Tiendal's hand, though undamaged, was bleeding profusely. Red trickles flowed down his fingers and the inside of his palm. The streams of blood appeared out of nowhere, multiplying by the second.

For a few seconds, I stood there, staring at his palm, spellbound. Then I snapped out of it and checked my pockets. My mother always told me to take a handkerchief whenever I left home. To her, it was more important than keys or a phone—like some kind of amulet. I never believed in a handkerchief's life-saving power and never shared my mom's enthusiasm for it. To me, it was a relic of the past, something I only carried to keep my mom calm. When I started living on my own, I ditched handkerchiefs, replacing them with wet wipes and paper tissues. But on the day I expected to be kidnapped, I remembered my mom's words and slipped a handkerchief into my pocket before heading to university. Just in case.

"My gut feeling didn't fail me," I thought, pulling out the 'magical' cloth and kneeling beside Tiendal.

Recalling every first aid lesson I'd ever taken, I bandaged his hand as tightly as I could and looked at him questioningly. Tiendal clenched his bandaged hand into a fist and rose to his feet. I followed suit.

"It won't help," he said thoughtfully, staring at his hand. "It's a sign. We're running out of time."

His voice was calm, though tinged with a faint sorrow. He stood straighter, his face no longer as pale, but he looked like a tree with sawn roots. It was strange to see him like that. This weary, pitiful look didn't suit him at all. The person standing before me wasn't the Jenkins I knew—it was a stranger, someone in need of help but too proud to ask.

I glanced at his hand and sighed. The bandage hadn't helped much. Within seconds, the edges of the handkerchief turned red, blood dripping onto the ground once more. I winced, shifting my gaze from his hand to his face. "Does it hurt?" I asked.

"No more than an ordinary wound," he replied calmly, showing no signs of discomfort. Yet, for some reason, I knew it was worse than he let on.

"This should help," I said with a small smile, gently taking Tiendal's bleeding, clenched fist into my hands. I brought it to my lips and kissed his knuckle softly.

Tiendal shuddered as if shocked, quickly pulling his hand away. He unclenched his fist and examined his palm, distrustful. He moved his fingers, clenching and unclenching them several times. Still in disbelief, he untied the handkerchief. The bleeding had stopped, and the traces of blood vanished before our eyes.

Tiendal's eyes widened, his brows shooting up so high it seemed his forehead wasn't big enough for them.

I smiled. "Better?"

Tiendal turned his astonished gaze from his hand to my face. "How did you do this?"

"Love is its own kind of magic, Tiendal. A magic you're not capable of. I'm still your charger. So, you're welcome."

Tiendal stared at his palm in wonder once more. "Unbelievable," he murmured in genuine surprise. "But why, Tayra?"

"You wouldn't understand. Let's just say, I'm invested. I need you to reach the Source of Force."

"Okay," he shrugged. "Let's go."

"Still far?" I asked, looking ahead, trying to gauge the remaining distance.

"I think nearly as much as we've covered. Are you tired?"

"Not really. Ew... wait, did you just show some care?"

"In vain as I see."

"Do you think you feel good enough to speak while we walk?"

"Yes, why?"

"I'd like to hear more about your childhood. What happened next? Where did the old man take you?"

"He took me to a cave where an ancient magic book was hidden. He also gave me a seal that granted access to the book's contents. The cave was near Tiamon, so I moved there and became an apprentice to one of the local scientists. I'd been working with him for ten years, and in my spare time, I studied magic from the book.

As I gained experience, I began using magic more often in my daily life. I quickly became famous for my extraordinary abilities. Around the same time, Pharaoh Milcentep was planning a new military campaign. However, both his commander-in-chief and his chief adviser were short-sighted fools, willing to sell out the country for their own ambitions. After carefully calculating all the possible risks, I realized Milcentep held the brightest future for the state. I had to open his eyes to what was happening behind his back before it was too late. I also saw opportunities in the upcoming campaign that could strengthen both our borders and Milcentep's throne with minimal losses.

With the help of some acquaintances, I managed to secure an audience with the Pharaoh. By then, word of my skills had already reached Milcentep, and he was curious about what I had to say. I wasn't much of an orator at the time, and my point of view must have seemed improbable. But surprisingly, Milcentep trusted my words and followed my advice. Soon, it brought him great success, just as I had predicted. Realizing my value, Milcentep decided to keep me close and made me a priest. Before long, I became the high priest and Pharaoh's advisor. And the rest, you already know."

As Tiendal finished speaking, he turned his gaze to me, and I felt my jaw drop.

"What happened?" he asked, "Why are you looking at me like this?"

"Your eyes..." I whispered in amazement, "they've turned green."

Tiendal chuckled, shrugged, but said nothing.

"You know what..." I said thoughtfully, "maybe I was wrong. Maybe there's still a chance for you to let love into your heart and do something good. Tiendal sold his ability to love for magical knowledge. But even after that, I can't say he became purely evil. Though his decisions were mostly guided by calculation, he could still act nobly, and it often led to good things. Anyway, you have Robert's heart now. And Robert was a good man—he loved his father, his friends, and his factory. Stop suppressing him. Let him out. Who knows... maybe the eleventh life is the perfect time for change. Doing good can bring satisfaction. You might even like it."

Tiendal smiled. "Never thought I'd say this, but... I enjoy talking to you, Tayra. It can be as pleasurable as sex with you."

I laughed. "Thanks. That might be the most sophisticated compliment I've ever heard."

CHAPTER 41: AMHITIEMAR

We covered the rest of the way quickly and without incident. Along the way, I managed to ask Tiendal about the events and customs of ancient times, as well as the most remarkable memories from each of his reincarnations. Yes, our relationship was complicated, and I had plenty of reasons to hold a grudge against him, but I couldn't deny that, from a scientific standpoint, Tiendal was priceless. Not only did he live thousands of years ago, but his existence spanned several centuries. For me, as a historian and archaeologist, it was a double jackpot. Missing the chance to personally communicate with such a unique figure would've been unthinkable.

Fortunately, Tiendal seemed to relax and was more talkative than usual. He answered general questions willingly, providing me with information you won't find in any history book. I prayed my memory could hold all this knowledge, as losing even a tiny drop would be a shame.

Getting to know him on a deeper level proved difficult. He was in no hurry to open up and answered personal questions evasively. Still, I managed to get a general picture of his personality, which turned out to be even more complex and contradictory than I'd imagined.

Lost in conversation, time passed unnoticed, and at some point, I realized the area around me was familiar. We were in the vicinity of our former camp. The tents, the people, and all the gear were gone, but the places where the temporary structures had stood were still clearly visible.

Soon, the temple came into view, proud and majestic as ever, still towering over the daily bustle and inspiring awe in the hearts of all who saw it. To me, though, it didn't seem as formidable as before; it was more like an old friend I hadn't seen in a while. I greeted the temple with a smile and looked up at the sky, trying to gauge the time.

Meanwhile, Tiendal climbed the steps and stopped at the temple door, examining the lock. Four of its slots were filled with keys, leaving only the fifth recess empty.

I'd had enough of that lock during the expedition, so unlike Tiendal, I had no desire to study it again. I was more interested in finding Tony and consulting him on how to proceed with the rest of our plan, given the new information I'd gathered.

The sun was already high in the sky, though it hadn't reached its zenith yet. At this time of day, the back of the temple was the only side cloaked in shadow, making it the perfect spot to wait. While Tiendal was preoccupied with the locked door, I carefully snuck around the corner and hurried to the back wall.

To my relief, Tony stood exactly where I expected, in the narrow strip of shadow cast by the building. He must have heard me approaching because he was already on alert. But the moment he recognized me, Tony smiled and rushed toward me.

"Are you okay?" he asked, pulling me into his embrace.

"Yeah, seems so," I replied, hugging him back and resting my head on his shoulder.

I was about to tell Tony about our next steps when a voice suddenly thundered behind me, "Gotcha!"

I turned and saw Tiendal, slowly walking toward us. His appearance wasn't a surprise, but his menacing look sent shivers down my spine. No, dragon wings didn't sprout from his back, and he didn't tower like a ten-story building, as in the final scenes of action movies. There were no devil's flames, and no threads from the underworld stretched from his hands. Yet there was something hypnotic about his movements, making it impossible to look away. He looked like a madman holding a nuclear launch button, seriously considering pressing it. Hellish lights danced in his black eyes, and he radiated an incomprehensible power, invisible to the eye but sensed as something dangerous. He was a bomb, ready to explode at any moment, waiting only for the perfect time to maximize the devastation.

"Interesting, isn't it?" he continued. "Why do I have this déjà vu?"

"You always knew about him," I replied. "So, what exactly are you angry about?"

"Angry? No, Tayra, I'm furious. You two destroyed my throne and turned me into a fugitive. It's your damn alliance that's landed me in this mess."

"You brought this on yourself, Jenkins," Tony said coldly. "No one forced you to choose a life of crime."

"You know nothing about me," Tiendal snapped. "You thought you could outplay me, but crossing me never goes unpunished."

I drew a breath to retort, but before I could speak, Tiendal theatrically raised his hand, as if preparing to throw an invisible ball. In the next moment, Tony doubled over in pain.

Keeping his hand raised, Tiendal smirked. "Even if I can't change anything, I can still have my revenge. Tayra, you and I have unfinished business, but we don't need him for that, do we? Killing him will give me quite a bit of power, as long as I do it slowly... and painfully. You'll have to watch him suffer, but isn't that a fair price for my humiliation?"

With a satisfied grin, Tiendal nodded toward Tony, who couldn't straighten up despite all his efforts. Tony clenched his teeth, enduring the pain stoically, without making a sound. He desperately tried to hide how much pain he was in, but it was impossible.

I stepped forward quickly, shielding Tony, and said, "Stop it, Tiendal. You can't kill him."

"Oh really?" Tiendal chuckled, feigning surprise. "Just wait a little longer, and I'll prove how wrong you are!"

He flashed a malevolent grin, gesturing as Tony dropped to one knee, resting his hand on the ground. It was getting harder for him to breathe.

I drew air into my lungs and yelled, "The last temple cache is empty!"

"What?!" Tiendal exclaimed, stepping back, lowering his hand in shock.

I shot a glance at Tony, who managed a short breath but still couldn't get up, then turned my gaze back to Tiendal. "Yes, Tiendal, you heard me right. I know how to open it, but it's already empty."

"Impossible!" he said, eyes wide with disbelief. "I'm sure you weren't lying when you said..."

"That I didn't have the key and didn't know where it was? I still don't, but Tony does."

"Shit!" Tiendal shouted, dropping his hands in frustration.

"I suppose a murder for the sake of energy is canceled. Today isn't your day, Tiendal."

I turned to Tony and saw him slowly rising, struggling to catch his breath.

I was gasping for air too, barely holding my racing heart inside my chest. I'd never been as terrified as just a moment ago. I knew that to have the desired effect the performance needed to reach its climax. But the price for it seemed way too high—Tiendal could have killed Tony before I managed to deliver my lines. Still, even after it all worked out as planned, I felt guilty for every second that Tony had to suffer.

Tiendal looked up at me, swallowing hard. "You're much cleverer than I thought, Tayra. And you used your wits against me. Why?"

"I had no reason to trust you, and the gut feeling didn't fail me."

Tiendal winced, staying silent. Just then, I felt Tony's hand touch my waist, heard his heartbeat behind me, still fast, but steady. I smiled and placed my hand over his.

Tiendal glanced indifferently at Tony's hand and grunted. He looked back at me and asked, "The expedition team tried everything but couldn't find it. What's the secret, Tayra?"

"Time. The caches appeared at different times of the day. The last pattern, which turned out to be a hexagon, could only be seen under the moonlight, as the symbols appeared different in those light conditions."

Tiendal sighed thoughtfully and lowered his gaze to the ground. The next moment, he doubled over coughing, and several drops of blood fell onto the grass.

"Hold on, Tiendal!" I said, wrapping my arm around his back and giving him a reassuring pat on the shoulder. Then I looked up at Tony and said, "Tony, I'll explain everything to you later. We need to open the temple and let him take what he needs. After that, we must get to the Tiamon Catacombs as quickly as possible."

Tony replied with an intense stare, as if making sure I meant what I'd just said. The genuine plea in my eyes seemed to convince him. He shrugged and, with a muttered "Under your responsibility," turned around and walked away.

Tiendal and I made our way to the temple entrance and sat down on the steps. He no longer coughed, but he didn't look well, to put it mildly. Clearly, he was suffering from some kind of internal pain, and I truly felt sorry for him, despite the fact that only a couple of minutes ago, he had almost killed my boyfriend.

The memory of Tony falling to his knee, unable to catch his breath, pierced my mind again, and I shuddered. *What a blessing that I foresaw this*, I thought, exhaling with relief. *What a blessing.*

After the stressful experience, my hands still shook, and my heart continued to race at breakneck speed. But other than that, I felt no discomfort.

Strange, I thought, glancing at Tiendal, who sat with his head in his hands, staring at the ground. *He said we were connected, yet he's obviously feeling bad now, while I seem to be okay. I wonder if this is temporary or if he was bluffing after all.*

After a moment's hesitation, I decided to voice my doubts. "Look," I said smoothly, "Are we really connected, or did you lie just to get the fifth key?"

"Really," he said without raising his head. "I didn't lie."

"And why are you feeling bad, but I'm not?"

He turned his head and looked at me. "Because this is my payback, not yours."

He grimaced, probably in pain, and returned his expression to neutral.

Heck! I thought. *Even though he's a jerk, I can't just stand by knowing he's suffering.*

I moved closer and firmly took his hand in mine.

He raised his head in surprise and looked at me, bewildered. "Tayra, listen, you don't have to help me..."

"So, you admit that it's helping?"

"I do, but..."

"So shut up and sit quietly, or I might change my mind. Thanks to your centuries-old efforts, we're all held hostage by this idiotic situation."

He sighed and turned his gaze back to the ground, leaving his hand in mine. We had been sitting like that for a while when Tony finally appeared at the temple wall.

He quickly walked to the steps and, rounding us indifferently, proceeded to the temple door. We stood up and followed him. Tony took the fifth key from his backpack and slid it into the corresponding hole. We heard a characteristic click, followed by a slight vibration under our feet, and slowly the door leaves began to part.

Incredible! I thought. *It's scary to even consider how old this mechanism is, but it still works.*

When the doors were fully open, Tony gloomily nodded toward the entrance and, addressing Tiendal, said, "Go."

Tiendal entered the temple while we remained outside.

"How are you?" I asked, stepping closer to Tony.

"I don't know," Tony replied. "More or less, I think. Alright, tell me."

"Well, the Source of Force is a magical book hidden in the Secret Room in Tiamon. To access it, you need a special seal, one copy of which must be inside this temple. His vitality is running out, and if he doesn't reach the Source of Force, he'll die, and I'll die with him because we're connected. If he makes it there, our connection will break, but my insensitivity will remain forever. In short, that's it."

"Wow!" Tony said, rubbing his forehead. "Yeah... it'd be hard to find a more wacky situation."

I shrugged and nodded in agreement.

"Okay," Tony continued, gazing thoughtfully at the dark entrance to the temple. "Let's say he comes out with the seal. Then at least two questions arise. First, how do we get to Tiamon unnoticed? It's a four-hour drive from here, and our ancient friend is on the wanted list, with the traffic police on alert. And secondly, what do we do with the temple? Should we just leave it open?"

"I have no idea how to get to Tiamon, let alone unnoticed. But as for the temple... Maybe it'd make sense to close it."

"Yep," Tony smiled. "And better while he's inside."

"Good point," I giggled. "And the problem with the drive to Tiamon would be solved right away. Okay, let's ask him when he gets back. It's his element, after all."

"**If** he comes back... God knows what's inside—and whether that damn seal is there."

"If he doesn't come back, I'll die too..."

"Are you sure he didn't lie?"

"Well... about eighty percent."

"Okay, don't worry," Tony said, pulling me to him. "I hope everything will be fine. We'll get to Tiamon somehow and deal with the temple. We're not stopping now."

"Tony, I don't know if I'll get another chance to say this, but I love you. And if I die soon..."

"You won't," a familiar voice interrupted from behind. "If we don't waste time talking."

"Found it?" Tony asked, slightly moving me aside and eyeing the package in Tiendal's hands.

"As you see."

"Okay, what now with the temple?" Tony continued, nodding toward the open door.

Tiendal shrugged. "We can leave it as is. Nothing dangerous inside."

"Are you sure? I've had enough of your ancient tricks."

Tiendal met Tony's gaze, his black eyes cold and calm. "I'm sure. Relax."

"Okay," Tony said just as coldly, turning around. "And now to Tiamon."

CHAPTER 42: THE SOURCE OF FORCE

We were lucky not to attract unwanted attention on the way, so the trip to Tiamon went smoothly, though it took much longer than Tony had expected. By the time we reached the entrance gate of the museum complex, it was getting dark outside. As expected, the museum was closed to visitors.

I don't know what Jenkins's plan to get inside looked like, but at this point, Tony took the initiative. He stepped out of the car and carefully scanned the area, focusing especially on the CCTV cameras. He paused for a moment, likely weighing the choice between a legal and an illegal approach, before heading toward the guard station.

A few minutes later, the guard unlocked the gate and escorted us to the catacomb entrance. He opened the door and left without a word.

"Surprised" doesn't even begin to describe my expression when the guard left. Despite a sleepless night and a crazy day, my eyes seemed to grow wide, and my jaw hit the floor in an instant. In recent days, I'd seen so many miracles that I was starting to grow numb to them. But the guard's behavior was so unexpected that curiosity overwhelmed me, and the question, "What did you say to him?" slipped out before I even decided to ask.

Tony met my amazed stare with a soft smile and deflected, "You're better off not knowing." He shifted his gaze to Tiendal and said, "Okay, what's next?"

"Tayra comes with me, and you stay here."

"Seriously? Do you think I'll let her go with a psycho like you?"

"Otherwise, the connection won't be ruined. Just Tayra and I."

"And how can I be sure you won't use her for one more human sacrifice?"

"You can't. You just have no choice."

Tony shot Tiendal a devastating look, and I knew it was time for me to step in.

"Tony, don't worry. I'll be fine," I said softly, wrapping my arms around his neck and kissing him.

Tony kissed me back, twining his arms around my waist and pulling me closer.

At that moment, we heard Tiendal cough. "Sorry to interrupt," he said with feigned indifference. "But time's running out."

"Well, let's go," I said, pulling away from Tony and turning around.

I knew Tony's eyes followed us until we disappeared into the catacombs, so I tried to appear fearless and confident. Truthfully, I was scared as hell. First, because my last visit to that building ended badly, and I had no idea what to expect this time. Second, Tiendal—due to obvious reasons—didn't inspire confidence as a partner, and the thought of relying on him drove me crazy.

Without him, though, I had zero chance of getting out of those catacombs alive. The guard opened the door for us, but didn't turn on the light—leaving us in impenetrable darkness. Knowing how winding those corridors were, I figured lights wouldn't help much. Fortunately, Tiendal didn't need Ariadne's thread to find the way, and the absence of light didn't seem to bother him at all. In that pitch darkness, he was like a fish in water. Just a few minutes later, we reached the Dark Isthmus, and in some incredible way, he found a button to open the swivel door.

We entered the cell with three doors—well, four, counting the swivel door we came through. Light flickered on either side of the door in front of us. It wasn't very bright, but enough to make out the rest of the doors and the levers nearby. The cell looked exactly as I remembered it and as it had appeared in my flashbacks. The fact I could doubt its existence and tried to convince myself it was just a hallucination now seemed ridiculous.

"Has it stayed open all this time?" I asked, studying the central door, trying to guess what could be producing the light behind it.

"Well, yes," Tiendal replied. "There was no one to close it."

"What's behind the side doors?"

"Nothing special," he shrugged. "Just the engineering system that powers the code lock mechanism."

I also wanted to ask about the restrictions on the number of code combinations, but Tiendal slipped into one of the slots behind the front door, and I followed him.

The room we found ourselves in was spacious, dimly lit. I looked around with interest. Everything seemed new, and I could hardly remember anything from my previous visit.

Tiendal read the doubt in my eyes. "It's the same room, you can be sure. Your conscience was fogged. You couldn't remember."

"Will I remember it this time?"

"Who knows?" Tiendal shrugged. "We'll see."

I looked around the eerie, half-dark room again and asked, "Where's the book?"

Tiendal gestured for me to walk deeper inside. I took a few hesitant steps forward and stopped a couple of meters from a stone stand, something lying on it. That must have been the book. I turned around again, trying to identify the sources of the dim light filling the room. But before I could see anything, Tiendal's voice came. "Stay where you are and don't ask any questions."

I didn't feel like walking around that creepy place, so I followed the order without reservation and fixed my gaze on Tiendal. By then, he had already reached the stand, bent over the book, and was trying to make something out on the cover.

The stand was decorated with intricate patterns carved into the stone. They seemed to be formed from special symbols, and I recognized a few, having seen something similar on the walls of the Amhitiemar temple. The stand was a work of art in itself and could be studied for hours, but time was limited, so I had to focus on the Source of Force.

Although I had heard a lot about it by then, I still had no clear image of the magical book in my mind, so there were no expectations to live up to. When I saw the Source of Force, the first thing that struck me was its size. It looked like an ordinary book with a leather-like cover and metal corner reinforcements, but it was about twice as wide and tall as a standard book. There was a recess in the smooth surface of the cover. The bottom and the seal had the same patterns.

Carefully, as if it were something precious and fragile, Tiendal placed the seal into the recess and stared at it. I focused on it too, but to my surprise, nothing happened. I feared the seal had lost its magical power, but then a blue light began to glow around the book. I glanced from the book to Tiendal's face. He looked focused, his lips moving. He was probably pronouncing a spell.

Wow, it boots up like my laptop after an update, I thought, but refrained from commenting.

The light around the book grew brighter and brighter. Finally, a beam shot from the stone, piercing the room. It was so bright, I couldn't look at it and had to close my eyes.

I felt warmth fill my body. At first, it was pleasant, but with each passing second, it grew hotter. Soon, it felt as though I were burning. I wanted to scream, but no sound came. My body ached. The sensation was torturous, almost unbearable. I struggled, then surrendered, slipping into darkness.

I don't know how long I was unconscious, but the first thing I saw when I woke was Robert Jenkins's green eyes. He reached out, helping me to my feet.

"Are you okay?" he asked, his voice soft.

I took a breath and rubbed my head. "I don't know," I shrugged. "What happened?"

"Haven't I warned you about asking questions?" Jenkins said with a slight smile.

I sighed again and snapped, "You could've warned me it would hurt like that."

"I could," he agreed. "But it wouldn't have changed anything, so I didn't think it was necessary."

"What now?"

"I can congratulate you: from now on, my death won't cause your demise."

"Good news, thank you. Is that all? I mean… you're not going to kill me, are you?"

"Well, I thought of it, can't deny," he said with a smile. "The temptation was strong. But since I promised you wouldn't die, I had to resist and change my plans. Let's go."

"Where to?"

"Outside. I need to talk to Tony."

"You may be full of magic now, but you're not immortal! If you touch him..."

"Tayra, calm down. I've never been a good person, but I've never been a liar. I promise, I won't hurt him. I just want to ask for a favor."

"You tried to kill him hours ago. Are you sure this is a good idea?"

"Everyone makes mistakes. I admit mine. But we were all held hostage in an idiotic situation. And I have a proposal he can't refuse, so I doubt he'll be vindictive."

"Look at me," I said, amazed as I studied his eyes.

"Why?" he asked, smiling as he turned his gaze to me.

"Your eyes are green again."

"I know. Do you think this color suits me?"

"It does."

"Glad you like it."

***

"Thank God, Tayra!" Tony exclaimed as soon as Jenkins and I appeared at the door. He rushed to me, hugging me tightly, his face buried in my hair. It seemed like he couldn't believe I was real, as if he needed confirmation. "Oh my God," he whispered, "Thank goodness!"

We must have been gone a long time; it was already dark outside. I could only imagine how Tony felt while we were away—blaming himself, no doubt. It's awful, knowing someone you love is in danger and being powerless to help.

Jenkins gave us a few minutes before stepping over. "Tony, can I have a word?" he asked.

Tony lifted his head from my hair, gently moved me aside, and looked at Jenkins, clearly ready to listen.

"Eye to eye," Jenkins said, nodding for Tony to follow him.

"Okay, fine," Tony replied, following Jenkins across the museum grounds.

They walked a few dozen meters away. The museum grounds were lit, so I could see them, but they stood far enough that I couldn't hear their conversation. Time dragged as I stood there, torn between curiosity and anxiety, every second feeling like an eternity.

Tony finally came back, leaving Jenkins where they had been talking.

"What did he want?" I asked.

"Just a trifle, nothing special. Let's go."

"Where?"

"Home."

"Uh... eh..."

"He's no longer our problem," Tony said with a smirk. "And the rest will become clear soon enough. Just be patient."

CHAPTER 43: A CALL

I returned to the dorm and resumed classes the day after we got back from our adventure. Of course, I could've taken a short break to rest and recover, but I didn't feel like it. I knew I'd spend days of idleness, reflecting on everything that had happened, and that was exactly what I didn't want. The events had been so emotionally overwhelming that I wanted to forget them for a while and focus on something else. So, diving back into university life seemed like the best choice.

After a few days, I settled back into my routine, balancing studies and social life like any other student. Between classes and meeting friends, I discussed my master's thesis topic with Portonapoulos and started working on it. My life finally settled back into its calm, even rhythm, just like it was before my first trip to Tiamon. I was sure nothing could break that harmony again. I was wrong.

Five days after my encounter with the Source of Force, I got an unexpected phone call on my way home from university. The number was unidentified.

"Hello?" I answered.

"Miss Melfuri?" a voice asked.

"Yes, this is she."

"My name is Stephen Colter. I'm Mr. Robert Jenkins's lawyer. I have some important information for you. Could you come to Mr. Jenkins's office tomorrow?"

"Uh... What time?"

"At 11 a.m."

"Okay, but what's this about?"

"I'll explain everything at the appointment."

"Okay, I'll come."

I said goodbye to Colter and hung up, feeling discouraged. The walk back to the dormitory felt long, and I couldn't think of anything else. My imagination spun out the most incredible scenarios for what could happen next—and, of course, none of them were rosy.

I thought this was over, I muttered. *Lord, what else could possibly connect me to Jenkins? Why do I need to meet his lawyer? Where's Jenkins, anyway? He should've been arrested by now. I've been avoiding the whole mess so well that I didn't even think to ask Tony about it. I'll ask him tonight when he gets here. I should tell him about the call too—maybe he knows something I don't.*

When I finally got home, I decided to push the call out of my mind and focus on something more useful. Tony and I had realized that in the two months we'd known each other, we'd been through a lot, but we hadn't gone on a real date yet. We were planning to fix that tonight. But first, I had some study tasks to finish, so I threw myself into those instead.

As usual, I got carried away and completely lost track of time. By the time I finished, there were only 15 minutes left before Tony was supposed to arrive—and I still needed to shower, get dressed, and do my makeup. It was a date after all.

Obviously, the shower was my first priority. I rushed in but unlocked the door first so Tony wouldn't be stuck in the hallway if he showed up early. That turned out to be a good call, because just as I turned off the water, I heard a knock at the door.

"Come in! It's unlocked," I called out, drying myself quickly and wrapping a towel around me.

Tony walked in, and though I couldn't see him, I heard the door click shut behind him.

I stepped out of the bathroom, shrugging apologetically. "Hey! Sorry, I'm not ready yet. I got a little too caught up in studying—had to catch up on some stuff... uh, whatever. I'll be quick, just give me five, maybe ten minutes."

"Relax, it's fine," Tony said with a grin. "No rush. I like you in the towel, though... and I wouldn't mind if you took it off."

"Tony, stop it—you're embarrassing me."

"Oh, am I? I'm just being sincere—hoping you'll take pity on me and let me kiss that gorgeous shoulder of yours."

"I'd love to, but if you do that, our date will definitely fail—we'll end up staying home..."

Tony chuckled. "Because of you, or because of me?"

"Because of you, of course," I laughed. "Tricks like that don't work on me. Being insensitive has its perks, you know. At least I'm not tied to 'you know who' anymore. By the way, has he been arrested?"

"Uh... why?"

"I got a call from an unknown number today. The guy said he's Robert Jenkins's lawyer and scheduled a meeting for tomorrow."

"Hmm..." Tony rubbed his chin, looking thoughtful.

"Tony, explain what's going on—now! I feel like an idiot."

"Wait until tomorrow. You'll probably get all your answers then, and you can stop worrying that beautiful head of yours."

"Why can't you just tell me? Why all the secrecy? Haven't we had enough of that lately?"

"Tayra, you're beautiful, kind, and smart—but patience? Definitely not your strong suit."

"Is it that bad?"

"Sometimes. But honestly? I'm curious too."

"So, you don't know what's going on either?"

"I don't know exactly, but I have a few guesses. I'm not really curious about your meeting tomorrow, but I'd still like to go with you, if that's okay."

"Yeah, of course. I've been freaking out and wanted to ask you to come, but I was worried you'd be busy."

"I'll make time for this, don't worry. What time's the meeting?"

"11 a.m."

"Okay. Where?"

"Jenkins's office."

"Got it."

"So, what were you curious about?"

"Come closer."

"Uh..." I froze, hesitating.

"Don't worry, I won't bite. Although, with you looking this sexy in that towel, I can't make any promises."

I giggled and stepped closer to Tony. "Well, here I am."

"Close your eyes and relax."

I blinked, skeptical. But Tony smiled and nodded, so I hesitated, then closed my eyes and took a deep breath.

Tony's soft lips brushed my neck, sending a gentle warmth spreading from where he touched. Instinctively, I tilted my head, giving him more room to explore. He pressed his lips harder, teasing my skin with his tongue as he slowly moved down to my shoulder. A wave of warmth rippled from his kiss, making me crave more, and a soft moan escaped my lips.

At that moment, Tony exclaimed, "Wow, it worked!" and then grabbed me, planting a quick, excited kiss on my cheek.

I blinked, bewildered, and looked at Tony in confusion. Then it hit me—my body had just responded to his touch, physically, not just because of our emotional bond, but because I could feel it. I stared at him, speechless, silently asking for an explanation. But he just smiled, looking thrilled.

I took a breath, my voice shaky. "Do you think... my sensitivity is back? That I can feel again?"

"I do. And I'm more than happy to give you as many tests as you need to believe it."

"How is it possible? He said that…"

"He didn't know. We'll figure it out tomorrow. But for tonight... we could always change plans and stay in."

"Mmm... sounds perfect," I said with a mischievous smile, pulling Tony further into the room.

"Let's lock the door and draw the curtains first," Tony protested.

"Why so shy?" I teased, giggling, but I headed for the door anyway—Tony made sense.

"I'm not shy, I'm careful. I don't want my personal life to become public. Is it bad?"

"It's not. I'm just kidding."

I bit my lip, giving Tony a playful look. He stepped closer, sliding one arm around my waist while intertwining the fingers of his free hand with mine. He brought our hands to his lips, pressing a soft kiss to the back of my palm before gently kissing each finger. A soft moan escaped me, and Tony smiled. "So, now I can count on my runway lights too?"

"I believe so," I whispered, releasing his hand and starting to unbutton his shirt. "And if you keep teasing me like this, the neighbors might get a show as well."

"Let them envy."

I closed my eyes and pressed my lips to Tony's neck, slipping his shirt off his shoulders. My lips were no longer blind and impassive; they greedily trailed over Tony's chest, savoring the heat that his skin returned to each kiss. My hands felt the warmth and slight tremble of his excitement, while my mind instinctively mapped out where to move next. I could feel now—not just with my heart, but with my body—and the return of that lost harmony filled me with a unique sense of freedom and happiness.

Things were probably different for Tony as well. My body responded readily and gratefully to his tenderness, which felt both inspiring and uplifting. Tony's hands and lips never skimped on affection; they knew no boundaries or prohibitions in their pursuit of the voluptuous moans he drew from my lips. Each of Tony's touches sent a sweet shiver through me, quickening my heartbeat. Tony's movements grew more confident, more passionate. His hands and lips were hot, yet they remained uniquely gentle, every touch filled with boundless care and love.

We shared that deep mental and physical unity that transforms sex into lovemaking. We gave ourselves to each other completely, dissolving into one another and, without exaggeration, becoming a single whole.

Imagine a flame that never scorches, no matter how close you bring your hand to it—that is the flame of our passion. A flame only one force on earth is able to ignite—sincere, unconditional love.

CHAPTER 44: ANSWERS

I opened the door to Jenkins's office and found a stranger, a man in his fifties, seated at Jenkins's desk. It had to be the man who called me yesterday—the one I was supposed to meet.

I stepped into the room and greeted him. "Good morning, Mr. Colter."

Sunlight poured through the windows, filling the room with bright light. Yet, the atmosphere inside was far from sunny. I'd never liked that office. It always felt cold, unwelcoming. I was certain Jenkins and his aura were to blame. I loathed his business suit, his poker face, and, most of all, those black eyes that flashed with hellish fire. Every time I saw him, I wished him straight to hell where he belonged. But now, in his absence, I felt an emptiness, as if something was missing. Oddly, without Jenkins, the room felt even colder.

I glanced around, and my mind conjured Jenkins's image. There he was, rising from his chair, pacing around the desk. He'd walk to the window, look out, smirk, then cross his arms. The absence of all that just wouldn't settle in my mind. I'd felt anxious before opening the door, but the strange emptiness caused by Jenkins's absence made it even worse. Thankfully, Tony was close, his presence grounding me, helping me stay in control.

The man offered a polite smile. "Good morning, Miss Melfuri and..."

"Tony Weiler," Tony prompted, introducing himself.

"And Mr. Weiler," the man concluded.

We walked over to the table and sat in the chairs beside it.

"Mr. Jenkins contacted me a few days ago and asked me to give you this three days after our meeting," Mr. Colter said, handing me an envelope.

"What is it?" I asked, accepting the envelope.

"You should probably open it and read to find out," Mr. Colter replied with an encouraging smile.

I opened the envelope and pulled out a folded sheet of paper. Handwritten text covered the inside of the paper. My hands began to shake uncontrollably, impossible to hide. I felt embarrassed but helpless to stop it. I took a deep breath, counted to ten on the exhale, and finally gathered the courage to unfold the sheet and begin reading.

"Dear Tayra,

By the time you read this, I will no longer exist. But it doesn't matter, for I've already lived far longer than the most famous centenarian.

I reflected on your words and realized you were right. I've always cared only for fame, money, power, and my own desires, never considering the consequences of my decisions for others. Unfortunately, even the ancient magical book can't undo the mistakes I've made in eleven lifetimes. I've experienced much, yet I've never known love, nor has anyone ever loved me.

For centuries, my heart remained stone, and I believed it could never change. But the truth is, I never really tried to change it. As unbelievable as it seems, plants can grow through stone. Thanks to you, I realized the stone of my heart was no different. The seeds of love buried deep within me, long forgotten, might still survive—and perhaps, even grow. Still, I've decided that the end of my eleventh life isn't too late to try.

The magic book offered me a solution that should help lift your curse. But to make it work, I must allow the book to devour me. I've never done anything like this before, so I don't know what to expect. It will probably hurt, and it will probably be frightening. But I'm willing to suffer if it means your happiness. Because you deserve happiness far more than I deserve to live.

Once I disappear, all copies of the seal will be destroyed, and no one will be able to use the book. All the magic in the Secret Room will be erased as well. If anyone enters, the mechanism for my reincarnation won't activate. But if, by any chance, my soul escapes its magical captivity and inhabits the body of another man, I promise to live that life differently. I will dedicate it to doing good and bringing happiness to others. Still, I fear it may never happen, so I must start doing good immediately.

I'm leaving all my confectionery factories to my manager, William Walden. He's a good man. He's worked alongside Robert and Christopher Jenkins for many years. He will transfer a portion of the factory revenues to rehabilitation centers for drug addicts, as my actions have greatly contributed to their rise.

I know you will successfully complete your graduate studies and continue your research. Walden will provide financial support to the scientific teams you work with, and he will assist in organizing expeditions. I trust him completely, but surprises happen. To ensure he fulfills the conditions of this agreement, I've documented everything, and my lawyer will soon provide it for your review.

Who knows where your curiosity may lead. As a gift, I'm leaving you with a special ability. You will be able to sense the presence of ancient magic, allowing you to avoid objects that may hold danger.

Goodbye, Tayra. I doubt our acquaintance brought you much

happiness, but I ask for your forgiveness for all the harm I've caused you.

Sincerely yours,
Tiendal Jenkins"

I lifted my tear-filled eyes to Colter, swallowing hard, and asked, "Is there anything else I should read? He mentioned there should be an agreement."

"Yes, there is," Colter replied with the same polished politeness, then added, his tone softening, "But I don't think it's a good idea to deal with it now. We'll schedule another appointment where I'll introduce you to Mr. Walden and go over the key points of the agreement Mr. Jenkins mentioned."

"Okay, thank you, Mr. Colter," I said, struggling to keep my voice from trembling. "I'll be waiting for your call. May we take our leave now?"

"Yes, of course," Colter replied with a polite nod, then Tony and I quickly rose and left.

The emotions overfilling me in that moment urgently needed to be released. But I didn't want to cry in that place, especially not in front of someone I barely knew. I needed fresh air and a safe place to process the overwhelming information I had just received.

We stepped out onto the street, and as the cool autumn air touched my face, hot, salty streams ran down my cheeks. Tony silently offered me his handkerchief, but I waved it away, trying unsuccessfully to wipe the tears from my face with my hand. Without a word, Tony wrapped his arm around my shoulders and gently guided me somewhere. Through my tears, I could barely see the way, but honestly, I didn't care where we were going. Lost in my thoughts, I followed Tony blindly, brushing away tears whenever they tickled my nose.

Soon, we reached a park and sat down on a bench. At this point, Tony caringly offered me his handkerchief again. I accepted it, handing him the envelope in return. Tony took it and glanced at me, his eyes questioning, making sure I truly wanted him to read it. I nodded, bringing the handkerchief to my eyes, hoping to wipe away another round of salty tears. Tony unfolded the paper and began reading.

As Tony read, I calmed down a bit. Although my eyes were still wet, no more tears fell. I fixed my gaze on the ground, sitting there until Tony moved the paper aside, signaling he was finished.

I turned my head, swallowing hard, and asked, "Did you know about this?"

"Partly," Tony shrugged. His voice was calm, but I caught a faint note of guilt.

"Why didn't you tell me?"

"Because he asked me not to."

"What else did he ask you?"

"Well, our conversation went something like this.

'Would you jeopardize your career for Tayra's happiness?' he asked.

'What are you getting at?' I frowned.

'I know how to lift her curse, but I need your help.'

'Seriously? What is it?'

'I've found a gap in the magic field that might allow me to reverse the spell. But to use it, I'll have to go to the deepest level. Without going into detail, it means the book will devour me, leaving no trace of me behind in this world.'

'Wow, that's... interesting. But how can I help?'

'I need you to hold off on the arrest for a few days so I can finish some business and arrange a believable suicide for Robert Jenkins.'

'Aren't you going to kill someone to provide the body?'

'No, it will be clean. No one will be harmed, I promise.'

'How many days do you need?'

'How many can you arrange?'

'Can't you just give me a number?'

'Three should be enough.'

'Okay, I think it's possible. Your office and home are under surveillance, so don't even think about showing up there.'

'I'm not going to.'

'Good. Need a ride?'

'No, I'm not done here yet.'

'What about the guard?'

'He won't remember our visit. Other than that, he'll be fine.'

'Fine. Good luck, I guess.'

'Yes, thank you. One more thing—don't tell Tayra until I've implemented it.'

'Do you think she'll mind?'

'Maybe. She might. Anyway, it's better if she finds out after it's done. There's always a chance it could fail, but I'll give it 100% to make it work.'

'Okay. How will I know if you did it?'

'I'll take care of it.'

'Good. Farewell, Tiendal.'

'Goodbye, Tony. Take care of her.'

'I will.'"

Tony made a hand gesture, as if to say "that's it," then looked at me, waiting for my reaction.

I sighed and shrugged. "Well, I… I didn't expect him to do something like this."

"When he made his request, I was surprised too. I can't even imagine what you did to him on the way to Amhitiemar that could've changed his worldview this much."

"Nothing, nothing special, really. Honestly, he wasn't that bad. He just made a wrong decision as a teenager, and that mistake haunted all his future lives."

I sighed and glanced at the ground. Tony moved closer, wrapping an arm around my back, silently inviting me to rest my head on his shoulder. After the emotional storm from Tiendal's letter, I felt drained, so I gladly accepted. But the thoughts in my head had no intention of resting. They whirled and buzzed like a swarm of angry bees, and it was one of those rare times when even Tony's closeness couldn't calm me.

"You know..." I said after a few minutes of silence. "Everyone knows, or will know, the story of Tiendal as an evil priest who did terrible things. But no one knows the other Tiendal—the one who revealed himself only to me."

"I think I know how to fix that," Tony said with a soothing smile, pulling me into his embrace.

CHAPTER 45: EPILOGUE

"Honey, I'm back!" Tony's voice called from the hallway.

"Oh my God, finally!" I exclaimed, rushing out of the kitchen to meet him.

I wrapped my arms around Tony's neck and pressed my face into his shirt, rubbing my cheek against his shoulder. Tony returned my hug with a passionate kiss before smiling. "I've only been gone a week! Did you really miss me that much?"

"More!" I kissed him again. "This week felt longer than a year!"

"I bet it did. I missed you too. I've got a few days off starting today, so we can finally enjoy some real time together."

"Wow, that sounds promising," I said, running my hand through Tony's hair. "Well, we're not spending the rest of the evening in the hallway, are we? Let's go—I'll treat you to a new dish. It's an experiment, so you'll be the first to try it."

"Should I be honored or afraid?"

"It looks and smells fine, so I think you're safe," I said with a giggle. "Anyway, I'll be in the kitchen waiting."

"Roger that," Tony said, heading for the bathroom.

I watched Tony and smiled. I feared our love, born in the midst of a thunderstorm, might not survive the calm. I was afraid we'd grow bored of a peaceful life, and worse, that we'd grow tired of each other. I don't know what fueled these fears, but they influenced many of my decisions. I think that's why I delayed moving in with Tony throughout my master's program, offering ridiculous excuses each time he brought it up. It's a blessing that Tony has angelic patience. However, his patience ran out as soon as I started graduate school. That's when Tony stopped accepting excuses like "the dorm is closer to the university" and finally pushed me to finish my driving course and get my license. Afterward, he bought me a car. I still often choose public transport, but now it's my choice, not a necessity.

It's been two years since we moved in together, and there's no sign of us growing tired—if anything, it's the opposite. We're still just as crazy about each other and cherish every minute we spend together. Still, our life can hardly be called calm. Though we no longer deal with ancient magic and its keepers, there are still plenty of tasks and worries. We both have busy work schedules and frequent business trips, some of which can last a while. Being apart might be easier if Tony's work weren't so dangerous. Though Tony often downplays his investigations and missions, I know they're far from trivial. Sometimes, I think it might be better if he changed jobs, but if he ever does, I want it to be entirely his decision, free from my influence. After all, he loves his work as much as I love mine, and love isn't something I'd ever want to hinder.

For now, facing everyday challenges together only brings us closer. Whether it stays this way, only time will tell. The main thing is, I'm no longer afraid of the future. The most important lesson I've learned is that fearing what might happen only poisons your life. Problems often seem much worse from a distance than they do up close, so there's no need to worry prematurely.

"Mmm," Tony said, sitting down at the table. "The smell is amazing. Now I don't know what to do first—try this delicious-smelling food or hear your news."

"I'll make sure you get both," I said, placing a slice of casserole on

Tony's plate. "Though I don't know where to start either. Catelyn showed me the sales report last week, and I was shocked. It's only been two months since sales started, and the numbers have already exceeded my wildest expectations."

"Wow, that's amazing! Congrats! I told you it would work."

"Yeah, you were right. If it wasn't for you, I never would've dared to try. I should've credited you as a co-author or at least as the one who came up with the idea."

"Oh, stop it," Tony laughed. "It's all your doing. I'm just glad the information reached the audience."

"Yeah, it's true. Catelyn told me the readers bombarded the publishing house with questions and requests for a meeting with the author. You know, I didn't write the book for fame. I never wanted any publicity or any of that. But Catelyn insisted, and I couldn't hold out any longer. She was so kind, taking the book on and publishing it out of turn. Refusing just felt wrong. The meeting's tomorrow, and I'm freaking out. I can't even sit still."

"Well, you've spoken in front of an audience before. It can't be scarier than teaching your students."

"I always know what my students will ask. But what will *they* want to know?"

"I'd ask about your inspiration and what's next for the main characters."

"Exactly! Those are the two questions I'm terrified of. What should I say?"

"Something that would convince me," Tony laughed.

"You're no help, you know."

"I'm trying my best," Tony shrugged, "but I'm out of creative ideas for today."

"Will you come support me? You still owe me for missing my master's thesis defense!"

“Oh, Tayra… Will you remind me of this forever? You know I’d have come if I could!”

“I know, but it’s just too fun watching you justify yourself every time.”

“How could I let the readers tear you apart? Of course I’ll go with you.”

“That’s exactly what I wanted to hear,” I said, standing up and walking toward Tony from behind. I placed my hands on Tony’s shoulders, leaned in, and, with a gentle kiss on his ear, whispered seductively, “I hope you’re not too tired, because it’s going to be a long night…”

“I am, but that’s not going to stop you, is it?”

“Okay, so how do you think I’ll fight off your fatigue?”

“Um… I guess… you’ll join me in the shower…”

“Maybe… for the beginning…”

“I like the beginning,” Tony said, closing his eyes and giving me a chance to kiss him.

***

“There’s such a crowd at the entrance,” Tony said, glancing out the bookstore window.

“Wow,” I agreed, peeking through a gap in the blinds.

“Just relax and breathe,” Tony said, coming up behind me and gently resting his hands on my shoulders. “You’ve got this.”

I shrugged, staying silent.

Tony smiled and walked over to the desk stacked with books. He picked one up and read, “Taira Weiler: *Unknown Story of Tiendal*: *Fiery Heart Without Love.*” He turned the book in his hands, then looked at me and said, “I love the cover. Especially the author’s name."

“I’m not used to it yet, but I think I will,” I said, blushing.

“You should’ve said ‘yes’ sooner, then you’d have had more time to adjust.”

"I said yes the moment you asked. So, you should've proposed sooner."

"You never admit you're wrong, do you?" Tony said, gently kissing my head.

"That's because I'm not," I retorted, barely holding back a giggle.

"Well, anyway, I'm glad you said it," Tony murmured, pecking the top of my head again.

"I'm glad you asked… more than once," I said with a smile, resting my head on Tony's shoulder.

At that moment, the clock struck ten, and the guard moved to unlock the bookstore door.

I've got this, I whispered to myself, settling in at the desk, readying for a long, hard day of work.

The flow of visitors began as soon as the bookstore opened and didn't stop until closing time. I could hardly recall a day when I had to write or speak as much as I did then. I hadn't imagined my version of Tiendal's story would stir such a response in readers' hearts. Still, the steady stream of people wanting to ask for details or simply thank me for a job well done made it clear: even with sharp intuition, some things in life remain unpredictable, and there's always room for surprises.

Naturally, on the journey to Amhitiemar, Tiendal hadn't shared enough about his life to fill an entire book, so many parts of his biography had to be imagined. Still, I believe the story didn't lose its value because of it.

Despite his flaws, Tiendal was certainly an extraordinary man, willing to work tirelessly toward his goals, which, when you think about it, weren't always bad. He truly made the impossible possible, showing that the boundaries of our consciousness are far wider than we often believe. Though goodness wasn't the path Tiendal walked in most of his lives, his controversial personality still left a good trace in my heart.

He reached the Source of Force, yet remained doomed, as the other threats to his life hadn't vanished. But when he faced all the possible ways to end his eleventh life, he chose the most unexpected—and the noblest—path. His gesture moved me so deeply that, despite all the harm Tiendal had done to me and others, gratitude overshadowed the animosity I'd felt toward him. This book, written to soften the dark halo around his name, was my thanks.

However, the book ended with Tiendal's death at the hands of Pilzernat's mercenary, with no mention of his eleventh life or his sacrifice. So it wasn't clear why I chose to rethink a well-known legend and view Tiendal's character from a different angle. Obviously, the true story deserves another book, and it's even more incredible than what I'd written in Tiendal's tale. That's why I decided to keep the truth between Tony and myself, never sharing it with anyone else. But aside from the truth, I couldn't come up with any convincing explanation, though I'd been obsessing over it ever since I learned the time and date of the reader event.

The first few hours passed smoothly. Most people came for autographs and to express their gratitude. A few questions came up about the plot, but since they focused on fictional events and characters, they were easy to answer. I relaxed during this time, beginning to believe that the scariest questions might not come after all. But, as you might guess, my hope was in vain. At one point, a pretty, red-haired, middle-aged woman approached the table and, handing me a book for an autograph, asked, "Mrs. Weiler, may I ask you a question?"

"Sure, you're welcome," I replied, glancing up at her.

"When I first saw the title and description of your book in a promotional email from the publisher, I was surprised. I thought, 'Tiendal? That evil priest from the legend, who made women addicted to him? What more could be added to this story?' But your book turned my world upside down. Before reading it, I saw Tiendal in a purely negative light, but now I actually feel sorry for him. So, I'm curious—what prompted you to view Tiendal's personality this way? Why do you defend him rather than condemn him?"

Here it comes, I thought with frustration. But I quickly remembered how easily my thoughts show on my face, so I forced a smile and asked, "Have you been to the Tiamon catacombs?"

"Yes, I have."

"Was that before or after you read the book?"

"It was a long time ago. I was quite young."

"So, you haven't been to Tiendal's Secret Room, then. It was only discovered less than five years ago, and it's only been open to the public for about three. It's a fascinating tour, one I highly recommend. But I was lucky enough to visit it before it was open to the public. Back then, before the reconstruction, the room looked different, and it held something that inspired me to write this story."

"Really? What was it?"

"Tiendal's diary. Well, parts of it. They were incredibly fragile and, unfortunately, were destroyed during transport, so they're no longer accessible. But some information was salvaged, then deciphered and processed. After comparing the legend with the diary's contents, my heart filled with pity. So, I decided to write the book to share those feelings with others."

"Oh, now I understand. Thank you, Mrs. Weiler, both for your answer and for the amazing book."

"I'm so glad you enjoyed it. With this book, I wanted to show that the meaning of love should never be underestimated. Tiendal's life perfectly illustrates that love can't be replaced by power, money, or loveless lust. I hope you have true love in your life. If not, I hope you find it. And when you do, cherish and hold on to it."

The end.

www.ingramcontent.com/pod-product-compliance
Lightning Source LLC
LaVergne TN
LVHW091252150826
845673LV00006B/1394

* 9 7 8 6 0 9 0 8 0 6 8 2 1 *